THE
COLLECTED
STORIES
OF
ISAAC BABEL

The

COLLECTED
STORIES

of

Isaac Babel

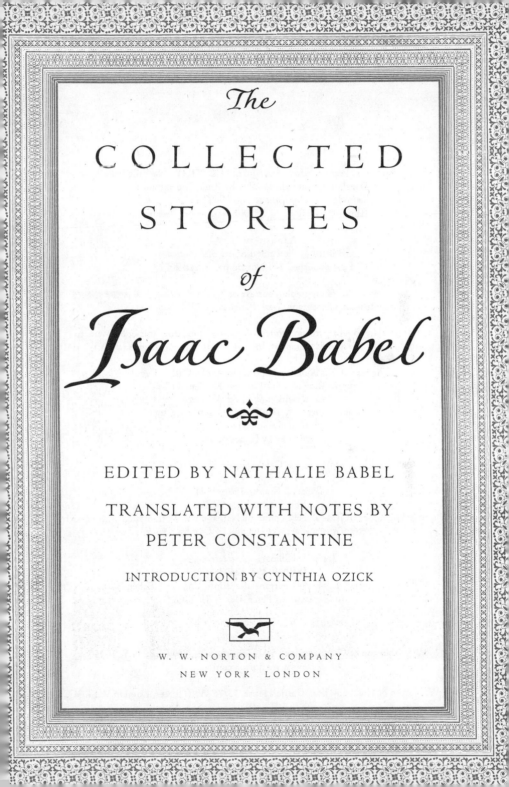

EDITED BY NATHALIE BABEL

TRANSLATED WITH NOTES BY
PETER CONSTANTINE

INTRODUCTION BY CYNTHIA OZICK

W. W. NORTON & COMPANY
NEW YORK   LONDON

Compilation, Preface, Afterword copyright © 2002 by Nathalie Babel
Translation copyright © 2002 by Peter Constantine
Introduction copyright © 2002 by Cynthia Ozick
Chronology copyright © 2002 by Gregory Freidin

All photographs courtesy of Nathalie Babel
Frontispiece photograph: Isaac Babel, circa 1931, Molodenovo

For information about permission to reproduce selections from this book, write to
Permissions, W. W. Norton & Company, Inc., 500 Fifth Avenue, New York, NY 10110

The text of this book is composed in Adobe Caslon Regular
with the display set in Florens and Centaur MT
Composition by Gina Webster
Manufacturing by The Haddon Craftsmen, Inc.
Book design by Mary Wirth
Cartography by Jacques Chazaud

Library of Congress Cataloging-in-Publication Data

Babel', I. (Isaak), 1894–1941.
[Short stories. English]
The collected stories of Isaac Babel / edited by Nathalie Babel ; translated with notes by
Peter Constantine ; introduction by Cynthia Ozick.
p. cm.
Includes bibliographical references.
ISBN 0-393-32402-8
1. Babel', I. (Isaak), 1894–1941—Translations into English. I.Babel, Nathalie.
II. Constantine, Peter, 1963– III. Title.
PG3476.B2 A23 2002
891.73'42—dc21   2002012200

W. W. Norton & Company, Inc., 500 Fifth Avenue, New York, N.Y. 10110
www.wwnorton.com

W. W. Norton & Company Ltd., Castle House, 75/76 Wells Street, London W1T 3QT

3 4 5 6 7 8 9 0

To the memory of my father,
Isaac Emmanuelovich Babel,
and of my mother,
Evgenia Borisovna Babel.

"You are lucky, Alexander Konstantinovich. A few centuries ago your forebears were still running around covered in animal skins, while I too often feel the weight of the centuries of my people's ancient culture, and it suffocates me."
—*Isaac Babel to his friend and editor, Alexander Konstantinovich Voronsky,*
who was arrested in February 1937 and executed in August 1937

CONTENTS

Contents

The Odessa Stories

The Red Cavalry Stories

CONTENTS

The Red Cavalry Cycle: Additional Stories 335

Stories, 1925–1938 363

Contents

INTRODUCTION

by Cynthia Ozick

O n May 15, 1939, Isaac Babel, a writer whose distinction had earned him the Soviet privilege of a dacha in the country, was arrested at Peredelkino and taken to Moscow's Lubyanka prison, headquarters of the secret police. His papers were confiscated and destroyed—among them half-completed stories, plays, film scripts, translations. Six months later, after three days and nights of hellish interrogation, he confessed to a false charge of espionage. The following year, a clandestine trial was briefly held in the dying hours of January 26; Babel recanted his confession, appealed to his innocence, and at 1:40 the next morning was summarily shot by a firing squad. He was forty-five. His final plea was not for himself, but for the power and truth of literature: "Let me finish my work."

What Kafka's art hallucinates—trial without cause, an inescapable predicament directed by an irrational force, a malignant social order—Babel is at last condemned to endure in the living flesh. Kafka and Babel can be said to be the twentieth century's European coordinates: they are separated by language, style, and temperament; but where their fevers intersect lies the point of infection. Each was an acutely conscious Jew. Each witnessed a pogrom while still very young, Kafka in enlightened Prague, Babel under a Czarist regime that promoted harsh legal disabilities for Jews. Each invented a type of literary modernism, becoming a movement in himself, indelible, with no possibility of successors. To be influenced by Kafka is to end in parody; and because the wilderness of an astoundingly variegated experience is incised, unduplicatably, in the sinews of Babel's prose, no writer can effectively claim to be his disciple.

But of course they are opposites: Kafka ingrown, self-dissatisfied, indifferent to politics; hardly daring, despite genius, to feel entitlement to his own language; endlessly agonizing over a broken engagement; rarely leaving home. And here is Babel, insouciant, reckless, a womanizer, half a vagabond, a horseman, a propagandist, the father of three by three different women, only one of them legally his wife. Then why bring up Kafka when speaking of Babel? Kafka at least died in his bed. Babel was murdered by the criminal agency of a cynically criminal government. Kafka requested that his writing be destroyed, and was not obeyed. Babel's name and work were erased—as if he had never written at all—until 1954, when, during a "thaw," he was, in Soviet terminology, rehabilitated.

Yet taken together, they tell us what we in our time are obliged to know about the brutal tracings of force and deception, including self-deception. Kafka alone is not enough; his interiors are too circumscribed. Babel alone is not enough; his landscapes are too diffuse. Kafka supplies the grandly exegetical metaphor: the man who thinks but barely lives, the metaphysician who is ultimately consumed by a conflagration of lies. Babel, by contrast, lives, lives, lives! He lives robustly, inquisitively, hungrily; his appetite for unpredictable human impulse is gargantuan, inclusive, eccentric. He is trickster, rapscallion, ironist, wayward lover, imprudent impostor—and out of these hundred fiery selves insidious truths creep out, one by one, in a face, in the color of the sky, in a patch of mud, in a word. Violence, pity, comedy, illumination. It is as if he is an irritable membrane, subject to every creaturely vibration.

Babel was born in Odessa, a cosmopolitan and polyglot city that looked to the sea and beyond. It was, he wrote,

the most charming city of the Russian Empire. If you think about it, it is a town in which you can live free and easy. Half the population is made up of Jews, and Jews are a people who have learned a few simple truths along the way. Jews get married so as not to be alone, love so as to live through the centuries, save money so they can buy houses and give their wives astrakhan jackets, love children because, let's face it, it is good and important to love one's children. The poor Odessa Jews get very confused when it comes to officials and regulations, but it isn't all that easy to get them to budge in their opinions, their very antiquated opinions. You might not be able to budge these Jews, but there's a whole lot you can learn from them. To a large extent it is because of them that Odessa has this light and easy atmosphere.

There is much of the affectionate and mirthful Babel in this paragraph: the honest yet ironic delight in people exactly as they are, the teasing sense of laughing entitlement ("so as to live through the centuries"), prosperity and poverty rubbing elbows, ordinary folk harried by officialdom, confusion and stubbornness, love and loneliness. As for poor Jews, Babel began as one of these, starting life in the Moldavanka, a mixed neighborhood with a sprinkling of mobsters. What he witnessed there, with a bright boy's perceptiveness, catapulted him early on into the capacious worldliness that burst out (he was twenty-nine) in the exuberant tales of Benya Krik and his gang—tough but honorable criminals with a Damon Runyonesque strain.

Lionel Trilling, among the first to write seriously about Babel in English, mistook him for "a Jew of the ghetto." If "ghetto" implies a narrow and inbred psyche, then Babel stands for the reverse. Though he was at home in Yiddish and Hebrew, and was familiar with the traditional texts and their demanding commentaries, he added to these a lifelong infatuation with Maupassant and Flaubert. His first stories were composed in fluent literary French. The breadth and scope of his social compass enabled him to see through the eyes of peasants, soldiers, priests, rabbis, children, artists, actors, women of all classes. He befriended whores, cabdrivers, jockeys; he knew what it was to be penniless, to live on the edge and off the beaten track. He was at once a poet of the city ("the glass sun of Petersburg") and a lyricist of the countryside ("the walls of sunset collapsing into the sky"). He was drawn to spaciousness and elasticity, optimism and opportunity, and it was through these visionary seductions of societal freedom, expressed politically, that he welcomed the Revolution.

He not only welcomed it; he joined it. In order to be near Maxim Gorky, his literary hero, Babel had been living illegally in St.

Petersburg, one of the cities prohibited to Jews under the hobbling restrictions of the Czarist Pale of Settlement. With the advent of the Revolution the Pale dissolved, discriminatory quotas ceased, censorship vanished, promises multiplied, and Babel zealously attached himself to the Bolshevik cause. In 1920, as a war correspondent riding with the Red Calvary to deliver Communist salvation to the reluctant Polish villages across the border, he fell into disenchantment. "They all say they're fighting for justice and they all loot," he wrote in his diary. "Murderers, it's unbearable, baseness and crime. . . . Carnage. The military commander and I ride along the tracks, begging the men not to butcher the prisoners." Six years later, Babel published his penetratingly authoritative *Red Cavalry* stories, coolly steeped in pity and blood, and found instant fame.

With Stalin's ascension in 1924, new tyrannies began to mimic the old. Postrevolutionary literary and artistic ferment, much of it experimental, ebbed or was suppressed. Censorship returned, sniffing after the subversive, favoring the coarse flatness of Socialist Realism. Babel's wife, Evgenia, whom he had married in 1919, emigrated to Paris, where his daughter Nathalie was born in 1929. His mother and sister, also disaffected, left for Brussels. Babel clung to Moscow, hotly wed to his truest bride, the Russian tongue, continuing his work on a cycle of childhood stories and venturing into writing for theater and film. The film scripts, some designed for silent movies, turned out to be remarkable: they took on, under the irresistible magnetism of the witnessing camera and the innovation of the present tense, all the surreal splendor of Babel's most plumaged prose. Several were produced and proved to be popular, but eventually they failed to meet Party guidelines, and the director of one of them, an adaptation of Turgenev, was compelled to apologize publicly.

Unable to conform to official prescriptiveness, Babel's publications grew fewer and fewer. He was charged with "silence"—the sin of Soviet unproductivity—and was denied the privilege of traveling abroad. His last journey to Paris occurred in 1935, when André Malraux intervened with the Soviet authorities to urge Babel's attendance at a Communist-sponsored International Congress of Writers for the Defense of Culture and Peace—after which Babel never again met with his wife and daughter. Later that year, back in Moscow, he set up a second household with Antonina Pirozhkova, with whom he fathered a second daughter; through an earlier liaison, he was already the father of a son. But if Babel's personal life was unpredictable, disorganized, and rash, his art was otherwise. He wrested his sentences out of a purifying immediacy. Like Pushkin, he said, he was in pursuit of "precision and brevity." His most pointed comment on literary style appears in "Guy de Maupassant," a cunning seriocomic sexual fable fixed on the weight and trajectory of language itself. The success of a phrase, the young narrator instructs, "rests in a crux that is barely discernible. One's fingertips must grasp the key, gently warming it. And then the key must be turned once, not twice." But even this is not the crux. The crux (Babel's severest literary dictum) is here: "No iron spike can pierce a human heart as icily as a period in the right place."

A writer's credo, and Babel's most intimate confession. Stand in awe of it, yes—but remember also that this same master of the white bone of truth, this artist of the delicately turned key, was once a shameless propagandist for the Revolution, capable of rabid exhortations: "Beat them, Red Fighters, clobber them to death, if it is the last thing you do! Right away! This minute! Now!" "Slaughter them, Red Army fighters! Stamp harder on the rising lids of their rancid coffins!" While it is a truism that every utopia contains the seeds of dystopia, Babel, after all, was granted skepticism almost from the start. Out of skepticism came disillusionment; out of disillusionment, revulsion. And in the end, as the tragic trope has it, the Revolution devoured its child.

Babel's art served as a way station to the devouring. He was devoured because he would not, could not, accommodate to falsehood; because he saw and he saw, with an eye as merciless as a klieg light; and because, like Kafka, he surrendered his stories to voices and passions tremulous with the unforeseen. If we wish to complete, and transmit, the literary configuration of the twentieth century—the image that will enduringly stain history's retina—now is the time (it is past time) to set Babel beside Kafka. Between them, they leave no nerve unshaken.

CYNTHIA OZICK

❧

PREFACE

by Nathalie Babel

*S*o, who was Isaac Emmanuelovich Babel? Was he a Soviet writer, a Russian writer, or a Jewish writer?

As a Soviet writer, he shows and experiences a profound dichotomy between acceptance of the ideals of the Revolution and repulsion for its methods. As a Russian writer, he expresses both nostalgia for the old world and desire for the new. As a Jewish writer, he was well versed in Hebrew and the Talmud. Yet he wrote in Russian. His work reveals what many have called a "Jewish sensibility." However, when he used the typical Jewish themes found in Yiddish literature, they were always interwoven with Russian cultural archetypes.

Babel's work defies categorization. Simply put, in my personal view, the juxtaposition of compatibles and incompatibles keeps Babel's prose in a state of constant tension and gives it its unique character. Approaching Babel with expectations based on traditional Russian literature might lead either to disappointment or to a feeling of discovery. His prose does not merely draw on past themes and forms, but is the forging of a new manner of writing, which reflected new times. Babel's readers are not only students of Russian literature and history or of the Russian Revolution. They belong to different cultures, different religions, and different social classes. They have no single national tradition.

Critics have taken various positions and a great deal of research and passion has been invested in solving questions of Babel's personal convictions and literary style. Actually, the critical literature on Babel's works fills bookcases, compared to the mere half shelf of his own writings. Babel started writing as an adolescent, but he himself considered that his career as a man of letters, writing "clearly and concisely," began only in 1924. It was then that his stories, which were to become the volumes entitled *Red Cavalry* and *The Odessa Stories* started to appear. The young writer burst upon the literary scene and instantly became the rage in Moscow. The tradition in Russia being to worship poets and writers, Babel soon became one of the happy few, a group that included Soviet writers, who enjoyed exceptional status and privileges in an otherwise impoverished and despotic country. He was allowed to travel abroad and to stay in Western Europe for relatively long periods of time. In the late 1930s, he was given a villa in the writers' colony of Peredelkino, outside Moscow. No secret was ever made of his having a wife and daughter in Paris. At the same time, hardly anyone outside of Moscow knew of two other children he had fathered. As a matter of fact, Babel had many secrets, lived with many ambiguities and contradictions, and left many unanswered questions behind him.

During his lifetime, Babel was loved, admired, and respected as a writer. The following entry from the first volume of the second edition of the *Small Soviet Encyclopedia* of March 1937 provides an insightful description of the man and the writer. I will quote from this article, since I find it well documented, critically sound, and psychologically perceptive. It shows what Babel was striving for and what he in fact achieved. Moreover, it is astonishing to note the date of publication, the year 1937, when the ground was very shaky for Jews and intellectuals. It seems that when the books were already printed in March 1937, the publishers did not have time to revise the contents of the encyclopedia according to the Party's latest interpretations of Soviet history. They did, however, manage to glue by hand an addendum of "corrections" into each of the sixty-one thousand copies of the first volume before they were distributed, explaining the need for the revision of several of the articles. Fortunately for us, the entry on Babel was neither "corrected" nor removed.

> **Babel, Isaac Emmanuelovich** (born 1894)—Soviet writer; son of an Odessa merchant. His first stories appeared in 1916, although the height of his literary activity occurred during the years 1923–1924. Babel's literary output is small in volume. His basic genre was the "novella" or short story, most of which can be grouped into three the-

matic cycles: "Odessa Stories," mainly about the exploits of the gang-
sters of Odessa (the film scenario of "Benya Krik" and the play
"Sunset" also fall under this theme); the collection of stories "Red
Cavalry"—impressions of the 1920 campaign of the army of
Budyonny, in which Babel took part; and autobiographical stories
("The Story of My Dovecote," etc.). . . .

An aesthete with a heightened interest in all the colorful revelations of the human character, inclined towards the abstract intellectual humanism and to romanticism, expressing through his whole life
and work the agonizing sensation of his own dilettante weaknesses,
Babel admired the heroic spirit of the Revolutionary and saw the
Revolution as essentially elemental, accepting it without fear.

In his portrayal of Red Cavalry soldiers, as with the gangsters of
Odessa, Babel expresses both admiration and horror of their strength and
natural daring, through his own intellectual's skeptical irony. This creates
an original combination of heroics and humor. Characteristically, in his
book "Red Cavalry," Babel focuses his attention less on the colorful
episodes of military life, and more on the wild escapades of the partisans.

Typical for Babel is his primordial florid imagery, his original syn-
thesis of romanticism and sharp naturalism, of the physiological and
the erotic, which at times becomes pathological. His great mastery is
in his concise picturesque story telling, his bright and witty commu-
nication of local color and life (for example—the subtly humorous
depiction of Jewish life in "Odessa Stories").

The stories which he published after his long silence in
1931–1932, including the fragment "Gapa Guzhva"—which touches
separately on the theme of collectivization, are similar in nature to his
earlier literary work.

L. KAGAN

Indeed, the author of this "politically incorrect" article was on dangerous ground. One wonders whatever happened to Mr. Kagan.

By this time, the Great Purges were in full swing. Stalin held the
country in his fist. His Revolutionary comrades, his generals, writers,
anarchists, so-called Trotskyites, and their associates were arrested, tortured, and shot. The political terror penetrated all spheres of life, including literary and cultural circles. It was only a matter of time before my
father's turn would come. He surely must have known that he himself had
been under the vigilant surveillance of the secret police for some years.

On May 15, 1939, Babel was arrested. He disappeared. Not a trace, not a word. He vanished. His lodgings were searched and every scrap of paper was confiscated—correspondence, drafts, manuscripts, everything. None of it has ever resurfaced. His name, his works, were officially erased as though he had never existed. There was only silence. How could a man so friendly, so socially astute, so famous, not be able to pass a word to the outside? And so the guessing began, and slowly, a sort of myth emerged. He never existed, but by his nonexistence, he became famous. I have been asked many times in my life, "Do you know how he died? Do you know where? Do you know why?" There is another question also often asked. "Why did he go back to the Soviet Union? The times were already bad. Didn't he know it? Why didn't he stay in Paris with his family?" Babel came to Paris in the summer of 1935, as part the delegation of Soviet writers to the International Congress of Writers for the Defense of Culture and Peace. He probably knew this would have been his last chance to remain in Europe. As he had done numerous times for some ten years, he asked my mother to return with him to Moscow. Although he knew the general situation was bad, he nevertheless described to her the comfortable life that the family could have there together. It was the last opportunity my mother had to give a negative answer, and she never forgot it. Perhaps it helped her later on to be proven completely right in her fears and her total lack of confidence in the Soviet Union. My mother described to me these last conversations with my father many times.

So, why did he go back to Moscow in 1935? For many years, Babel had battled with the dilemma of his life situation. During his lengthy visits to Paris dating from 1926, he could express his thoughts without fear of possible betrayal. According to his close friend Boris Souvarine,* for example, Babel had a great knowledge of high political spheres in

*Boris Souvarine (1895–1984), historian and writer of Russian origin, who settled in Paris. On Lenin's personal recommendation, he became a member of the Committee for the Third International (1919), later a member of the Executive Committee of the Komintern (1921-1924), and a member of the French Communist Party, which he helped to create and from which he was expelled in 1924. Author of *Staline: Aperçu historique du Bolchevisme* (1935), the first biography and historical study of Joseph Stalin, and *Dernières conversations avec Babel*, Ed. Counterpoint, 1979, later a chapter in his book *Souvenirs sur Panait Istrati, Isaac Babel, et Pierre Pascal*, Ed. Gérard Lebovici, Paris, 1985. Souvarine was considered the foremost French specialist on Kremlin politics. The first monograph on his life and work, *Boris Souvarine: le premier désenchanté du communisme*, by Jean Louis Panné, was published in Paris in 1993 by Robert Laffont. The title speaks for itself.

the Soviet Union, of its plots, manipulations and daily practices. He knew very well the nature of Stalin's character and private life, and had no illusions about Stalin's monstrous intentions and crimes.

Another person with intimate knowledge of Babel's political views at the time was Yuri Annenkov.* In his memoirs, Annenkov wrote of his many encounters with Babel in Paris and of the letters he received from him through the early 1930s. In 1932, Babel returned to Paris to visit his family, after an absence of three years. Annenkov wrote, "Babel's moods had changed significantly in the past months. It's true, he was still a big joker, but his topics of conversation were different. The last stay in the Soviet Union and the growing repression of creative art through the demands and instructions of the State had completely disillusioned him. To write within the framework of 'the barrack mentality of Soviet ideology' was intolerable for him, yet he didn't know how he could manage to live otherwise."[†]

Annenkov described another visit with Babel in 1932, noting that the conversation had just one subject: how to manage to live further.

"I have a family: a wife and daughter," said Babel, "I love them and have to provide for them. Under no circumstances do I want them to return to Sovietland. They must remain here in freedom. But what about myself? Should I stay here and become taxi driver, like the heroic Gaito Gazdanov? But you see, he has no children! Should I return to our proletarian revolution? Revolution indeed! It's disappeared! The proletariat? It flew off, like an old buggy with a leaky roof, that's lost its wheels. And it stayed wheelless. Now, dear brother, it's the Central Committees that are pushing forward—they'll be more effective. They don't need wheels—they have machine guns instead. All the rest is clear and needs no further commentary, as they say in polite society. . . . Maybe I won't become a taxi driver after all, although, as you know, I passed the driving test long ago. Here a taxi driver has more freedom than the rector of a Soviet university. . . . Driver or no driver, I'm going to become a free man."**

*Yuri Pavlovich Annenkov (1889–1974), famous Russian portraitist, painter, printmaker, scientific draftsman, theater designer, cartoonist, writer, critic, stage manager. Left the USSR in 1924 and settled in Paris. His memoirs of his meetings with well-known artists, writers, and political figures were published in 1996 (*People and Portraits: A Tragic Cycle*, Vols. 1–2, published by the Inter-Language Literary Associates, New York, 1996).

[†]Annenkov, pp. 305–306.

*As above.

On July 27, 1933, Babel wrote to Annenkov that he had received a strange summons from Moscow and was departing immediately, "in the most dramatic conditions and no money and a lot of debts everywhere. . . . Live well without me. Don't forget Evgenia Borisovna* while I'm gone. . . . I kiss you. I'm glad that I'm going to Moscow. All the rest is bitter and uncertain."†

This turned out to be the last letter Yuri Annenkov ever received from my father. In their correspondence, Babel sounds to me like a man divided in his heart, a man pulled with equal force in two different directions.

In 1933, Babel still had a powerful political protector, his beloved mentor Alexei Maximovich Gorky. Gorky had played a critical and irreplaceable role in Babel's life. Babel wrote in 1924, "At the end of 1916, I happened to meet Gorky. I owe everything to this meeting and to this day speak the name of Alexei Maximovich with love and reverence. He published my first stories in the November 1916 issue of *Letopis*. Alexei Maximovich taught me extremely important things and sent me into the world, at a time when it was clear that my two or three tolerable attempts as a young man were at best successful by accident, that I would not get anywhere with literature, and that I wrote amazingly badly."**

During a trip to Italy in the spring of 1933, shortly before returning to the Soviet Union, my father visited Gorky in Sorrento. His death in 1936 was a great personal loss for Babel and signaled the inevitable coming tragedy.

One of Babel's main preoccupations was money. All his adult life, Babel had money problems and worried about them. Not that he did not make money. On the contrary, he made a lot of money. In the 1920s, his stories were published and republished in book form. In one year (1924–1925), four collections of stories and two screenplays were published. He also received payment for foreign editions. In the 1930s,

---

*Evgenia Borisovna Babel, born Gronfein. My parents were married on August 9, 1919, in Odessa.

†Annenkov, p. 307.

**Excerpt from an autobiographical sketch by Babel that appeared in Lidin, Vladimir (ed.), "*Pisateli: avtobiografii i portrety sovremennykh russkikh prozaikov*" ("Authors: Autobiographies and Portraits of Contemporary Russian Writers") Sovremennyie Problemi (Contemporary Problems), Moscow, 1926, pp. 27–29.

he worked for film studios in Moscow, Kiev, and Leningrad and was extremely well paid for his efforts. He not only wrote original scripts, but also revised the screenplays of others, without attribution to himself. Apparently, he was the main author of *The Gorky Trilogy*, which appeared only after his arrest and without his name in the film credits.

Babel's problem was not the absence of money, but his inability to manage it. Above all, he felt the obligation to take care of his relatives abroad. His sister Meri Emmanuelovna Chapochnikoff had left in 1924 to join her fiancé, who was studying medicine in Belgium; my mother Evgenia Borisovna had left in 1925, taking with her a lifelong hatred of the Bolsheviks; and his mother, the last one to leave, joined her daughter in Brussels in 1926.

As I noted in my introduction to *The Lonely Years*, "Money matters tormented him. To make more money, he had to work under increasingly difficult conditions. Moreover, the impractical Babel would let his generosity run away with him. Whether he was in Moscow or in Paris, distant relatives, friends and friends of friends were continually imploring him for financial assistance. A few weeks after his return to the Soviet Union from a trip abroad, he would find himself totally impoverished, his Soviet friends having finished the job that had begun in Paris. Above all, Babel feared that his economic position would affect his work. His life centered on writing."*

His inability to imagine himself as anything but a writer played a critical role in his refusal to leave the USSR. His stays abroad made him understand that he could not make a comfortable living as an émigré writer.

As Cynthia Ozick observed in a review of Babel's *1920 Diary*, "By remaining in the Soviet Union and refusing finally to bend his art to Soviet directives, Babel sacrificed his life to his language."†

Souvarine remembers what he called Babel's leitmotiv, "I am a Russian writer. If I did not live with the Russian people, I would cease being a writer. I would be like a fish out of water."** Actually, my mother would use these words almost verbatim to explain my father's

---

Isaac Babel: The Lonely Years 1925–1939. Unpublished Stories and Private Correspondence. Edited with an Intoduction by Nathalie Babel, published by Farrar, Straus and Co., 1964.

†Cynthia Ozick, "The Year of Writing Dangerously," *The New Republic*, May 8, 1995.

**Boris Souvarine, *Souvenirs sur Panait Istrati, Isaac Babel, et Pierre Pascal*, Ed. Gérard Lebovici, Paris 1985, p. 34.

absence and why I had no brothers and sisters, whom I had always wanted. This romantic ideal of the writer, which was only part of the story, stayed with me for a very long part of my life. It took many years to let it go.

For Babel, it is clear that there was no one ideal solution. In the end, a man's destiny is his own.

In 1954, after many years of official silence, Babel's name was heard again. A typed half sheet of ordinary paper, accepted as an official document, declared, "The sentence of the Military College dated 26 January 1940 concerning Babel I. E. is revoked on the basis of newly discovered circumstances and the case against him is terminated in the absence of elements of a crime." The news took a couple of years to leak out of Moscow to the rest of Europe. Several decades later in the early 1990s, following the breakup of the Soviet Union, some brave souls were able to get access to the KGB's archives on Babel. Minute records had been kept about the arrest and interrogations of the accused.

As we now know, his trial took place on January 26, 1940, in one of Lavrenti Beria's private chambers. It lasted about twenty minutes. The sentence had been prepared in advance and without ambiguity: death by firing squad, to be carried out immediately. Babel had been accused and convicted of "active participation in an anti-Soviet Trotskyite organization" and of "being a member of a terrorist conspiracy, as well as spying for the French and Austrian governments."

Babel's last recorded words in the proceedings were, "I am innocent. I have never been a spy. I never allowed any action against the Soviet Union. I accused myself falsely. I was forced to make false accusations against myself and others. . . . I am asking for only one thing—let me finish my work." He was shot the next day and his body was thrown into a communal grave. All of this horrific information was revealed in the early 1990s, a relatively short time ago.

Considering that revelations about my father have been coming to light for almost fifty years, a large portion of my life, I understand why it has never been possible to put an end to grieving. For many years now, I have been involved with attempting to bring together and to light what is recognized as the body of Babel's work. I hope the present project will provide further insights into his personality, as well as a greater knowledge and appreciation of his literary legacy.

NATHALIE BABEL
Washington, D.C.
March 2001

FOREWORD
by Peter Constantine

*O*ne of the great tragedies of twentieth century literature took place in the early morning hours of May 15, 1939, when a cadre of agents from the Soviet secret police burst into the house of Isaac Babel in Peredelkino, arrested him, and gathered up the many stacks of unpublished manuscripts in his office. From that day on, Babel, one of the foremost writers of his time, became a nonperson in the Soviet Union. His name was blotted out, removed from literary dictionaries and encyclopedias, and taken off school and university syllabi. He became unmentionable in any public venue. When the film director Mark Donskoi's famous Gorky trilogy premiered the following year, Babel, who had worked on the screenplay, had been removed from the credits.

Babel was executed in 1940. It was only in 1954, fourteen years later, that he was officially exonerated, but his books were only warily republished in the Soviet Union, and in censored form. And yet today, sixty-two years after his arrest and the subsequent silence surrounding his name, Babel is considered, both inside and outside Russia, to be among the most exciting—and at times unsettling—writers of the twentieth century.

Babel is one of the great masters of the short story, and for the translator a great and challenging master of style. It has been fascinating to see his style change from work to work. We are familiar with terms such as Proustian, Chekhovian, and Nabokovian, but, as I soon realized, the term "Babelian" is harder to define.

Babel burst onto the literary scene after the Bolshevik Revolution of 1917, becoming within a few years one of Russia's most original and highly regarded authors—"the best Russia has to offer," as Maxim Gorky wrote to André Malraux in 1926. Babel began his career during a time when Russian culture, society, and language were in total upheaval. World War I, the February and October Revolutions of 1917, and the Civil War left in their wake poverty, hunger, and social instability. At the same time, the promise of limitless change was in the air. The people of Russia felt that they were being given the opportunity to participate in an exhilarating and unprecedented social experiment which, if World Communism was to have its way, would be a global one.

The abrupt social changes on all levels, the abolition of imperial censorship, and the new feeling of liberty drove writers of Babel's generation—Mayakovsky, Pasternak, Zamyatin, Bulgakov—to write in new ways about new topics with an unprecedented vigor. Babel did this with a vengeance. His themes were steeped in the brutal realism of the times: In the arctic night of Petersburg a Chinese man, seeing a desperate prostitute, holds up a loaf of bread—"With his blue fingernail he draws a line across the crust. One pound. Glafira [the prostitute] raises two fingers. Two pounds." A teenage girl tries to help her younger sister abort her baby with a clothes hanger—their mother walks in on them just in time. These were contemporary topics that before Babel nobody had dared touch. When the valiant Red Cavalry rode into Poland, in what was intended to be the first step that would carry the glories of Communism to Europe and the world, Babel rode along. He brought back with him a series of stories that presented a literary portrait of war that has awed and haunted readers for almost eighty years.

One apt definition of "Babelian" might be: a trenchant and unrelenting literary re-creation of a world in war and turmoil. And yet this is a limited definition, for it leaves out Babel's irrepressible sense of humor.

In translating Babel I was constantly struck by the different registers of Babel's voice in different stories. Babel's first published piece, "Old Shloyme," which opens this volume, has little in common with the style, content, language, or rhythm of the second story, "At Grandmother's," or with the story after that, or with any of the other stories. The Odessa stories, traditionally thought of as a stylistic unit threaded through with feisty Babelian color, are, on closer scrutiny, just as disparate. In the first Odessa story, "The King," the author-narrator draws us into the wild gangster world of Odessa with his elegant and surprising prose: "The tables, draped in velvet, coiled through the yard like a snake on whose belly patches of every color had been daubed, and these orange and red velvet patches sang in deep voices." The second Odessa story, "Justice in Parentheses," begins on a very different note: "My first run-in was with Benya Krik, my second with Lyubka Shneiweis. Do you understand the meaning of these words? Can you drink in their full essence?" Here the narrator Zudechkis, a small-time wheeler-dealer who operates on the fringes of Odessa's Jewish underworld, suddenly steps into the foreground. The story is told from his perspective and in his subtly Yiddling words, "At five o'clock in the morning—or no, it must have been four, and then again, maybe it wasn't even four yet—the King entered my bedroom, grabbed me, if you will pardon the expression, by my back, dragged me out of bed. . . ." In the next story, "How Things Were Done in Odessa," the primary narrator is an unworldly Jew, described as having glasses on his nose and autumn in his heart.

The Red Cavalry stories are, stylistically speaking, just as varied. There is the "I" of Isaac Babel and the "I" of Kiril Lyutov, the very Russian war correspondent (who might go as far as admitting that his mother is Jewish). "Lyutov" was also the identity that Babel assumed in real life as a way of surviving among the fiercely anti-Semitic Cossacks of the Red Cavalry. There are also other narrators, such as the murderous Cossack Balmashov. When these characters are the narrators, the tone, style, and grammar in the stories begin to go awry. Babel is a master at re-creating the Cossacks' wild, ungrammatical speech filled with skewed and half-understood Communist doctrine. In "Salt," for instance, the entire story is narrated in the voice of a Cossack whose ranting jumble ranges from Communist jargon to folk verse:

> I want to tell you of some ignorant women who are harmful to us. I set my hopes on you, that you who travel around our nation's fronts have not overlooked the far-flung station of Fastov, lying afar beyond

the mountains grand, in a distant province of a distant land, where many a jug of home-brewed beer we drank with merriment and cheer.

Babel's later stories are very different in plot and structure. They are longer and more complex, and though they are among his most brilliant works, they lack some of the wildness and innovation of his earlier writing. Though Babel had achieved international fame, as the Stalin regime became increasingly repressive it grew harder for him to publish his work: Babel was not the kind of writer to conform to the prescribed formulas of Socialist Realism. His growing caution and ensuing well-publicized "silence" were the result of the increasing stringency of Stalin's censor. The freedom and creative euphoria of the early 1920s were over.

PETER CONSTANTINE
New York
March 2001

ACKNOWLEDGMENTS

*T*he realization of this volume, and the larger *Complete Works* upon which it is based, has been a long-term dream and struggle. The struggle has been made easier by my good fortune in working with Peter Constantine, who took it upon himself to translate anew all available original manuscripts and the first publications in Russian—a long and arduous task. Peter was not only meticulous in his choice of words and phrasing, but also in his research in order to clarify the text and provide notes where necessary. He also was of great help to me in organizing and editing this large and unwieldy collection of materials, and in supporting me with frequent practical advice and unflagging enthusiasm.

I approached Gregory Freidin without warning to request that he prepare a biographical and literary chronology of Babel's life and works. Gregory's exceptional knowledge allowed us to sort out many conflicting or incomplete items of information. I thank him for his graciousness in completing this task.

Special thanks are also due to Robert Weil, my editor at W. W. Norton, who embraced the challenge of giving new life to Babel's work through what he knew would be a difficult project. His editorial advice and his steadfast guidance have earned my heartfelt gratitude. Without the professional perseverance and affectionate encouragement of my friend and literary agent, Jennifer Lyons, this work would not have been completed. I thank her warmly. I also cannot hope to acquit my debt merely with thanks, or even the feelings of profound gratitude and affection that I feel for my friend, Christine Galitzine. As she became more and more interested in this project, she also became more indispensable to my being able to advance it. Through her knowledge of English, French, and Russian, as well as her own literary and administrative gifts, she was able to understand my thoughts and sentiments deeply and to help me render them onto the printed page. Indeed, her involvement in this work has been invaluable.

This publication is also the realization of a dream of my husband, Richard Harvey Brown, who for over thirty years has hoped that I would be able to master my memories sufficiently to bring these volumes to print. His benevolence and loving support throughout these struggles also should be publicly acknowledged.

NATHALIE BABEL BROWN

I would like to thank Nathalie Babel for offering me this project, and for her constant support and encouragement. I owe particular thanks to my Russian editor, Anneta Greenlee, for her tireless checking of my translation against the Russian original for stylistic nuance. My translation owes much to her specialized knowledge of early-twentieth-century Russian language and literature. I am also grateful to Katya Ilina for the weeks she spent studying the many editions of Babel works, checking for editorial variations and instances of Soviet censorship.

I am also indebted to my editor at Norton, Robert Weil, for his insightful and knowledgeable editing and particularly for his expertise in American and European Jewish literature. I am also grateful to Jason Baskin and Nomi Victor, editors at Norton, and to David Cole for copyediting the manuscript.

I am indebted to Professor Gregory Freidin for his help and advice, and for his specialized knowledge of Isaac Babel's life and works, and to Christine Galitzine for her knowledge of pre-Revolutionary Russia.

I am thankful to Peter Glassgold for his initial suggestion that I translate Isaac Babel, and for his helpful editorial advice. I am thankful also to my agent, Jessica Wainwright, for her encouragement and constant support as I worked on the translation. I also wish to thank Jennifer Lyons, the agent of the Babel estate, for her help and input.

I am deeply indebted to the resources of the New York Public Library, where I did all my research and annotation. I owe special gratitude to Edward Kasinec, curator of the Slavic and Baltic Division, for his erudite advice and for the many times he personally located materials for me that were hidden in obscure Soviet publications of the 1920s and 1930s. I am also grateful to Tanya Gizdavcic, librarian of the Slavic and Baltic Division, for her help in locating material, and to Serge Gleboff, Robert Davis, Lev Chaban, and Hee-Gwone Yoo for their help and advice.

I would like to thank Paul Glasser at YIVO for his helpful explanations of Yiddish expressions. I would also like to express my appreciation to Karina Vamling from the Linguistics Department of the University of Lund, Sweden, for her explanations of Georgian expressions in Isaac Babel's texts and the information she provided on aspects of Georgian and Caucasian politics that Babel referred to, and to Peter Gasiorowski of the University of Poznan, Poland, for his linguistic advice. I am also grateful to Thomas Fiddick for his help—I benefited greatly from his books and articles on the Russian-Polish war of 1920. I am thankful as well to Patricia Herlihy for her encouragement: I found her book *Odessa: A History, 1794–1914* a great help in putting early-twentieth-century Odessa—the Odessa of Babel's early years— into perspective. I found the extensive annotations in the German translation of the *1920 Diary* by Peter Urban very helpful, as I did the scholarly and bibliographical work on Babel by Efraim Sicher.

My very special thanks to Burton Pike, who inspired, helped, and advised me throughout the project.

PETER CONSTANTINE

THE
COLLECTED
STORIES
OF
ISAAC BABEL

Early Stories

❧

When the twenty-one-year-old Isaac Babel arrived in St. Petersburg in 1916, he found the city in wild but stimulating upheaval. It was still the capital of Russia and the center of Russian literature and art, where the foremost writers of the day lived and published. But the city was shaken by World War I. The Imperial government was losing control, and calls for change, which were to lead to the Revolution and Civil War, were in the air. Perhaps most important for a young writer was that the Czarist censorship was crumbling, which meant that daring new subjects could be treated in new ways, a characteristic that was to stay with Babel throughout his writing career. His first published story, "Old Shloyme" (1913), dealt with the subversive subject of Jews forced by officially sanctioned anti-Semitism to renounce their religion. In the story, a young Jew gives in to the pressure to Russianize himself, "to leave his people for a new God," while the old Jew, though never interested in religion or tradition, cannot bring himself to give them up. In the subsequent stories, Babel touches on other taboo subjects: Jewish men mixing with Christian women, prostitution, teenage pregnancy, and abortion.

These early stories also reveal Babel's growing interest in using language in new and unusual ways. He has a young woman offer herself to her lover, "and the lanky fellow wallowed in businesslike bliss." Odessa matrons, "plump with idleness and naively corseted are passionately squeezed behind bushes by fervent students of medicine or law." Babel describes the Czarina as "a small woman with a tightly powdered face, a consummate schemer with an indefatigable passion for power." In a forest scene, "green leaves bent toward one another, caressed each other with their flat hands." We also see the recurring motifs of sun and sunset, which are to play an important role in Babel's later writing.

Babel's piquant brand of realism soon caught the eye of Maxim Gorky, who was to be the single most influential literary figure in the Soviet Union during the 1920s and 1930s, and who was particularly instrumental in helping young Soviet writers. Gorky published Babel's stories "Elya Isaakovich and Margarita Prokofievna," and "Mama, Rimma, and Alla" in 1916 in his literary magazine LETOPIS, which marked the beginning of Gorky's mentoring of Babel's career. This mentoring was to last until Gorky's death exactly twenty years later.

OLD SHLOYME

*A*lthough our town is small, its inhabitants few in number, and although Shloyme had not left this town once in sixty years, you'd be hard-pressed to find a single person who was able to tell you exactly who Shloyme was or what he was all about. The reason for this, plain and simple, is that he was forgotten, the way you forget an unnecessary thing that doesn't jump out and grab you. Old Shloyme was precisely that kind of thing. He was eighty-six years old. His eyes were watery. His face—his small, dirty, wrinkled face—was overgrown with a yellowish beard that had never been combed, and his head was covered with a thick, tangled mane. Shloyme almost never washed, seldom changed his clothes, and gave off a foul stench. His son and daughter-in-law, with whom he lived, had stopped bothering about him—they kept him in a warm corner and forgot about him. His warm corner and his food were all that Shloyme had left, and it seemed that this was all he needed. For him, warming his old broken bones and eating a nice, fat, juicy piece of meat were the purest bliss. He was the first to come to the table, and greedily watched every bite with unflinching eyes, convulsively cramming food into his mouth with his long bony fingers, and he ate, ate, ate till they refused to give him any more, even a tiny little piece. Watching Shloyme eat was disgusting: his whole puny body quivered, his fingers covered with grease, his face so pitiful, filled with the dread that someone might harm him, that he might be forgotten. Sometimes his daughter-in-law would play a little trick on Shloyme. She would serve the food, and then act as if she had overlooked him.

The old man would begin to get agitated, look around helplessly, and try to smile with his twisted, toothless mouth. He wanted to show that food was not important to him, that he could perfectly well make do without it, but there was so much pleading in the depths of his eyes, in the crease of his mouth, in his outstretched, imploring arms, and his smile, wrenched with such difficulty, was so pitiful, that all jokes were dropped, and Shloyme received his portion.

And thus he lived in his corner—he ate and slept, and in the summer he also lay baking in the sun. It seemed that he had long ago lost all ability to comprehend anything. Neither his son's business nor household matters interested him. He looked blankly at everything that took place around him, and the only fear that would flutter up in him was that his grandson might catch on that he had hidden a dried-up piece of honey cake under his pillow. Nobody ever spoke to Shloyme, asked his advice about anything, or asked him for help. And Shloyme was quite happy, until one day his son came over to him after dinner and shouted loudly into his ear, "Papa, they're going to evict us from here! Are you listening? Evict us, kick us out!" His son's voice was shaking, his face twisted as if he were in pain. Shloyme slowly raised his faded eyes, looked around, vaguely comprehending something, wrapped himself tighter in his greasy frock coat, didn't say a word, and shuffled off to sleep.

From that day on Shloyme began noticing that something strange was going on in the house. His son was crestfallen, wasn't taking care of his business, and at times would burst into tears and look furtively at his chewing father. His grandson stopped going to high school. His daughter-in-law yelled shrilly, wrung her hands, pressed her son close to her, and cried bitterly and profusely.

Shloyme now had an occupation, he watched and tried to comprehend. Muffled thoughts stirred in his long-torpid brain. "They're being kicked out of here!" Shloyme knew why they were being kicked out. "But Shloyme can't leave! He's eighty-six years old! He wants to stay warm! It's cold outside, damp. . . . No! Shloyme isn't going anywhere! He has nowhere to go, nowhere!" Shloyme hid in his corner and wanted to clasp the rickety wooden bed in his arms, caress the stove, the sweet, warm stove that was as old as he was. "He grew up here, spent his poor, bleak life here, and wants his old bones to be buried in the small local cemetery!" At moments when such thoughts came to him, Shloyme became unnaturally animated, walked up to his son, wanted to talk to him with passion and at great length, to give him advice on a couple of things, but . . . it had been such a long time since he had spoken to anyone, or given anyone advice. And the words froze in his toothless mouth, his raised arm dropped weakly. Shloyme, all huddled up as if ashamed at his outburst, sullenly went back to his corner and listened to what his son was saying to his daughter-in-law. His hearing was bad, but with fear and dread he sensed something terrifying. At such moments his son felt the heavy crazed look of the old man, who was being driven insane, focused on him. The old man's two small eyes with their accursed probing, seemed incessantly to sense something, to question something. On one occasion words were said too loudly—it had slipped the daughter-in-law's mind that Shloyme was still alive. And right after her words were spoken, there was a quiet, almost smothered wail. It was old Shloyme. With tottering steps, dirty and disheveled, he slowly hobbled over to his son, grabbed his hands, caressed them, kissed them, and, not taking his inflamed eyes off his son, shook his head several times, and for the first time in many, many years, tears flowed from his eyes. He didn't say anything. With difficulty he got up from his knees, his bony hand wiping away the tears; for some reason he shook the dust off his frock coat and shuffled back to his corner, to where the warm stove stood. Shloyme wanted to warm himself. He felt cold.

From that time on, Shloyme thought of nothing else. He knew one thing for certain: his son wanted to leave his people for a new God. The old, forgotten faith was kindled within him. Shloyme had never been religious, had rarely ever prayed, and in his younger days had even had the reputation of being godless. But to leave, to leave one's God completely and forever, the God of an oppressed and suffering people—that he could not understand. Thoughts rolled heavily inside his head, he comprehended things with difficulty, but these words remained unchanged, hard, and terrible before him: "This mustn't happen, it mustn't!" And when Shloyme realized that disaster was inevitable, that his son couldn't hold out, he said to himself, "Shloyme, old Shloyme! What are you going to do now?" The old man looked around helplessly, mournfully puckered his lips like a child, and wanted to burst into the bitter tears of an old man. But there were no relieving tears. And then, at the moment his heart began aching, when his mind grasped the boundlessness of the disaster, it was then that Shloyme looked at his warm corner one last time and decided that no one was going to kick him out of here, they would never kick him out. "They will not let old Shloyme eat the dried-up piece of honey cake lying under his pillow! So what! Shloyme will tell God how he was wronged! After all, there is a God, God will take him in!" Shloyme was sure of this.

In the middle of the night, trembling with cold, he got up from his bed. Quietly, so as not to wake anyone, he lit a small kerosene lamp. Slowly, with an old man's groaning and shivering, he started pulling on his dirty clothes. Then he took the stool and the rope he had prepared the night before, and, tottering with weakness, steadying himself on the walls, went out into the street. Suddenly it was so cold. His whole body shivered. Shloyme quickly fastened the rope onto a hook, stood up next to the door, put the stool in place, clambered up onto it, wound the rope around his thin, quivering neck, kicked away the stool with his last strength, managing with his dimming eyes to glance at the town he had not left once in sixty years, and hung.

There was a strong wind, and soon old Shloyme's frail body began swaying before the door of his house in which he had left his warm stove and the greasy Torah of his forefathers.

AT GRANDMOTHER'S

*O*n Sabbaths after six classes I came home late. Walking through the streets didn't seem to me pointless. I could daydream remarkably well as I walked, and I felt that everything, everything around me was part of my being. I knew the signs, the stones of the houses, the windows of the stores. I knew them in a very special way, a very personal way, and I was firmly convinced that I saw the fundamental secret within them—what we grown-ups call the "essence" of things. Everything about them was deeply imprinted on my soul. When grown-ups mentioned a store in my presence, I envisioned its sign, the worn, golden letters, the little scratch in the left corner, the young lady with the tall coiffure at the cash register, and I remembered the air around this store that was not around any other. I pieced together from these stores, from the people, the air, the theater posters, my own hometown. To this day I remember, feel, and love this town—feel it, as one feels one's mother's scent, the scent of her caresses, words, and smiles, and I love this town because I grew up in it, was happy, melancholy, and dreamy in it. Passionately and singularly dreamy.

I always walked down the main street—that is where most of the people were.

The Sabbath I want to tell you about was a Sabbath in early spring. At that time of year, our air does not have the quiet tenderness, so sweet in central Russia, resting upon its peaceful streams and modest valleys. Our air has a sparkling, light coolness that blows with a shallow, chilly passion. I was no more than a young boy then and didn't understand a thing, but I felt the spring, and I blossomed and reddened in the chill.

The walk lasted a long time. I stared at the diamonds in the jeweler's window, read the theater posters from A to Z, and once I even studied the pale pink corsets with their long, wavy suspenders in Madam Rosalie's store. As I was about to walk on, I collided with a tall student who had a big black mustache. He smiled at me and asked, "So you're examining these closely, are you?" I was mortified. Then he patronizingly patted me on the back and said in a superior tone, "Keep up the good work, dear colleague! My compliments! All the best!" He roared with laughter, turned, and walked away. I felt very flustered, avoided looking at Madam Rosalie's display window, and quickly headed for home.

I was supposed to spend the Sabbath at my grandmother's. She had her own room at the very end of the apartment, behind the kitchen. A stove stood in the corner of this room, Grandmother always felt cold. The room was hot and stuffy, which made me feel melancholy and want to escape, to get out into the open.

I dragged my belongings over to Grandmother's, my books, my music stand, and my violin. The table had already been set for me. Grandmother sat in the corner. I ate. We didn't say a word. The door was locked. We were alone. There was cold gefilte fish for dinner with horseradish (a dish worth embracing Judaism for), a rich and delicious soup, roasted meat with onions, salad, compote, coffee, pie, and apples. I ate everything. I was a dreamer, it is true, but a dreamer with a hearty appetite. Grandmother cleared away the dishes. The room became tidy. There were wilting flowers on the windowsill. What grandmother loved best among all living things were her son, her grandson, Mimi her dog, and flowers. Mimi came over, rolled herself up on the sofa, and immediately fell asleep. She was kind of a lazy pooch, but a splendid dog, good, clever, small, and pretty. Mimi was a pug dog. Her coat was light-colored. Even in old age she didn't get flabby or heavy, but managed to remain svelte and slim. She lived with us for a long time, from birth to death, the whole fifteen years of her dog life, and, needless to say, she loved us, and most of all our severe and unbending grandmother. I shall tell about what tight-mouthed, secretive friends they were another time. It is a very interesting and tender story.

So there we were, the three of us—Grandmother, Mimi, and me.
Mimi slept. Grandmother, kind, wearing her holiday silk dress, sat in
the corner, and I was supposed to study. That day was difficult for me.
There were six classes in the high school, and Mr. Sorokin, the music
teacher, was supposed to come, and Mr. L., the Hebrew teacher, to
make up the lesson I had missed, and then maybe Peysson, my French
teacher. I had to prepare for all these lessons. I could deal with L. eas-
ily enough, we were old friends, but the music and the scales—what
anguish! First of all, I started on my homework. I spread out my notebooks and painstakingly began to do my mathematics problems.
Grandmother didn't interrupt me, God forbid. The tension inside her,
and her reverence for my work, gave her face a dazed look. Her eyes,
round, yellow, transparent, never left me. I would turn a page—and her
eyes would slowly follow my hand. Another person might have suffered
greatly under her persistent, watchful, unwavering stare, but I was used
to it.

Then Grandmother listened to me recite my lessons. It has to be
said that her Russian was bad—she had her own peculiar way of man-
gling words, mixing Russian with Polish and Hebrew. Needless to say,
she couldn't read or write Russian, and would hold books upside down.
But that didn't deter me from reciting my lesson from beginning to
end. Grandmother listened without understanding a word, but to her
the music of the words was sweet, she bowed before science, believed
me, believed in me, and wanted me to become a "bogatir"*—that is
what she called a rich man. I finished my lessons and began reading a
book. At the time, I was reading "First Love" by Turgenev. I liked
everything in it, the clear words, the descriptions, the conversations, but
the scene that made me shiver all over was the one in which Vladimir's
father strikes Zinaida's cheek with a whip. I could hear the whip's
whistling sound—its lithe leather body sharply, painfully, instantly biting into me. I was seized by an indescribable emotion. At that point in
the book I had to stop reading, and pace up and down the room. And
Grandmother sat there stock-still, and even the hot, stupefying air did
not stir, as if it sensed I was studying and shouldn't be disturbed. The
heat in the room kept rising. Mimi began snoring. Until then there had

---

*The grandmother is mixing up *Bogatir*, a Herculean hero in Russian folklore, with *bogaty*,
"rich man."

been silence, a ghostly silence, not a sound. Everything seemed uncanny at that moment and I wanted to run away from it all, and yet I wanted to stay there forever. The darkening room, Grandmother's yellow eyes, her tiny body wrapped in a shawl silent and hunched over in the corner, the hot air, the closed door, and the clout of the whip, and that piercing whistle—only now do I realize how strange it all was, how much it meant to me. I was snatched out of this troubled state by the doorbell. Sorokin had come. I hated him at that moment, I hated the scales, the incomprehensible, pointless, shrill music. I must admit that Sorokin was quite a nice fellow. He wore his black hair cropped very short, had large red hands, and beautiful thick lips. On that day, under Grandmother's watchful stare, he had to work for a whole hour, even longer, he had to push himself to the limit. For all of this he got absolutely no recognition. The old woman's eyes coldly and persistently followed his every move, remaining distant and indifferent. Grandmother had no interest in outside people. She demanded that they fulfill their obligations to us, and nothing more. We began our lesson. I wasn't frightened of Grandmother, but for a full hour I had to brave poor Sorokin's boundless zeal. He felt extremely ill-at-ease in this remote room, in the presence of a dog peacefully asleep and a coldly watchful, hostile old woman. Finally he took his leave. Grandmother gave him her hard, wrinkled, large hand with indifference, without shaking it. On his way out, he stumbled into a chair.

I also survived the following hour, Mr. L.'s lesson, longing for the moment that the door would close behind him too.

Evening came. Faraway golden dots ignited in the sky. Our courtyard, a deep cage, was dazzled by the moon. A woman's voice next door sang the ballad "Why I Am Madly in Love." My parents went to the theater. I became melancholy. I was tired. I had read so much, studied so much, seen so much. Grandmother lit a lamp. Her room immediately became quiet. The dark, heavy furniture was softly illuminated. Mimi woke up, walked through the room, came back to us again, and waited for her supper. The maid brought in the samovar. Grandmother was a tea lover. She had saved a slice of honey cake for me. We drank large quantities. Sweat sparkled in Grandmother's deep, sharp wrinkles. "Are you sleepy?" she asked. "No," I said. We began to talk. And once more I heard Grandmother's stories. Long ago, many, many years ago, there was a Jew who ran a tavern. He was poor, married, burdened with children, and traded in bootleg vodka. The commissar came and tormented him. Life became difficult. He went to the *tsaddik* and said, "Rabbi! The commissar is vexing me to death! Speak to God on my behalf!" "Go in peace," the *tsaddik* said to him. "The commissar will calm down." The Jew left. At the threshold of his tavern he found the commissar. He was lying there dead, with a purple, swollen face.

Grandmother fell silent. The samovar hummed. The woman next door was still singing. The moon still dazzled. Mimi wagged her tail. She was hungry.

"In olden times, people had beliefs!" Grandmother said. "Life on earth was simpler. When I was a girl, the Poles rebelled. Near where we lived was a count's estate. Even the Czar came to visit the count. Seven days and seven nights they made merry. At night I ran over to the count's castle and looked through the bright windows. The count had a daughter and the finest pearls in the world. Then came the uprising. Soldiers dragged him out onto the square. We all stood there crying. The soldiers dug a pit. They wanted to blindfold the old man. He said, "That will not be necessary!" The count stood before the soldiers and ordered, "Fire!" He was a tall, gray-haired man. The muzhiks loved him. Just as they began burying him, a messenger came galloping up. He brought a pardon from the Czar.

The samovar had gone out. Grandmother drank her last, cold glass of tea, and sucked on a piece of sugar with her toothless mouth.

"Your grandfather," she began, "knew many stories, but he had no beliefs whatsoever, he only believed in people. He gave away all his money to his friends, and when his turn came to ask them for something they kicked him down the stairs, and he lost his mind."

And then Grandmother told me about my grandfather, a tall, haughty, passionate, and despotic man. He played the violin, wrote literary works at night, and knew all the languages. He was governed by an unquenchable thirst for knowledge and life. A general's daughter fell in love with their eldest son, who traveled a lot, played cards, and died in Canada at the age of thirty-seven. All Grandmother had left was one son and me. It was all over. Day slips into evening, and death slowly approaches. Grandmother falls silent, lowers her head, and begins crying.

"Study!" she suddenly said forcefully. "Study and you can have everything—wealth and glory. You must know everything. Everyone will fall on their knees before you and bow to you. Let them envy you. Don't believe in people. Don't have friends. Don't give them your money. Don't give them your heart!"

Grandmother stops talking. Silence. Grandmother is thinking of bygone years and sorrows, is thinking about my fate, and her severe testament rests heavily, eternally, on my weak, young shoulders. In the dark corner, the incandescent cast-iron stove is blazing intensely. I'm suffocating, I can't breathe, I want to run out into the air, into the open, but I don't have the strength to lift my drooping head.

Dishes clatter in the kitchen. Grandmother goes there. We're going to have supper. I hear her angry, metallic voice. She is shouting at the maid. I feel strange and troubled. Just a short while ago she had been breathing peace and sorrow. The maid snaps back at her. Grandmother's unbearably shrill voice rings out in an uncontrollable rage, "Get out of here, you dreck! I'm the mistress here. You are destroying my property. Get out of here!" I cannot bear her deafening voice of steel. I can see Grandmother through the half-open door. Her face is distorted, her lips are trembling thinly and relentlessly, her throat has thickened, as if it were bulging out. The maid answers back. "Get out of here," Grandmother says. Then there is silence. The maid bows, and quietly, as if she were afraid of offending the silence, slips out of the room.

We eat our dinner without talking. We eat our fill, abundantly and long. Grandmother's transparent eyes are staring immovably—what they are staring at, I do not know. After supper, she [. . .]*

* * *

More than that I do not see because I fall into a deep sleep, a child's sleep behind seven locks in Grandmother's hot room.

---

*Gap in manuscript.

ELYA ISAAKOVICH
AND
MARGARITA PROKOFIEVNA

*G*ershkovich came out of the police chief's office with a heavy heart. He had been informed that if he didn't leave Oryol on the first train, he would have to leave town in a chain gang. And leaving meant he would lose business.

With briefcase in hand, gaunt, unhurried, he walked down the dark street. At the corner, a tall female figure called out to him, "Will you come with me, sweetie?"

Gershkovich raised his head, looked at her through his shimmering spectacles, thought it over, and guardedly said, "I'll come."

The woman took him by the arm. They walked around the corner. "So where will we go? To a hotel?"

"I want something for the whole night," Gershkovich answered. "How about your place?"

"That'll cost you three rubles, Papa."

"Two," Gershkovich said.

"Not worth my while, Papa!"

• • •

He managed to haggle her down to two-and-a-half rubles. They began walking.

The prostitute's room was small, nice, and clean, with frayed curtains and a pink lamp.

When they entered, the woman took off her coat, unbuttoned her blouse, and winked at him.

"Hey!" Gershkovich said, knitting his brow. "Stop messing around!"

"You're in a bad mood, Papa."

She came over and sat on his knee.

"Well, I'll be damned!" Gershkovich said. "You must weigh at least five *pood*!"

"Four-point-three *pood*!"

She gave him a long kiss on his graying cheek.

•   •   •

"Hey!" Gershkovich said, knitting his brow again. "I'm tired, I want to go to sleep."

The prostitute stood up. Her face had become hard.

"You a Jew?"

He looked at her through his spectacles and answered, "No."

"Papa," the prostitute said slowly, "that'll be ten rubles."

He got up and walked to the door.

"Five," the woman said.

Gershkovich came back.

"Make up the bed for me," the Jew said wearily, then took off his jacket and looked for a place to hang it. "What's your name?"

"Margarita."

"Change the sheets, Margarita."

The bed was wide and covered with a soft eiderdown.

Gershkovich slowly started undressing. He took off his white socks, stretched his sweaty toes, locked the door with the key, put the key under his pillow, and lay down. Margarita yawned, and slowly took off her dress, squinted, squeezed out a pimple on her shoulder, and began plaiting a thin braid for the night.

"Papa, what's your name?"

"Eli. Elya Isaakovich."

"A tradesman?"

"Well, if you want to call it a trade . . ." Gershkovich answered vaguely.

Margarita blew out the night-light and lay down. . . .

•   •   •

"Well, I'll be damned!" Gershkovich said. "That's a whole lot of woman here."

Soon they were asleep.

• • •

Next morning the sun's bright light filled the room. Gershkovich woke up, dressed, and walked to the window.

"We have sea, and you have fields," he said. "Great."

"Where you from?" Margarita asked.

"Odessa," Gershkovich answered. "The number-one town, a good town." And he smiled slyly.

"It looks like you pretty much feel nice and fine everywhere," Margarita said.

"You can say that again," Gershkovich said. "Wherever there's people it's nice and fine."

"You're such a fool!" Margarita said, propping herself up on the bed. "People are evil."

"No," Gershkovich said. "People are good. They've been taught to think that they're evil, and they ended up believing it."

Margarita thought for a while, and then smiled.

"You're funny," she said slowly, and she ran her eyes carefully over him.

"Turn around, I'm going to get dressed."

Then they ate breakfast, drank tea with hard rolls. Gershkovich taught Margarita how to spread butter on a roll in a special way and to put the sausage on top.

"Try it! Though I have to be on my way now.

"Here are three rubles for you, Margarita," he said on his way out. "Believe me, rubles don't come easy nowadays."

Margarita smiled.

"You skinflint, you! So give me three. You coming back this evening?"

"Yes, I am."

That evening Gershkovich brought dinner with him—a herring, a bottle of beer, sausages, apples. Margarita was wearing a dark, high-buttoned dress. They talked as they ate.

"Nowadays you can't get by on fifty rubles a month," Margarita said. "And what with this job, if you don't dress up, you don't get no cabbage soup. You have to take into account that I have to pay fifteen for this room."

"Back in Odessa," Gershkovich said pensively, straining to cut the herring into equal parts, "for ten rubles you can get a room in the Moldavanka fit for a Czar."

"You have to take into account that people tumble all over the place in my room, what with the drunks and everything."

"Every man must bear his burden," Gershkovich said, and started talking about his family, his faltering business dealings, his son who had been called up by the army.

Margarita listened, resting her head on the table, and her face was attentive, quiet, and thoughtful.

After supper, he took off his jacket, painstakingly wiped his spectacles with a piece of cloth, and sat down at the table to write some business letters. Margarita washed her hair.

Gershkovich wrote unhurriedly, carefully, raising his eyebrows, stopping to think, and when he dipped his pen into the inkwell, he never once forgot to shake off the extra ink.

After he finishing writing he had Margarita sit down on his notebook.

"Well, I'll be damned, but you sure are a lady with bulk! Do me a favor and keep sitting there, Margarita Prokofievna."

Gershkovich smiled, his spectacles shimmered, and his eyes became small, more sparkling, full of laughter.

The next day he left town. As he paced up and down the platform, a few minutes before the train was to leave, Gershkovich noticed Margarita walking quickly toward him with a small parcel in her hands. There were pies in the parcel, and oily blotches had seeped through the paper.

Margarita's face was red, pitiful, her chest agitated from walking so quickly.

"Greetings to Odessa!" she said. "Greetings. . . ."

"Thank you," Gershkovich answered. He took the pies, raised his eyebrows, thought about something for a moment, and bent forward.

The third bell rang. They stretched their hands out to each other.

"Good-bye, Margarita Prokofievna."

"Good-bye, Elya Isaakovich."

Gershkovich went inside the railway car. The train began moving.

MAMA, RIMMA,
AND ALLA

*F*rom early in the morning the day had been going badly.

The day before, the maid had begun putting on airs and walked out. Barbara Stepanovna ended up having to do everything herself. Then the electric bill came first thing in the morning. And then the student boarders, the Rastokhin brothers, came up with a completely unexpected demand. They had allegedly received a telegram from Kaluga in the middle of the night informing them that their father had been taken ill, and that they had to come to him at all costs. They were therefore vacating the room, and could they have the sixty rubles back that they had given Barbara Stepanovna "on loan."

To this Barbara Stepanovna answered that it was quite irregular to vacate a room in April, when there is no one to rent it to, and that it was difficult for her to return the money, as it was given to her not on loan but as a payment for the room, regardless of the fact that the payment had been made in advance.

The Rastokhin brothers disagreed with Barbara Stepanovna. The discussion became drawn-out and unfriendly. The students were stubborn, infuriating louts in long, clean frock coats. When they realized that getting their money back was a lost cause, the older brother suggested that Barbara Stepanovna give them her sideboard and pier glass as collateral.

Barbara Stepanovna turned purple, and retorted that she would not tolerate being spoken to in such a tone, that the Rastokhins' suggestion was utter rubbish, that she knew the law, her husband being a member of the district court in Kamchatka, and so on. The younger Rastokhin flared up and told her that he didn't give a hoot that her husband was a member of the district court in Kamchatka, that it was quite obvious that once she got her hands on a kopeck there was no prying it loose, that they would remember their stay at Barbara Stepanovna's—with all that clutter, dirt, and mess—to their dying day, and that although the district court in Kamchatka was quite far away, the Moscow Justice of the Peace was just around the corner.

And that was how the discussion ended. The Rastokhins marched out haughtily and in silent fury, and Barbara Stepanovna went to the kitchen to make some coffee for her other boarder, a student by the name of Stanislaw Marchotski. There had been loud and insistent ringing from his room for quite a few minutes.

Barbara Stepanovna stood in front of the spirit stove in the kitchen. A nickel pince-nez, rickety with age, sat on her fat nose; her graying hair was disheveled, her pink morning coat full of stains. She made the coffee, and thought how these louts would never have spoken to her in such a tone if there hadn't been that eternal shortage of money, that unfortunate need to constantly snatch, hide, cheat.

When Marchotski's coffee and fried eggs were ready, she brought his breakfast to his room.

Marchotski was a Pole—tall, bony, light blond, with long legs and well-groomed fingernails. That morning he was wearing a foppish gray dressing gown with ornamental military clasps.

He faced Barbara Stepanovna with resentment.

"I've had enough of there never being a maid around!" he said. "I have to ring for a whole hour, and then I'm late for my classes."

It was true that all too often the maid wasn't there, and that Marchotski had to ring and ring, but this time he had a different reason for his resentment.

The evening before, he had been sitting on the living room sofa with Rimma, Barbara Stepanovna's oldest daughter. Barbara Stepanovna had seen them kissing two or three times and hugging in the darkness. They sat there till eleven, then till midnight, then Stanislaw laid his head on Rimma's breast and fell asleep. After all, who in his youth has not dozed off on the edge of a sofa with his head propped on the breast of a high school girl, met by chance on life's winding path? It is not necessarily such a bad thing, and more often than not there are no consequences, but one does have to show a little consideration for others, not to mention that the girl might well have to go to school the next day.

It wasn't until one-thirty in the morning that Barbara Stepanovna declared quite sourly that it was time to show some consideration. Marchotski, brimming with Polish pride, pursed his lips and took umbrage. Rimma cast an indignant look at her mother.

The matter had ended there. But the following morning it was quite clear that Stanislaw hadn't forgotten the incident. Barbara Stepanovna gave him his breakfast, salted the fried eggs, and left.

It was eleven in the morning. Barbara Stepanovna opened the drapes in her daughters' room. The gentle rays of the weak sun gleamed on the dirty floor, on the clothes scattered throughout the room, on the dusty bookshelf.

The girls were already awake. The eldest, Rimma, was thin, small, quick-eyed, black-haired. Alla was a year younger—she was seventeen—larger than her sister, pale, sluggish in her movements, with delicate, pudgy skin, and a sweetly pensive expression in her blue eyes.

When her mother left the room, she started speaking. Her heavy bare arm lay on the blanket, her little white fingers hardly moving.

"I had a dream, Rimma," she said. "Imagine—a strange little town, small, Russian, mysterious. . . .The light gray sky is hanging very low, and the horizon is very close. The dust in the streets is also gray, smooth, calm. Everything is dead. Not a single sound can be heard, not a single person can be seen. And suddenly I feel like I'm walking down some side streets I don't know, past quiet little wooden houses. I wander into blind alleys, then I find my way out into the streets again, but I can only see ten paces ahead, and I keep walking on and on. Somewhere in front of me is a light cloud of whirling dust. I approach it and see wedding carriages. Mikhail and his bride are in one of them. His bride is wearing a veil, and her face is happy. I walk up to the carriages, I seem to be taller than everyone else, and my heart aches a little. Then they all notice me. The carriages stop. Mikhail comes up to me, takes me by the arm, and slowly leads me into a side street. 'Alla, my friend,' he says in a flat voice, 'all this is very sad, I know. But there's nothing I can do, because I don't love you.' I walk next to him, my heart shudders, and more gray streets keep opening up before us."

Alla fell silent.

"A bad dream," she added. "But, who knows? Maybe because it's bad, everything will turn out well and he'll send me a letter."

"Like hell he will!" Rimma answered. "You should have been a little more clever and not run off to see him. By the way, I intend to have a word or two with Mama today!" she said suddenly.

Rimma got up, dressed, and went over to the window.

Spring lay over Moscow. The long somber fence outside their window, which stretched almost the whole length of the side street, glistened with warm dampness.

Outside the church, in its front yard, the grass was damp, green. The sun softly gilded the lackluster chasubles, and twinkled over the dark face of the icon standing on the slanting column by the entrance to the churchyard.

The girls went into the dining room. Barbara Stepanovna was sitting there, carefully eating large portions of food, intently studying the rolls, the coffee, the ham, through her spectacles. She drank the coffee with loud short gulps, and ate the rolls quickly, greedily, almost furtively.

"Mama!" Rimma said to her severely, proudly raising her pretty little face. "I'd like to have a little chat with you. You needn't blow up. We can settle this quietly, once and for all. I can no longer live with you. Set me free."

"Fine," Barbara Stepanovna answered calmly, raising her colorless eyes to look at Rimma. "Is this because of yesterday?"

"Not because of yesterday, but it has to do with yesterday. I'm suffocating here."

"And what do you intend to do?"

"I'll take some classes, learn stenography, right now the demand—"

"Right now stenographers are crawling out of the woodwork! You think the jobs will come running—"

"I won't come to you for help, Mama!" Rimma said shrilly. "I won't come to you for help. Set me free!"

"Fine," Barbara Stepanovna said again. "I'm not holding you back."

"I want you to give me my passport."

"I'm not giving you your passport."

The conversation had been unexpectedly restrained. Now Rimma felt that the passport matter gave her a reason to start yelling.

"Well, that's marvelous!" she shouted, with a sarcastic laugh. "I can't go anywhere without my passport!"

"I'm not giving you your passport!"

"I'll go turn myself into a kept woman!" Rimma yelled hysterically. "I shall give myself to a policeman!"

"Who do you think will want you?" Barbara Stepanovna answered, critically eyeing her daughter's shivering little body and flushed face. "You think a policeman can't find a better—"

"I'll go to Tverskaya Street!" Rimma shouted. "I'll find myself some old man—I don't want to live with her, with this stupid, stupid, stupid—"

"Ah, so this is how you speak to your mother," Barbara Stepanovna said, standing up with dignity. "We can't make ends meet, everything is falling apart around us, we're short of everything, all I ask is for a few minutes of peace and quiet, but you . . . Wait till your father hears about this!"

"I'm going to write him myself, to Kamchatka!" Rimma shouted in a frenzy. "I'll get my passport from him!"

Barbara Stepanovna walked out of the room. Rimma, small and disheveled, paced excitedly up and down the room. Angry, isolated phrases from her future letter to her father tore through her brain.

"Dear Papa!" she would write. "You are busy, I know, but I have to tell you everything. May the allegation that Stanny dozed on my breast lie heavy on Mama's conscience! It was an embroidered cushion that he was dozing on, but the center of gravity lies elsewhere. As Mama is your wife, you will doubtless side with her, but I can't stay here any longer, she is a difficult person! If you want, Papa, I can come to you in Kamchatka, but I will need my passport!"

Rimma paced up and down, while Alla sat on the sofa and watched her. Quiet and mournful thoughts lay heavily on her soul.

"Rimma is fussing about," she thought, "while I am completely desolate! Everything is painful, nothing makes sense!"

She went to her room and lay down. Barbara Stepanovna came in wearing a corset. She was thickly and naively powdered, flushed, perplexed, and pitiful.

"I just remembered that the Rastokhins are leaving today. I have to give them back their sixty rubles. They threatened to take me to court. There are some eggs in the cupboard. Make some for yourself—I'm going down to the pawnbroker.

.   .   .

When Marchotski came home from his classes at around six in the evening, he found the entrance hall filled with packed suitcases. There was noise coming from the Rastokhins' rooms—they were obviously arguing. Right there in the entrance hall Barbara Stepanovna, some-how, with lightning speed and desperate resolution, managed to borrow ten rubles from Marchotski. It was only when he got back to his room that he realized how stupid he had been.

His room was different from all the other rooms in Barbara Stepanovna's apartment. It was neat, filled with bibelots, and covered with carpets. Drawing utensils, foppish pipes, English tobacco, ivory paper knives were carefully laid out on the tables.

Before Stanislaw even managed to change into his dressing gown, Rimma quietly slipped into his room. He gave her a chilly reception.

"Are you angry, Stanny?" the girl asked.

"I am not angry," the Pole answered. "It is just that in the future I would prefer not to be encumbered with having to bear witness to your mother's excesses."

"It'll all be over very soon," Rimma said. "Stanny, I'm going to be free!"

She sat down next to him on the sofa and embraced him.

"I am a man," Stanny began. "This platonic business is not for me, I have a career before me."

He gruffly told her the things that men more or less say to certain women when they've had enough. There's nothing to talk to them about, and flirting with them is pointless, as it is quite obvious they are not prepared to get down to business.

Stanny said that he was consumed by desire; it was hampering his work, making him nervous. The matter had to be settled one way or the other—he didn't care in the least which, as long as it was settled.

"Why are you saying such things to me?" Rimma asked him pen-sively. "What is all this 'I am a man' about, and what do you mean by 'the matter has to be settled'? Why is your face so cold and nasty? And why can we talk about nothing else but that one thing? This is so sad, Stanny! Spring is in the streets, it's so beautiful, and we are in such an ugly mood."

Stanny didn't answer. They both remained silent.

A fiery sunset was sinking over the horizon, flooding the distant sky with a scarlet glow. On the opposite horizon a volatile, slowly thickening darkness was descending. The room was illuminated by the last glowing light. On the sofa, Rimma leaned more and more tenderly toward the student. They were doing what they always did at this exquisite hour of the day.

Stanislaw kissed the girl. She rested her head on the pillow and closed her eyes. They both burst into flame. Within a few minutes, Stanislaw was kissing her incessantly, and in a fit of malicious, unquenchable passion began shoving her thin, burning body about the room. He tore her blouse and her bodice. Rimma, with parched mouth and rings under her eyes, offered her lips to be kissed, while with a distorted, mournful grin she defended her virginity. Suddenly there was a knock at the door. Rimma began rushing about the room, clutching the hanging strips of her torn blouse to her breast.

They eventually opened the door. It turned out to be a friend of Stanislaw's. He eyed Rimma with ill-concealed derision as she rushed past him. She slipped into her room furtively, changed into another blouse, and went to stand by the chilly windowpane to cool down.

• • •

The pawnbroker only gave Barbara Stepanovna forty rubles for the family silver. Ten rubles she had borrowed from Marchotski, and the rest of the money she got from the Tikhonovs, walking all the way from Strastny Boulevard to Pokrovka. In her dismay, she forgot that she could have taken a tram.

At home, besides the raging Rastokhins, she found Mirlits, a barrister's assistant, waiting for her. He was a tall young man with decaying stumps for teeth, and foolish, moist gray eyes.

Not too long ago, the shortage of money had driven Barbara Stepanovna to consider mortgaging a cottage her husband owned in Kolomna. Mirlits had brought over a draft of the mortgage. Barbara

Stepanovna felt that something was wrong with the draft, and that she ought to get some more advice before signing. But she told herself that she was being beset by altogether too many problems of every kind. To hell with everything—boarders, daughters, rudeness.

After the business discussion, Mirlits uncorked a bottle of Crimean Muscat-Lunelle that he had brought with him—he knew Barbara Stepanovna's weakness. They drank a glass each and right away had another. Their voices rang louder, Barbara Stepanovna's fleshy nose grew red, and the stays of her corset expanded and bulged out. Mirlits was telling a jovial story and burst out laughing. Rimma sat silently in the corner, wearing the blouse into which she had changed.

After Barbara Stepanovna and Mirlits finished the Muscat-Lunelle, they went for a walk. Barbara Stepanovna felt that she was just a tiny bit tipsy. She was a little ashamed about this, but at the same time couldn't care less because there was simply too much hardship in life, so everything could go to hell.

Barbara Stepanovna came back earlier than she had anticipated, because the Boikos, whom she had intended to visit, had not been home. She was taken aback by the silence that lay over the apartment. Usually at this time of the day the girls were always fooling around with the students, giggling, running about. The only noise came from the bathroom. Barbara Stepanovna went to the kitchen. There was a little window there from which one could see what was going on in the bathroom.

She went to the little window and saw a strange and most unusual scene.

The stove for boiling the bathwater was red-hot. The bath was filled with steaming water. Rimma was kneeling next to the stove. In her hands she held a pair of curling irons. She was heating them over the fire. Alla was standing naked next to the bath. Her long braids were undone. Tears were rolling down her cheeks.

"Come here," Alla told Rimma. "Listen, can you maybe hear its heart beating?"

Rimma laid her head on Alla's soft, slightly swollen belly.

"It's not beating," she answered. "Anyway there's no doubt about it."

"I'm going to die," Alla whispered. "I'm going to get scalded by the water! I won't be able to bear it! Not the curling irons! You don't know how to do it!"

"Everyone does it this way," Rimma told her. "Stop whimpering, Alla. You can't have that baby."

Alla was about to climb into the tub, but she didn't manage to, because at that very moment she heard the unforgettable, quiet, wheezing voice of her mother call out. "What are you doing in there, girls?"

Two or three hours later, Alla was lying on Barbara Stepanovna's wide bed, tucked in, caressed, and wept over. She had told her mother everything. She felt relieved. She felt like a little girl who had overcome a silly childish fear.

Rimma moved about the bedroom carefully and silently, tidying up, making tea for her mother, forcing her to eat something, seeing to it that the room would be clean. Then she lit the icon lamp in which the oil had not been refilled for at least two weeks, undressed, trying hard not to make any noise, and lay down next to her sister.

Barbara Stepanovna sat at the table. She could see the icon lamp, its even, darkish red flame dimly illuminating the Virgin Mary. Her tipsiness, somehow strange and light, still bubbled in her head. The girls quickly fell asleep. Alla's face was broad, white, and peaceful. Rimma nestled up against her, sighed in her sleep, and shuddered.

Around one in the morning, Barbara Stepanovna lit a candle, placed a sheet of paper in front of her, and wrote a letter to her husband:

Dear Nikolai,
Mirlits came by today, a very decent Jew, and tomorrow I'm expecting a gentleman who will give me money for the house. I think I'm doing things right, but I'm getting more and more worried, because I lack confidence.

I know you have your own troubles, your work, and I shouldn't be bothering you with this, but things at home, Nikolai, are somehow not going all too well. The children are growing up, life nowadays is more demanding—courses, stenography—girls want more freedom. They need their father, they need someone to maybe yell at them, but I simply don't seem to be able to. I can't help thinking that your leaving for Kamchatka was a mistake. If you were here, we would have moved to Starokolenny Street, where there is a very bright little apartment available.

Rimma has lost weight and looks rather bad. For a whole month we were ordering cream from the dairy across the street, and the girls started looking much better, but now we have stopped ordering it. At times my liver acts up a little, and at times it doesn't. Write me more often. After your letters I am a bit more careful, I don't eat herring and my liver doesn't bother me. Come and see us, Kolya, we could all unwind. The children send you their greetings. With loving kisses,

Your Barbara.

THE PUBLIC LIBRARY

*O*ne feels right away that this is the kingdom of books. People working at the library commune with books, with the life reflected in them, and so become almost reflections of real-life human beings.

Even the cloakroom attendants—not brown-haired, not blond, but something in between—are mysteriously quiet, filled with contemplative composure.

At home on Saturday evenings they might well drink methylated spirits and give their wives long, drawn-out beatings, but at the library their comportment is staid, circumspect, and hazily somber.

And then there is the cloakroom attendant who draws. In his eyes there is a gentle melancholy. Once every two weeks, as he helps a fat man in a black vest out of his coat, he mumbles, "Nikolai Sergeyevich approves of my drawings, and Konstantin Vasilevich also approves of them. . . . In the first thing I was originating . . . but I have no idea, no idea where to go!"

The fat man listens. He is a reporter, a married man, gluttonous and overworked. Once every two weeks he goes to the library to rest. He reads about court cases, painstakingly copies out onto a piece of paper the plan of the house where the murder took place, is very pleased, and forgets that he is married and overworked.

The reporter listens to the attendant with fearful bewilderment, and wonders how to handle such a man. Do you give him a ten-kopeck coin on your way out? He might be offended—he's an artist. Then again, if you don't he might also be offended—after all, he's a cloak-room attendant.

In the reading room are the more elevated staff members, the librarians. Some, the "conspicuous ones," possess some starkly pronounced physical defect. One has twisted fingers, another has a head that lolled to the side and stayed there. They are badly dressed, and emaciated in the extreme. They look as if they are fanatically possessed by an idea unknown to the world.

Gogol would have described them well!

The "inconspicuous" librarians show the beginnings of bald patches, wear clean gray suits, have a certain candor in their eyes, and a painful slowness in their movements. They are forever chewing something, moving their jaws, even though they have nothing in their mouths. They talk in a practiced whisper. In short, they have been ruined by books, by being forbidden from enjoying a throaty yawn.

Now that our country is at war, the public has changed. There are fewer students. There are very few students. Once in a blue moon you might see a student painlessly perishing in a corner. He's a "white-ticketer," exempt from service. He wears a pince-nez and has a delicate limp. But then there is also the student on state scholarship. This student is pudgy, with a drooping mustache, tired of life, a man prone to contemplation: he reads a bit, thinks about something a bit, studies the patterns on the lampshades, and nods off over a book. He has to finish his studies, join the army, but—why hurry? Everything in good time.

A former student returns to the library in the figure of a wounded officer with a black sling. His wound is healing. He is young and rosy. He has dined and taken a walk along the Nevsky Prospekt. The Nevsky Prospekt is already lit. The late edition of the *Stock Exchange News* has already set off on its triumphal march around town. Grapes lying on millet are displayed in the store window at Eliseyev's. It is still too early to make the social rounds. The officer goes to the public library for old times' sake, stretches out his long legs beneath the table where he is sitting, and reads *Apollon*. It's somewhat boring. A female student is sitting opposite him. She is studying anatomy, and is copying a picture of a stomach into her notebook. It looks like she might be of Kalugan origin—large-faced, large-boned, rosy, dedicated, and robust. If she has a lover, that would be perfect—she's good material for love.

Beside her is a picturesque tableau, an immutable feature of every public library in the Russian Empire: a sleeping Jew. He is worn out. His hair is a fiery black. His cheeks are sunken. There are humps on his forehead. His mouth is half open. He is wheezing. Where he is from, nobody knows. Whether he has a residence permit or not, nobody knows. He reads every day. He also sleeps every day. There is a terrible, ineradicable weariness in his face, almost madness. A martyr to books—a distinct, indomitable Jewish martyr.

Near the librarians' desk sits a large, broad-chested woman in a gray blouse reading with rapturous interest. She is one of those people who suddenly speaks with unexpected loudness in the library, candidly and ecstatically overwhelmed by a passage in the book, and who, filled with delight, begins discussing it with her neighbors. She is reading because she is trying to find out how to make soap at home. She is about forty-five years old. Is she sane? Quite a few people have asked themselves that.

There is one more typical library habitué: the thin little colonel in a loose jacket, wide pants, and extremely well-polished boots. He has tiny feet. His whiskers are the color of cigar ash. He smears them with a wax that gives them a whole spectrum of dark gray shades. In his day he was so devoid of talent that he didn't manage to work his way up to the rank of colonel so that he could retire a major general. Since his retirement he ceaselessly pesters the gardener, the maid, and his grandson. At the age of seventy-three he has taken it into his head to write a history of his regiment.

He writes. He is surrounded by piles of books. He is the librarians' favorite. He greets them with exquisite civility. He no longer gets on his family's nerves. The maid gladly polishes his boots to a maximal shine.

Many more people of every kind come to the public library. More than one could describe. There is also the tattered reader who does nothing but write a luxuriant monograph on ballet. His face: a tragic edition of Hauptmann's. His body: insignificant.

There are, of course, also bureaucrats riffling through piles of *The Russian Invalid* and the *Government Herald*. There are the young provincials, ablaze as they read.

It is evening. The reading room grows dark. The immobile figures sitting at the tables are a mix of fatigue, thirst for knowledge, ambition.

Outside the wide windows soft snow is drifting. Nearby, on the Nevsky Prospekt, life is blossoming. Far away, in the Carpathian Mountains, blood is flowing.

C'est la vie.

NINE

*T*here are nine people. All waiting to see the editor. The first to enter the editor's office is a broad-shouldered young man with a loud voice and a bright tie. He introduces himself. His name: Sardarov. His occupation: rhymester. His request: to have his rhymes published. He has a preface written by a well-known poet. And if need be, an epilogue, too.

The editor listens. He is an unruffled, pensive man, who has seen a thing or two. He is in no rush. The upcoming issue has gone to press. He reads through the rhymes:

> *O, dolefully the Austrian Kaiser groans,*
> *And I too emit impatient moans.*

The editor says that, unfortunately, for this reason and that, and so on. The magazine is currently looking for articles on cooperatives or foreign affairs.

Sardarov juts out his chest, excuses himself with exquisite politeness bordering on the caustic, and noisily marches out.

The second person to enter the editor's office is a young lady—slim, shy, very beautiful. She is there for the third time. Her poems are not intended for publication. All she wants to know, and absolutely nothing more, is if there's any point in her continuing to write. The editor is extremely pleasant to her. He sometimes sees her walking along the Nevsky Prospekt with a tall gentleman who, from time to time, gravely buys her half a dozen apples. His gravity is ominous. Her poems testify to this. They are a guileless chronicle of her life.

"You want my body," the girl writes. "So take it, my enemy, my friend! But where will my soul find its dream?"

"He'll be getting his hands on your body any day now, that's pretty clear!" the editor thinks. "Your eyes look so lost, weak, and beautiful. I doubt your soul will be finding its dream anytime soon, but you'll definitely make quite a spicy woman!"

In her poems the girl describes life as "madly frightening" or "madly marvelous," in all its little aggravations: "Those sounds, sounds, sounds that me enfold, those sounds eternal, so drunken and so bold."

One thing is certain: once the grave gentleman's enterprise comes to fruition, the girl will stop writing poetry and start visiting midwives.

After the girl, Lunev, a small and nervous man of letters, enters the editor's office. Here things get complicated. On a former occasion Lunev had blown up at the editor. He is a talented, perplexed, hapless family man. In his fluster and scramble for rubles he is unable to discriminate who he can afford to shout at and who not. First he blew up at the editor, and then, to his own and the editor's amazement, handed over the manuscript, suddenly realizing how foolish all this was, how hard life was, and how unlucky he was, oh, how very unlucky! He had already begun having palpitations in the waiting room, and now the editor informed him that his "little daubs" weren't all that bad, but, *au fond,* you couldn't really classify them as literature, they were, well . . . Lunev feverishly agreed, unexpectedly muttering, "Oh, Alexander Stepanovich! You are such a good man! And all the while I was so horrible to you! But it can all be seen from another perspective! Absolutely! That is all I want to elucidate, there is more to it than meets the eye, I give you my word of honor!" Lunev turns a deep crimson, scrapes together the pages of his manuscript with quaking fingers, endeavoring to be debonair, ironic, and God knows what else.

After Lunev, two stock figures found in every editorial office come in. The first is a lively, rosy, fair-haired lady. She emits a warm wave of perfume. Her eyes are naive and bright. She has a nine-year-old son, and this son of hers, "you wouldn't believe it, but he simply writes and writes, day and night, at first we didn't pay any attention, but then all our friends and acquaintances were so impressed, and my husband, you know, he works in the Department of Agricultural Betterment, a very practical man, you know, he will have nothing to do with modern literature, not Andreyev, not Nagrodskaya, but even he couldn't stop laughing—I have brought along three notebooks. . . ."

The second stock figure is Bykhovsky. He is from Simferopol. He is a very nice, lively man. He has nothing to do with literature, he doesn't really have any business with the editor, he doesn't really have anything to say to him, but he is a subscriber, and has dropped by for a little chat and to exchange ideas, to immerse himself in the hurly-burly of Petrograd life. And he *is* immersing himself. The editor mumbles something about politics and cadets, and Bykhovsky blossoms, convinced that he is taking an active part in the nation's public life.

The most doleful of the visitors is Korb. He is a Jew, a true Ahasuerus. He was born in Lithuania, and had been wounded in a pogrom in one of the southern towns. From that day on his head has been hurting very badly. He went to America. During the War he somehow turned up in Antwerp and, at the age of forty-four, joined the French Foreign Legion. He was hit on the head in Maubeuge. Now it won't stop shaking. Korb was somehow evacuated to Russia, to Petrograd. He gets a pension from somewhere, rents a ramshackle little place in a stinking basement in Peski, and is writing a play called *The Czar of Israel*. Korb has terrible headaches, he cannot sleep at night, and paces up and down in his basement, deep in thought. His landlord, a plump, condescending man who smokes black four-kopeck cigars, was angry at first, but then was won over by Korb's gentleness and his diligence at writing hundreds of pages, and finally came to like him. Korb wears an old, faded Antwerp frock coat. He doesn't shave his chin, and there is a tiredness and fanatical determination in his eyes. Korb has headaches, but he keeps on writing his play, and the play's opening line is: "Ring the bells, for Judah hath perished!"

After Korb, three remain. One is a young man from the provinces. He is unhurried, lost in thought, takes a long time to settle into a chair, and stays settled there for a long time. His sluggish attention comes to rest on the pictures on the wall, the newspaper clippings on the table, the portraits of the staff. What is it exactly that he wants?—It is not that he really wants anything . . . He worked for a newspaper—What newspaper?—A newspaper in the provinces . . . Well, all he really wants to know is what the circulation of this magazine is and how much it pays. The young man is told that such information is not handed out to just anybody. If he were a writer, that would be another matter, if not, well then . . . The young man says that he isn't really a writer or anything, and that he hasn't really done this kind of work before, but he could take to, well, working as an editor, for instance.

The young "editor" exits, and Smursky enters. He too is a man with a background. He worked as an agriculturist in the district of Kashin in the province of Tver. A tranquil district, a wonderful province! But Smursky was drawn to Petrograd. He applied for a position as an agriculturist, and also submitted twenty manuscripts to an editor. Two had been accepted, and Smursky had come to the conclusion that his future lay in literature. Now he is no longer applying for a position as an agriculturist. He walks about town in a morning coat with his briefcase in hand. He writes a lot, and every day, but little is ever published.

The ninth visitor is none other than Stepan Drako, "the man who walked around the world on foot, bon vivant extraordinare, and public speaker."

ODESSA

Odessa is a horrible town. It's common knowledge. Instead of saying "a great difference," people there say "two great differences," and *"tuda i syuda,"** they pronounce *"tudoyu i syudoyu"*! And yet I feel that there are quite a few good things one can say about this important town, the most charming city of the Russian Empire. If you think about it, it is a town in which you can live free and easy. Half the population is made up of Jews, and Jews are a people who have learned a few simple truths along the way. Jews get married so as not to be alone, love so as to live through the centuries, hoard money so they can buy houses and give their wives astrakhan jackets, love children because, let's face it, it is good and important to love one's children. The poor Odessa Jews get very confused when it comes to officials and regulations, but it isn't all that easy to get them to budge in their opinions, their very antiquated opinions. You might not be able to budge these Jews, but there's a whole lot you can learn from them. To a large extent it is because of them that Odessa has this light and easy atmosphere.

The typical Odessan is the exact opposite of the typical Petrogradian. Nowadays it is a cliché how well Odessans do for themselves in Petrograd. They make money. Because they are dark-haired, limpid blondes fall in love with them. And then, Odessans have a tendency to settle on the Kamenno-Ostrovsky Prospect. People will claim that what I am saying smacks of tall tales. Well, I assure you that these are not tall

*"Here and there."

71

tales! There is much more to this than meets the eye. Dark-haired Odessans simply bring with them a little lightness and sunshine.

But I have a strong hunch that Odessa is about to provide us with much more than gentlemen who bring with them a little sunshine and a lot of sardines packed in their original cans. Any day now, we will fully experience the fecund, revivifying influence of the Russian south, Russian Odessa—perhaps, *qui sait*, the only Russian town where there is a good chance that our very own, sorely needed, homegrown Maupassant might be born. I can even see a small, a very small sign, heralding Odessa's great future: Odessa's chanteuses (I am referring to Izya Kremer*). These chanteuses might not have much in the way of a voice, but they have a joy, an expressive joy, mixed with passion, lightness, and a touching, charming, sad feeling for life. A life that is good, terrible, and, *quand même et malgré tout*, exceedingly interesting.

I saw Utochkin,[†] a *pur sang* Odessan, lighthearted and profound, reckless and thoughtful, elegant and gangly, brilliant and stuttering. He has been ruined by cocaine or morphine—ruined, word has it, since the day he fell out of an airplane somewhere in the marshes of Novgorod. Poor Utochkin, he has lost his mind. But of one thing I am certain: any day now the province of Novgorod will come crawling down to Odessa.

The bottom line is: this town has the material conditions needed to nurture, say, a Maupassantesque talent. In the summer, the bronze, muscular bodies of youths who play sports glisten on beaches, as do the powerful bodies of fishermen who do not play sports, the fat, potbellied, good-natured bodies of the "businessmen," and the skinny, pimply dreamers, inventors, and brokers. And a little distance from the sea, smoke billows from the factories, and Karl Marx plies his familiar trade.

In Odessa there is an impoverished, overcrowded, suffering Jewish ghetto, an extremely self-satisfied bourgeoisie, and a very Black Hundred** city council.

In Odessa there are sweet and oppressive spring evenings, the spicy aroma of acacias, and a moon filled with an unwavering, irresistible light shining over a dark sea.

---

*Izya Kremer, 1885–1956, Odessan Jewish folksinger.

[†] Sergei Isayevich Utochkin, 1874–1916, aviation pioneer, was the first to fly from Moscow to St. Petersburg, in 1911.

**Chernosotyensi (Black Hundred), a right-wing, anti-Semitic group responsible for pogroms.

In Odessa the fat and funny bourgeois lie in the evenings in their white socks on couches in front of their funny, philistine dachas, digesting their meals beneath a dark and velvety sky, while their powdered wives, plump with idleness and naively corseted, are passionately squeezed behind bushes by fervent students of medicine or law.

In Odessa the destitute *"luftmenshen"* roam through coffeehouses trying to make a ruble or two to feed their families, but there is no money to be made, and why should anyone give work to a useless person—a *"luftmensh"*?

In Odessa there is a port, and in the port there are ships that have come from Newcastle, Cardiff, Marseilles, and Port Said; Negroes, Englishmen, Frenchmen, and Americans. Odessa had its moment in the sun, but now it is fading—a poetic, slow, lighthearted, helpless fading.

"But Odessa is just a town like any other," the reader will argue. "The problem is that you are extremely biased, that's all."

Well, fine. So I am biased, I admit it. Maybe I'm even extremely biased, but *parole d'honneur*, there *is* something to this place! And this something can be sensed by a person with mettle who agrees that life is sad, monotonous—this is all very true—but still, *quand même et malgré tout*, it is exceedingly, exceedingly interesting.

And now my thoughts move on from my Odessan discourse to higher matters. If you think about it, doesn't it strike you that in Russian literature there haven't been so far any real, clear, cheerful descriptions of the sun?

Turgenev poeticized the dewy morning, the calm night. With Dostoyevsky you feel the uneven, gray high road along which Karamazov walks to the tavern, the mysterious and heavy fog of Petersburg. The gray roads and the shrouds of fog that stifle people and, stifling them, distorts them in the most amusing and terrible way, giving birth to the fumes and stench of passions, making people rush around frenetically in the hectic humdrum pace. Do you remember the life-giving, bright sun in Gogol, a man who, by the way, was from the Ukraine? But such descriptions are few and far between. What you always get is "The Nose," "The Overcoat," "The Portrait," and "Notes of a Madman." Petersburg defeated Poltava. Akaki Akakiyevich, modestly enough but with terrible competence, finished off Gritsko, and

Father Matvei finished off what Taras began.* The first person to talk about the sun in a Russian book, to talk about it with excitement and passion, was Gorky. But precisely because he talks about it with excitement and passion, it still isn't quite the real thing.

Gorky is a forerunner, and the most powerful forerunner of our times. Yet he is not a minstrel of the sun, but a herald of the truth. If anything is worth singing the praises of, then you know what it is: the sun! There is something cerebral in Gorky's love for the sun. It is only by way of his enormous talent that he manages to overcome this obstacle.

He loves the sun because Russia is rotten and twisted, because in Nizhny, Pskov, and Kazan, the people are pudgy, heavy, at times incomprehensible, at times touching, at times excessive, and at times boring to the point of distraction. Gorky knows why he loves the sun, why the sun must be loved. It is this very awareness that hides the reason why Gorky is a forerunner, often magnificent and powerful, but still a forerunner.

And on this point Maupassant is perhaps off the mark, or right on the mark. A stagecoach rumbles along a road scorched by the heat, and in it, in this stagecoach, sits a fat, crafty young man by the name of Polyte, and a coarse, healthy peasant girl. What they are doing there and why, is their business. The sky is hot, the earth is hot. Polyte and the girl are dripping with sweat, and the stagecoach rumbles along the road scorched by the bright heat. And that's all there is to it.

In recent times there has been a growing trend of writing about how people live, love, kill, and how representatives are elected in the provinces of Olonetsk, or Vologodsk, not to mention Arkhangelsk. All this is written with total authenticity, verbatim, the way people speak in Olonetsk and Vologodsk. Life there, as it turns out, is cold, extremely wild. It is an old story. And the time is approaching where we will have had more than enough of this old story. In fact, we have already had enough. And I think to myself: the Russians will finally be drawn to the

---

*Babel is implying that a cold, northern Petersburg frame of mind overpowered Gogol's earlier brighter southern "Poltavan" style, and that the somber and tragic Akaki Akakiyevich, the protagonist of "The Overcoat," superseded Gritsko, the lively and witty protagonist of "Evenings on a farm near Dikanka." Father Matvei Konstantinovsky was a fanatical ascetic priest who influenced Gogol's later writing. Taras is the protagonist of Gogol's story "Taras Bulba."

south, to the sea, to the sun! "Will be drawn," by the way, is wrong. They already *have* been drawn, for many centuries. Russia's most important path has been her inexhaustible striving toward the southern steppes, perhaps even her striving for "the Cross of Hagia Sophia."*

It is high time for new blood. We are being stifled. Literature's Messiah, so long awaited, will issue from there—from the sun-drenched steppes washed by the sea.

---

* Constantinople's Cathedral of Hagia Sophia, the seat of Russian and Greek Orthodox Christianity.

THE AROMA OF
ODESSA

I am wandering between tables, making my way through the crowd, catching snippets of conversation. S., a female impersonator, walks past me. In his pale youthful face, in his tousled soft yellow hair, in his distant, shameless, weak-spirited smile is the stamp of his peculiar trade, the trade of being a woman. He has an ingratiating, leisurely, sinuous way of walking. His hips sway, but barely. Women, real women, love him. He sits silently among them, his face that of a pale youth and his hair soft and yellow. He smiles faintly at something, and the women smile faintly and secretively back—what they are smiling at only S. and the women know.

On the other side of the café a man in a blue caftan and a peasant shirt tied with a strap hurries past in patent-leather boots. They call him the "Bard of Russian Song." On the bard's nose is a pince-nez, and in his soul the petty anxiety of a petty man. The bard's face is that of a worldly pharmacist. Why even mention his name.

I make my way between tables where retired colonels with brilliantined mustaches have found a haven for their shamed Czarist uniforms and play lotto with Jewish boys. Fat, serene wives of movie-theater owners, thin cash-register girls ("true union members"), and fleshy, flabby, sagacious café-chantant agents, currently unemployed, also sit with the colonels.

Our times have knocked these people off their feet, misfortune has driven them to the Palais Royal, and to Paraskeva and other Greek cafés to make a quick ruble trading in turquoise rings. At the club you can learn a lot about their desires and ideals, and who their idols are. Go to the reading room, where portraits of Gorky, Vinaver, and Linovsky* hang on the walls. On the table you will find an old issue of *Divertissement*. Take it from me, a very interesting magazine! A life filled with mirth, wine, love, and death will open out before you. You can read about the clever and beautiful Jenny Molten, who came to Russia in the bloom of her youth. You can read about her successes and her admirers, of the papa's boys who love her body, and the little men, downtrodden by life, who love her soul. You can read of her nomadic life, of the barrels of wine she has drunk, the crates of oranges she has eaten, of her husband, the husband of a café-chantant diva, and of her death. About the death of Jenny Molten you will read at the end. Someone else besides Jenny Molten who has died is Naumenko or Karasulenko, our passionate, trusting, drunk, kindhearted, hysterical Russian chanteuse. She died on a bed strewn with flowers and doused in perfume. Telegrams were found in her room from officials, warrant officers, and second lieutenants. According to these telegrams the second lieutenants were about to rush to her side, to kiss her. They were indignant about something, even threatening.

But in *Divertissement* you will also find serious articles with advice on professional matters and portraits of the editor, a handsome man with a black mustache and languid eyes. His mustache, his eyes, his noble demeanor point unmistakably to one thing: the editor was loved, and never squandered his money on little chanteuses. There are also stories in *Divertissement* about wrestling champions, of their first victories, the arenas bathed in light, the Parisian crowds, the Parisian women applauding ecstatically, the crowd carrying the smooth, powerful body of the wrestler on its shoulders. In every issue of *Divertissement* there are also jokes about Odessa Jews, about Café Fankoni,[†] about brokers taking dance classes and Jewesses riding trams.

Divertissement smells of Odessa and Odessa's hot, homegrown lingo. The whole club on Preobrazhenskaya Street smells of Odessa, and that might well be the only reason I began talking about it. These

---

* Maxim Moseyevich Vinaver, 1863–1923, Jewish politician, activist, and writer who emigrated to Paris, where he became the editor of the Russian-French Jewish journal *Evreiskaya Tribuna*. Nikolai Osipovich Linovsky, a Jewish writer who wrote under the pseudonym Pruzhansky.

† An elegant and expensive Odessan café that attracted a wealthy international clientele.

days the aroma of one's native town is very important. This is the fourth year that warriors from afar have flooded it without respite. The horns of large ocean liners no longer roar, fine coal dust no longer wafts over the harbor. The brilliant sun lights the quiet, untroubled waters. There is no *Bavaria* pulling into port, there are no money changers, no tall, strong German and American sailors roaming through the town in packs, there are no taverns in the port where through waves of tobacco smoke one can see the drunk drooping heads of Englishmen, while a gramophone, rasping and proud, plays "Rule Britannia." During the war, ruined people have flocked to our town, strange Jews who are foreign to us—refugees from Latvia and Poland. Serbs and Rumanians have come. But nobody who loves Odessa can say a word against these Rumanians. They have brought life back to Odessa. They remind us of the days when the streets were full of trade, when we had Greeks trading in coffee and spices, German sausage makers, French book peddlers, and Englishmen in steamship offices. The Rumanians have opened restaurants, play music with cymbals, fill taverns with their fast, foreign speech. They have sent us handsome officers with yellow boots and tall, elegant women with red lips. These people fit the style of our town.

Not that it is a problem if the other newcomers do not fit Odessa's style. Odessa stands strong, she hasn't lost her astonishing knack for assimilating people. A proud, cunning Polish Jew comes to Odessa, and before long we've turned him into a loud, gesticulating fellow who is as quick to flare up or calm down as the best of us. We're still busy grinding them down. Soon the time will come when all the ex-Czarist officers who are used to life in the capital and their regiments in Mezhibozh will leave, and then all the red-bearded Jews, who walk dully down our streets, littering them dully with sunflower-seed shells, will go back to their gray Kozlovs and Tulas. The horns of ocean liners will once more blare in our harbor, and in our taverns old gramophones will once more croak words about Britannia ruling the waves. Our storehouses will be filled with oranges, coconuts, pepper, and Málaga wine, and in our granaries the greenish dust of pouring grain will rise.

INSPIRATION

*I*felt sleepy and was in a bad mood. Just then Mishka dropped in to read me the novella he had written. "Lock the door," he said, and pulled a bottle of wine out of his coat pocket. "This is an evening to celebrate! I have finished my novella! I think this is the real thing. Let's drink to it!"

Mishka's face was pale and clammy.

"Only fools will say that there's no such thing as happiness on earth," he said. "Happiness is inspiration! Yesterday I wrote the whole night through and didn't even notice the sun rising. Then I walked through town. Early in the morning it's striking: dew, silence, and almost nobody out and about. Everything is limpid, and the day begins bluish cold, spectral, and gentle. Let's drink to it! There's no mistake, this novella is definitely a turning point in my life."

Mishka poured himself some wine and drank. His fingers trembled. He had remarkably beautiful hands—slim, white, and smooth, with fingers delicately pointed at the tip.

"You know, I have to place this novella," he continued. "They'll all want it. They print such rubbish nowadays. Connections are the most important thing. I've already put out feelers. Sukhotin will take care of everything."

"Mishka," I said to him. "You need to go through your novella again; I don't see a single correction."

"Nonsense! There'll be time enough for that! Back home, everyone's making fun of me. *Rira bien, qui rira le dernier.* I'm not going to say anything. Just wait a year, then they'll all come running!"

The bottle was almost empty.

"You've already had enough to drink, Mishka!"

"I need to get myself on a roll," he answered. "Last night I smoked forty cigarettes."

He took out his notebook. It was very thick, very thick indeed. I thought of asking him to leave it with me. But then I saw his pale forehead, with a swollen vein protruding, and his dangling tie, crooked and pitiful.

"Well, Mr. Tolstoy," I said to him. "When you write your memoirs, don't forget to include me."

Mishka smiled.

"You bastard!" he said. "You don't value our friendship at all!"

I made myself comfortable. Mishka leaned over his notebook. The room was quiet and the lights were dim.

"My aim in this novella," Mishka said, "has been to come up with a new way of writing that is filled with cloudy dreams, subtle shadows and allusions. . . . How I loathe, loathe life's folly!"

"Enough preamble, start reading!" I said to him.

He began. I listened carefully. It wasn't easy. The story was clumsy and boring. A clerk had fallen in love with a ballerina and kept lounging around under her window. She left town. The clerk fell ill because his dreams of love had come to nothing.

It wasn't long before I stopped listening. The words were trite and boring, slippery as polished wood. Nothing was clear—not what the clerk was like, not what she was like.

I looked at Mishka. His eyes were sparkling. He was grinding his dead cigarette butts between his fingers. His dull, gaunt face, horribly distorted with sterile creative ardor, his yellow, fat, protruding nose, and puffy, pale-pink lips, all gradually brightened as he was gripped by the burgeoning power of his creative rapture.

He read with agonizing slowness, and when he finished, he awkwardly put his notebook away and looked at me.

"Well, Mishka," I said to him slowly. "You see, you need to think it through a little . . . The idea is quite original, it is very tender and everything, but, you see, it does need a little work . . . you see, it sort of needs to be edited down a little."

"I've been working on it for three years!" Mishka said. "Of course there are still a few rough edges, but as a whole it's fine, isn't it?"

Mishka had sensed something. His lips trembled. He hunched forward and took a terribly long time to light a cigarette.

"Mishka," I said to him. "What you've written is marvelous. Your technique isn't quite there yet, but *ça viendra*. Damn it, there's so much in that head of yours!"

Mishka turned around, looked at me, and his eyes were like those of a child—tender, radiant, and happy.

"Let's go out into the street," he said. "Let's go out, I can't breathe." The streets were dark and quiet.

Mishka squeezed my hand hard and said, "The one thing that I feel with utter conviction is that I have talent! My father wants me to look for a position somewhere. But I won't! In autumn I'm off to Petrograd. Sukhotin will take care of everything." He fell silent, lit another cigarette with the one he was just finishing, and spoke more quietly. "At times my inspiration is so strong that I'm in agony! At such times I know that what I am doing I am doing right! I sleep badly, always nightmares and anguish. I toss and turn for hours before I fall asleep. In the morning my head feels heavy, painful, terrible. I can only write at night, when I am alone, when there is silence, when my soul is burning. Dostoyevsky always wrote at night, drinking a whole samovar of tea—me, I have my cigarettes . . . you know, there's a blanket of smoke beneath my ceiling."

We reached Mishka's house. His face was lit by a street lamp. A fierce, thin, yellow, happy face.

"We'll get there, damn it!" he said, and squeezed my hand tighter. "Everyone makes it big in Petrograd!"

"Anyway, Mishka," I said, "you've got to keep working."

"Sashka, my friend!" he replied, grinning at me broadly and patronizingly. "I'm no fool, I know what I know. Don't worry, I'm not about to start resting on my laurels. Come by tomorrow. We'll go through it again."

"Very well," I said. "I'll come by."

We parted. I went home. I felt very depressed.

DOUDOU

*B*ack in those days I was a medical orderly in the hospital in the town of N. One morning General S., the hospital administrator, brought in a young girl and suggested she be taken on as a nurse. Needless to say, she was hired.

The new nurse was called *la petite Doudou*. She was kept by the general, and in the evenings danced at the café chantant.

She had a lithe, springy gait, the exquisite, almost angular gait of a dancer. In order to see her, I went to the café chantant. She danced an amazing *tango acrobatique*, with what I'd call chastity mixed with a vague, tender passion.

At the hospital she worshiped all the soldiers, and looked after them like a servant. Once, when the chief surgeon was walking through the halls, he saw Doudou on her knees trying to button up the underpants of a pockmarked, apathetic little man called Dyba.

"Dyba! Aren't you ashamed of yourself?" the surgeon called out. "You should have gotten one of the men to do that!"

Doudou raised her calm, tender face and said: "*Oh, mon docteur*, do you think I have never seen a man in his underpants before?"

I remember on the third day of Passover they brought us a badly injured French airman, a Monsieur Drouot. Both his legs had been smashed to bits. He was a Breton—strong, dark, and taciturn. His hard cheeks had a slight bluish tint. It was so strange to see his powerful torso, his strong, chiseled neck, and his broken, helpless legs.

They put him in a small, private room. Doudou would sit with him for hours. They spoke warmly and quietly. Drouot talked about his flights and how he was all alone, none of his family was here, and how sad it all was. He fell in love with her (it was clear to all), and looked at her as was to be expected: tenderly, passionately, pensively. And Doudou, pressing her hands to her breast, told Sister Kirdetsova in the corridor with quiet amazement: "*Il m'aime, ma soeur, il m'aime.*"*

That Saturday night she was on duty and was sitting with Drouot. I was in a neighboring room and saw them. When Doudou arrived, he said: "*Doudou, ma bien aimée!*" He rested his head on her breast and slowly started kissing her dark blue silk blouse. Doudou stood there without moving. Her fingers quivered and picked at the buttons of her blouse.

"What is it you want?" Doudou asked him.

He answered something.

Doudou looked at him carefully and pensively, and slowly undid her lace collar. Her soft, white breast appeared. Drouot sighed, winced, and clung to her. Doudou closed her eyes in pain. But still, she noticed that he was uncomfortable, and so she unhooked her bodice. He clasped Doudou close, but moved sharply and moaned.

"You're in pain!" Doudou said. "You must stop. You mustn't—"

"Doudou!" he said. "I'll die if you leave!"

I left the window. But I still saw Doudou's pale, pitiful face. I saw her try desperately not to hurt him, I heard the moan of passion and pain.

The story got out. Doudou was dismissed—in short, she was fired. The last I saw of her she was standing in the hall, bidding me farewell. Heavy, bright tears fell from her eyes, but she was smiling so as not to upset me.

"Good-bye!" Doudou said, stretching out her slim, white-gloved hand to me. "*Adieu, mon ami!*" She fell silent and then added, looking me straight in the eye: "*Il géle, il meurt, il est seul, il me prie, dirai-je non?*"†

At that moment, Dyba, filthy and small, hobbled in at the end of the hall. "I swear to you," Doudou said to me in a soft, shaking voice. "I swear to you, if Dyba had asked me to, I would have done the same for him."

* "He loves me, Sister, he loves me."
† "He is cold, he is dying, he is alone, he begs me to, would I say no?"

SHABOS-NAKHAMU

*M*orning came, evening came—it was the fifth day of the week. Morning came, evening came—the sixth day of the week. On the sixth day, on Friday evening, one prays. Having prayed, one puts one's best hat on and goes for a stroll through the shtetl and then hurries home for dinner. At home a Jew will empty a glass of vodka—and neither God nor the Talmud forbid him to empty two—he will eat gefilte fish and raisin cake. After dinner he feels quite jovial. He talks to his wife and then dozes off, one eye shut, his mouth hanging open. He dozes, but in the kitchen Gapka, his wife, hears music—as if a blind fiddler had come from the shtetl and was playing beneath the window.

This is how things go with your average Jew. But Hershele is not your average Jew. It wasn't by chance that he was famous in all of Ostropol, in all of Berdichev, and in all of Vilyuisk.

Hershele celebrated only one Friday evening in six. On other Fridays he sat in the cold darkness with his family. His children cried. His wife hurled reproaches at him, each as heavy as a cobblestone. Hershele answered her with poetry.

Once, word has it, Hershele decided to act with foresight. He set off on a Wednesday to go to a fair to make some money by Friday. Where there's a fair there's a goyish gentleman, where there's a goyish gentleman there are sure to be ten Jews hovering about. But you'll be lucky to squeeze three *groschen* out of ten Jews. They all listened to Hershele's routine, but quickly disappeared into thin air when the time came to pay up.

His stomach empty as a wind instrument, Hershele shuffled back home.

"What did you earn?" his wife asked him.

"Everlasting life," he answered. "Both the rich and the poor promised it to me."

Hershele's wife had only ten fingers, but she had many more curses. Her voice boomed like mountain thunder.

"Other women have husbands who are like husbands! All my husband knows how to do is feed his wife jokes! Come New Year, may God rip out his tongue, his arms, and his legs!"

"Amen!" Hershele said.

"Candles burn in every window as if people were burning oak trees in their houses. My candles are thin as matchsticks, and they give off so much smoke that it rises all the way to heaven! Everyone has made their white bread already, but my husband brings me firewood as wet as newly washed hair!"

Hershele did not say a word. First, why throw kindling on a fire when it is blazing brightly? Second, what can one say to a ranting wife when she is absolutely right?

The time came when his wife got tired of shouting. Hershele went to lie down on his bed and think.

"Why don't I go see Rabbi Boruchl?" he thought.

(As is common knowledge, Rabbi Boruchl had a tendency to fall into a black melancholia, and there was no better cure for him than Hershele's jokes.)

"Why don't I go see Rabbi Boruchl? It's true that the *tsaddik's* helpers keep the meat and only give me bones. Meat is better than bones, but bones are better than air. Let's go to Rabbi Boruchl!"

Hershele got up and went to harness his mare. She looked at him severely and morosely.

"This is great, Hershele!" her eyes said. "Yesterday you didn't give me any oats, the day before yesterday you didn't give me any oats, and I didn't get anything today either. If I don't get any oats by tomorrow, I'm going to have to give my life some serious thought."

Hershele could not bear her penetrating stare. He lowered his eyes and patted her soft lips. Then he sighed so loudly that the horse understood. Hershele decided to go to Rabbi Boruchl on foot.

When Hershele set out, the sun stood high in the sky. The hot road ran on ahead. White oxen slowly pulled carts piled high with fragrant hay. Muzhiks sat on these piles, their legs dangling, and waved their long whips. The sky was blue and the whips were black.

About five versts down the road, Hershele came to a forest. The sun was beginning to set. Soft fires raged in the sky. Barefoot girls chased cows from the pastures. The cows' pink udders swung heavily with milk.

In the forest, Hershele was met by a cool, quiet twilight. Green leaves bent toward one another, caressed each other with their flat hands, and, softly whispering high in the trees, returned to their places, rustling and quivering.

Hershele did not notice their whispering. An orchestra as large as the ones at Count Potocki's feasts was playing in his belly. The road before him was long. An airy darkness drifted from the edges of the earth, closed over Hershele's head, and scattered over the world. Unmoving lamps lit up in the sky. The world fell silent.

It was night when Hershele came to the inn. A light flickered through the small window by which Zelda the landlady was sitting, sewing swaddling clothes in the warm room. Her belly was so large it looked as if she were about to give birth to triplets. Hershele looked at her small red face and blue eyes and greeted her.

"May I rest here awhile, mistress?"

"You may."

Hershele sat down. His nostrils flared like a blacksmith's bellows. Hot flames were burning in the stove. In a large cauldron water was boiling, pouring steam over the waiting, snow-white dumplings. A plump chicken was bobbing up and down in a golden soup. The aroma of raisin pie wafted from the oven.

Hershele sat on the bench writhing like a woman in labor. His mind was hatching more plots in a minute than King Solomon had wives.

It was quiet in the room; the water was boiling, and the chicken bobbing in the golden soup.

"Where is your husband?"

"My husband went to the goyish gentleman to pay the money for the rent." The landlady fell silent. Her childish eyes widened. Suddenly she said, "I am sitting here at the window, thinking. And I would like to ask you a question, Mr. Jew. I am sure you wander about the world quite a bit, and that you've studied with a rabbi and know about our Jewish ways. Me, I never studied with anyone. Tell me, Mr. Jew, will Shabos-Nakhamu come to us soon?"

"Aha!" Hershele thought. "Not a bad little question! In God's garden all kinds of potatoes grow!"

"I am asking this because my husband promised that when Shabos-Nakhamu comes to us, we will go visit my mother, and he said I'll buy you a new dress, and a new wig, and we'll go to Rabbi Motalemi to ask that a son be born to us, and not a daughter, all of this when Shabos-Nakhamu comes. I think he's someone from the other world."

"You are not mistaken!" Hershele answered. "God placed these words in your mouth. You will have a son and a daughter. I am Shabos-Nakhamu, mistress!"

The swaddling clothes slipped from Zelda's knees. She rose and banged her small head against a beam, for Zelda was tall and plump, flushed and young. Her breasts jutted up like two taut sacks filled with seed. Her blue eyes opened wide, like those of a child.

"I am Shabos-Nakhamu, mistress!" Hershele said again. "This is the second month that I am walking the earth helping people. It is a long path from heaven down to earth. My shoes are falling apart. I have brought you greetings from all your loved ones."

"From Auntie Pesya?" the woman shouted. "And from Papa, and Auntie Golda? You know them?"

"Who doesn't?" Hershele answered. "I was speaking to them just the way I'm speaking to you now!"

"How are they doing up there?" the woman asked, clutching her belly with trembling fingers.

"They are doing badly," Hershele said dolefully. "How should a dead person be doing? There are no feasts up there!"

The woman's eyes filled with tears.

"It is cold up there," Hershele continued. "They are cold and hungry. They eat just what angels eat, nobody in that world is allowed to eat more than angels. And what do angels need? All they need is a swig of water—up there, you won't see a glass of vodka in a hundred years!"

"Poor Papa!" the devastated woman whispered.

"At Passover he gets one *latke*. And a blin has to last him a day and a night!"

"Poor Auntie Pesya!" the woman stammered.

"I myself have to go hungry!" Hershele said, turning his head away as a tear rolled down his nose and fell into his beard. "And I'm not allowed to complain, as they think of me as one of them."

Hershele didn't get any further.

With fat feet slapping over the floor, the woman ran to get plates, bowls, glasses, and bottles. When Hershele started eating, the woman was completely convinced that he was a man from the other world.

To start with, Hershele ate chopped liver with finely diced onions doused in fat. Then he had a glass of the best vodka (orange peels floated in it). Then he had fish, mashing soft potatoes into the aromatic broth, and he poured on the side of his plate half a jar of red horseradish—a horseradish that would have driven five fully decked-out counts to tears of envy.

After the fish, Hershele busied himself with the chicken, and spooned down the soup in which droplets of fat swam. The dumplings, dipped in melted butter, fled into Hershele's mouth like hares fleeing a hunter. I need not dwell on what happened to the pies—what else could have happened to them if one takes into account that at times a whole year would pass without Hershele ever seeing a pie?

After the meal, the woman collected all the things she wanted to send with Hershele to the other world for Papa, Auntie Golda, and Auntie Pesya. For her father she packed a new prayer shawl, a bottle of cherry liqueur, a jar of raspberry jam, and a pouch of tobacco. For Auntie Pesya she brought out some warm gray stockings. For Auntie Golda she packed an old wig, a large comb, and a prayerbook. She also gave Hershele some shoes for himself, a loaf of bread, fat cracklings, and a silver coin.

"Greet everyone from me, Mr. Shabos-Nakhamu! Greet everyone from me!" she called after Hershele as he left, carrying the heavy bundle. "Or why don't you stay a little longer, until my husband comes back?"

"No," Hershele said. "I must hurry! Do you think you are the only one I have to see?"

In the dark forest the trees were sleeping, the birds were sleeping, the green leaves were sleeping. The stars that stand watch over us had gone pale and began flickering.

After about a verst, Hershele stopped to catch his breath, heaved the bundle off his shoulder, sat on it, and thought things through.

"One thing I must tell you, Hershele!" he said to himself. "There's no lack of fools in this world! The mistress of the inn is a fool, but her husband might well be a clever man with big fists and fat cheeks—and a long whip! What if he comes home and then hunts you down in the forest?"

Hershele did not waste time weighing the odds. He immediately buried his bundle and marked the place so that he could find it again.

Then he ran off toward the opposite side of the forest, took off all his clothes, threw his arms around the trunk of a tree, and waited. He did not have to wait long. As dawn approached he heard the lashes of a whip, the smacking lips of a horse, and the clattering of hooves. It was the innkeeper in full pursuit of Mr. Shabos-Nakhamu.

The innkeeper pulled his cart up to Hershele, who stood naked, hugging the tree. He reined in his horse and looked at Hershele with an expression as foolish as that of a monk coming face-to-face with the devil.

"What are you doing?" the innkeeper asked him in a cracked voice.

"I am a man from the other world," Hershele told him dolefully. "I was robbed—they took some important papers which I was taking to Rabbi Boruchl."

"I know who robbed you!" the innkeeper shouted. "I myself have some accounts to settle with him! Which way did he go?"

"I cannot tell you which way he went!" Hershele whispered bitterly. "But give me your horse, and I shall catch him in an instant! Just wait for me here. Undress, stand by the tree, hug it, and don't move an inch until I return! This tree is a holy tree! Many things in our world depend on it!"

Hershele had been quick to size this man up. One glance had been enough to tell him that husband and wife were not all that far apart. And, sure enough, the innkeeper took off his clothes, went over to the tree, and stood by it. Hershele jumped into the cart and rode off. He dug up his things, put them in the cart, and rode to the edge of the forest.

Hershele left the horse, slung the bundle over his shoulder, and continued along the road that led to Rabbi Boruchl's house.

The sun had already risen. The birds sang, closing their eyes. The innkeeper's mare, her head hanging low, pulled the empty cart back to where she had left her master.

The innkeeper, naked beneath the rays of the rising sun, stood waiting for her huddled against the tree. He felt cold. He was shifting from one foot to the other.

ON THE FIELD
OF HONOR

*T*he following stories are the beginning of my notes on the War. Their plots were taken from books written by French soldiers and officers who took part in the battles. In some passages I have altered the plot and the narrative form, in others I tried to stay as close as possible to the original.

On the Field of Honor

The German batteries were shelling the villages with heavy artillery. The peasants were running for Paris. They dragged with them cripples, freaks, women in labor, dogs, sheep, goods and chattels. The sky, sparkling with heat and azure, slowly turned crimson, heavy, and clouded with smoke.

The sector near N was occupied by the Thirty-seventh Infantry Regiment. Losses were great. The regiment was preparing to counter-attack. Captain Ratin was making his rounds of the trenches. The sun was at its zenith. The neighboring sector sent word that all the officers of the Fourth Company had fallen. The Fourth Company was continuing its resistance.

Ratin saw the shape of a man about three hundred meters from the trenches. It was private Bidou, Simpleton Bidou. He was cowering in a wet pit, which had been made by an exploding shell. The soldier was doing what obscene old men in villages and depraved boys in public lavatories do. I don't think I need say more.

"Bidou! Button yourself up!" the captain yelled in disgust. "Why are you here?"

"I . . . I can't tell you . . . I'm frightened, Captain!"

"You've found yourself a wife here, you swine! You have the gall to tell me to my face that you're a coward? You have abandoned your comrades just when the regiment is about to attack? *Bien, mon cochon!*"

"I swear to you, Captain, I've tried everything! 'Bidou!' I said to myself. 'Be reasonable!' I drank a whole bottle of pure spirits for courage! *Je ne peux pas, capitaine.* I'm frightened, Captain!"

The simpleton lay his head on his knees, clutched it with both hands, and began to cry. Then he looked up at the captain, and through the slits of his porcine eyes flickered timid, tender hope.

Ratin was a quick-tempered man. He had lost two brothers in the war and had a wound in his neck that hadn't healed. A wave of blasphemous abuse poured over the soldier, a dry hot torrent of the repulsive, frenzied, and nonsensical words that send blood pounding to the temples, and drive one man to kill another.

Instead of answering, Bidou quietly shook his round, red-haired, tousled head, the heavy head of the village idiot.

No power on earth could have made him stand up. The captain came right to the edge of the pit and whispered very quietly.

"Get up, Bidou, or I will piss on you from head to toe."

He did as he said. Captain Ratin was not a man to joke with. A reeking stream splashed forcefully over the soldier's face. Bidou was an idiot, a village idiot, but he could not bear this insult. He gave a long, inhuman howl. The miserable, solitary, forlorn howl spread over the harrowed fields. He jumped up, wrung his hands, and bolted over the field toward the German trenches. An enemy bullet struck him in the chest. Ratin finished him off with two shots from his revolver. The soldier's body didn't even twitch. It was left lying in no-man's-land, between enemy lines.

Thus died Celestin Bidou, a Norman peasant from Ori, twenty-one years of age, on the bloodstained fields of France.

The story I have told here is true. Captain Gaston Vidal wrote of it in his book *Figures et anecdotes de la Grand Guerre*. He had witnessed the event. He also fought for France, Captain Vidal did.

The Deserter

Captain Gémier was an outstanding man, and a philosopher too. On the battlefield he never hesitated, in private life he was capable of overlooking minor offenses. It is no small thing for a man to be able to overlook minor offenses. He loved France with a soul-devouring fervor, and his hatred for the barbarians who were defiling her ancient soil was relentless, unquenchable, and lifelong.

What more can one say about Gémier? He loved his wife, brought up his children to be good citizens, was a Frenchman, a patriot, a Parisian, and a lover of books and beautiful things.

Then one fine rosy spring morning, Captain Gémier was informed that an unarmed soldier had been found between French and enemy lines. The soldier's intention to defect was obvious, his guilt clear, and he was brought back under guard.

"Is that you, Beaugé?"

"Yes, Captain!" the soldier replied, saluting.

"I see you took advantage of the dawn to catch a breath of fresh air!" Silence.

"*C'est bien!* You may leave the two of us alone!"

The other soldiers left. Gémier locked the door. The soldier was twenty years old.

"You know what awaits you! *Voyons,* explain yourself!"

Beaugé told him everything. He said that he was sick of war.

"I'm sick of war, *mon capitaine.* No sleep for six nights because of the shelling!"

He had a horror of war. He had not wanted to go to the other side as a traitor, but to give himself up.

In a word, our little Beaugé was unexpectedly eloquent. He told the captain that he was only twenty—*mon dieu, c'est naturel,* one makes mistakes at twenty. He had a mother, a fiancée, *des bons amis.* His whole life lay before him, before twenty-year-old Beaugé, and he would have ample time to make up for his transgression against France.

"Captain, what would my mother say if she found out that I was shot like a wretched criminal?"

The soldier fell to his knees.

"Don't try that with me, Beaugé!" the captain told him. "The other soldiers saw you. We get five soldiers like you, and the whole company is poisoned. *C'est la défaite. Cela jamais.** You are going to die, Beaugé, but I shall save your honor. The local authorities will not be informed of your disgrace. Your mother will be told that you fell on the field of honor. Let's go!"

The soldier followed his superior officer. When they got to the forest, the captain stopped, took out his revolver, and held it out to Beaugé.

"This is how you can avoid a court-martial. You will shoot yourself! I will come back in five minutes. By then everything must be over!"

Gémier walked away. Not a sound interrupted the silence of the forest. The captain returned. Beaugé was waiting for him, hunched over.

"I can't, Captain!" he whispered. "I don't have the strength."

And he recommenced the same long story—his mother, his fiancée, his friends, the life that lay before him.

"I am giving you another five minutes, Beaugé! Don't waste my time!"

When the captain returned, he found the soldier lying on the ground, sobbing, his fingers twitching weakly on the revolver.

Gémier helped the soldier to his feet and, looking him in the eye, said in a quiet, friendly voice, "Beaugé, my friend. Could it be that you don't know how to do it?"

He slowly took the revolver from the young boy's wet hands, walked away three paces, and shot him in the head.

• • •

This incident is also described in Gaston Vidal's book. And the soldier was in actual fact called Beaugé. I am not fully sure if this captain's name really was Gémier. Vidal's story is dedicated "with deep reverence" to a certain Firmin Gémier—and I believe this dedication might well indicate that the captain's name was indeed Gémier. Furthermore, Vidal maintains that the captain was "a patriot, a soldier, a good father and a man who was capable of overlooking minor offences." And that is quite a commendable trait in a man—being able to overlook minor offenses.

*"That would mean defeat. Never."

Papa Marescot's Family

We occupy a village that we have taken from the enemy. It is a tiny Picardy village, lovely and modest. Our company has been bivouacked in the cemetery. Surrounding us are smashed crucifixes and fragments of statues and tombstones wrecked by the sledgehammer of an unknown defiler. Rotting corpses have spilled out of coffins shattered by shells. A picture worthy of you, Michelangelo!

A soldier has no time for mysticism. A field of skulls has been dug up into trenches. War is war. We're still alive. If it is our lot to increase the population of this chilly little hole, we should at least make these decaying corpses dance a jig to the tune of our machine guns.

A shell had blown off the cover of one of the vaults. This so I could have a shelter, no doubt about it. I made myself comfortable in that hole, *que voulez vous, on loge ou on peut.**

So—it's a wonderful, bright spring morning. I am lying on corpses, looking at the fresh grass, thinking of Hamlet. He wasn't that bad a philosopher, the poor prince. Skulls spoke to him in human words. Nowadays, that kind of skill would really come in handy for a lieutenant of the French army.

"Lieutenant, there's some civilian here who wants to see you!" a corporal calls out to me.

What the hell does a civilian want in these nether regions?

A character enters. A shabby, shriveled little old man. He is wearing his Sunday best. His frock coat is bespattered with mud. A half-empty sack dangles from his cowering shoulders. There must be a frozen potato in it—every time he moves, something rattles in the sack.

"*Eh bien*, what do you want?"

"My name, you see, is Monsieur Marescot," the civilian whispers, and bows. "That is why I've come . . ."

"So?"

"I would like to bury Madame Marescot and the rest of my family, Monsieur Lieutenant."

"What?"

"My name, you see, is Papa Marescot." The old man lifts his hat

*"What do you expect, one holes up where one can."

from his gray forehead. "Perhaps you have heard of me, Monsieur Lieutenant!"

Papa Marescot? I have heard this name before. Of course I have heard it. This is the story: Three days ago, at the beginning of our occupation, all nonenemy civilians had been issued the order to evacuate. Some left, others stayed. Those who stayed hid in cellars. But their courage was no match for the bombardment—the stone defense proved hopeless. Many were killed. A whole family had been crushed beneath the debris of a cellar. It was the Marescot family. Their name had stuck in my mind, a true French name. They had been a family of four, the father, mother, and two daughters. Only the father survived.

"You poor man! So you are Marescot? This is so sad. Why did you have to go into that damned cellar, why?"

The corporal interrupted me.

"It looks like they're starting up again, Lieutenant!"

That was to be expected. The Germans had noticed the movement in our trenches. The volley came from the right flank, then it moved farther left. I grabbed Papa Marescot by the collar and pulled him down. My boys ducked their heads and sat quietly under cover, no one as much as sticking his nose out.

Papa Marescot sat pale and shivering in his Sunday best. A five-inch kitten was meowing nearby.

"What can I do for you, Papa? This is no time to beat about the bush! As you can see, we're at each other's throats here!"

"*Mon lieutenant,* I've told you everything. I would like to bury my family."

"Fine, I'll send the men to collect the bodies."

"I have the bodies with me, Monsieur Lieutenant!"

"What?"

He pointed to the sack. In it were the meager remains of Papa Marescot's family.

I shuddered with horror.

"Very well, Papa, I will have my men bury them."

He looked at me as if I had just uttered the greatest idiocy.

"When this hellish din has died down," I continued, "we shall dig an excellent grave for them. Rest assured, *père Marescot,* we will take care of everything."

"But I have a family vault."

"Splendid, where is it?"

"But . . . but . . ."

" 'But what?

"But we're sitting in it as we speak, *mon lieutenant.*"

The Quaker

"Thou shalt not kill" one of the Commandments dictates. This is why Stone, a Quaker, enlisted in the Drivers Corps. He could serve his country without committing the mortal sin of murder. His wealth and education could have secured him a higher post, but, a slave to his conscience, he humbly accepted an insignificant position and the company of people he found coarse.

Who was Stone? He was a bald dome on top of a long stick. The Lord had given him this body with only one objective: to raise Stone's thoughts above the sorrows and cares of this world. His every move was nothing more than a victory of spirit over matter. Regardless of how bad things were, when he was sitting at the wheel of his car he bore himself with the wooden firmness of a preacher in his pulpit. No one ever saw him laugh.

One morning Stone was off duty and decided to go for a walk to pay homage to the Lord in the midst of His creation. An enormous Bible under his arm, Stone strode with his long legs over meadows revived by spring. The blue sky, the twittering of the sparrows in the grass, filled him with joy.

Stone sat down, opened his Bible—but at that very moment he saw an untethered horse, its scrawny ribs jutting out, appear by the bend in the path. Stone immediately heard the powerful voice of duty calling him from within. Back home, he was a member of the Society for the Protection of Animals. He went up to the beast, patted its soft lips, and, forgetting his walk, set off for the stables, clutching his Bible. On the way, he stopped to let the horse drink at a well.

The stableboy was a young man named Bekker. His ways had always triggered righteous indignation in Stone: at every posting, Bekker left inconsolable fiancées.

"I could report you to the major!" the Quaker told him. "But I hope that this time a simple warning will be enough! You are going to look after this poor sick horse, which deserves a much better fate than you do!"

And he marched off with a measured, solemn gait, ignoring the guffaws behind him. The young man's square, protruding chin convincingly testified of his invincible stubbornness.

A few days passed. The horse was still wandering about neglected. This time, Stone told Bekker severely, "Son of Satan!" this is more or less how he started his speech. "The Lord Almighty may well allow you to destroy your soul, but your grievous sins should not be allowed to fall upon an innocent mare! Look at her, you wretch! She is stomping about, greatly unsettled. I am certain you are treating her roughly, as is to be expected from a criminal like you! I shall say this one last time, you Devil's progeny: head to your own damnation as fast as you see fit, but look after this horse, or you will have me to answer to!"

From that day on, Stone felt that Providence had invested him with a special mission: to care for the fate of the abused quadruped. He felt that people, sinful as they were, were unworthy of respect. But for animals he felt an indescribable compassion. His exhausting duties did not hinder him from keeping his inviolable promise to God.

At night the Quaker would often get out of his car (he slept in it, huddled on the seats) in order to make sure that the horse was at a suitable distance from Bekker's nail-studded boot. In good weather, Stone would even mount the beloved animal. The poor nag, trotting along with an air of importance, would carry Stone's long, scrawny body over the green fields, while Stone, his face yellowish and sallow and his lips pressed tight, would picture the immortal, toy-soldierlike figure of the Knight of the Mournful Countenance trotting on his mare Rosinante, over flowers and pastures green.

Stone's zeal bore fruit. The stableboy felt Stone's relentless eyes upon him, and used every trick in the book not to be caught in the act, but when he was alone with the mare, he vented on her all the fury of his base soul. He felt an inexplicable dread of the taciturn Quaker, and he hated him because of this, and despised himself. The only way he could raise himself in his own esteem was to taunt the horse which the Quaker had taken under his wing. Such is the despicable pride of man. Locking himself in the stables with the horse, the stableboy pricked her hairy, sagging lips with red-hot needles, lashed her across the spine with a wire whip, and threw salt in her eyes. When he finally let the tortured animal totter fearfully to its stall, blinded by stinging salt and swaying like a drunkard, the stableboy threw himself in the hay and laughed his heart out, enjoying his revenge to the fullest.

There was a change at the front. Stone's division was relocated to a more dangerous position. His religious beliefs did not permit him to kill, but they did permit him to be killed. The Germans were advancing on the Isère. Stone was transporting the injured. All around him, men of various nationalities were dying at an incredible rate. Old generals, spotlessly clean, their faces swollen, stood on hilltops and monitored the area with field glasses. There was a ceaseless barrage of cannon fire. A stench rose from the earth, the sun rummaged through the mangled corpses.

Stone forgot his horse. But within a week his conscience began gnawing at him, and he found an opportunity to return to the area where he had been stationed before. He found the horse in a dark shed made of a few rickety planks. The mare was so weak she could barely stand. Her eyes were covered with a grimy film. She neighed weakly when she saw her true friend, and lay her faltering muzzle on his hand.

"It isn't my fault," the stableboy told Stone cheekily. "We're not being given any oats."

"Fine," Stone said. "I'll go get some oats."

He looked up at the sky that shone through a hole in the roof, and went outside.

I came across him a few hours later and asked him whether the road he was driving down wasn't too dangerous. He seemed more intense than usual. The last few blood-drenched days had left a deep mark on him, it was as if he were in mourning for himself.

"I haven't run into any trouble this far," he mumbled. "But things might well end up badly." And suddenly he added, "I'm heading for the forage stores. I need some oats."

The following morning a search party of soldiers that was sent out to look for him found him dead at the wheel of his car. A bullet had penetrated his forehead. The car had crashed into a ditch.

Thus died Stone, the Quaker, on account of his love for a horse.

THE SIN OF JESUS

*A*rina had a little room by the grand stairway near the guest rooms, and Sergei, the janitor's assistant, had a room near the service entrance. They had done a shameful deed together. Arina bore Sergei twins on Easter Sunday. Water flows, stars shine, muzhiks feel lust, and Arina again found herself in a delicate condition. She is in her sixth month, the months just roll by when a woman is pregnant, and Sergei ends up being drafted into the army—a fine mess! So Arina goes to him and says, "Listen, Sergunya, there's no point in me sitting around waiting for you. We won't see each other for four years, and I wouldn't be surprised if I had another brood of three or four by the time you come back. Working in a hotel, your skirt is hitched up more often than not. Whoever takes a room here gets to be your lord and master, Jews or whatever. When you come back from the army my womb will be worn out, I'll be washed up as a woman, I don't think I'll be of any use to you."

"True enough," Sergei said, nodding his head.

"The men who want to marry me right now are Trofimich the contractor, he's a rude roughneck, Isai Abramich, a little old man, and then there's the warden of Nilolo-Svyatskoi Church, he's very feeble, but your vigor has rattled my soul to pieces! As the Lord is my witness, I'm all chewed up! In three months I'll be rid of my burden, I'll leave the baby at the orphanage, and I'll go marry them."

When Sergei heard this he took off his belt and gave Arina a heroic beating, aiming for her belly.

"Hey!" the woman says to him. "Don't beat me on the gut, remember it's your stuffing in there, not no one else's!"

She received many savage wallops, he shed many a bitter tear, the woman's blood flowed, but that's neither here nor there. The woman went to Jesus Christ and said:

"This and that, Lord Jesus. Me, I'm Arina, the maid from the Hotel Madrid & Louvre on Tverskaya Street. Working in a hotel, your skirt is hitched up more often than not. Whoever takes a room there gets to be your lord and master, Jews or whatever. Here on earth walks a humble servant of Yours, Sergei the janitor's assistant. I bore him twins last year on Easter Sunday."

And she told him everything.

"And what if Sergei didn't go to the army?" the Savior pondered.

"The constable would drag him off."

"Ah, the constable," the Savior said, his head drooping. "I'd forgotten all about him. Ah!—and how about if you led a pure life?"

"For four years!" the woman gasped. "Do you mean to say that everyone should stop living a life? You're still singing the same old tune! How are we supposed to go forth and multiply? Do me a favor and spare me such advice!"

Here the Savior's cheeks flushed crimson. The woman had stung him to the quick, but he said nothing. You cannot kiss your own ear, even the Savior knew that.

"This is what you need to do, humble servant of the Lord, glorious maidenly sinner Arina!" the Savior proclaimed in all his glory. "I have a little angel prancing about up in heaven, his name is Alfred, and he's gotten completely out of hand. He keeps moaning, 'Why, O Lord, did you make me an angel at twenty, a fresh lad like me?' I'll give you, Arina, servant of God, Alfred the angel as a husband for four years. He'll be your prayer, your salvation, and your pretty-boy, too. And there's no way you'll get a child from him, not even a duckling, because there's a lot of fun in him, but no substance."

"That's just what I need!" maid Arina cried. "It's their substance that has driven me to the brink of the grave three times in two years!"

"This will be a sweet respite for you, child of God, a light prayer, like a song. Amen."

And thus it was decided. Alfred, a frail, tender youth, was sent down, and fluttering on his pale blue shoulders were two wings, rippling in a rosy glow like doves frolicking in the heavens. Arina hugged him, sobbing with emotion and female tenderness.

"My little Alfredushka, my comfort and joy, my one-and-only!"

The Savior gave her instructions that, before going to bed, she had to take off the angel's wings, which were mounted on hinges, just like door hinges, and she had to take them off and wrap them in a clean sheet for the night, because at the slightest frolic the wings could break, as they were made of infants' sighs and nothing more.

The Savior blessed the union one last time, and called over a choir of abbots for the occasion, their voices thundering in song. There was nothing to eat, not even a hint of food—that wouldn't have been proper—and Arina and Alfred, embracing, descended to earth on a silken rope ladder. They went to Petrovka, that's were the woman dragged him to, she bought him lacquered shoes, checkered tricot trousers (by the way, not only was he not wearing pants, he was completely in the altogether), a hunting frock, and a vest of electric-blue velvet.

"As for the rest, sweetie," she said, "we'll find that at home."

That day Arina did not work in the hotel, she took the day off. Sergei came and made a big to-do outside her room, but she wouldn't open, and called out from behind her door, "Sergei Nifantich, I'm busy washing my feet right now and would be obliged if you would distance yourself without all that to-do!"

He left without saying a word. The angelic power was already taking effect.

Arina cooked a meal fit for a merchant—ha, she was devilishly proud, she was! A quart of vodka, and even some wine, Danube herring with potatoes, a samovar filled with tea. No sooner had Alfred eaten this earthly abundance than he keeled over into a deep sleep. Arina managed to snatch his wings off their hinges just in time. She wrapped them up, and then carried Alfred to her bed.

Lying on her fluffy eiderdown, on her frayed, sin-ridden bed, is a snow-white wonder, an otherworldly brilliance radiating from him. Shafts of moonlight mix with red rays and dart about the room, trippling over their feet. And Arina weeps, rejoices, sings, and prays. The unheard of, O Arina, has befallen you in this shattered world, blessed art thou among women!

They had drunk down the whole quart of vodka. And it was pretty obvious, too. As they fell asleep, Arina rolled over onto Alfred with the hot, six-month gut that Sergei had saddled her with. You can imagine the weight! It wasn't enough that she was sleeping next to an angel, it wasn't enough that the man next to her wasn't spitting on the wall, or snoring, or snorting—no it wasn't enough for this lusty, crazed wench! She had to warm her bloated, combustible belly even more. And so she crushed the Lord's angel, crushed him in her drunken bliss, crushed him in her rapture like a week-old infant, mangled him beneath her, and he came to a fatal end, and from his wings, wrapped in the sheet, pale tears flowed.

Dawn came, the trees bowed down low. In the distant northern woods, every fir tree turned into a priest, every fir tree genuflected.

The woman comes again before the throne of the Savior. She is strong, her shoulders wide, her red hands carrying the young corpse.

"Behold, Lord!"

This was too much for Jesus' gentle soul, and he cursed the woman from the bottom of his heart.

"As it is in the world, Arina, so it shall be with you!"

"But Lord!" the woman said to him in a low voice. "Was it I who made my body heavy, who brewed the vodka, who made a woman's soul lonely and stupid?"

"I do not wish to have anything further to do with you," Lord Jesus exclaimed. "You have crushed my angel, you trollop, you!" And Arina was hurled back down to earth on a purulent wind, to Tverskaya Street, to her sentence at the Madrid & Louvre. There all caution had been thrown to the winds. Sergei was carousing away the last few days before he had to report as a recruit. Trofimich, the contractor, who had just come back from Kolomna, saw how healthy and red-cheeked she was.

"Ooh what a nice little gut!" he said, among other things.

Isai Abramich, the little old man, came wheezing over when he heard about the little gut.

"After all that has happened," he said, "I cannot settle down with you lawfully, but I can definitely still lie with you."

Six feet under, that's where he should be lying, and not spitting into her soul like everyone else! It was as if they had all broken loose from their chains—dishwashers, peddlers, foreigners. A tradesman likes to have some fun.

And here ends my tale.

Before she gave birth—the remaining three months flew by quickly—Arina went out into the backyard behind the janitor's room, raised her horribly large belly to the silken skies, and idiotically uttered, "Here you are, Lord, here is my gut! They bang on it as if it were a drum. Why, I don't know! And then, Lord, I end up like this again! I've had enough!"

Jesus drenched Arina with his tears. The Savior fell to his knees.

"Forgive me, my Arinushka, sinful God that I am, that I have done this to you!"

"I will not forgive you, Jesus Christ!" Arina replied. "I will not!"

AN EVENING WITH
THE EMPRESS

Siberian salmon caviar and a pound of bread in my pocket. Nowhere to go. I am standing on Anichkov Bridge, huddling against Klodt's horses. A heavy evening is descending from Morskaya. Orange lights wrapped in gauze roam along the Nevsky Prospekt. I need shelter. Hunger is plucking at me the way a clumsy brat plucks at the strings of a violin. My mind skims over all the apartments abandoned by the bourgeoisie. The Anichkov Palace shimmers into view in all its squat splendor. There's my shelter!

It isn't hard to slip into the entrance hall unnoticed. The palace is empty. An unhurried mouse is scratching away in one of the chambers. I am in the library of the Dowager Empress Maria Fyodorovna.* An old German is standing in the middle of the room, stuffing cotton wool in his ears. He is about to leave. Luck kisses me on the lips! I know this German! I once typed a report for him, free of charge, about the loss of his passport. This German belongs to me, from his puffy head to his good-natured toes. We decide that I have an appointment with Lunacharsky† in the library, and that I am waiting for him.

The melodic ticking of the clock erases the German from the room. I am alone. Balls of crystal blaze above me in the silky yellow

---

* Empress Maria Fyodorovna (Princess Dagmar of Denmark), 1847–1928, wife of Czar Alexander III.
  † Anatoly Lunacharsky, 1875–1933, Marxist critic and playwright, was the USSR's first Commissar of Education.

light. A warmth beyond description rises from the steam pipes of the central heating. The deep divans wrap my frozen body in calm.

A quick inspection yields results. I discover a potato pie in the fireplace, a saucepan, a pinch of tea and sugar. And behold! The spirit stove just stuck its bluish little tongue out.

That evening I ate like a human being. I spread the most delicate of napkins on an ornate little Chinese table glittering with ancient lacquer. I washed down each piece of my brown ration bread with a sip of sweet, steaming tea, its coral stars dancing on the faceted sides of the glass. The bulging velvet palms of the cushion beneath me caressed my bony hips. Outside the windows, fluffy snow crystals fell on the Petersburg granite deadened by the hard frost.

Light streamed down the warm walls in glittering lemon torrents, touching book spines that responded with a bluish gold twinkle.

The books, their pages molding and fragrant, carried me to faraway Denmark. Over half a century ago they had been given to the young princess as she left her small, chaste country for savage Russia. On the austere title pages, the ladies of the court who had raised her bade her farewell in three slanting lines, in fading ink, as did her friends from Copenhagen, the daughters of state councilors, her tutors, parchment professors from the Lycée, and her father, the King, and her mother, the Queen, her weeping mother. Long shelves of small plump books with blackened gilt edges, children's Bibles speckled with timid ink splotches, clumsy little prayers written to Lord Jesus, morocco-leather volumes of Lamartine and Chénier containing dried flowers crumbling to dust. I leaf through the gossamer pages that have survived oblivion, and the image of a mysterious country, a thread of exotic days, unfurls before me: low walls encircling the royal gardens, dew on the trimmed lawns, the drowsy emerald canals, the tall King with chocolate sideburns, the calm ringing of the bell above the palace cathedral and, maybe, love—a young girl's love, a fleeting whisper in the heavy halls. Empress Maria Fyodorovna, a small woman with a tightly powdered face, a consummate schemer with an indefatigable passion for power, a fierce female among the Preobrazhensky Grenadiers, a ruthless but attentive mother, crushed by the German woman,* unfurls the scroll of her long, somber life before me.

* Empress Maria Fyodorovna's daughter-in-law, Empress Alexandra, 1872–1918, wife of Czar Nicholas II.

It was very late that night when I tore myself from this sorrowful and touching chronicle, from the specters with their blood-drenched skulls. The balls of crystal covered in swirls of dust were still blazing peacefully above me on the ornate brown ceiling. Next to my tattered shoes, leaden rivulets had crystallized on the blue carpet. Exhausted by my thoughts and the silent heat, I fell asleep.

In the depths of the night I made my way toward the exit over the dully glinting parquet of the corridors. Alexander III's study was a high-ceilinged box with boarded-up windows facing the Nevsky Prospekt. Mikhail Alexandrovich's* rooms were the lively apartment of a cultivated officer who likes his exercise. The walls were decorated with bright, pink-patterned wallpaper. Little porcelain bibelots, of the naive and redundantly fleshy genre of the seventeenth century, lined the low mantelpieces.

Pressed against a column, I waited for a long time for the last court lackey to fall asleep. He dropped his wrinkled jowls, clean-shaven out of age-old habit, the lantern weakly gilding his high, lolling forehead.

At one in the morning I was out in the street. The Nevsky Prospekt welcomed me into its sleepless womb. I went to the Nikolayevsky Station to sleep. Let those who have fled this city know that there is still a place in Petersburg where a homeless poet can spend the night.

---

* Grand Duke Mikhail Alexandrovich, 1878–1918, brother of Czar Nicholas II.

CHINK

A vicious night. Slashing wind. A dead man's fingers pluck at the frozen entrails of Petersburg. The crimson pharmacies on street corners freeze over. A pharmacist's prim head lolls to the side. The frost grips the pharmacy by its purple heart. And the pharmacy's heart dies.

The Nevsky Prospekt is empty. Ink vials shatter in the sky. It is two in the morning. The end. A vicious night.

A young girl and a gentleman are sitting by the railing of the Café Bristol. Two whimpering backs. Two freezing ravens by a leafless bush.

"If, with the help of Satan, you manage to succeed the deceased Czar, then see if the masses will follow you, you mother-killers! Just you try! The Latvians will back them, and those Latvians are Mongols, Glafira!"

The man's jowls hang on both sides of his face like a rag peddler's sacks. In the man's reddish brown pupils wounded cats prowl.

"I beg you, for the love of Christ, Aristarkh Terentich! Please go to Nadezhinskaya Street! Who will walk up to me if I'm sitting with a man?"

A Chinese in a leather jacket walks past. He lifts a loaf of bread above his head. With his blue fingernail he draws a line across the crust. One pound. Glafira raises two fingers. Two pounds.

A thousand saws moan in the ossified snow of the side streets. A star twinkles in the hard, inky firmament.

The Chinese man stops and mumbles to her through clenched teeth, "You a dirty one? Huh?"

"I'm a nice clean girl, comrade!"

"Pound."

On Nadezhinskaya Street, Aristarkh looks back with sparks in his eyes.

"Darling," the girl says to the Chinese man in a hoarse voice, "I've got my godfather with me. Will you let him sleep in a corner?"

The Chinese man slowly nods his head. O great wisdom of the East!

"Aristarkh Terentich," the girl yells casually, leaning against the smooth leather shoulder. "My acquaintance is inviting you to join us for company!"

Aristarkh Terentich immediately livens up.

"For reasons beyond the control of management, he is currently not employed," she whispers, wriggling her shoulders. "But he had a past with meat and potatoes in it!"

"Definitely. I am pleased to make your acquaintance. Aristarkh Terentich Sheremetsev."

At the hotel they were served Chinese liquor and weren't even asked to pay.

Late at night, the Chinese man slipped out of bed into the darkness of the room.

"Where are you going?" Glafira asked gruffly, twisting her legs.

There was a large sweat stain under her back.

The Chinese man went over to Aristarkh, who was sleeping on the floor by the washstand. He shook the old man's shoulders and pointed to Glafira.

"Oh, yes, yes, pal!" Aristarkh prattled from the floor, "A definite yes!" And with quick little steps he hobbled over to the bed.

"Get away from me, you dog!" Glafira shouted. "Your Chinaman's finished me off already!"

"She won't do it, pal!" Aristarkh hissed quickly. "You ordered her to, but she isn't obeying!"

"He friend!" the Chinese man said. "He do! Big harlot!"

"You are an elderly gentleman, Aristarkh Terentich," the girl whispered, letting the old man climb into bed with her. "What's got into your head?"

Period.

A TALE ABOUT
A WOMAN

*O*nce upon a time there was a woman, her name was Xenia. Large bosom, round shoulders, blue eyes. That was the kind of woman she was. If only you and I had such a woman!

Her husband was killed on the battlefield. Three years she lived without a husband, working in the house of a rich family. The rich family wanted a hot meal three times a day. Wood they never burned, nothing but coal. The heat from the coals was unbearable—in coals fiery roses glow.

For three years the woman cooked for the rich family, and she was virtuous with the menfolk. But where do you hide a gigantic bosom like that? Can you tell me?

The fourth year she goes to the doctor. "My head feels all heavy," she says to him. "One minute I'm ablaze with fire, the next I'm all weak."

And this, believe it or not, is what the doctor tells her: "Is there no menfolk running around in your courtyard? *Oy*, woman!"

"I wouldn't dare," Xenia said, bursting into tears. "I'm a delicate girl!"

And indeed she was a delicate girl. Xenia's bitter tears made her eyes bluer.

Old mother Morozikha took matters in hand.

Old mother Morozikha was the midwife and potion-maker for the whole street. The likes of her are ruthless with a woman's insides. Give her half a chance to steam them out, and you'll be lucky if even a blade of grass will ever grow there again.

"Xenia," she says, "I'll fix things for you! A dryness has cracked the soil. All it needs is some God-sent rain. A mushroom needs to sprout up in a woman, all soggy and rank."

And she brought him. Valentin Ivanovich was his name. Not much to look at, but quite a joker, and he could make up nice ditties. He didn't have a body worth mentioning, his hair was long, and he was covered with a rainbow scattering of pimples. But did Xenia need a bull? He was a man, and could make up nice ditties. Could you find anything better in the world? Xenia cooked a hundred blini and raisin pies. Three eiderdowns were laid on her bed, and six pillows, all nice and fluffy—all for you to roll around in, Valentin!

Evening came, the guests squeezed into the tiny room behind the kitchen, everyone downed a glass of vodka. Old mother Morozikha had put on a silk kerchief, you wouldn't believe how respectable she looked. And Valentin spoke wonderful words to Xenia: "Ah, Xenia, my sweet one! I am a neglected man in this world, a dog-tired youth! Do not think of me lackadaisically! Night will descend with stars and black fans—O can a man express his soul in a poem? O, timid man that I am!"

Word upon word. Needless to say, they emptied two whole bottles of vodka and three of wine. Not to mention five rubles' worth of food—no joke!

Our Valentin's face flushed to a dark maroon, and he began hollering poetry.

Old mother Morozikha got up from the table.

"Well, I'll be off, may the Lord be with me!" she said. "There'll be love between the two of you, so when you lie down together on the stove bench, pull off his boots. With men, you can wash sheets till you're blue in the face."

But the liquor was beginning to kick in. Valentin grabbed his hair and started tearing at it. "I," he shouts, "am having visions. The moment I have a few drinks, I start having visions. Xenia, I can see you lying dead, your face looks sickening. And I am the priest, I am walking behind your coffin, swinging the censer!"

At this point, needless to say, he raised his voice.

Well, Xenia was only human. She too had loosened her blouse, unfastening a button or two.

"Don't shout, Valentin Ivanovich," she whispered. "Don't shout, the master and mistress will hear."

But tell me, can you hold a man back once he is seized by melancholia?

"You have offended me most deeply!" Valentin wept convulsively. "Oh, what snakes people are! What did they want? They wanted to buy my soul! I," he went on, "was born out of wedlock, but I am still a nobleman's son! Are you listening to me, you scullery maid, you?"

"I will be sweet to you, Valentin Ivanovich."

"Leave me be!"

He rose and flung open the door.

"Leave me be! I am going out into the world!"

But how was he to go out into the world, poor soul, soused out of his mind as he was? He collapsed onto the bed, puked on the, if you will pardon the expression, sheets, and fell asleep, the humble servant of God.

Old mother Morozikha was already rolling up her sleeves.

"Well, that's the end of that," she said. "We'd better carry him outside."

The women carried Valentin out into the street and laid him down outside the gate. They went back in, and there stood the mistress, in a nightcap and the most elegant pantaloons.

"You entertain men here at night and act most scandalously!" she scolded her cook. "I want you to pack your bags and leave my God-fearing household by tomorrow morning! I have my unmarried daughter to think of!"

Xenia sat in the hall, weeping till dawn.

"Grandma Morozikha, ah, Grandma Morozikha," she whimpered, "what have you done to me, poor young woman that I am! I'm ashamed of myself, how can I even dare look at God's world, and what can I expect to see in God's world now?"

Xenia cried and carried on, surrounded by raisin pies, snowy featherbeds, holy icon lamps, and wine. And her warm shoulders shook.

"It was a blunder," old mother Morozikha said to her. "We should have gone for a simpler fellow, we should have gone for Mitya."

And morning set up shop once more. The girls carrying milk went from house to house. It was a blue and frosty morning.

THE BATHROOM WINDOW

I have an acquaintance, a Madam Kebchik. In her day, Madam Kebchik assures me, "nothing in the world" would have induced her to take less than five rubles.

Now she has a nice, respectable apartment, and in this apartment she has two girls, Marusya and Tamara. There are more requests for Marusya than for Tamara. One of the windows of the girls' room has a view of the street, the other window, just an air vent near the ceiling, has a view of the bathroom. When I realized this, I said to Fanya Osipovna Kebchik, "How about putting a ladder by the little window in the bathroom in the evenings, so I can climb up and peek into Marusya's room? I'll give you five rubles."

"You rogue, you!" Fanya Osipovna said, and agreed.

She got her five rubles quite often. I made use of the little window when Marusya had clients.

Everything went without a hitch, but one time an extremely foolish thing happened. I was standing on the ladder. Luckily, Marusya hadn't turned off the light. Her guest was a pleasant, unassuming fellow with one of those large, harmless mustaches. He undressed in a prim and proper fashion: he took off his collar, looked in the mirror, noticed a pimple under his mustache, studied it, and pressed it out with a handkerchief. He took off a boot and examined it too—was there a scratch on the sole?

They kissed, undressed, and smoked a cigarette. I got ready to climb down. At that moment I felt the ladder sliding away under me. I tried to grab hold of the window, but it gave way. The ladder fell with a crash and there I was, dangling in the air.

Suddenly the whole apartment exploded with alarm. Everyone came running, Fanya Osipovna, Tamara, and an official I didn't know in a Ministry of Finance uniform. They helped me down. My situation was pitiful. Marusya and her lanky client came into the bathroom.

The girl looked at me, froze, and said quietly, "What a bastard, oh, what a bastard!"

She fell silent, stared at us foolishly, went over to the lanky man, and for some reason kissed his hand and started crying.

"My dear, O God, my dear!" she said, between kisses and sobs.

The lanky man stood there like a total idiot. My heart was pounding wildly. I dug my nails into my palms and went over to Madam Kebchik.

Within a few minutes, Marusya knew everything. All was forgiven and forgotten. But I was still wondering why she had kissed the lanky fellow.

"Madam Kebchik," I said. "Put up the ladder one last time, and you can have ten rubles."

"Your mind's even more unsteady than that ladder of yours!" the landlady answered, and agreed.

So there I was again, standing by the little window. I looked through it and saw Marusya, her thin arms wrapped around her client, kissing him with slow kisses, tears flowing from her eyes.

"My darling!" she whispered. "O God, my sweet darling!" And she gave herself to him with all the passion of a woman in love. She looked at him as if he, this lanky fellow, were the only man in the world.

And the lanky fellow wallowed in businesslike bliss.

BAGRAT-OGLY AND
THE EYES OF HIS BULL

I saw a bull of unparalleled beauty lying by the side of the road. A boy was bending over it, crying.

"This boy is Bagrat-Ogly," said a snake charmer who was eating his scanty meal nearby. "Bagrat-Ogly, son of Kazim."

"He is as exquisite as twelve moons," I said.

"The green cloak of the Prophet will never cover the rebellious whiskers of Kazim," the snake charmer said. "He was a quarrelsome man, and left his son nothing but a pauper's hut, his plump wives, and a bull that was unrivaled. But Allah is great!"

"*Allah il'Allah!*" I said.

"Allah is great," he repeated, pushing away his basket of snakes. "The bull grew up to become the mightiest bull in Anatolia. Memed-khan, a neighbor, sick with envy, castrated it last night. Now no one will bring their cows to Bagrat-Ogly in the hope of conception. Now no one will pay Bagrat-Ogly a hundred piasters for the love of his bull. He is a pauper, Bagrat-Ogly. He weeps by the side of the road.

The silence of the mountains unfurled its violet banners above us. The snows glittered on the peaks. Blood trickled down the legs of the mutilated bull and bubbled onto the grass. And, hearing the bull moan, I looked into its eyes and saw the bull's death and my own death, and I fell to the ground in measureless torment.

"Traveler!" the boy then called, his face as rosy as the dawn. "You writhe, and foam bubbles from the corners of your lips. A black illness is fettering you with the ropes of its convulsions."

"Bagrat-Ogly!" I answered, sunk in exhaustion. "In the eyes of your bull I saw the reflection of the ever-watchful malice of our neighbors, the Memed-khans of this world. In the moist depths of its eyes I saw mirrors in which rage the green fires of the treachery of our neighbors, the Memed-khans of this world. In the eyes of the mutilated bull I saw my youth, barren and cut down, the prime of my life thrashing its way through the thorny undergrowth of indifference. The deserts of Syria, Arabia, and Kurdistan, which I have fathomed thrice, I saw within the eyes of your bull, O Bagrat-Ogly, and their flat sands leave me no hope. The hatred of the whole world has penetrated the eye sockets of your bull. Flee from the malice of our Memed-khan neighbors, O Bagrat-Ogly, and may the old snake charmer hoist his basket of pythons onto his back and flee at your side!"

And filling the ravines with my moans, I rose to my feet. I drank in the fragrance of the eucalyptus and walked away. A many-headed dawn soared above the mountains like a thousand swans. The steel waters of the Bay of Trebizond sparkled in the distance, and I saw the sea and the yellow decks of the feluccas. The freshness of the grass poured over the ruins of a Byzantine wall. The bazaars of Trebizond and the carpets of Trebizond rose before me. I came across a young highlander at a fork in the road outside the city. On his outstretched hand sat a pigeon hawk chained by its talon. The highlander walked with a light gait. The sun surfaced above our heads. And a sudden calm descended on my wanderer's soul.

LINE AND COLOR

I first met Alexander Fyodorovich Kerensky* on December 20, 1916, in the dining room of the Ollila Spa. We were introduced by Zatsareni, a barrister from Turkestan. I had heard that Zatsareni had had himself circumcised at the age of forty. That disgraced imbecile Grand Duke Peter Nikolayevich, who was banished to Tashkent, prized Zatsareni's friendship very highly. The Grand Duke used to walk about Tashkent stark naked, married a Cossack woman, lit candles before a portrait of Voltaire as if it were an icon of Jesus Christ, and had the boundless flatlands of Amu-Dari drained. Zatsareni was a good friend to him.

So, there we were at the Ollila Spa. Ten kilometers away shimmered the blue granite walls of Helsingfors.† O Helsingfors, love of my heart! O sky, pouring down onto the esplanades and soaring high like a bird!

So, there we were at the Ollila Spa. Northern flowers were withering in vases. Antlers spread across the murky ceilings. The air of the dining room was filled with the fragrance of pine trees, the cool breasts of Countess Tyszkiewicz, and the British officers' silk underwear.

At the table, a courteous converted Jew from the police department was sitting next to Kerensky. To his right, a Norwegian by the name of

---

* Alexander Fyodorovich Kerensky, 1881–1970, served as Minister of Justice, Minister of War, and provisional Prime Minister of Russia after the 1917 Russian Revolution.
   † A former name (Swedish) for Helsinki, which until Finland's declaration of independence in 1917 was Russian.

Nickelsen, the owner of a whaling vessel. To his left, Countess Tyszkiewicz, as beautiful as Marie Antoinette.

Kerensky ate three pieces of cake and went with me for a walk in the forest. Fröken Kristi hurried past us on skis.

"Who was that?" Kerensky asked me.

"That was Nickelsen's daughter, Fröken Kristi," I said. "She's beautiful, isn't she?"

Then we saw old Johannes's sledge.

"Who was that?" Kerensky asked.

"That was old Johannes," I said. "He brings cognac and fruit from Helsingfors. Can it be that you don't know old Johannes the coachman?"

"I know everyone here," Kerensky replied, "but I can't see anyone."

"Are you nearsighted, Alexander Fyodorovich?"

"Yes, I'm nearsighted."

"You need glasses, Alexander Fyodorovich."

"Never!"

"If you think about it," I said to him with the brashness of youth, "you are not merely blind, you are as good as dead. The line—that divine trait, that queen of the world—has escaped you forever. You and I are walking through this enchanted garden, this marvelous Finnish forest. To our dying day we will not encounter anything better, and you, you cannot even see the rosy, ice-crusted edges of the waterfall, over there, on the river. The weeping willow, leaning over the waterfall—you cannot see its Japanese delicacy. The red trunks of the pine trees heaped with snow! The granular sparkle that scintillates over the snows! It begins as a frozen line above the tree's wavy surface, like Leonardo's line, crowned by the reflection of the blazing clouds. And what about Fröken Kristi's silk stockings, and the line of her maturing legs? I beg of you, Alexander Fyodorovich, buy some spectacles!"

"My dear boy," he answered, "don't waste your gunpowder! That half-ruble coin you want me to squander on a pair of spectacles is the one coin that will never leave my pocket! You can keep that line of yours with its repulsive reality. You are living the sordid life of a trigonometry teacher, while I am enveloped by wonders, even in a hole like Klyazma! Why do I need the freckles on Fröken Kristi's face when I, who can barely make her out, can imagine everything I want to imagine about her? Why do I need these clouds in the Finnish sky, when I can see a dreamy ocean above my head? Why do I need lines when I have colors? For me the whole world is a gigantic theater in which I am the only spectator without opera glasses. The orchestra plays the prelude to the third act, the stage is far away as in a dream, my heart swells with delight, I see Juliet's crimson velvet, Romeo's violet silk, and not a single false beard—and you want to blind me with a pair of half-ruble spectacles?"

That evening I left for town. O Helsingfors, refuge of my dreams!

I saw Alexander Fyodorovich again half a year later, in June of 1917, after he had become Supreme Commander of the Russian army and master of our fate.

That day the Troitsky drawbridge had been lifted. The Putilov workers were heading for the arsenal. Burning tramcars lay in the streets like dead horses.

The mass rally had gathered at the House of the People. Alexander Fyodorovich gave a speech on Russia, our mother and our wife. The crowd smothered him with its sheepskin-coat passion. Could he, the only spectator without opera glasses, even see the bristling passion of the sheepskin coats? I have no idea. But after him, Trotsky came to the podium, twisted his lips, and, in a voice that chased away one's last hopes, said:

"My Comrades and Brothers!"

YOU MISSED THE BOAT, CAPTAIN!

*T*he *Halifax* pulled into Odessa's port. It had come from London for a cargo of Russian wheat.

On the twentieth-seventh of January, the day of Lenin's funeral, the ship's colored crew—three Chinese, two Negroes, and a Malay— called the captain to the deck. In town orchestras were thundering and a blizzard howled.

"Captain O'Nearn!" the Negroes said. "As there's no loading to do today, can we go ashore this evening?"

"You will stay where you are!" O'Nearn told them. "A wind-force-nine gale is blowing right now, and it's getting stronger. The *Beaconsfield* has gotten stuck in the ice at Sanzheyka, and the barometer is pointing to where I wish it weren't! In weather like this, the crew has to stay with the vessel. Stay where you are!"

And Captain O'Nearn went off to see the first mate. The two had a good laugh, lit cigars, and pointed at the city, where the blizzard and the orchestras writhed and howled in abject grief.

The two Negroes and the three Chinese loitered about the deck. They blew on their frozen palms, stamped their rubber boots, and peered into the captain's cabin, the door of which stood ajar. The velvet of the sofas, the heated cognac, and the soft tobacco fumes came wafting out into the wind-force-nine gale.

"Boatswain!" O'Nearn yelled, seeing the sailors. "Our deck is not a boulevard! Throw them in the hold!"

"Yes, sir!" shouted the boatswain, a pillar of red meat covered with red hair. "Yes, sir!" And he grabbed the Malay by the scruff of his neck. He dragged him to the side of the deck facing the open sea, and shoved him onto a rope ladder. The Malay jumped down and went scampering over the ice. The three Chinese and the two Negroes followed close at his heels.

"Did you throw them in the hold?" the captain yelled from his cabin, which was warmed by cognac and delicate smoke.

"I threw them, sir!" shouted the boatswain, a pillar of red meat, standing in the storm by the gangway like a sentinel.

The wind blew in from the sea at force nine, like nine rounds of fire discharged by the frozen batteries of the sea. White snow raged above the mounds of ice. And over the hardened waves five contorted commas with singed faces and flapping jackets frantically scampered toward the shore, toward the piers. They clambered onto the icy embankments with scraping hands, and ran through the port and into the town, which was quaking in the wind.

A detachment of stevedores with black flags was marching over the square to the pedestal where Lenin's monument was to be raised. The two Negroes and the Chinese marched beside the stevedores, panting, shaking hands with people, overcome with the joy of escaped convicts.

That very minute in Moscow, on Red Square, Lenin's body was being lowered into his tomb. Back in Odessa, sirens wailed, the blizzard howled, and the crowds marched in columns. And on board the *Halifax* the impermeable boatswain was standing alone in the storm by the gangway like a sentinel. Under his equivocal guard, Captain O'Nearn drank cognac in his smoky cabin.

He had relied on his boatswain, Captain O'Nearn had, and so the captain had missed the boat.

THE END OF
ST. HYPATIUS

*Y*esterday I was at the St. Hypatius Monastery, and Father Hillarion, the last of the resident monks, showed me the abode of the Romanov boyars.

The Muscovites had come here in 1613 to ask Mikhail Fyodorovich* to ascend the throne.

I saw the worn corner where Sister Martha, the Czar's mother, used to pray, her gloomy bedchamber, and the turret from which she watched the wolf hunts in the Kostroma forests.

Father Hillarion and I crossed the ancient little bridges on which the snow was piled high, and startled the ravens that had nested in the boyars' tower. We went up to the church, which was indescribably beautiful.

The church, painted carmine and azure, encircled by a wreath of snows, stood out against the smoke-blackened northern sky like a peasant woman's motley kerchief with its design of Russian flowers.

The lines of the modest cupolas were chaste, the blue side buildings potbellied, and the patterned transom of the windows sparkled in the sun with a needless brilliance.

In this deserted church I found the iron gates that had been a gift of Ivan the Terrible, and looked at the ancient icons, the dank decay of ruthless holiness.

The saints—possessed, naked muzhiks with withered thighs—

---

* Mikhail Fyodorovich Romanov, 1596–1645, was the first Czar of the Romanov dynasty.

---

writhed on the flaking walls, and next to them the Russian Holy Virgin was portrayed, a thin peasant woman with parted knees and sagging breasts that looked like two extra green arms.

The ancient icons wrapped my cheerful heart in the chill of their deathly passions, and I barely managed to escape them and their sepulchral saints.

Their God lay in the church, cleansed and ossified, like a cadaver that has been washed on its deathbed but left unburied.

Father Hillarion wandered alone among his corpses. His left foot had a limp; he tended to doze off, kept scratching his dirty beard, and soon began to bore me.

I threw open Ivan the Terrible's gates and ran under the black arches out onto the square, where the Volga, shackled in ice, twinkled at me.

Kostroma's smoke rose high, cutting through the snow. Muzhiks clothed in a yellow halo of frost were dragging flour on sledges, and their dray-horses slammed their iron hooves into the ice.

On the river the chestnut dray-horses, covered with hoarfrost and steam, breathed noisily, the rosy lightning flashes of the north darted into the pines, and the crowds, the faceless crowds, crawled over the frozen slopes.

A fiery wind blew on them from the Volga. Many of the women tumbled into the snowdrifts, but they kept climbing higher, heading for the monastery like invading columns.

Women's laughter thundered over the mountain, samovar pots and tubs traveled up the slope, impish sleighs groaned as they veered.

Ancient crones were hauling great loads up the high mountain, the mountain of St. Hypatius, and dragged goats on leashes and infants sleeping in little sledges.

"Damn you all!" I shouted when I saw them, and stepped back from the outrageous invasion. "You're all going to Sister Martha to ask her son, Mikhail Romanov, to ascend the throne!"

"Get out of our way!" one of the women yelled, stepping forward. "Stop wasting our time! We're not here to have babies with you!" And, harnessing herself again to her sleigh, she hauled it into the courtyard of the monastery, practically knocking the confused monk off his feet. She dragged her washtubs, her geese, and her hornless gramophone into the cradle of the Muscovite Czars, declaring that her name was

Savicheva, and demanding that she be allotted apartment number nineteen in the archbishop's chambers.

To my amazement, Savicheva *was* allotted an apartment, as were all the others behind her. I was told that the Union of Textile Workers had constructed forty apartments in the burned-out building for the workers of the Kostroma United Flax Mills, and that today was the day they were moving into the monastery.

Father Hillarion stood at the gates counting goats and women. Then he invited me in to drink tea, and silently laid out the table with cups he had stolen in the courtyard when the treasures of the Romanov boyars were being packed off to the museum.

We drank tea from these cups till sweat dripped from our faces, while the women's bare feet trampled on windowsills in front of us: the women were washing the windows of their new apartments.

Then, as if by prearrangement, smoke billowed from all the chimneys, and a cock scampered onto the tomb of Abbot Sioni and began squawking. The accordion of one of the women, having labored its way through a prelude, sang a tender song, and some little old woman in a homespun overcoat poked her head into Father Hillarion's cell and asked him to lend her a pinch of salt for her cabbage soup.

Evening had already fallen when the little old woman appeared. Purple clouds surged above the Volga, the thermometer on the outside wall registered forty degrees below zero, gigantic fires died out, flashing over the river. A determined young man obstinately climbed a frozen ladder to the iron bar above the gates in order to hang up a flimsy lamp and a sign with a legion of letters on it, "USSR—RSFSR," along with the emblem of the Textile Union, the hammer and sickle, and the figure of a woman standing at a loom from which rays surged in all directions.

A STORY

This story is an earlier version of "The Bathroom Window."

I have an old acquaintance—Fanya Osipovna Kebchik. She had been a prostitute in her youth, but she assures me that "nothing in the world" would have induced her to take less than five rubles.

Now she has a "nice, respectable apartment." There are two girls there, Marusya and Tamara. Marusya is really nice, gentle, and with a delicate build. There are many requests for her. One of the windows in her room has a view of the street, the other—just a small one up by the ceiling—has a view of the bathroom. When I noticed this, I suggested the following deal to Fanya Osipovna Kebchik: for five rubles she would put a ladder by the little window in the bathroom, I would climb up the ladder, and for an hour or two, or for however long I wanted, I would peek into Marusya's room.

At first Fanya Osipovna was astonished at my suggestion, but then she said, "Oy, you rogue, you!" And . . . agreed.

She got her five rubles quite often. Needless to say, I only made use of the little window when Marusya had clients.

For me there is no greater bliss than passionlessly following the play of passion on people's faces.

What astonishing moments I spent! I remember an old, thickset man crying quietly on the edge of the bed, a drunken English soldier, coldly beating the girl with icy malice. There were disgusting types too. I particularly remember a drooling high school boy, his body covered with pimples, shivering with impatience and muttering bookishly, "Oh, how I want you! Give yourself to me!"

Recently something very unpleasant happened. I was standing on the ladder. Marusya had a client. Luckily they hadn't turned off the light. (They often do, which is bothersome.) Her guest was a fine fellow, cheerful, unassuming, with one of those large, harmless mustaches. He undressed in a funny way, very prim and proper: he took off his collar, looked in the mirror, noticed a pimple under his mustache, went closer to the mirror, studied the pimple, pressed it out, and then quite cheerfully made a few faces. He took off his boots and again rushed to the mirror—might there be a scratch? They lay down, kissed, tickled one another. All very ordinary. I was about to climb down, when I slipped. The ladder fell with a crash, and there I was, dangling in the air. The apartment was suddenly full of commotion. A hysterical screech came from Marusya's room. Everyone came running, Fanya Osipovna, Tamara, some official in a Ministry of Education uniform. They helped me down. My situation was pitiful. Marusya ran in half dressed, her lanky client in tow, his clothes thrown on hastily. Marusya guessed what had happened, and froze. She looked at me long and hard, and said quietly, and with surprise, "What a bastard, oh, what a bastard!"

She fell silent, stared at all of us, went over to the lanky man, and for some reason kissed his hand and started to cry softly.

"My dear, oh, God, my dear!" she said, between kisses and sobs, caressing him.

The lanky man stood there like a total idiot. My soul turned inside out. I went over to Madam Kebchik.

Within half an hour, Marusya knew the secret. All was forgiven and forgotten. But I was still wondering why Marusya had kissed the lanky fellow.

"Madam Kebchik," I said. "I'll give you ten rubles if you let me look again."

Madam Kebchik assured me that I was out of my mind, but ten rubles is ten rubles. So I stood again on top of the ladder, looked into the room, and saw Marusya, her thin white arms wrapped around her client, kissing him with long, slow kisses.

Tears were flowing from her eyes.

"My darling!" she whispered. "Oh, God, my sweet darling!" And she gave herself to him with all the passion of a woman in love.

She looked at him as if he, the lanky fellow, were the only man in the world.

And the lanky fellow wallowed in businesslike bliss.

The Odessa Stories

In 1921, Isaac Babel's first two Odessa stories, "The King" and "Justice in Parenthesis," were published in the Odessa magazines MORYAK and NA POMOSHCH, beginning a series of stories that was to continue into the 1930s about the city and its strange and colorful Jewish gangster class that were to become some of Babel's most acclaimed stories. This section contains all these stories.

Babel was particularly fascinated by the new Jewish classes emerging from the social upheavals of the early twentieth century. The RED CAVALRY stories, published during the same period as the Odessa stories, reveal Babel's fascination with the new Jewish fighters who have managed to break out of the strictures of the Jewish shtetl culture and transform themselves into wild, horse-riding Cossack commanders. The Jewish characters of the Odessa stories are just as unconventional and surprising. The carters, peddlers, cantors, and not-so-pious synagogue SHAMASES who "jumped onto the tables and sang out above the din of the seething flourishes" at a gangster wedding, are not the conventional Jewish figures one might expect to find in even the wildest of Jewish shtetls. There is Benya the King with his "refined gangster

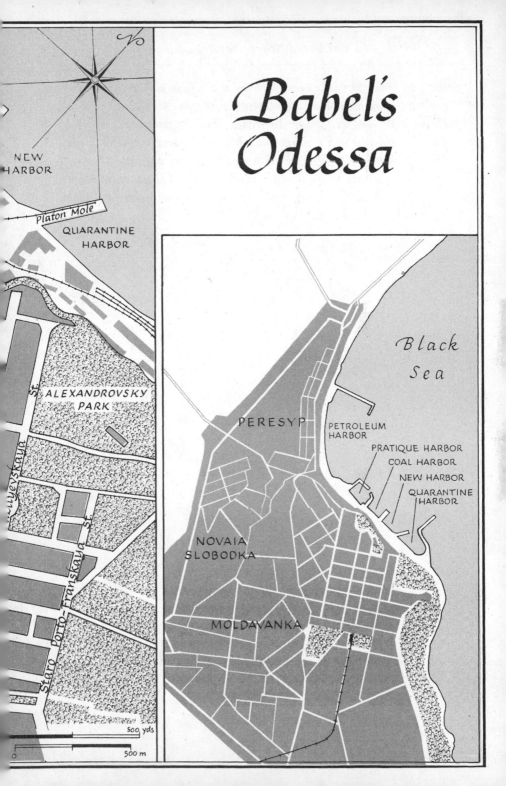

Babel's Odessa

NEW HARBOR

Platon Mole

QUARANTINE HARBOR

ALEXANDROVSKY PARK

...levskaya St.

Staro Porto-Franskaya St.

Black Sea

PERESYP

PETROLEUM HARBOR

PRATIQUE HARBOR

COAL HARBOR

NEW HARBOR

QUARANTINE HARBOR

NOVAIA SLOBODKA

MOLDAVANKA

500 yds

500 m

chic"; his father, Mendel, a carter "known as a ruffian even in carting circles"; the murderous Madam Shneiweis (Snow-white in Yiddish), who is known as Lyubka the Cossack; Yid-and-a-Half, the millionaire; little old Pesya-Mindl, cook and procuress; and Manka, the aged matriarch of the Jewish bandits from the shantytowns beyond the factory districts.

The stories are set in the Moldavanka, a real Odessa neighborhood "crowded with suckling babies, drying rags, and conjugal nights filled with big-city chic and soldierly tirelessness."

THE KING

*T*he wedding ceremony ended, the rabbi sank into a chair, then he left the room and saw tables lined up the whole length of the courtyard. There were so many of them that the end stuck out of the gates onto Gospitalnaya Street. The tables, draped in velvet, coiled through the yard like a snake on whose belly patches of every color had been daubed, and these orange and red velvet patches sang in deep voices.

The rooms had been turned into kitchens. A rich flame, a drunk, plump flame, forced its way through the smoke-blackened doors. Little old women's faces, wobbly women's chins, beslobbered breasts, baked in the flame's smoky rays. Sweat, red as blood, pink as the foam of a rabid dog, dripped from these blobs of rampant, sweet-odored human flesh. Three cooks, not counting the scullery maids, prepared the wedding feast, and over them eighty-year-old Reizl reigned, traditional as a Torah scroll, tiny and hunchbacked.

Before the feast began, a young man unknown to the guests wormed his way into the courtyard. He asked for Benya Krik. He took Benya Krik aside.

"Listen, King!" the young man said. "I have a couple of words I need to tell you. Aunt Hannah from Kostetskaya Street, she sent me."

"So?" Benya Krik, nicknamed "the King," answered. "So what's these couple of words?"

"Aunt Hannah, she sent me to tell you that a new chief of police took over at the police station yesterday."

"I've known that since the day before yesterday," Benya Krik answered. "Well?"

"The chief of police called the whole station together and gave a speech . . ."

"A new broom is always eager to sweep," Benya Krik answered. "He wants a raid. So?"

"But when does he want to raid, King, do you know that?"

"Tomorrow."

"King, it's going to be today!"

"Who told you that, boy?"

"Aunt Hannah, she said so. You know Aunt Hannah?"

"I know Aunt Hannah. So?"

"The chief called the whole station together and gave them a speech: 'We must finish off Benya Krik,' he said, 'because when you have His Majesty the Czar, you can't have a King too. Today, when Krik gives away his sister in marriage, and they will all be there, is when we raid!'"

"So?"

"Then the stool pigeons began to get worried. They said, 'If we raid them today, during his feast, Benya will get angry and a lot of blood will flow.' But the chief said, 'Our self-respect is more important to me!'"

"Good, you can go," the King said.

"So what do I tell Aunt Hannah about the raid?"

"Tell her Benya he knows from the raid."

And the young man left. Three or four of Benya's friends followed him. They said they would be back in about half an hour. And they were back in half an hour. That was that.

At the table, the guests did not sit in order of seniority. Foolish old age is just as pitiful as cowardly youth. Nor in order of wealth. The lining of a heavy money bag is sewn with tears.

The bride and groom sat at the table's place of honor. It was their day. Beside them sat Sender Eichbaum, the King's father-in-law. That was his due. You should know the story of Sender Eichbaum, because it's a story definitely worth knowing.

How did Benya Krik, gangster and King of gangsters, make himself Eichbaum's son-in-law? How did he make himself the son-in-law of a man who owned one milch cow short of sixty? It all had to do with a robbery. A year or so earlier Benya had written a letter to Eichbaum.

"Monsieur Eichbaum," he wrote. "I would be grateful if you could place twenty thousand rubles by the gate of number 17, Sofiyefskaya Street, tomorrow morning. If you do not, then something awaits you, the like of which has never before been heard, and you will be the talk of all Odessa. Sincerely yours, Benya the King."

Three letters, each clearer than the one before, remained unanswered. Then Benya took action. They came by night, ten men carrying long sticks. The sticks were wound with tarred oakum. Nine burning stars flared up in Eichbaum's cattle yard. Benya smashed the barn's locks and started leading the cows out, one by one. They were met by a man with a knife. He felled the cows with one slash and plunged his knife into their hearts. On the ground drenched with blood the torches blossomed like fiery roses, and shots rang out. The dairy maids came running to the cowshed, and Benya chased them away with shots. And right after him other gangsters began shooting into the air because if you don't shoot into the air you might kill someone. And then, as the sixth cow fell with a death bellow at the King's feet, it was then that Eichbaum came running out into the courtyard in his underpants.

"Benya! Where will this end?" he cried.

"If I don't have the money, you don't have the cows, Monsieur Eichbaum. Two and two make four."

"Benya, come into my house!"

And inside the house they came to an agreement. They divided the slaughtered cows between them, Eichbaum was promised immunity and given a certificate with a stamp to that effect. But the miracle came later.

At the time of the attack, that terrible night when the slashed cows bellowed and calves skidded in their mothers' blood, when torches danced like black maidens, and the milkmaids scattered and screeched before the barrels of the amicable Brownings—that terrible night, old Eichbaum's daughter, Zilya, had run out into the yard, her blouse torn. And the King's victory turned into his downfall.

Two days later, without warning, Benya gave back all the money he had taken from Eichbaum, and then came in the evening on a social call. He wore an orange suit, and underneath his cuff a diamond bracelet sparkled. He entered the room, greeted Eichbaum, and asked him for the hand of his daughter, Zilya. The old man had a small stroke, but recovered—there were at least another twenty years of life in him.

"Listen, Eichbaum," the King told him. "When you die, I'll have you buried in the First Jewish Cemetery, right by the gates. And, Eichbaum, I will have a monument of pink marble put up for you. I will make you the Elder of the Brodsky Synagogue. I will give up my career, Eichbaum, and I will go into business with you as a partner. We will have two hundred cows, Eichbaum. I will kill all the dairymen except you. No thief shall walk the street you live in. I shall build you a dacha at the Sixteenth Stop* . . . and don't forget, Eichbaum, you yourself were no rabbi in your youth. Who was it who forged that will? I think I'd better lower my voice, don't you? And your son-in-law will be the King, not some snotface! The King, Eichbaum!"

And he got his way, that Benya Krik, because he was passionate, and passion holds sway over the universe. The newlyweds stayed for three months in fertile Bessarabia, among grapes, abundant food, and the sweat of love. Then Benya returned to Odessa to marry off Dvoira, his forty-year-old sister, who was suffering from goiter. And now, having told the story of Sender Eichbaum, we can return to the marriage of Dvoira Krik, the King's sister.

For the dinner at this wedding, they served turkeys, roasted chicken, geese, gefilte fish, and fish soup in which lakes of lemon shimmered like mother-of-pearl. Above the dead goose heads, flowers swayed like luxuriant plumes. But do the foamy waves of the Odessan Sea throw roasted chickens onto the shore?

On this blue night, this starry night, the best of our contraband, everything for which our region is celebrated far and wide, plied its seductive, destructive craft. Wine from afar heated stomachs, sweetly numbed legs, dulled brains, and summoned belches as resonant as the call of battle horns. The black cook from the *Plutarch*, which had pulled in three days before from Port Said, had smuggled in big-bellied bottles of Jamaican rum, oily Madeira, cigars from the plantations of Pierpont Morgan, and oranges from the groves of Jerusalem. This is

* Bolshoi Fontan, an elegant resort spa outside Odessa.

what the foamy waves of the Odessan Sea throw onto the shore, and this is what Odessan beggars sometimes get at Jewish weddings. They got Jamaican rum at Dvoira Krik's wedding, and that's why the Jewish beggars got as drunk as unkosher pigs and began loudly banging their crutches. Eichbaum unbuttoned his vest, mustered the raging crowd with a squinting eye, and hiccuped affectionately. The orchestra played a flourish. It was like a regimental parade. A flourish, nothing more than a flourish. The gangsters, sitting in closed ranks, were at first uneasy in the presence of outsiders, but soon they let themselves go. Lyova Katsap smashed a bottle of vodka over his sweetheart's head, Monya Artillerist fired shots into the air. But the peak of their ecstasy came when, in accordance with ancient custom, the guests began bestowing gifts on the newlyweds. The synagogue *shamases* jumped onto the tables and sang out, above the din of the seething flourishes, the quantity of rubles and silver spoons that were being presented. And here the friends of the King proved what blue blood was worth, and that Moldavanka chivalry was still in full bloom. With casual flicks of the hand they threw gold coins, rings, and coral necklaces onto the golden trays.

The Moldavanka aristocrats were jammed into crimson vests, their shoulders encased in chestnut-colored jackets, and their fleshy legs bulged in sky-blue leather boots. Drawing themselves up to their full height and sticking out their bellies, the bandits clapped to the rhythm of the music and, shouting "Oy, a sweet kiss for the bride!," threw flowers at her, and she, forty-year-old Dvoira, Benya Krik's sister, the sister of the King, deformed by illness, with her swollen goiter and eyes bulging out of their sockets, sat on a mountain of pillows next to a frail young man who was mute with melancholy who had been bought with Eichbaum's money.

The gift-giving ceremony was coming to an end, the *shamases* were growing hoarse, and the bass fiddle was clashing with the violin. A sudden faint odor of burning spread over the courtyard.

"Benya," Papa Krik, the old carter, known as a ruffian even in carting circles, shouted. "Benya! You know what? I think the embers have blazed up again!"

"Papa!" the King said to his drunken father. "Please eat and drink and don't let these foolish things be worrying you!"

And Papa Krik followed his son's advice. He ate and drank. But the cloud of smoke became ever more poisonous. Here and there patches of sky were turning pink, and suddenly a tongue of fire, narrow as a sword, shot high into the air. The guests got up and started sniffing, and their women yelped. The gangsters looked at one another. And only Benya, who seemed not to notice anything, was inconsolable.

"My feast! They're ruining it!" he shouted in despair. "My friends, please, eat, drink!"

But at that moment the same young man who had come at the beginning of the feast appeared again in the courtyard.

"King!" he said. "I have a couple of words I need to tell you!"

"Well, speak!" the King answered. "You always got a couple words up your sleeve!"

"King!" the young man said with a snigger. "It's so funny—the police station's burning like a candle!"

The storekeepers were struck dumb. The gangsters grinned. Sixty-year-old Manka, matriarch of the Slobodka* bandits, put two fingers in her mouth and whistled so shrilly that those sitting next to her jumped up.

"Manka! You're not at work now!" Benya told her. "Cool down!"

The young man who had brought this startling news was still shaking with laughter.

"About forty of them left the station to go on the raid," he said, his jaws quivering. "They hadn't gone fifteen yards when everything went up in flames! Run and see for yourselves!"

But Benya forbade his guests to go look at the fire. He himself went with two friends. The police station was in flames. With their wobbling backsides, the policemen were running up and down the smoke-filled staircases, throwing boxes out of the windows. The prisoners made a run for it. The firemen were bristling with zeal, but it turned out that there wasn't any water in the nearby hydrant. The chief of police, the new broom so eager to sweep, stood on the opposite sidewalk, chewing on his mustache which hung into his mouth. The new broom stood completely still. Benya walked past and gave him a military salute.

---

* Slobodka was a rough shantytown neighborhood on the outskirts of Odessa.

"A very good day to you, Your Excellency!" he said sympathetically. "What bad luck! A nightmare!" He stared at the burning building, shook his head, and smacked his lips: "Ai-ai-ai!"

. . .

When Benya came back home, the lantern lights in the courtyard were already going out and dawn was breaking across the sky. The guests had dispersed, and the musicians were asleep, their heads leaning against the necks of their bass fiddles. Only Dvoira hadn't gone to sleep yet. With both hands she was edging her timid husband toward the door of their nuptial chamber, looking at him lustfully like a cat which, holding a mouse in its jaws, gently probes it with its teeth.

JUSTICE IN
PARENTHESES

My first run-in was with Benya Krik, my second with Lyubka Shneiweis. Do you understand the meaning of these words? Can you drink in their full essence? On this road to hell, Seryozhka Utochkin* was missing. I did not run into him this time around, which is why I am still here to tell the tale. Like a bronze colossus, he will tower above the town—red-haired, gray-eyed Utochkin. Everyone will have to scamper through his bronze legs.

But I must not send my tale down side streets, even if on these side streets chestnuts are ripening and acacias are in bloom. I'll start with Benya, and then go on to Lyubka Shneiweis. And that will be that. Then I can say I put the period where it belongs.

I became a broker. Becoming an Odessan broker, I sprouted leaves and shoots. Weighed down with leaves and shoots, I felt unhappy. What was the reason? The reason was competition. Otherwise I would not have even wiped my nose on Justice. I never learned a trade. All there is in front of me is air, glittering like the sea beneath the sun, beautiful, empty air. The shoots need to be fed. I have seven of them, and my wife is the eighth shoot. I did not wipe my nose on Justice. No, Justice wiped its nose on me. What was the reason? The reason was competition.

The cooperative store had been given the name "Justice." Nothing

---

* Sergei Isayevich Utochkin, 1874–1916, aviation pioneer, was the first man in Odessa to own a car and had a reputation for devil-may-care driving.

bad can be said about that store. Sinful is he who speaks ill of it. It was run by six partners, *"primo di primo,"* specialists, if anything, in their line. Their store was full of merchandise, and the policeman they had standing outside was Motya from Golovkovskaya. What more do you want? Can you want more? This deal was suggested to me by the Justice bookkeeper. I give you my word of honor, it was a proper deal, an honest deal! With a clothes brush I brushed my body and sent it over to Benya. The King acted as if he did not notice my body. So I cleared my throat and said: "Ready when you are, Benya."

The King was having light refreshments. A carafe of vodka, a fat cigar, a big-bellied wife in her seventh or eighth month, I wouldn't want to lie to you. The terrace was surrounded by nature and wild vines.

"Ready when you are, Benya," I said.

"When?" he asked me.

"Well, now that you ask me," I said to the King, "I have to tell you my opinion. If you ask *me,* the best time of all would be Sabbath night going on Sunday. By the way, none other than Motya from Golovkovskaya will be on guard. We *could* do this on a weekday, but why turn a nice and easy job into a job that isn't nice and easy?"

That was my opinion. And the King's wife also agreed.

"Baby," Benya said to her. "I want you to go take a rest on the sofa now."

Then with slow fingers he tore the gold band off his cigar and turned to Froim Stern.

"Tell me, Grach, are we busy on the Sabbath, or are we not busy on the Sabbath?"

But Froim Stern is quick-witted. He is a red-haired man with only one eye in his head. Froim cannot afford to give an open answer.

"On the Sabbath," he said, "you were thinking of dropping by the Mutual Credit Society."

Grach acted as if he had nothing more to say, and calmly turned his one eye to the farthest corner of the terrace.

"Excellent," Benya Krik said to him. "Remind me about Zudechkis on the Sabbath, make yourself a note, Grach!" Then the King turned to me: "Go back to your family, Zudechkis. Sabbath evening, I might very well be dropping in at the Justice. Take my words with you, Zudechkis, and get going."

The King speaks little and speaks politely. This frightens people so much that they never question him. I left his courtyard and set off down Gospitalnaya Street, turned on Stepovaya, and then stopped to ponder Benya's words. I probed them by touch and by weight, bit down on them with my front teeth, and realized that they had not been the words that I needed.

"I might very well," the King had said, pulling the gold band off his cigar with slow fingers. The King speaks little and speaks politely. Who can fathom the meaning of the King's few words? I might very well be dropping by, or I might very well not be dropping by? Between yes and no, a five-thousand-ruble commission hangs in the air. Not to mention the two cows that I keep for my needs—I have nine mouths at home snatching for food! Who gave me the right to run risks? After the Justice bookkeeper came to see me, didn't he drop by at Bunzelmann's? And then didn't Bunzelmann run straight to Kolya Shtift? And Kolya is a fellow who is hotheaded beyond belief. The words of the King lay like a stone block across the road where hunger roamed, multiplied by nine. To make a long story short, I whispered a little warning in Bunzelmann's ear. He was going in to see Kolya just as I was coming out from seeing Kolya. It was hot, and he was sweating. "Relax, Bunzelmann," I said to him. "You're rushing for nothing, and you're sweating for nothing! This is my deal, *und damit Punktum*, like the Germans say!"

And then the fifth day came. And then the sixth day came. The Sabbath came strolling through the streets of the Moldavanka. Motya was already standing guard, and I was already asleep in my bed, and Kolya was busy working at the Justice. He had loaded half a cart, and was aiming to load another half. Suddenly there was a rumpus in the alley, the clattering of iron-reinforced wheels, and Motya from Golovkovskaya grabbed hold of the telegraph pole and yelled, "Shall I push it over?"

"Not yet!" Kolya yelled back. (The thing is, the telegraph pole could be toppled when push came to shove.)

A cart rolled slowly into the alley and pulled up in front of the store. Kolya thought the police were on their way, and his heart tore itself to shreds, because he really hated the idea of the deal going sour.

"Motya!" he yelled. "When I fire my gun, the pole topples!"

"Understood!"

Kolya Shtift went back into the store, and all his helpers followed him. They lined up against the wall and drew their revolvers. Ten eyes and five revolvers were trained on the door, and outside there was the booby-trapped telegraph pole. The youths were bristling with impatience.

"Scram, you cops, you!" one of the eager youths hissed. "Scram or we'll finish you off!"

"Shut up!" Benya Krik growled, jumping down from the loft. "Where d'you see cops, you lunkhead? It's me, the King!"

A bit more and there would have been trouble. Benya knocked Shtift down and snatched the revolver from his hands. Men started descending from the loft like rain. You couldn't tell who was who in the darkness.

"Ha! Interesting!" Kolya shouted. "So now Benya is out to kill me!"

It was the first time in his life that the King had been mistaken for a policeman. This was worth a good laugh. The gangsters laughed out loud. They turned on their flashlights, splitting their sides with laughter, rolling on the floor, gasping for air.

Only the King did not laugh.

"They will be saying in Odessa," he began in a serious tone, "in Odessa they will be saying the King was tempted by his friend's earnings."

"They will say it only once," Shtift said. "No one will dare say it twice."

"Kolya," the King continued in a solemn, quiet voice. "Do you believe me, Kolya?"

And here the gangsters stopped laughing. Each of them was holding a burning lantern, but laughter wormed its way out of the Justice store.

"What do you want me to believe you about, King?"

"Do you believe me, Kolya, that I had nothing to do with all of this?"

And the King sat down sadly on a chair, covered his eyes with a dusty sleeve, and began to cry. This was how proud this man was, he should burn in hell! And all the gangsters, each and every one of them, saw their King crying because his pride was hurt.

Then the two men stood opposite each other. Benya stood, and Shtift stood. They apologized to each other, they kissed each other on the lips, and they shook hands with such force that it looked as if they were trying to tear each other's arms off. Dawn was already beginning to blink its bleary eye, Motya had already left for the police station to sign out, two full carts had hauled off what had once been known as the Justice Cooperative Store, while the King and Kolya were still distraught, still bowing to each other, still throwing their arms around each other's necks, kissing each other tenderly like drunks.

Who was Fate hunting down that morning? Fate was hunting down me, Zudechkis, and Fate cornered me.

"Kolya!" the King finally said. "Who arranged for you to come here to the Justice?"

"Zudechkis. What about you, Benya? Who had you come here?"

"Zudechkis!"

"Benya!" Kolya exclaimed. "Is he to be left alive?"

"Most definitely not," Benya said, and he turned to one-eyed Stern, who was chuckling in a corner because the two of us don't see eye to eye. "Froim! You go order a brocaded coffin, and I'll go over to Zudechkis. And you, Kolya, once you've started something you have to finish it, which is why my wife and I would like to cordially invite you to visit us in our home in the morning, to partake of breakfast with us and our family."

At five o'clock in the morning—or no, it must have been four, and then again, maybe it wasn't even four yet—the King entered my bedroom, grabbed me, if you will pardon the expression, by my back, dragged me out of bed, laid me down on the floor, and placed his foot on my nose. Hearing various sounds and so on, my wife jumped out of bed and asked Benya, "Monsieur Krik, why have you taken umbrage at my Zudechkis?"

"What do you mean, 'why'?" Benya said, without removing his foot from the bridge of my nose, and tears began to trickle from his eyes. "He has cast a shadow on my name, he has disgraced me before my companions, you can bid him farewell, Madam Zudechkis, because my honor is more important to me than my happiness, which is why he cannot live!"

Continuing to cry, he began stomping on me. My wife, seeing that

I was quite distressed, started yelling. This occurred at four-thirty, but she didn't finish with Benya until around eight. She let him have it— *oy!*—how she let him have it! It was a joy to behold!

"Why are you angry at my Zudechkis?" she shouted, standing on the bed, while I, writhing on the floor, looked up at her with admiration. "Why beat up my Zudechkis? Why? Because he wanted to feed nine little hungry fledglings? You—ha!—you're so very grand! The King! The son-in-law of a rich man, rich yourself, and your father rich too! You are a man with the world at your feet! What is one bungled deal for Benchik, when next week will bring seven successful ones? How dare you beat my Zudechkis! How dare you!"

She saved my life.

The children woke up and began yelling in unison with my wife. Benya still ruined as much of my health as he knew he needed to ruin. He left two hundred rubles for my doctor's bill, and walked out. I was taken to the Jewish hospital. On Sunday I was dying, on Monday I felt better, on Tuesday I took a turn for the worse.

This is my first story. Who was to blame, and what was the reason? Was Benya really to blame? Let us not try to pull the wool over each other's eyes. There is no other like Benya the King! He stamps out lies in his quest for justice—justice in parentheses as well as justice without parentheses. But what are you to do when everyone else is as unruffled as a pickled fish? The others don't care for justice, and don't look for it, which is even worse!

I recovered—escaping from Benya's hands only to fall into Lyubka's! I have told you about Benya, and I will tell you about Lyubka Shneiweis. But let us stop here. Then I can say I put the period where it belongs.

HOW THINGS WERE
DONE IN ODESSA

I was the one who began.

"Reb Arye-Leib," I said to the old man. "Let's talk about Benya Krik. Let's talk about his lightning-quick beginning and his terrible end. Three shadows block the path of my thoughts. There is Froim Grach. The steel of his actions—doesn't it bear comparison to the power of the King? There is Kolka Pakovsky. The rage of that man had everything it takes to rule. And could not Chaim Drong tell when a star was on the rise? So why was Benya Krik the only one to climb to the top of the ladder while everyone else was clinging to the shaky rungs below?"

Reb Arye-Leib remained silent as he sat on the cemetery wall. Before us stretched the green calm of the graves. A man thirsting for an answer must stock up with patience. A man in possession of facts can afford to carry himself with aplomb. That is why Arye-Leib remained silent as he sat on the cemetery wall. Finally he began his tale:

"Why him? Why not the others, you want to know? Well then, forget for a while that you have glasses on your nose and autumn in your heart. Forget that you pick fights from behind your desk and stutter when you are out in the world! Imagine for a moment that you pick fights in town squares and stutter only among papers. You are a tiger, you are a lion, you are a cat. You can spend the night with a Russian woman, and the Russian woman will be satisfied by you. You are twenty-five years old. If the sky and the earth had rings attached to them, you would grab these rings and pull the sky down to the earth. And your papa is the carter Mendel Krik. What does a papa like him think about? All he thinks about is downing a nice shot of vodka, slugging someone in their ugly mug, and about his horses—nothing else. You want to live, but he makes you die twenty times a day. What would you have done if you were in Benya Krik's shoes? You wouldn't have done a thing! But he did. Because he is the King, while you only thumb your nose at people when their back is turned!

"He, Benchik, went to Froim Grach, who even back then peered at the world with only one eye and was just what he is now. And Benya told Froim, 'Take me on. I want to come on board your ship. The ship I end up on will do well by me.'

"Grach asked him, 'Who're you, where d'you come from, what's your bread and butter?'

"'Try me, Froim,' Benya answered, 'and let's stop wasting time spreading kasha on the table.'

"'Fine, we won't waste time spreading kasha on the table,' Grach said. 'I'll try you.'

"And the gangsters called a council together to decide about Benya Krik. I wasn't at that council, but word has it that they did call together a council. The elder back then was the late Lyovka Bik.

"'Anyone know what's going on under Benchik's hat?' the late Bik asked.

"And one-eyed Grach gave his opinion.

"'Benya talks little, but he talks with zest. He talks little, but you want that he'll say more.'

"'If that's so, we'll try him out on Tartakovsky,' the late Bik pronounced.

"'We'll try him out on Tartakovsky,' the council decided, and those who still housed a trace of conscience turned red when they heard this decision. Why did they turn red? If you listen, you'll find out.

"Tartakovsky was known as 'Yid-and-a-Half' or 'Nine-Raids.' They called him 'Yid-and-a-Half' because there wasn't a single Jew who had as much chutzpah or money as Tartakovsky had. He was taller than the tallest Odessa policeman, and heavier than the fattest Jewess. And they called Tartakovsky 'Nine-Raids' because the firm of Lyovka Bik and Company had launched not eight raids and not ten, but exactly nine raids against his business. To Benya, who was not yet King, fell the honor of carrying out the tenth raid on Yid-and-a-Half. When Froim informed Benya of this, Benya said yes, and left, slamming the door behind him. Why did he slam the door? If you listen, you'll find out.

"Tartakovsky has the soul of a murderer, but he's one of us. He sprang forth from us. He is our blood. He is our flesh, as if one mama had given birth to us. Half of Odessa works in his stores. Not to mention, his own Moldavankans have given him quite a bit of grief. They abducted him twice and held him for ransom, and once, during a pogrom, they buried him with chanters. The Slobodka* thugs were beating up Jews on Bolshaya Arnautskaya. Tartakovsky ran away from them and came across the funeral march with chanters on Sofiyskaya Street.

"'Who are they burying with chanters?' he asked.

"The passersby told him that Tartakovsky was being buried. The procession marched to the Slobodka Cemetery. Then our boys yanked a machine gun out of the coffin and started shooting at the Slobodka thugs. But Yid-and-a-Half had not foreseen this. Yid-and-a-Half got the fright of his life. What boss in his place would not have been frightened?

"A tenth raid on a man who had already been buried once was a crass deed. Benya, who back then wasn't yet the King, knew this better than anyone else. But he said yes to Grach and on that very same day wrote Tartakovsky a letter, typical of those letters:

Most esteemed Rubin Osipovich,

I would be grateful if by the Sabbath you could place by the rainwater barrel a . . . , and so on. Should you choose to refuse, which you have opted to do lately, a great disappointment in your family life awaits you.

Respectfully yours,
Ben Zion Krik

"Tartakovsky, not one to dither, was quick to answer:

* A poor neighborhood on the outskirts of Odessa.

Benya,

If you were an idiot, I would write you as to an idiot. But from what I know of you, you aren't one, and may the Lord prevent me from changing my mind. You, as is plain to see, are acting like a boy. Is it possible that you are not aware that this year the crop in Argentina has been so good that we can stand on our heads but we still can't unload our wheat? And I swear to you on a stack of Bibles that I'm sick and tired of having to eat such a bitter crust of bread and witness such trouble after having worked all my life like the lowliest carter. And what do I have to show for my life sentence of hard labor? Ulcers, sores, worries, and no sleep! Drop your foolish thoughts, Benya.

Your friend, a far better one than you realize,
Rubin Tartakovsky

"Yid-and-a-Half had done his part. He had written a letter. But the mail didn't deliver it to the right address. Getting no answer, Benya became angry. The following day he turned up at Tartakovsky's office with four friends. Four masked youths with revolvers burst into the room.

"'Hands up!' they shouted, waving their pistols.

"'Not so loud, Solomon!' Benya told one of the youths, who was yelling louder than the rest. 'Don't get so jumpy on the job!' and he turned to the shop assistant, who was white as death and yellow as clay, and asked him:

"'Is Yid-and-a-Half in the factory?'

"'He's not in the factory,' said the shop assistant, whose family name was Muginshtein, his first name Josif, and who was the unmarried son of Aunt Pesya, the chicken seller on Seredinskaya Square.

"'So who's in charge when the boss is out?' they asked poor Muginshtein.

"'I'm in charge when the boss is out,' the shop assistant said, green as green grass.

"'In that case, with God's help, please open the safe!' Benya ordered, and a three-act opera began.

"Nervous Solomon stuffed money, papers, watches, and jewelry into a suitcase—the late Josif Muginshtein stood in front of him with his hands in the air, while Benya told stories from the life of the Jewish people.

"'Well, ha! If he likes playing Rothschild,' Benya said about Tartakovsky, 'then let him roast in hell! I ask you, Muginshtein, as one asks a friend: he gets my business letter—so how come he can't take a five-kopeck tram to come visit me at home, drink a shot of vodka with my family, and eat what God has seen fit to send us? What stopped him from baring his soul to me? Couldn't he have said—Benya, you know, such and such, but here's my balance sheet, just give me a couple of days to catch my breath, to get things rolling—don't you think I'd have understood? Pigs at a trough might not see eye to eye, but there is no reason why two grown men can't! Do you see what I'm saying, Muginshtein?'

"'I see what you're saying,' Muginshtein answered, lying, because he was at a loss as to why Yid-and-a-Half, a respected, wealthy man, one of the foremost men in town, should want to take a tram so he could have a bite to eat with the family of Mendel Krik, a carter.

"But all the time misfortune was loitering beneath the windows, like a beggar at dawn. Misfortune burst loudly into the office. And though this time it came in the guise of the Jew Savka Butsis, it was as drunk as a water carrier.

"'Ooh, ooh, ah!' Savka the Jew shouted. 'I'm sorry I'm so late, Benchik!' And he stamped his feet and waved his hands. Then he fired, and the bullet hit Muginshtein in the stomach.

"Are words necessary here? There was a man, and now there's none. An innocent bachelor, living his life like a little bird on a branch, and now he's dead from sheer idiocy. In comes a Jew looking like a sailor and doesn't shoot at a bottle in a fairground booth to win a prize—he shoots at a living man! Are words necessary here?

"'Everyone out!' Benya shouted, and as he ran out last, managed to tell Butsis, 'On my mother's grave, Savka, you'll be lying next to him!'

"So tell me, a young gentleman like you who cuts coupons on other people's bonds, how would you have acted in Benya Krik's position? You wouldn't know what to do? Well, he did! That's why he was King, while you and I are sitting here on the wall of the Second Jewish Cemetery, holding up our hands to keep the sun out of our eyes.

"Aunt Pesya's unfortunate son didn't die right away. An hour after they got him to the hospital, Benya turned up. He had the senior doctor called in and the nurse, and, without taking his hands out of the pockets of his cream-colored pants, told them, 'I have a whole lot of interest that your patient, Josif Muginshtein, recovers. Just in case, let me introduce myself—Ben Zion Krik. Give him camphor, air cushions, a private room, from the depths of your heart! If you don't, then every doctor here, even if they're doctors of philosophy, will be doled out six feet of earth!'

"And yet, Muginshtein died that same night. It was only then that Yid-and-a-Half raised hell in all Odessa. 'Where do the police begin and Benya end?' he wailed.

"'The police end where Benya begins,' levelheaded people answered, but Tartakovsky wouldn't calm down, and to his amazement saw a red automobile with a music box for a horn playing the first march from the opera *I Pagliacci* on Seredinskaya Square. In broad daylight the car raced over to the little house in which Aunt Pesya lived. Its wheels thundered, it spat smoke, gleamed brassily, reeked of gasoline, and honked arias on its horn. A man jumped out of the automobile and went into the kitchen where little Aunt Pesya was writhing on the earthen floor. Yid-and-a-Half was sitting on a chair waving his arms. 'You ugly hooligan!' he shouted, when he saw the man. 'You damn bandit, may the earth spit you out! A nice style you've picked for yourself, going around murdering live people!'

"'Monsieur Tartakovsky,' Benya Krik said to him quietly. 'For two days and nights I have been crying for the dear deceased as if he were my own brother. I know that you spit on my young tears. Shame on you, Monsieur Tartakovsky! What fireproof safe have you hidden your shame in? You had the heart to send a paltry hundred rubles to the mother of our dear deceased Josif. My hair, not to mention my brain, stood on end when I got word of this!'

"Here Benya paused. He was wearing a chocolate jacket, cream pants, and raspberry-red half boots.

"'Ten thousand down!' he bellowed. 'Ten thousand down, and a pension till she dies—may she live to be a hundred and twenty! If it's 'no,' then we leave this house together, Monsieur Tartakovsky, and go straight to my car!'

"Then they started arguing. Yid-and-a-Half swore at Benya. Not that I was present at this quarrel, but those who were, remember it well. They finally agreed on five thousand cash in hand, and fifty rubles a month.

"'Aunt Pesya!' Benya then said to the disheveled old woman rolling on the floor. 'If you want my life, you can have it, but everyone makes mistakes, even God! This was a giant mistake, Aunt Pesya! But didn't God Himself make a mistake when he settled the Jews in Russia so they could be tormented as if they were in hell? Wouldn't it have been better to have the Jews living in Switzerland, where they would've been surrounded by first-class lakes, mountain air, and Frenchmen galore? Everyone makes mistakes, even God. Listen to me with your ears, Aunt Pesya! You're getting five thousand in hand and fifty rubles a month till you die—may you live to be a hundred and twenty! Josif's funeral will be first-class. Six horses like lions, two hearses with garlands, chanters from the Brodsky Synagogue, and Minkovsky himself will come to chant the burial service for your departed son!'

"And the funeral took place the next morning. Ask the cemetery beggars about this funeral! Ask the synagogue *shamases*, the kosher poultry sellers, or the old women from the Second Poorhouse! Such a funeral Odessa had never seen, nor will the world ever see the like of it. On that day the policemen wore cotton gloves. In the synagogues, draped with greenery, their doors wide open, the electricity was on. Black plumes swayed on the white horses pulling the hearse. Sixty chanters walked in front of the procession. The chanters were boys, but they sang with women's voices. The elders of the Kosher Poultry Sellers Synagogue led Aunt Pesya by the hand. Behind the elders marched the members of the Society of Jewish Shop Assistants, and behind the Jewish shop assistants marched the barristers, the doctors, and the certified midwives. On one side of Aunt Pesya were the chicken sellers from the Stary Bazaar, and on the other the esteemed dairymaids from the Bugayevka, wrapped in orange shawls. They stamped their feet like gendarmes on parade. From their broad hips came the scent of sea and milk. And behind them plodded Rubin Tartakovsky's workers. There were a hundred of them, or two hundred, or two thousand. They wore black frock coats with silk lapels, and new boots that squeaked like piglets in a sack.

"And now I will speak as God spoke on Mount Sinai from the burning bush! Take my words into your ears. Everything I saw, I saw with my own eyes, sitting right here on the wall of the Second Cemetery, next to lisping Moiseika and Shimshon from the funeral home. I, Arye-Leib, a proud Jew living among the dead, saw it with my own eyes.

"The hearse rolled up to the synagogue in the cemetery. The coffin was placed on the steps. Aunt Pesya was shaking like a little bird. The cantor climbed out of the carriage and began the funeral service. Sixty chanters supported him. And at that very moment the red automobile came flying around the corner. It was honking *I Pagliacci* and came to a stop. The people stood, silent as corpses. The trees, the chanters, the beggars stood silent. Four men got out from under the red roof, and with quiet steps carried to the hearse a wreath of roses of a beauty never before seen. And when the funeral ended, the four men lifted the coffin onto their steel shoulders, and with burning eyes and protruding chests, marched with the members of the Society of Jewish Shop Assistants.

"In front walked Benya Krik, who back then nobody was yet calling the King. He was the first to approach the grave. He climbed onto the mound, and stretched out his arm.

"'What are you doing, young man?' Kofman from the Burial Brotherhood shouted, running up to him.

"'I want to give a speech,' Benya Krik answered.

"And he gave a speech. All who wanted to hear it heard it. I, Arye-Leib, heard it, as did lisping Moiseika, who was sitting next to me on the wall.

"'Ladies and gentlemen,' Benya Krik said. 'Ladies and gentlemen,' he said, and the sun stood above his head, like a guard with a rifle. 'You have come to pay your last respects to an honest toiler, who died for a copper half-kopeck. In my own name, and in the name of all those who are not present, I thank you. Ladies and gentlemen! What did our dear Josif see in his life? One big nothing! What did he do for a living? He counted someone else's money. What did he die for? He died for the whole working class. There are men who are already doomed to die, and there are men who still have not begun to live. And suddenly a bullet, flying toward the doomed heart, tears into Josif, when all he has seen of life is one big nothing. There are men who can drink vodka, and there are men who can't drink vodka but still drink it. The former get pleasure from the agony and joy, and the latter suffer for all those who drink vodka without being able to drink it. Therefore, ladies and gentlemen, after we have prayed for our poor Josif, I ask you to accompany Saveli Butsis, a man unknown to you but already deceased, to *his* grave.'

"Having finished his speech, Benya Krik came down from the mound. The people, the trees, and the cemetery beggars stood silent. Two gravediggers carried an unpainted coffin to an adjacent grave. The cantor, stuttering, ended the prayer. Benya threw the first spadeful of earth and walked over to Savka. All the barristers and ladies with brooches followed him like sheep. He had the cantor chant the full funeral rites for Savka, and sixty chanters sang with him. Savka had never dreamt of such a funeral—you can trust the word of Arye-Leib, an aged old man.

"Word has it that it was on that day that Yid-and-a-Half decided to close shop. Not that I myself was there. But I saw with my own eyes, the eyes of Arye-Leib—which is my name—that neither the cantor, nor the choir, nor the Burial Brotherhood asked to. get paid for the funeral. More I couldn't see, because the people quietly slipped away from Savka's grave and started running, as if from a fire. They flew off in carriages, in carts, and on foot. And the four men who had arrived in the red automobile left in it. The musical horn played its march, the car lurched and hurtled off.

"'The King!' lisping Moiseika, who always grabs the best seat on the wall, said, following the car with his eyes.

"Now you know everything. You know who was the first to pronounce the word 'King.' It was Moiseika. Now you know why he didn't call one-eyed Grach that, nor raging Kolka. You know everything. But what use is it if you still have glasses on your nose and autumn in your heart? . . ."

LYUBKA THE COSSACK

*I*n the Moldavanka, on the corner of Dalnitskaya and Balkovskaya Streets, stands Lyubka Shneiweis's house. In this house there is a wine cellar, an inn, an oat store, and a dovecote for a hundred Kryukov and Nikolayev doves. All these as well as lot number forty-six in the Odessa quarry belong to Lyubka Shneiweis, nicknamed Lyubka the Cossack—only the dovecote is the property of Yevzel, a retired soldier with a medal. On Sundays, Yevzel goes to Okhotnitskaya Square and sells doves to officials from town and to the boys of the neighborhood. Also living in Lyubka's courtyard, besides the watchman, are Pesya-Mindl, cook and procuress, and Zudechkis, the manager, a small Jew with a build and beard like those of our Moldavanka Rabbi, Ben Zkharia. There are many stories I can tell about Zudechkis. The first is the story of how Zudechkis became the manager of the inn that belonged to Lyubka, nicknamed the Cossack.

About ten years ago Zudechkis was the middleman in the sale of a horse-drawn threshing machine to a landowner, and in the evening he brought the landowner over to Lyubka's to celebrate the sale. This landowner had not only a mustache, but also a goatee, and wore lacquered shoes. Pesya-Mindl served him gefilte fish, followed by a very nice young lady by the name of Nastya. The landowner stayed the night, and in the morning Yevzel woke Zudechkis, who was lying curled up by Lyubka's door.

"Well!" Yevzel said to him. "Last night you were boasting about how the landowner bought a threshing machine through you! Well, let me inform you that he stayed the night and then at dawn, like the lowest of the low, made a run for it. That'll be two rubles for the food and four rubles for the young lady. I can see you're a slippery old con!"

But Zudechkis wouldn't pay. So Yevzel shoved him into Lyubka's room and locked the door.

"Well!" the watchman said. "You're going to stay right here till Lyubka gets back from the quarry, and with the help of God she will beat the soul out of you! Amen!"

"Jailbird!" Zudechkis shouted after the soldier, and looked around the room. "All you know about is your doves, you jailbird! But I still have some faith in God who will lead me out of here, the way He led all the Jews first out of Egypt and then out of the desert!"

There was much more that the little middleman wanted to tell Yevzel, but the soldier had taken the key and left, his shoes thumping. Then Zudechkis turned around and saw the procuress, Pesya-Mindl, sitting by the window reading *The Miracles and Heart of Baal-Shem*. She was reading the Hasidic book with gilt edges, and rocking an oak cradle with her foot. In the cradle lay Lyubka's son, Davidka, crying.

"I see you have a nice setup here in this Sakhalin prison camp!" Zudechkis said to Pesya-Mindl. "The child lies there, bawling its lungs out so that a man feels pity at the sight of it, while you, you fat woman, sit here like a stone in the woods and don't even give him a bottle."

"*You* give him a bottle!" Pesya-Mindl answered, without looking up from her book. "That's if he'll take a bottle from you, you old crook! He's as big as a pork butcher, and all he wants is his mama's milk, while his mama gallops around her quarries, drinks tea with Jews in the Medved Tavern, buys contraband down by the harbor, and thinks of her son as she might think of last year's snow!"

"*Oy*, poor Zudechkis!" the small middleman then said to himself. "You have fallen into the hands of the Pharaoh himself!" And he went over to the eastern wall of the room, muttered the whole Morning Prayer with addenda, and then took the crying infant in his arms. Davidka looked at him in bewilderment and waved his little crimson legs covered in infant's sweat, and the old man started walking up and down the room and, rocking like a *tsaddik* in prayer, began singing an endless song.

"Ah-ah-ah," he began singing. "Now all the children will get nothing-and-a-half, but our little Davidka will get some buns, so he will sleep both night and day . . . ah-ah-ah, now all the children will get a good punch in the . . ."

Zudechkis showed Lyubka's son his fist with its gray hairs, and repeated the song about getting nothing-and-a-half and buns until the boy fell asleep and the sun had reached the middle of the shining sky. It reached the middle and began quivering like a fly weakened by the heat. Wild muzhiks from Nerubaiska and Tatarka who were staying at Lyubka's inn crawled under their carts and fell into a wild and sonorous sleep; a drunken workman went out to the gates and, dropping his plane and his saw, collapsed on the ground and began snoring then and there, surrounded by the golden flies and the blue lightning of July. Wrinkled German settlers who had brought Lyubka wine from the borders of Bessarabia sat nearby in the shade. They lit their pipes, and the smoke from their curved chibouks blended with the silver stubble of their old, unshaven cheeks. The sun hung from the sky like the pink tongue of a thirsty dog, the immense sea rolled far away to Peresip, and the masts of distant ships swayed on the emerald water of Odessa Bay. The day sat in an ornate boat, the day sailed toward evening, and halfway toward evening, at five o'clock, Lyubka came back from town. She rode in on a little roan horse with a large belly and an overgrown mane. A fat-legged young man in a calico shirt opened the gate for her, Yevzel grabbed hold of the bridle of her horse, at which point Zudechkis called down to Lyubka from his prison cell, "My respects, Madam Shneiweis, and good day to you! You simply go off on a three-year trip, and throw your hungry child at me!"

"Shut your ugly trap!" Lyubka shouted back at the old man, and jumped off the horse. "Who's that yelling out my window?"

"It's Zudechkis, a slippery old con," the soldier with the medal explained to his mistress, and began telling her the whole story about the landowner, but didn't get to the end because Zudechkis interrupted him, yelling with all his might.

"This is an outrage!" he yelled, hurling down his skullcap. "This is an outrage to throw a child at a stranger and simply go off on a three-year trip! Come here this instant and give him your breast!"

"You wait till I come up there, you crook!" Lyubka muttered, and ran to the stairs. She came into the room and pulled her breast out of her dusty blouse.

The child stretched toward her and gnawed at her monstrous nipple, but didn't strike milk. A vein protruded on the mother's brow, and, shaking his skullcap, Zudechkis said to her, "You're such a greedy woman, Lyubka! You want everything for yourself! You snatch at the whole world, the way a child snatches at a tablecloth to get at breadcrumbs! You always have to have the best wheat and the best grapes! You want to bake white bread in the blaze of the sun, while your little baby, your sweet little pumpkin, is drying up without milk!"

"How am I supposed to have milk!" the woman yelled, kneading her breast. "The *Plutarch* pulled into port today and I had to cover fifteen versts in the heat! But don't think you can hoodwink me with your stories, you old Jew! Give me my six rubles!"

But again Zudechkis wouldn't pay. He rolled up his sleeve, and jabbed his thin, dirty elbow into Lyubka's mouth.

"Choke, you jailbird!" he shouted, and spat into the corner.

Lyubka stood there for a while with the foreign elbow in her mouth, then took it out, locked the door, and went out into the courtyard. Waiting for her there was Mr. Trottyburn, who resembled a pillar of red meat. Mr. Trottyburn was the chief engineer on the *Plutarch*. He had brought Lyubka two sailors. One of the sailors was an Englishman, the other a Malay. The three of them were lugging into the courtyard contraband they had brought from Port Said. The box was heavy. They dropped it on the ground, and out of the box tumbled cigars tangled with Japanese silk. A horde of women came running to the box, and two wandering gypsy women came slyly edging nearer.

"Get out of here! Scum!" Lyubka yelled at them, and led the sailors to the shade of an acacia tree.

They sat down at a table. Yevzel brought them wine, and Mr. Trottyburn began unwrapping his merchandise. Out of his bale he took cigars and delicate silks, cocaine and metal jiggers, uncut tobacco from the state of Virginia, and black wine bought on the Island of Chios. Each item had a special price, and each figure was washed down with Bessarabian wine with its bouquet of sunshine and bedbugs. Twilight was already flooding the courtyard, twilight was flooding in like an evening wave over a wide river, and the drunken Malay, completely taken aback, poked Lyubka's breast with his finger. He poked it with one finger, then with each of his fingers, one after the other.

His yellow and tender eyes hung above the table like paper lanterns on a Chinese street. He started singing, barely audibly, and toppled onto the ground as Lyubka punched him with her fist.

"A nice literate fellow, that one!" Lyubka said to Mr. Trottyburn. "That Malaysian's making me lose my last drop of milk, while that Jew up there won't stop badgering me for it!"

And she pointed at Zudechkis, who was standing by the window, washing his socks. A small lamp was smoking in Zudechkis's room, his tub frothed and hissed, he leaned out the window sensing that they were talking about him, and in despair started yelling down to them.

"Save me, you people!" he yelled, waving his hands.

"Shut your ugly trap!" Lyubka yelled back, and burst out laughing. "Shut up!"

She threw a stone at the old man, but didn't manage to hit him. She then grabbed an empty wine bottle. But Mr. Trottyburn, the chief engineer, took the bottle away from her, aimed, and flung it through the open window.

"Miss Lyubka," the chief engineer said, rising, pulling his drunken legs toward himself. "Many worthy individuals have come to me, Miss Lyubka, to trade, but I trade with no one, not with Mr. Kuninson nor with Mr. Bats, nor with Mr. Kupchik, no one but you, because I find your conversation so agreeable, Miss Lyubka."

And, gaining a foothold on his wobbly legs, he grabbed his sailors by their shoulders—the one an Englishman, the other a Malay—and began dancing with them through the cooling courtyard. The men from the *Plutarch* danced in deeply pensive silence. An orange star had slid right down to the edge of the horizon and was staring them in the face. Then they took their money, grabbed each other by the hand, and went out into the street, swaying the way hanging lamps sway on a ship. From the street they could see the sea, the black waters of Odessa Bay, little toy flags on sunken masts, and piercing lights that had ignited in the spacious depths. Lyubka walked her dancing guests to the intersection. She stayed back alone in the empty street, laughed to herself, and went home. The sleepy young man in the calico shirt locked the gates behind her, Yevzel brought his mistress the proceeds of the day, and she went upstairs to sleep. There Pesya-Mindl, the procuress, was already slumbering, and Zudechkis was rocking the oak cradle with his bare feet.

"How you've tortured us, you shameless woman!" he said, and took the child out of the cradle. "But here, watch me and you might learn a thing or two, you foul mother, you!"

He laid a thin comb on Lyubka's breast and put her son into her bed. The child stretched toward his mother, pricked himself on the comb, and started to cry. Then the old man pushed the bottle toward him, but Davidka turned away from the bottle.

"Is this some spell you're putting on me, you old swindler?" Lyubka muttered, dozing off.

"Shut up, you foul mother, you!" Zudechkis said to her. "Shut up and learn, may the devil take you!"

The baby pricked himself on the comb again, hesitantly took the bottle, and began sucking.

"There!" Zudechkis said, and burst out laughing. "I have weaned your child! I can teach you a thing or two, may the devil take you!"

Davidka lay in his cradle, sucking on his bottle and dribbling blissfully. Lyubka woke up, opened her eyes, and closed them again. She saw her son, and the moon forcing its way through her window. The moon jumping into black clouds, like a straying calf.

"Well, fair enough," Lyubka said. "Unlock the door for Zudechkis, Pesya-Mindl, and let him come tomorrow for a pound of American tobacco."

And the following day Zudechkis came for a pound of uncut tobacco from the state of Virginia. He was given it, and a quarter pound of tea was thrown in. And within a week, when I came to buy a dove from Yevzel, I ran into the new manager of Lyubka's courtyard. He was tiny, like our Rabbi Ben Zkharia. Zudechkis was the new manager. He stayed at his post for fifteen years, and during that period I heard a great number of stories about him. And if I can manage, I will tell them one after another, because they are very interesting stories.

THE FATHER

Froim Grach had once been married. That was long ago—twenty years have passed since then. His wife had borne him a daughter and had died in childbirth. The girl was named Basya. Her grandmother on her mother's side lived in Tulchin. The old woman did not like her son-in-law. She said about him, "Froim is a carter by profession, he has black horses, but his soul is blacker than his horses' coats."

The old woman did not like her son-in-law and took away the newborn girl. She lived twenty years with the girl and then died. Then Basya came back to her father. That's how it happened.

On Wednesday, the fifth, Froim Grach was carting wheat from the Dreyfus Company warehouses down to the port to load on the *Caledonia*. As evening fell, he finished working and went home. At the corner of Prokhorovskaya Street he came across Ivan Pyatirubel, the blacksmith.

"My respects, Grach!" Ivan Pyatirubel said. "There's some woman banging on your door."

Grach drove on and saw a gigantic woman standing in his courtyard. Her hips were enormous, and her cheeks brick red.

"Papa!" the woman shouted in a deafening bass voice. "The devil is snatching at me already, I'm so bored! I've been waiting for you all day. . . . You know, Grandma died in Tulchin."

Grach stood in his cart staring at his daughter.

"Don't prance about in front of the horses!" he shouted in despair. "Grab the bridle there! You trying to finish off my horses?"

Grach stood on the cart waving his whip. Basya grabbed the shaft horse's bridle and led the horses to the stable. She unharnessed them and went to busy herself in the kitchen. She hung her father's foot bindings on a line, scrubbed the sooty teapot with sand, and warmed up a large meatball in the cast-iron pot.

"What unbearable dirt, Papa!" she said, grabbed the rancid sheepskins from the floor and threw them out the window. "But I'll get rid of this dirt!" she shouted, and gave her father his food.

The old man drank vodka out of an enameled teapot and ate his meatball, which smelled of happy childhood. Then he picked up his whip and walked out the gates. Basya came out after him. She had put on a pair of men's boots, an orange dress, and a hat covered with birds, and sat down next to him on the bench. The evening slouched past the bench; the shining eye of the sunset fell into the sea beyond Peresip, and the sky was red, like a red-letter day on a calendar. All trading had ended on Dalnitskaya Street, and the gangsters drove by on the shadowy street to Ioska Samuelson's brothel. They rode in lacquered carriages and were dressed up in colorful jackets, like hummingbirds. They were goggle-eyed, one leg resting on the running board, their steel hands holding bouquets of flowers wrapped in cigarette paper. The lacquered cabs moved at a walking pace, and in each carriage sat one man with a bouquet; the drivers, sticking out on their high seats, were covered in bows like best men at weddings. Old Jewish women in bonnets lazily watched the flow of this everyday procession—they were indifferent to everything, these old Jewish women, it was only the sons of shopkeepers and dockworkers who envied the kings of the Moldavanka.

Solomonchik Kaplun, the grocer's son, and Monya Artillerist, the smuggler's son, were among those who tried to turn their eyes away from the splendor of other men's success. Both of them walked past Basya swaying like girls who have just discovered love. They whispered to each other and mimicked with their arms how they would embrace her, if she wanted them to. And Basya immediately wanted them to, because she was a simple girl from Tulchin, that self-seeking, nearsighted little town. She weighed a good five *pood* and a few pounds over, had lived all her life among the viperous offspring of Podolian brokers, itinerant booksellers, and lumber dealers, and she had never before seen anyone like Solomonchik Kaplun. This is why when she saw him she started shuffling her fat feet, which had been squeezed into men's boots, and said to her father, "Papa!" she said in a thundering voice. "Look at that sweetie of a gentleman! Look at his little dolly feet! I could eat them up!"

"Aha, Mr. Grach," whispered an old Jew named Golubchik sitting next to them. "I see your child wants to roam in the pasture."

"That's all I need!" Froim told Golubchik, twirling his whip a little, and then went home to sleep, and slept soundly because he didn't believe the old man. He didn't believe the old man, but he turned out to be entirely wrong. Golubchik was the one who was right. Golubchik was the matchmaker on our street, at night he read prayers for the well-to-do who had passed away, and he knew all there was to know about life. Froim Grach was wrong. Golubchik was the one who was right.

And, truth to tell, from that day on Basya spent all her evenings outside the gates. She sat on the bench, sewing herself a trousseau. Pregnant women sat next to her. Heaps of sackcloth unfurled over her powerful, bandy knees. The pregnant women were filled with all kinds of things, the way a cow's udder in a pasture fills with the rosy milk of spring, and then their husbands, one by one, came from work. The quarrelsome women's husbands wrung out their tousled beards beneath the water fountain, and then made way for the hunchbacked old women. The old women washed fat babies in troughs, they slapped their grandsons' shiny bottoms, and bundled them up in their frayed skirts. And so Basya from Tulchin saw life in the Moldavanka, our generous mother, a life crowded with suckling babies, drying rags, and conjugal nights filled with big-city chic and soldierly tirelessness. The girl wanted such a life for herself too, but she was quick to realize that the daughter of one-eyed Grach could not count on a suitable match. That was when she stopped calling her father "Father."

"You redheaded thief!" she yelled at him in the evenings. "You redheaded thief! Come get your grub!"

And this went on until Basya had sewed herself six nightgowns and six pairs of bloomers with lace frills. Having finished sewing the hem of the lace, she began crying in a faint little voice not at all like her usual voice, and through her tears said to the unshakeable Grach: "Every girl has her interests in life!" she told him. "I'm the only one who has to live like a night watchman in someone else's warehouse. Either do something with me, Papa, or I shall kill myself off!"

Grach heard his daughter out, and on the following day put on a sailcloth cloak and went to visit Kaplun the grocer on Privoznaya Square.

A golden sign sparkled above Kaplun's store. It was the best store on Privoznaya Square. Inside was the aroma of many seas and wonderful lives unknown to us. A boy was sprinkling the cool depths of the store with a watering can, singing a song suitable only for adults to sing. Solomonchik, the owner's son, stood behind the counter. On the counter were olives that had come from Greece, Marseilles butter, coffee beans, Lisbon Malaga, sardines from the firm of "Philippe and Canot," and cayenne pepper. Kaplun himself was sitting in his vest in the sun on a glassed-in porch eating a watermelon, a red watermelon with black seeds, slanting seeds like the eyes of sly Chinese girls. Kaplun's stomach lay on the table in the sun, and there was nothing the sun could do with him. But then the grocer saw Grach in his sailcloth cloak and turned pale.

"Good day to you, Monsieur Grach," he said, and moved to the side. "Golubchik informed me that you'd be dropping by, and I have prepared a pound of tea for you, an absolute rarity!"

And he began talking about a new variety of tea that had been brought to Odessa on Dutch ships. Grach listened to him patiently, but then interrupted him, because he was a simple man with no tricks up his sleeve.

"I'm a simple man with no tricks up my sleeve," Froim said. "I stay with my horses and I work hard at my work. I'm ready to throw in some new linen and a few coins for Basya, and I needn't tell you that I myself stand behind her—and whoever thinks that's not enough can burn in hell!"

"Why should we burn?" Kaplun answered in a quick jabber, caressing the carter's arm. "No need for such words, Monsieur Grach. We know you well as a man who can lend another a helping hand, not to mention that your talk might offend a man—you're no Cracow rabbi, you know, and though I myself didn't stand beneath wedding wreaths with no niece of Moses Montefiore, we must consider . . . we must consider Madame Kaplun, a grand lady—God himself has no idea what that woman wants—"

"Me, I know, I know that Solomonchik wants my Basya," Grach interrupted the grocer. "But Madame Kaplun doesn't want me."

"That's right! I don't want you!" shouted Madame Kaplun, who had been listening by the door, and she came into the glass veranda, hot all over, her chest fluttering. "I don't want you, Grach, as man doesn't want death! I don't want you, as a bride doesn't want her face to be covered with pimples! Don't forget that our dear late granddaddy was a grocer, and we must keep up *la branche*."

"You can keep your *la branche*!" Grach told the heated Madame Kaplun, and went home.

Basya was waiting for him there in her orange dress. But without even glancing at her, the old man spread out a sheepskin coat under the cart and went to sleep, and he slept until Basya's powerful arm dragged him out from under the cart.

"You redheaded thief!" the girl said in a whisper, not at all like her usual whisper. "Why do I have to put up with your carter's ways, and why are you as mute as a log, you redheaded thief!"

"Basya!" Grach said to her. "Solomonchik wants you, but Madame Kaplun doesn't want me. She wants a grocer's girl."

The old man adjusted his sheepskin coat and crawled back under the cart, and Basya went running out of the courtyard.

All of this happened on a Sabbath, a day of rest. The purple eye of the sunset, rummaging over the earth, stumbled upon Grach in the evening, snoring under his cart. An impulsive ray bumped into the sleeping man, and with its blazing reproach led him to Dalnitskaya Street, which lay dusty and shimmering like green rye in the wind. Tatars were walking up Dalnitskaya Street, Tatars and Turks with their mullahs. They were returning from a pilgrimage to Mecca and going back to their homes on the Orenburg Steppes and in Transcaucasia. A steamship had brought them to Odessa, and they were going from the harbor to the inn of Lyubka Shneiweis, nicknamed Lyubka the Cossack. The Tatars wore striped, rigid robes, and they covered the streets with the bronze sweat of the deserts. White towels were wound around their fezzes, indicating they had worshiped at the shrine of the Prophet. The pilgrims walked to the corner of the street and headed for Lyubka's courtyard, but they couldn't get in because a big crowd of people had gathered by the gates. Lyubka Shneiweis, her bag by her side, was beating a drunken muzhik, pushing him out into the street. She was punching him in the face, her fist clenched like a tambourine, while with her other hand she was holding him up so he wouldn't collapse. Streams of blood were trickling between the muzhik's teeth and down past his ears. He was lost in thought, looking at Lyubka as if she were a complete stranger. Then he collapsed onto the stones and fell asleep. Lyubka gave him a kick and went back inside her store. Yevzel, her watchman, closed the gates behind her, and waved at Froim Grach, who was walking by.

"My respects, Grach!" he shouted. "If you want to see a real slice of life, come into our courtyard—you'll have a good laugh!"

And the watchman took Grach to a wall where the pilgrims who had arrived the night before had settled down. An old Turk in a green turban, an old Turk as green and light as a leaf, was lying on the grass. He was covered in pearly sweat, breathing with difficulty, and his eyes were rolling.

"There!" Yevzel said, adjusting the medal on his shabby jacket. "There you have a scene from the real-life opera 'Turkish Sickness.' He's dying, this old man is, but no one must call a doctor, because they think that whoever dies on the road back from the Muhammadan God is a fortunate and wealthy man. . . . Halvah!" Yevzel shouted at the dying man, and burst out laughing. "The doctor has come to cure you!"

The Turk looked up at the watchman with childish terror and hatred, and turned away. Yevzel, pleased with himself, took Grach to the wine cellar on the other side of the courtyard. In the cellar, lamps were already burning, and music was playing. Old Jews with massive beards were playing Rumanian and Jewish songs. Mendel Krik was at a table drinking wine from a green glass, describing how his own sons—Benya, the older one, and Lyovka, the younger—had maimed him. He yelled out his story in a hoarse and terrifying voice, showed his smashed teeth, and let those around him poke the wounds on his belly. The Volhynian *tsaddiks*, with their porcelain faces, stood behind his chair and listened to Mendel Krik's bragging with numb bewilderment. They were astonished at everything they heard, and Grach despised them for it.

"Old braggart!" he mumbled, and ordered wine.

Then Froim called over the owner, Lyubka the Cossack. She was standing by the door spouting curses and downing shots of vodka.

"What!" she shouted at Froim, squinting at him in fury.

"Madam Lyubka," Froim said, beckoning her to sit next to him. "You are a clever woman, and I have come to you as I would to my very own mama. I have faith in you, Madam Lyubka—first and foremost in God, then in you."

"What!" Lyubka yelled, and quickly marched around the cellar before coming to sit next to him.

And Grach said, "In the settlements," he said, "the Germans are having a rich wheat harvest, but in Constantinople groceries go for a song. In Constantinople you can buy a *pood* of olives for three rubles, and then sell them here for thirty kopecks a pound! The grocers are really doing well now, Madam Lyubka, they've grown big and fat, and if one approaches them with a delicate touch, one could come away quite happy. But I'm all alone now on the job, the late Lyovka Bik has died, and I have no one left to turn to, and I'm all alone, as God is alone in heaven.

"Benya Krik!" Lyubka said to him. "You tried Benya out on Tartakovsky, so why not Benya?"

"Benya Krik?" Grach repeated, full of amazement. "He's a bachelor too, now that I think of it!"

"He's a bachelor," Lyubka said. "Hook him up with Basya, give him money, make the rounds with him."

"Benya Krik," the old man repeated, like an echo, a distant echo. "I hadn't thought of him."

Froim Grach got up, muttering and stuttering, Lyubka marched off, and he tagged along behind her. They crossed the courtyard and went up to the second floor. There on the second floor lived the women that Lyubka kept for her guests.

"Our bridegroom is with Katyusha," Lyubka said to Grach. "Wait for me in the hall!" And she went to the room at the other end, where Benya was in bed with a woman named Katyusha.

"Enough slobbering!" Lyubka told the young man. "You have to set yourself up first, Benchik, and then you can slobber away. Froim Grach is looking for you. He needs a man for a job but can't find one."

Then she told him everything she knew about Basya and about Grach's business.

"I'll think it over," Benya told her, covering Katyusha's bare legs with the sheet. "I'll think it over. Let the old man wait a bit."

"Wait a bit," Lyubka told Grach, who was still standing in the hall. "Wait a bit, he's thinking it over."

Lyubka brought him a chair, and he sank into boundless waiting. He waited patiently, like a muzhik in a government office. Behind the wall, Katyusha moaned and burst out laughing. The old man dozed off for two hours, maybe more. Evening had long turned into night, the sky had turned black, and its Milky Ways had filled with gold, brilliance, and coolness. Lyubka's cellar was locked up already, the drunks lay like broken furniture in the courtyard, and the old mullah with the green turban had died around midnight. Then music came over the sea—hunting horns and trumpets from the English ships—the music came over the sea and faded away, but Katyusha, unfailing Katyusha, was still incandescing her rosy-painted Russian paradise for Benya Krik. She moaned behind the wall and burst out laughing. Old Froim sat motionless in front of her door. He waited till one in the morning, and then he knocked.

"Hey!" he called. "Are you making fun of me?"

Benya finally opened the door.

"Monsieur Grach!" he said, flustered, smiling, and covering himself with a sheet. "When we're young, we see girls like them's merchandise, but they're just straw that catches fire by itself."

He got dressed, made Katyusha's bed, shook out her pillow, and went out into the street with the old man. They walked until they came to the Russian cemetery, and there at the cemetery the interests of Benya Krik and gnarled old Grach the gangster intersected. Their interests intersected because Basya would bring her future husband three thousand rubles as a dowry, two thoroughbred horses, and a pearl necklace. They also intersected because Kaplun would have to pay two thousand rubles to Benya, Basya's bridegroom. Kaplun of Privoznaya Square was guilty of family pride. He had grown rich on Constantinople olives, he showed no mercy for Basya's first love, and that was why Benya decided to take on the task of relieving Kaplun of two thousand rubles.

"I'll take on this task, Papa!" he said to his future father-in-law. "With the help of God we shall punish all grocers!"

These words were uttered at dawn, after night had already past. And here now a new story begins, the story of the fall of the house of Kaplun, the tale of its slow ruin, of arson and gunshots in the night. And all this—the fate of arrogant Kaplun and the fate of Basya—was decided that night when Basya's father and her sudden fiancé sauntered past the Russian cemetery. Young men were pulling girls behind the fences, and kisses echoed on the gravestones.

FROIM GRACH

*I*n 1919, Benya Krik's men ambushed the rear guard of the Volunteer Army,* slit all the officers' throats, and captured part of their supply unit. As a reward, they demanded that the Odessa soviet allow them three days of "peaceful insurrection," but as they were not given permission, they looted all the stores lining the Alexandrovsky Boulevard. Then they set their sights on the Mutual Credit Society. They let all the customers enter first, and then requested that the porters carry all the bags of money and valuables outside to a car parked nearby. Within a month Benya Krik's men were being lined up and shot. There were people who said that Aron Peskin, a workshop owner, had had a hand in their capture and arrest. What kind of workshop it was, nobody knew. There was a machine in it—a long device with a warped lead roller—and on the floor, surrounded by sawdust, lay pasteboards for binding books.

One spring morning Misha Yablochko, one of Peskin's friends, knocked on the door of his workshop.

"The weather's great outside," Misha said to him. "You see before you a man who is about to grab a bottle of vodka along with some food and go for a ride to Arkadia.† Don't laugh—sometimes I love to just walk away from it all!"

Peskin put on his jacket and set out with Misha Yablochko in his

---

* The counterrevolutionary army (the Whites) fighting the Bolshevik forces in southern Russia and Ukraine from 1918–1920 under generals Kornilov, Denikin, and Wrangel.
† A resort area outside Odessa by the sea.

buggy to Arkadia. They rode about until evening. At dusk, Misha Yablochko entered the room in which Madame Peskin was bathing her fourteen-year-old daughter in a tub.

"Greetings," Misha said, lifting his hat. "We had such a nice time. The air there—simply out of this world! Though talking to your husband is like pulling teeth. What a tiresome man he is!"

"You can say that again!" Madame Peskin said, grabbing her daughter by the hair and yanking her head every which way. "Where is he, that vagabond?"

"He's unwinding outside in the garden."

Misha lifted his hat again, excused himself, and left in his buggy. Madame Peskin went straight outside. Her husband was sitting there in a Panama hat, leaning against the garden table with a grin on his face.

"You vagabond!" Madame Peskin said to him. "How dare you just sit there laughing, while that daughter of yours is driving me to an early grave! She won't wash her hair! I want you to go inside right now and have a word with her!"

Peskin sat there silently, still grinning.

"You fool!" Madame Peskin said. She peered under her husband's Panama hat and started screaming.

The neighbors came running.

"He's not alive," she told them. "He's dead!"

That wasn't true. Peskin had been shot twice in the chest and his skull was broken, but he was still alive. They took him to the Jewish hospital. Doctor Silberberg in person operated on the wounded man, but Peskin was out of luck. He died under the knife. That same night the Cheka* arrested a man nicknamed The Georgian, and his friend Kolya Lapidus. One of them was Misha Yablochko's coachman, the other had lain in wait for the buggy in Arkadia by the bend in the road that leads from the seashore out into the steppes. The two arrested men were shot after a brief interrogation. But Misha Yablochko managed to slip the net. He disappeared from sight, and a few days later an old woman selling sunflower seeds came hobbling into Froim Grach's yard.

---

* The Odessa branch of the "Extraordinary Commission" set up in 1917 to investigate counterrevolutionary activities. The Cheka later became the KGB.

She was carrying a basket of seeds on her arm. One of her eyebrows was arched in a furry, coal-black line above her eye, the other, barely visible, lay sagging on her eyelid. Froim Grach was sitting near the stable with his legs apart, playing with Arkadi, his grandson. The boy had come tumbling out of his daughter Basya's powerful womb three years ago. Froim held out his finger to Arkadi, who grabbed it and began to swing from it as if it were a crossbeam.

"You little scoundrel, you!" Froim said to his grandson, peering at him with his single eye.

The old woman came up to him with her furry eyebrow and her men's boots tied with string.

"Froim," she said. "I tell you these people have not a drop of soul in them. They don't say a word, they just kill us in their cellars like dogs. And they don't give us a chance to open our mouths before we die. We should tear these men to pieces with our teeth, and rip out their hearts! Why are you silent?" the old woman—Misha Yablochko—asked Froim. "Our men are waiting for you to break your silence!"

Misha got up, moved the basket to his other arm, and left, lifting his black eyebrow. He ran into three girls with braided hair walking with their arms around each other's waists outside the church on Alekseyevskaya Square.

"Hello girls," Misha Yablochko said to them. "Sorry I can't invite you for tea and cake."

He scooped up some sunflower seeds with a little glass mug, poured them into the pockets of their dresses, and walked off, disappearing around the church.

Froim Grach remained alone in his yard. He sat motionless, his single eye staring into the distance. Mules captured from imperialist troops were munching hay in the stables, and fattened mares were grazing with their foals on the meadow. Carters were playing cards in the shade of the chestnut trees and drinking wine from broken cups. Hot gusts of air swept over the whitewashed walls, and the sun in its blue rigidity poured over the yard. Froim got up and went out into the street. He crossed Prokhorovskaya Street, which was blackening the sky with the destitute, melting smoke of its kitchens, and Tolkuchy market, where people laden with curtains and drapes were trying to sell them to each other. He walked up Ekaterininskaya Street, made a turn by the statue of the Empress, and went inside the building of the Cheka.

"I am Froim," he told the commandant. "I want to see the boss."

The chairman of the Cheka back then was Vladislav Simen, who had come from Moscow. When he heard that Froim was there to see him, he called in Borovoi, one of his investigators, and asked for information on him.

"A first-rate fellow!" Borovoi told him. "Odessa begins and ends with him!"

And old Froim, in his canvas overalls, red-haired and big as a house, a patch over one eye and his cheek disfigured, was led into the office by the commandant.

"You know who you're killing off, boss?" he said as he walked into the room. "You're killing off all the lions! And you know what you'll be left with if you keep it up? You'll be left with shit!"

Simen leaned forward and opened his desk drawer.

"Don't worry, I'm clean," Froim told him. "Nothing in my hands, nothing in my boots—and I didn't leave nobody waiting outside neither. Let my boys go, boss! Just name your price!"

Simen had the old man sit down in an armchair, and offered him some cognac. Borovoi left the room and called together all the investigators who had come from Moscow.

Borovoi told them how it was one-eyed Froim and not Benya Krik who was the real boss of the forty thousand Odessa thugs. Froim might never show his hand, but he was the brains behind everything—the looting of the factories and the Odessa Treasury, and the ambushing of both the anti-Bolshevik army and its allies. Borovoi waited for Froim to come out of Simen's office so he could have a word with him. But Froim did not appear. Tired of waiting, Borovoi went to look for him. He searched through the whole building until he finally looked out into the backyard. Froim Grach was lying there stretched out under a tarpaulin by a wall covered in ivy. Two Red Army men stood by his body, smoking.

"Strong as an ox," the older of the two said when he saw Borovoi. "Strength like you wouldn't believe! If you don't butcher an old man like that, he'll live forever. He had ten bullets in him and he was still going strong!"

The Red Army man's face reddened, his eyes sparkled, and his cap slipped to the side.

"You're shooting your mouth off!" the second soldier cut in. "He died just like they all do!"

"No, not like they all do!" the older soldier shouted. "Some holler and beg, some don't say a word! So what do you mean, 'like they all do'?"

"To me they're all the same," the younger Red Army man repeated obstinately. "They all look the same, I can't even tell them apart!"

Borovoi bent down and pulled back the tarpaulin. The old man's face was frozen in a grimace.

Borovoi went back to his office. It was a round chamber with walls covered in satin. A meeting was under way about new rules for prosecuting cases. Simen was reprimanding the staff on the irregularities he had come upon, about the haphazard way verdicts were written up, and the absurd method with which protocols of the investigations were drawn up. The investigators were to split into groups and work with legal experts, so that from now on matters would be conducted according to the codes and statutes instituted by the Cheka headquarters in Moscow.

Borovoi sat in his corner, listening. He sat alone, far away from the rest. Simen came up to him after the meeting and took him by the hand.

"I know you're angry at me, Sasha," Simen said to him, "but you mustn't forget that now we are the power, the state power! You must remember that!"

"I'm not angry at you," Borovoi said, turning away. "It's just that you're not an Odessan, you can't understand what the old man represented."

They sat side by side, the chairman of the Cheka, who had just turned twenty-three, and his subordinate. Simen was holding Borovoi's hand in his and pressing it.

"Tell me one thing as a Chekist, as a revolutionary," Simen said to him after a moment of silence. "What use would that man have been to the society we are building?"

"I don't know," Borovoi said, staring motionlessly in front of him. "I suppose no use at all."

He pulled himself together and chased away his memories. Then, livening up, he continued telling the Chekists who had come from Moscow about the life of Froim Grach, about his ingenuity, his elusiveness, his contempt for his fellow men, all the amazing tales that were now a thing of the past.

THE END OF
THE ALMSHOUSE

*I*n the days of the famine, no one lived better in all Odessa than the almsfolk of the Second Jewish Cemetery. Kofman, the cloth merchant, had built an almshouse for old people by the wall of the cemetery in memory of his wife Isabella, a fact that became the butt of many a joke at Café Fankoni.* But Kofman turned out to be right in the end. After the Revolution, the old men and women who found refuge by the cemetery immediately grabbed positions as gravediggers, cantors, and body washers. They got their hands on an oak coffin with a silver-tasseled pall, and rented it out to the poor.

There were no planks to be found anywhere in Odessa in those days. The rental coffin did not stand idle. The dead would lie in the oak coffin at home and at the funeral service—but then they were pitched into their graves wrapped in a shroud. This was a forgotten Jewish custom.

Wise men had taught that one is not to hinder the union of worm and carrion—carrion is unclean. "For dust thou art and unto dust shalt thou return."

Because of the revival of the forgotten custom, the rations of the old folk grew in ways which in those days no one could even dream of. In the evenings they got drunk in Zalman Krivoruchka's cellar, and threw their leftover scraps to poorer companions.

Their prosperity remained undisturbed until the rebellion in the

* An elegant and expensive café that attracted a wealthy international clientele.

German settlements. The Germans killed Garrison Commander Gersh Lugovoy.

He was buried with honors. The troops marched to the cemetery with bands, field kitchens, and machine guns on *tachankas*. Speeches were given and vows made over his open grave.

"Comrade Gersh joined the Revolutionary Social Democratic Workers Party of the Bolsheviks in 1911, where he held the position of propagandist and liaison agent!" Lenka Broytman, the division commander, yelled at the top of his lungs. "Comrade Gersh was arrested along with Sonya Yanovskaya, Ivan Sokolov, and Monozon in the town of Nikolayev in 1913. . . ."

Arye-Leib, the elder of the almshouse, lay in waiting with his comrades. Lenka hadn't yet finished his farewell speech over the grave when the old men heaved up the coffin in order to tip it onto its side so that the deceased, covered with a flag, would come tumbling out. Lenka discreetly jabbed Arye-Leib with his boot spur.

"Beat it!" he hissed. "Go on, beat it! . . . Gersh served the Republic . . ."

Before the eyes of the horrified old folk, Lugovoy was buried along with the oak coffin, the tassels, and the black pall onto which the Star of David and verses from an ancient Hebrew prayer for the dead had been woven in silver.

"We've all just attended our own funeral!" Arye-Leib told his comrades after the burial. "We have fallen into Pharaoh's hands!" And he rushed off to see Broydin, the overseer of the cemetery, with a request that planks for a new coffin and cloth for a pall be issued immediately. Broydin made promises, but did nothing. His plans did not include the enrichment of the old folk.

"My heart aches more for the unemployed municipal employees than for these entrepreneurs," he told the others at the office.

Broydin made promises, but did nothing. In Zalman Krivoruchka's wine cellar, Talmudic curses rained down on his head and the heads of the Union of Municipal Workers. The old folk cursed Broydin's bone marrow and that of the members of the union, along with the fresh seed in the wombs of their wives. They called down every kind of paralysis and boil upon each and every one of them.

The old folk's income shrank. Their rations now consisted of bluish soup with boiled fish bones, with a second course of barley kasha without a single dab of butter in it.

An aged Odessan is ready enough to eat any kind of soup, regardless what it's made of, as long as there's garlic, pepper, and a bay leaf in it. There were none of these in the old folk's soup.

The Isabella Kofman Almshouse shared in the common lot. The rage of its famished inmates grew. Their rage rained down upon the head of the person who least expected it. This person was Dr. Judith Shmayser, who had come to the almshouse to administer smallpox vaccinations.

The Provincial Executive Committee had issued an order for mandatory vaccination. Judith Shmayser laid out her instruments on the table and lit a little alcohol burner. Outside the windows stood the emerald walls of the cemetery hedges. The blue tongue of the flame mingled with the June lightning.

Meyer Beskonechny, a haggard old man, stood closest to Judith. He watched her preparations sullenly.

"I'll give you a jab now," Judith said to him, beckoning him over with her tweezers. She pulled his thin, bluish strap of an arm out of his rags.

"There's nowhere for you to jab me," the old man said, jerking back his arm.

"It's not going to hurt," Judith exclaimed. "It doesn't hurt when you're given a jab in the flesh."

"I don't have no flesh!" Meyer Beskonechny said. "There's nowhere for you to jab."

Muffled sobs came from one of the corners. Doba-Leya, a former cook at circumcision feasts, was sobbing. Meyer twisted his decayed cheeks.

"Life is shit," he muttered. "The world's a brothel, everyone's a swindler!"

The pince-nez on Judith's nose bounced, her breasts swelled out of her starched coat. She opened her mouth to explain the benefits of vaccination, but Arye-Leib, the elder of the almshouse, stopped her.

"Young lady," he said. "Our mamas gave birth to us just like your mama gave birth to you! And this woman, our mama, gave birth to us so we would live, not so we would suffer! She wanted for us to live well, and she was as right as a mother can be. A person who is pleased with what Broydin provides him, that person is not worth the material that went into him. Your aim, young lady, is to inoculate smallpox, and with God's help, you are inoculating it. Our aim is to live out our life, not torture it! But we are not achieving our aim!"

Doba-Leya, a whiskered old woman with a leonine face, started sobbing even louder on hearing these words. She sobbed in a deep bass.

"Life is shit," Meyer Beskonechny repeated. "Everyone's a swindler!"

Paralyzed Simon-Volf, screeching and twisting his hands, clutched at the steering wheel of his invalid cart and went rolling toward the door. His yarmulke slid over his swollen, crimson head. Thirty growling and grimacing old men and women tumbled out onto the cemetery walk behind Simon-Volf. They shook their crutches and brayed like starving donkeys.

When he saw them, the watchman slammed the cemetery gates shut. The amazed gravediggers stopped digging and raised their shovels, clumps of earth and grass roots still clinging to them.

The noise brought out bearded Broydin in his tight little jacket, leggings, and cycling cap.

"You swindler!" Simon-Volf shouted. "There's nowhere for us to be jabbed! We've got no meat on our arms!"

Doba-Leya began snarling and growling. She grabbed Simon-Volf's invalid cart and tried to ram Broydin with it. Arye-Leib, as always, began spouting allegories and parables that crept up on byways toward an end that was not always clearly apparent.

He began with the parable about Rabbi Osiya, who had given his property to his children, his heart to his wife, his fear to God, and his levy to Caesar, keeping for himself only a place beneath an olive tree where the setting sun shone the longest. From Rabbi Osiya, Arye-Leib moved on to planks for a new coffin, and to rations.

Broydin spread his long-legginged legs, and listened without raising his eyes. The brown fringe of his beard lay motionless on his new jacket. He seemed immersed in sad, tranquil thought.

"Forgive me, Arye-Leib," Broydin sighed, turning to the cemetery sage. "Forgive me, but I must say that I cannot but see ulterior motives and political goals here. Standing behind you, I cannot but see people who know exactly what they are doing, just as you know exactly what you are doing."

Broydin raised his eyes. In a flash they filled with the white water of fury. He trained the trembling hills of his pupils on the old folk.

"Arye-Leib!" Broydin said in his powerful voice. "I want you to read this telegram from the Tatar Republic, where an immense number of Tatars are starving like madmen! Read the petition of the Petersburg proletariat who are working and waiting, hungering by their benches!"

"I don't have time to wait!" Arye-Leib interrupted Broydin. "I have no time!"

"There are people," Broydin continued without listening, "who have it worse than you do, and there are thousands of people who have it worse than the people who have it worse than you do! You are sowing trouble, Arye-Leib, and a whirlwind is what you shall reap. You are as good as dead if I turn my back on you. You will die if I go my way and you go yours. You will die, Arye-Leib. You will die, Simon-Volf. You will die, Meyer Beskonechny. But tell me one thing, just one thing, before you die—do we have a Soviet government, or could it be that we do not? If we do not have a Soviet government, if it's all in my imagination, then I would be grateful if you would be so kind as to take me back to Mr. Berzon's on the corner of Deribasovskaya and Ekaterininskaya Streets, where I worked as a tailor sewing vests all my life! Tell me, Arye-Leib, is the Soviet government all in my imagination?"

And Broydin came right up to the old cripples. His quivering pupils broke loose and went hurtling over the groaning, petrified herd like searchlights, like tongues of flame. Broydin's leggings crackled, and sweat stewed on his furrowed face. He came closer and closer to Arye-Leib, demanding an answer to whether it was all in his imagination that the Soviet government was now in power.

Arye-Leib remained silent. This silence might have been the end of him, had not Fedka Stepun appeared at the end of the walk, barefoot and in a sailor's shirt.

Fedka had been shell-shocked near Rostov and lived in a hut next to the cemetery, recovering. He wore a whistle on an orange police cord and carried a revolver without a holster.

Fedka was drunk. The locks of his rock-hard curls rested on his forehead. Beneath his locks his face, with its high cheekbones, was twisted by convulsions. He walked up to Lugovoy's grave, which was surrounded by wilted wreaths.

"Where were you, Lugovoy, when I took Rostov?" Fedka asked the dead man.

Fedka gnashed his teeth, blew his police whistle, and pulled the revolver from his belt. The revolver's burnished muzzle glittered.

"They've trampled on the czars," Fedka shouted. "There are no czars! Let them all lie without coffins!"

Fedka was clutching his revolver. His chest was bare. On it were tattooed the name "Riva" and a dragon, its head inclined toward a nipple.

The gravediggers crowded around Fedka with their raised shovels. The women who were washing corpses came out of their sheds ready to join Doba-Leya in her howling. Roaring waves beat against the locked cemetery gates.

People with dead relatives on wheelbarrows demanded to be let in. Beggars banged their crutches against the fence.

"They've trampled on the czars!" Fedka shouted, firing into the sky.

The people came hopping and jumping up the cemetery walk. Broydin's face slowly turned white. He raised his hand, agreed to all the demands of the almsfolk, and, with a soldierly about-turn, went back to his office. At that very instant the gates burst open. Pushing their wheelbarrows in front of them, the relatives of the dead briskly hurried down the paths. Self-proclaimed cantors sang "*El moley rakhim*"* in piercing falsettos over open graves. In the evening the old folk celebrated their victory at Krivoruchka's. They gave Fedka three quarts of Bessarabian wine.

"*Hevel havolim*," Arye-Leib said, clinking glasses with Fedka. "You're one of us, one of us! *Kuloy hevel*."†

The mistress of the wine cellar, Krivoruchka's wife, was washing glasses behind the partition.

"When a Russian man is blessed with a good character," Madame Krivoruchka commented, "it's a rare luxury!"

---

*Hebrew: *El maley rakhamim*, "God is filled with mercy." A prayer traditionally chanted at burials.

†Hebrew quotations from the Bible (Ecclesiastes 12:8), *Hevel havolim*, "vanity of vanities," and *Kuloy hevel*, "All is vanity."

Fedka was led out of the wine cellar after one in the morning. *"Hevel havolim."* He muttered the dire, incomprehensible words as he tottered along Stepovaya Street. *"Kuloy hevel."*

On the following day the old folk of the almshouse were each given four sugar cubes, and there was meat in their borscht. In the evening they were taken to the Odessa City Theater to a performance organized by the Department of Social Assistance. A performance of *Carmen*. It was the first time in their lives that these invalids and cripples saw an Odessa theater's gilt tiers, the velvet of its loges, and the oily sparkle of its chandeliers. During intermission they were given liver-sausage sandwiches.

An army truck took them back to the cemetery. It rolled through the deserted streets, banging and sputtering. The old folk slept with full stomachs. They belched in their sleep and shuddered with satiation, like dogs who have run so much they can run no more.

The next morning, Arye-Leib got up earlier than the rest. He faced east to say his prayers and saw a notice pinned to the door, in which Broydin announced that the almshouse was going to be closed for renovations and that all its wards were to report immediately to the local Department of Social Assistance for their employability to be reassessed.

The sun emerged over the green treetops of the cemetery grove. Arye-Leib raised his hand to his eyes. A tear dropped from the spent hollows.

The shining chestnut walk stretched toward the mortuary. The chestnuts were in bloom, the trees bore tall white blossoms on their spreading boughs. An unknown woman with a shawl tied tautly under her breasts was working in the mortuary. Everything had been redone—the walls decorated with fir branches, the tables scraped clean. The woman was washing an infant. She nimbly turned it from side to side, the water pouring in a diamond stream over its crushed, blotchy little back.

Broydin was sitting on the mortuary steps in his leggings. He sat there like a man of leisure. He took off his cap and wiped his forehead with a yellow handkerchief.

"That's exactly what I said to Comrade Andreychik at the union," said the melodious voice of the unknown woman. "We're not afraid of work! Let them go ask about us in Ekaterinoslav—Ekaterinoslav knows how we work.*

"Make yourself at home, Comrade Blyuma, make yourself at home," Broydin said placidly, sticking his yellow handkerchief into his pocket. "I'm easy enough to get along with, yes, I'm easy enough to get along with!" he repeated, and turned his sparkling eyes to Arye-Leib, who had dragged himself all the way up to the stoop. "As long as you don't spit in my kasha."

Broydin did not finish what he was saying. A buggy harnessed to a large black horse pulled up at the gate. Out of the buggy stepped the director of the Communal Economics Department, wearing a fine shirt. Broydin rushed over to help him out of the buggy and, bowing and scraping, took him to the cemetery.

The former tailor's apprentice showed his director a century of Odessan history resting beneath the granite tombstones. He showed him the vaults and memorials of the wheat exporters, shipping brokers, and merchants who had built Russia's Marseille on the site of Khadzhibei.† They all lay here, their faces toward the gate, the Ashkenazis, Gessens, and Efrussis—the lustrous misers and philosophical bon vivants, the creators of wealth and Odessa anecdotes. They lay beneath their labradorite and rose-marble memorials, shielded by chains of acacias and chestnut trees from the plebes clumped against the wall.

"They wouldn't let us live while they were alive," Broydin said, kicking a memorial with his boot. "And after their death they wouldn't let us die."

Inspired, he told the director of the Communal Economics Department about his reorganization program for the cemetery and his campaign plan against the Jewish Burial Brotherhood.

"And get rid of them over there too," the director said, pointing to the beggars who had gathered by the gate.

"I am already seeing to that," Broydin answered. "Step by step, everything's being taken care of."

---

* Broydin has hired cemetery workers from outside Odessa to take over the funerary duties of the old folk from the almshouse. Ekaterinoslav in Eastern Ukraine has been renamed Dnipropetrovsk.

†Khadzhibei was the small settlement where in 1794 Czarina Catherine II decided to build a powerful Black Sea harbor, which she then renamed Odessa.

"Well, keep up the good work," Mayorov,* the director, said. "I see you have things under control here. Keep up the good work!"

He placed his boot on the buggy's footboard, but suddenly remembered Fedka.

"By the way, who was that clown back there?"

"Just some shell-shocked fellow," Broydin said, lowering his eyes. "There are times when he loses control of himself—but he's been straightened out, and he apologizes."

"That Broydin knows his onions," Mayorov told his companion, as they drove off. "He's handling things well."

The large horse took Mayorov and the director of the Department of Public Services into town. On the way, they passed the old men and women who had been thrown out of the almshouse. They were hobbling along the road in silence, bent under their bundles. Spirited Red Army fighters were herding them into lines. The invalid carts of the paralyzed were screeching. Asthmatic whistling and humble wheezing tore from the chests of the retired cantors, wedding jesters, circumcision-feast cooks, and washed-up sales clerks.

The sun stood high in the sky. The heat tore into the hearts of the heaps of rags dragging themselves along the earth. Their journey lay along a joyless, scorched, stony high road, past shacks of straw and clay, fields smothered by rocks, gutted houses mangled by shells, and past the plague mound.† This inexpressibly sad Odessan high road led from the town to the cemetery.

---

*Mikhail Moisevich Mayorov (born Meyer Biberman), 1890–1938, like Broydin also originally a tailor by profession, became the director of the Communal Economics Department in July 1920.

†A huge sepulchral mound in which victims of the 1812 plague were buried.

SUNSET

*O*ne day Lyovka, the youngest of the Kriks, saw Lyubka's daughter Tabl. "Tabl" in Yiddish means dove. He saw her and left home for three days and nights. The dust of other streets and the geraniums in other people's windows were a comfort to him. After three days and nights, Lyovka came back home and found his father in the front garden. His father was eating supper. Madame Gorobchik was sitting next to her husband with murder in her eyes.

"Get out of here, you lout!" Papa Krik said to Lyovka when he saw him.

"Papa, pick up your tuning fork and tune your ears," Lyovka said to him.

"What might be the issue?"

"There is this girl," Lyovka said. "She's got blond hair on her head. Her name is Tabl. 'Tabl' in Yiddish means dove. I've clapped my eyes on that girl!"

"You've clapped your eyes on a slop bucket!" Papa Krik said. "And her mother is a gangster!"

On hearing these paternal words, Lyovka rolled up his sleeves and raised a sacrilegious hand to his father. But Madame Gorobchik jumped up from her chair and threw herself between them.

"Mendel!" she screeched. "Bash in Lyovka's ugly kisser! Lyovka, he ate eleven from my meatballs!"

"What? You ate eleven meatballs from your mother?" Mendel shouted, lunging at his son. But Lyovka dodged his blow and ran out of the yard, and Benchik, his older brother, ran with him. They roamed the streets until nightfall, seething like yeast in which vengeance is brewing, and finally Lyovka turned to his brother Benya, who within a few months was destined to become Benya the King: "Benchik," he said, "let's act now, and people will be lining up to kiss our feet. Let's kill Papa. The Moldavanka no longer calls him Mendel Krik. The Moldavanka is calling him Mendel the Pogrom. Let's kill Papa—can we wait any longer?"

"No, the time hasn't come yet," Benya answered. "But the time is coming. Listen to its footsteps and make way for it. You must step aside, Lyovka."

And Lyovka stepped aside to make way for time. Time, that ancient bookkeeper, set out, and along the way met Dvoira, the King's sister, Manasseh, the carter, and a Russian girl called Marusya Yevtushenko.

Ten years ago I still knew men who might have wanted Dvoira, the daughter of Mendel the Pogrom, but now goiter is dangling beneath her chin and her eyes are bulging from their sockets. Nobody wants Dvoira. And yet only recently an elderly widower with grown daughters appeared. He wanted a cart and two horses. When Dvoira heard the news, she rushed off to wash her green dress and hung it in the yard to dry. She wanted to call at the widower's to find out how old he was, what kind of horses he wanted, and whether she could get him. But Papa Krik didn't like widowers. He took the green dress, hid it in his cart, and left for work. Dvoira heated up the flatiron so she could press her dress, but the dress was nowhere to be found, and Dvoira threw herself on the ground and had a fit. Her brothers dragged her to the water pipe and poured water over her. So, my friends, can you see the workings of their father's, Mendel the Pogrom's, hand?

And now to Manasseh, the old carter, who harnessed Maid of Honor and Solomon the Wise. To his misfortune, he heard that old Butsis, Froim Grach, and Chaim Drong had their horses shod with rubber. Following their example, Manasseh went over to Pyatirubel and had Solomon the Wise shod with rubber. Manasseh loved Solomon the Wise, but Papa Krik told him, "I'm not Chaim Drong and I'm not Czar Nicholas II, that my horses should go to work in rubber soles!" And he grabbed Manasseh by the collar, lifted him up into his cart, and went riding out of the courtyard with him. Manasseh was dangling from Papa Krik's outstretched arm as from a gallows. The sunset was boiling in the skies, a sunset thick as jam, the bells of Alekseyevsky Church moaned, and the sun was sinking behind Blizhniye Melnitsy,* and Lyovka, the younger son of the house, ran after the cart like a dog running after its master.

An immense crowd followed the Kriks as if they were an ambulance cart, Manasseh still hanging from Papa Krik's iron grip.

"Papa, you are crushing my heart with your outstretched hand!" Lyovka shouted over to his father. "Drop my heart, let it roll in the dust!"

But Mendel didn't even turn around. The horses galloped, the wheels thundered, and the people enjoyed the circus. The cart veered into Dalnitskaya Street, to Ivan Pyatirubel the blacksmith. Mendel threw Manasseh against the wall of the smithy and then hurled him onto a heap of scrap iron. Lyovka ran off to get a bucket of water, and threw it over the old carter Manasseh. So, my friends, can you see the workings of Papa Krik's, Mendel the Pogrom's, hand?

"Time is coming," Benchik had said, and his brother had stepped aside to make way for time. And so Lyovka stood to the side until Marusya Yevtushenko got knocked up.

"Marusya's got knocked up," people whispered, and Papa Krik laughed when he heard them.

"Marusya's got knocked up," he said, laughing like a boy. "Woe unto Israel! And who is this Marusya?"

Benya was just coming out of the stables and laid his hand on his father's shoulder.

"I am a fan of women's!" Benchik said sternly to his papa, and gave him twenty-five rubles, because he wanted the cleanup to be done by a doctor in a hospital, and not at Marusya's house.

"I'll give her the money," his papa said, "and she can do a cleanup, or I won't live to see a happy day."

And the following morning, at the usual time, he harnessed Baby Burglar and Loving Wife, and drove off. But around lunchtime, Marusya Yevtushenko came to the Kriks' courtyard.

---

*"Near Mills," a poor factory and shantytown suburb.

"Benchik," she said, "I loved you, you bastard!"

And she hurled ten rubles in his face. Put two fivers together and they never come to more than a tenner.

"We're going to kill Papa," Benchik said to Lyovka, and they sat down on a bench by the gates, and next to them sat Semyon, Anisim the janitor's son, who was seven years old. And who would have thought that a little seven-year-old ragamuffin already has love in his heart as well as hatred? Who would think that he loved Mendel the Pogrom? But love him he did.

The brothers sat on the bench trying to figure out how old their papa was, and how long the hidden tail of years behind his admitted sixty might be, and Semyon, the janitor's son, was sitting next to them.

At that hour the sun had not yet reached Blizhniye Melnitsy. It poured into the clouds like the blood of a gouged boar, and the carts of old Butsis went rumbling through the streets, returning from work. The milkmaids were already milking the cows for the third time, and Madame Parabellum's women were dragging the pails of evening milk up onto her stoop. Madame Parabellum stood on the stoop and clapped her hands.

"Women! My own women, and the rest too!" she shouted. "Berta Ivanovna, ice-cream makers, and kefir makers! Come get your evening milk!"

Berta Ivanovna, a German language teacher who received two quarts of milk per lesson, was the first to be poured her portion. Right after her came Dvoira Krik, with an eye out to check how much water Madame Parabellum might have added to her milk and how much baking soda.

But Benya pulled his sister aside.

"This evening, if you see the old man has killed us, then go right up to him and smash his head in with your iron colander. And may that be the end of the firm of Mendel Krik and Sons!"

"Amen! And joyful the day will be!" Dvoira answered, and went outside the gates. And she saw that Semyon, Anisim's son, was no longer in the courtyard and that the whole of the Moldavanka was coming over to the Kriks'.

The Moldavanka was arriving in droves, as if a wake were being held in the Kriks' yard. The people came running as they come running to a country fair on the second day of Passover. Ivan Pyatirubel the blacksmith came with his pregnant daughter-in-law and his grandchildren. Old Butsis brought along his niece, who had just come on a boat from Kamenets-Podolsk. Tabl came with a Russian man. She was leaning on his arm and twirling the ribbon of her braid. Last of all came Lyubka, galloping in on her roan stallion. And only Froim Grach came all alone, redheaded as rust, one-eyed, and in a sailcloth cloak.

The people sat down in the front garden and unpacked the food they had brought with them. Workers took off their shoes, sent their children to get beer, and rested their heads on their wives' stomachs. And Lyovka said to Benchik, his brother, "Mendel the Pogrom is our father," he said, "Madame Gorobchik is our mother, and these people here are dogs! We are working for dogs!"

"We must think things through," Benya answered, but no sooner had he uttered these words than there was a roll of thunder on Golovkovskaya Street. The sun soared up into the sky and spun like a red bowl on the tip of a spear. Old Krik's cart came flying toward the gates. Darling Wife was covered in lather, and Baby Burglar was straining in his harness. The old man raised his whip over the crazed horses. His powerful legs were firmly planted on the cart, crimson sweat was seething on his face, and he was singing a song in a drunken voice. And suddenly Semyon, Anisim's son, slithered through somebody's legs like a snake and went scuttling out onto the street, shouting at the top of his voice, "Turn back the cart, Uncle Krik! Your sons want to give you a beating!"

But it was too late. Papa Krik flew into the courtyard with his foaming horses. He lifted his whip, opened his mouth, and—was struck dumb. The people sitting in his front garden were staring at him. Benya was standing on the left side of the yard by the dovecote. Lyovka was standing on the right side of the yard by the janitor's hut.

"People, neighbors!" Mendel Krik said barely audibly, lowering his whip. "Take a look at my own flesh and blood lifting a hand to strike me!"

And the old man jumped off the cart and hurled himself at Benya and smashed his nose with his fist. Lyovka came running, and did all he could do. He shuffled his father's face like a fresh deck of cards. But the old man was sewn of the devil's hide, and the stitches of this hide were reinforced with cast iron. The old man wrenched Lyovka's arms back and threw him on the ground next to his brother. He sat on Lyovka's chest, and the women closed their eyes so as not to see the old man's broken teeth and his face covered with blood. And at that moment the people of the indescribable Moldavanka heard Dvoira's voice and fast steps.

"This is for Lyovka," she said, "and for Benchik, and for me, Dvoira, and for all the others!" And she smashed her father's head with the heavy iron colander. The people jumped up and came running toward them, waving their arms. They dragged the old man to the water pipe as Dvoira had once been dragged, and turned on the faucet. Blood flowed like water into the gutter, and the water flowed like blood. Madame Gorobchik elbowed her way through the crowd, hopping up to them like a sparrow.

"Don't be silent, Mendel," she said in a whisper. "Yell something, Mendel.

But she heard the silence in the courtyard, and saw that the old man had just come from work, that the horses had not been unharnessed, and that nobody had poured water on the heated wheels, and so she went scuttling through the courtyard like a three-legged dog. And the honorable citizens drew closer. Papa Krik lay with his beard pointing upward.

"He's done for!" Froim Grach said, and turned away.

"Cashed in his rubles!" Chaim Drong said, but Ivan Pyatirubel the blacksmith waved his finger right in front of Chaim's nose.

"Three against one," Pyatirubel said. "A disgrace for all Moldavanka, but it's not night yet. I have yet to meet a fellow who could finish off old Krik!"

"It *is* night!" Arye-Leib cut in, suddenly appearing out of nowhere. "It *is* night, Ivan Pyatirubel. *Oy,* Russian man, do not say it isn't, when everything around you yells that it is!"

And Arye-Leib squatted down next to Papa Krik and wiped his mouth with a handkerchief, kissed his forehead, and told him about King David, the King of all the Jews, who had many wives, much land and treasure, and who could always weep when the time was right.

"Stop whining, Arye-Leib!" Chaim Drong shouted, thumping him on the back. "Don't read us a funeral service, you're not in your cemetery now!" He turned to Papa Krik and said, "Get up, you old drayman! Wet your whistle, say something foul like you always do, you old roughneck, and get a couple of carts ready for the morning—I have some trash I want carted off!"

And all the people waited to see what Mendel would say about the carts. But for a long time he said nothing. Then he opened his eyes and his mouth, caked with dirt and hair, blood seeping from his lips.

"I don't have no carts," Papa Krik said. "My sons have killed me. Let them take over."

And yet they who were to take over Mendel Krik's bitter inheritance were not to be envied. They were not to be envied because all the hay troughs in the stable had long been rotting away, and half the wheels needed to be refitted. The sign above the gates had fallen apart, you couldn't read a single word, and none of the carters had even a single pair of underpants left. Half the town owed money to Mendel Krik, but his horses licked the numbers written in chalk on the walls as they browsed for oats in their feeding troughs. All day long muzhiks came to the dumbfounded heirs demanding money for chaff and barley. All day long women came to get their golden rings and nickel-plated samovars out of pawn. Peace left the house of the Kriks, but Benya, who within a few months was destined to become Benya the King, did not give up, and ordered a new sign: "Horse-Carting Establishment Mendel Krik & Sons." He wanted this to be written in gold letters on a sky-blue background with garlands of horseshoes painted bronze surrounding them. He also bought a bale of sailcloth ticking so that underwear for his carters could be made, and an unheard-of amount of timber to repair the carts. He hired Pyatirubel for a whole week and wrote out receipts for each customer. And—you can believe what I am telling you—by the evening of the following day he was more worn out than if he had made fifteen trips from the Watermelon Docks to the Odessa Tovarnaya Railroad Depot. And in the evening—you can believe what I am telling you—he didn't find so much as a crumb of bread or a single washed plate. Try fathoming the passionate barbarism of Madame Gorobchik! The dirt lay unswept in the rooms, an unprecedented pot of jellied veal was thrown to the dogs. And Madame Gorobchik stood by her husband's bed like a mud-drenched crow on an autumn branch.

"Keep an eye on them," Benchik told his younger brother, "keep our two newlyweds under a microscope, because I tell you Lyovka, it looks to me like they're cooking something up."

That is what Lyovka was told by his brother Benchik, who could see through everything with the eyes of Benya the King, but Lyovka, the second fiddle, didn't believe him and went to sleep. His papa was already snoring on the boards, while Madame Gorobchik was tossing and turning. She kept spitting onto the wall and the floor. Her malicious character kept her from sleeping. But in the end she too fell asleep. The stars scattered in front of the window like urinating soldiers, green stars on a blue field. A gramophone at Petka Ovsyanitsy's house across the street played Jewish songs. Then the gramophone fell silent. The night went about its business, and the air, the rich air, poured through the window to Lyovka, the youngest of the Kriks. He loved the air, Lyovka did. He lay there, breathing, dozing, frolicking with the air. He savored this richness until he heard rustling and creaking from his father's bed. Lyovka closed his eyes and made his ears stand to attention. Papa Krik raised his head like a mouse sniffing the air, and got out of bed. The old man pulled a bag of money out from under his pillow and swung his boots over his shoulder. Lyovka let him go—for where could he get to, the old dog? So Lyovka crept after his father, and also saw Benchik come creeping along the wall on the other side of the courtyard. The old man stole quietly to the carts and stuck his head in the stable. He whistled to the horses, and the horses came running to rub their muzzles on Mendel's head. Night was in the courtyard, night filled with stars, blue air, and silence.

"Sh!" Lyovka said, laying his finger on his lips, and Benchik, who came creeping from the other side of the yard, also laid his finger on his lips. Papa whistled to the horses as if they were little children, and then went running between the carts and up to the gate.

"Anisim," he said in a soft voice, tapping against the window of the janitor's shed. "Anisim, dear friend, unlock the gates for me."

Anisim, rumpled as hay, came crawling out of the janitor's shed.

"I beg you, master," he said. "Don't grovel before me, a simple man. Go back to your bed, master."

"You will open the gates for me," Papa whispered even more softly. "I know you will, my friend."

"Go back inside, Anisim," Benchik said, coming over to the janitor's shed and laying his hand on his papa's shoulder. And right before his eyes Anisim saw Mendel the Pogrom's face, white as paper, and he turned away so that he would not see his master with such a face.

"Don't hit me, Benchik," old Krik said, stepping back. "When will your father's torture end?"

"Oh, low-down father!" Benchik said. "How could you say what you just said?"

"I could!" Mendel shouted, and banged his fist against his head. "I could, Benchik!" he yelled with all his might, staggering like an epileptic. "This courtyard around me, in which I have served a sentence for half my life. This courtyard has seen me be the father of my children, the husband of my wife, the master of my horses. It has seen my glory, and that of my twenty stallions and my twelve iron-reinforced carts. It has seen my legs, unshakable as pillars, and my arms, my evil arms. But now unlock the gates for me, my dear sons, today let me for once do as I wish! Let me leave this courtyard that has seen too much!"

"Papa," Benya said to him without raising his eyes. "Go back inside to your wife."

But there was no point in going back inside to Madame Gorobchik. She herself came rushing out and threw herself on the ground, kicking the air with her old yellow legs.

"Oy!" she shouted, rolling on the ground. "Mendel the Pogrom and bastard sons! What have you done to me, you bastards? What have you done to my hair, my body, where are my teeth, where is my youth?"

The old woman shrieked, tore her blouse from her shoulders, and, getting to her feet, went running in circles like a dog trying to bite its tail. She scratched her sons' faces, she kissed her sons' faces, and ripped at their cheeks.

"You old thief!" Madame Gorobchik yelled, hobbling around her husband, twisting his mustache and tugging at it. "You're an old thief, my darling Mendel!"

All the neighbors were awakened by her yelling. Everyone came running to the gate, and bare-bellied children began tooting on their whistles. All Moldavanka came running, eager for scandal. And Benya

Krik, gray with shame in front of everyone, barely managed to jostle his "newlyweds" back into the house. He chased the people away with a stick, herding them toward the gates, but Lyovka, his younger brother, grabbed him by the collar and shook him like a pear tree.

"Benchik," he said, "we are torturing the old man! Tears are gnawing at me, Benchik!"

"Tears are gnawing at you, are they?" Benchik said to Lyovka, and sucking the spit together in his mouth, spat in Lyovka's face. "You are the lowest of the low," he whispered. "You disgust me! Don't tie my hands, and don't get tangled between my feet!"

And Lyovka didn't tie his hands. He slept in the stables until dawn and then disappeared from the house. The dust of other streets and the geraniums in other people's windows were a comfort to him. The young man walked the roads of sorrow, disappeared for two days and nights, came back on the third day, and saw the blue sign floating above the Kriks' house. The blue sign struck him to the heart, and the velvet tablecloths knocked his eyes right off their feet. The velvet tablecloths were spread over tables, and a large crowd of guests was laughing in the front garden. Dvoira was walking among the guests in a white headdress, starched women glittered in the grass like enameled teapots, and staggering workmen, who had already thrown off their jackets, grabbed Lyovka and pushed him into the house. Mendel Krik, the eldest of the Kriks, was sitting there, his face bruised. Usher Boyarsky, the owner of the firm Chef d'oeuvre, his hunchbacked cutter Efim, and Benya Krik, were all circling around the disfigured father.

"Efim," Usher Boyarsky said to his cutter, "be so kind as to come a little closer and measure Monsieur Krik for one of our *prima* striped suits, like he's family, and make so bold as to inquire what material the gentleman would prefer—English naval double-breasted, English civilian single-breasted, Lodz *demi-saison*, or thick Moscow cloth?"

"What kind of suit would you prefer?" Benchik asked Papa Krik. "Confess to Monsieur Boyarsky."

"What you feel in your heart is good enough for your father," Papa Krik said, wiping away a tear, "that's the kind of suit you'll have him make."

"Well, since Papa isn't a navy man," Benya interrupted his father, "a civilian would suit him better. First of all choose a suit for him for everyday use."

Monsieur Boyarsky bent forward and cupped his ear.

"What, pray, might you have in mind?"

"This is what I have in mind. . . ."

The Red Cavalry Stories

In late May 1920, the First Cavalry of the Soviet Red Army, under the command of General Budyonny, rode into Volhynia, today the border region of western Ukraine and eastern Poland. The Russian-Polish campaign was under way, the new Soviet government's first foreign offensive, which was viewed back in Moscow as the first step toward spreading the doctrines of World Revolution to Poland, then to Europe, then to the world.

Babel chronicled this campaign in his RED CAVALRY stories, later to become the most well-known and enduring of his literary legacy. These loosely linked stories take the reader from the initial triumphant assault against the "Polish masters" to the campaigns of the summer of 1920, and the increasingly bitter defeats that led to the wild retreat of the cavalry in the autumn. Babel blends fiction and fact, creating a powerful effect that is particularly poignant in his rendering of the atrocities of war. The stories were published in magazines and newspapers between 1923 and 1926; the reading public was torn between delight at Babel's potent new literary voice and horror at the brutality portrayed in the stories. In 1926, thirty-four of the stories were included in the book KONARMIA (translated into English as

Volhynia
1920

Kovel

Zamosc Czesniki

Pniowek Komarov

Terebin

Laszczow

Vladimir-Volynsk

Budyatichi

Kivertsy

Lutsk

Novosel

Mali
Dorogos

Sokal

Belz

Vitkov

Berestechko

Demidoka

Du

Grzhimalovka

Boratin Pelch

Toporov Leshniov Khotin Verb

Bielavtsy Kozin

Adamy

Radzivillov

Brody

Kremene

Lvov

Milatin

Busk

Bug R.

PRESENT POLISH-UKRAINIAN BORDER

Dniester R.

RED CAVALRY), which quickly went into eight editions and was translated into English, French, Italian, Spanish, and German. It immediately turned Babel into an international literary figure and made him into one of the Soviet Union's foremost writers.

The stories, as Babel himself repeatedly stressed, were fiction set against a real backdrop. Literary effect was more important to Babel than historical fact. Babel might also have felt more comfortable reconfiguring military strategy that might still have been classified when the stories began appearing in newspapers and magazines in the first years after the war. Novograd-Volynsk, for instance, the town in the first story, lies on the river Slucz, not on the Zbrucz as the story indicates. (The Zbrucz runs along the western frontier of Volhynia, along the former border between the kingdom of Poland and Russia.) Also, Novograd-Volynsk was not occupied by the Red Cavalry, but by the Soviet 14th Army. As the historian Norman Davies has pointed out, a high road from Warsaw to Brest had been built by serfs under Nicholas I, but it lay two hundred miles beyond the front at Novograd-Volynsk, and so could not have been cluttered by the rear guard.

One of Babel's strategies for creating a sharper feeling of reality in his stories was to mix real people with fictional characters. This was to have serious repercussions. General Budyonny, for instance, the real-life commander of the cavalry, often comes across in the stories as brutal, awkward, and irresolute. Babel makes fun of his oafish and uneducated Cossack speech. In the story "Czesniki," Budyonny is asked to give his men a speech before battle: "Budyonny shuddered, and said in a quiet voice, 'Men! Our situations . . . well, it's . . . bad. A bit more liveliness, men!'"

Babel had, of course, no way of knowing that General Budyonny was to become a Marshal of the Soviet Union, First Deputy Commissar for Defense, and later "Hero of the Soviet Union." Another real character in the stories, Voroshilov, the military commissar, also does not always come across particularly well. The implication in "Czesniki" is that Voroshilov overrode the other commanders' orders, resulting in an overhasty attack that led to defeat. Voroshilov happened to be a personal friend of Stalin; he had become the People's Commissar of Defense by the time the RED CAVALRY collection was in print, and was destined to become Head of State. These were dangerous men to cross.

In these stories Babel uses different narrators, such as Lyutov, the young intellectual journalist, hiding his Jewishness and struggling to fit in with the Cossacks, and Balmashov, the murderous, bloodthirsty Cossack.

The Soviet Union wanted to forget this disastrous campaign, its first venture at bringing Communism to the world. Babel's RED CAVALRY stories, however, kept the fiasco in the public eye, both in the Soviet Union and abroad, throughout the 1920s and 1930s, and ever since.

CROSSING THE
RIVER ZBRUCZ

*T*he commander of the Sixth Division reported that Novograd-Volynsk was taken at dawn today. The staff is now withdrawing from Krapivno, and our cavalry transport stretches in a noisy rear guard along the high road that goes from Brest to Warsaw, a high road built on the bones of muzhiks by Czar Nicholas I.

Fields of purple poppies are blossoming around us, a noon breeze is frolicking in the yellowing rye, virginal buckwheat is standing on the horizon like the wall of a faraway monastery. Silent Volhynia is turning away, Volhynia is leaving, heading into the pearly white fog of the birch groves, creeping through the flowery hillocks, and with weakened arms entangling itself in the underbrush of hops. The orange sun is rolling across the sky like a severed head, gentle light glimmers in the ravines among the clouds, the banners of the sunset are fluttering above our heads. The stench of yesterday's blood and slaughtered horses drips into the evening chill. The blackened Zbrucz roars and twists the foaming knots of its rapids. The bridges are destroyed, and we wade across the river. The majestic moon lies on the waves. The water comes up to the horses' backs, purling streams trickle between hundreds of horses' legs. Someone sinks, and loudly curses the Mother of God. The river is littered with the black squares of the carts and filled with humming, whistling, and singing that thunders above the glistening hollows and the snaking moon.

Late at night we arrive in Novograd. In the quarters to which I am assigned I find a pregnant woman and two red-haired Jews with thin necks, and a third Jew who is sleeping with his face to the wall and a blanket pulled over his head. In my room I find ransacked closets, torn pieces of women's fur coats on the floor, human excrement, and fragments of the holy Seder plate that the Jews use once a year for Passover.

"Clean up this mess!" I tell the woman. "How can you live like this?"

The two Jews get up from their chairs. They hop around on their felt soles and pick up the broken pieces of porcelain from the floor. They hop around in silence, like monkeys, like Japanese acrobats in a circus, their necks swelling and twisting. They spread a ripped eiderdown on the floor for me, and I lie down by the wall, next to the third, sleeping Jew. Timorous poverty descends over my bed.

Everything has been killed by the silence, and only the moon, clasping its round, shining, carefree head in its blue hands, loiters beneath my window.

I rub my numb feet, lie back on the ripped eiderdown, and fall asleep. I dream about the commander of the Sixth Division. He is chasing the brigade commander on his heavy stallion, and shoots two bullets into his eyes. The bullets pierce the brigade commander's head, and his eyes fall to the ground. "Why did you turn back the brigade?" Savitsky, the commander of the Sixth Division, shouts at the wounded man, and I wake up because the pregnant woman is tapping me on the face.

"*Pan*,"* she says to me, "you are shouting in your sleep, and tossing and turning. I'll put your bed in another corner, because you are kicking my papa."

She raises her thin legs and round belly from the floor and pulls the blanket off the sleeping man. An old man is lying there on his back, dead. His gullet has been ripped out, his face hacked in two, and dark blood is clinging to his beard like a clump of lead.

"*Pan*," the Jewess says, shaking out the eiderdown, "the Poles were hacking him to death and he kept begging them, 'Kill me in the backyard so my daughter won't see me die!' But they wouldn't inconvenience themselves. He died in this room, thinking of me. . . . And now I want you to tell me," the woman suddenly said with terrible force, "I want you to tell me where one could find another father like my father in all the world!"

---

* Polish for "Sir" or "Mr."

THE CHURCH IN NOVOGRAD

*Y*esterday I took a report over to the military commissar who had been billeted to the house of a Catholic priest who had fled. In the kitchen I was met by *Pani** Eliza, the Jesuit's housekeeper. She gave me a cup of amber tea and some sponge cake. Her sponge cakes had the aroma of crucifixion. Within them was the sap of slyness and the fragrant frenzy of the Vatican.

In the church next to the house the bells were howling, tolled by the crazed bell ringer. It was an evening filled with the stars of July. *Pani* Eliza, shaking her attentive gray hair, kept on heaping cookies on my plate, and I delighted in the Jesuitical fare.

The old Polish woman addressed me as *"Pan,"* gray old men with ossified ears stood to attention near the door, and somewhere in the serpentine darkness slithered a monk's soutane. The *Pater* had fled, but he had left behind his curate, *Pan* Romuald.

Romuald was a eunuch with a nasal voice and the body of a giant, who addressed us as "Comrade." He ran his yellow finger along the map, circling the areas where the Poles had been defeated. He counted the wounds of his fatherland with rasping ecstasy. May gentle oblivion engulf the memory of Romuald, who betrayed us without pity and was then shot without so much as a second thought. But that evening his tight soutane rustled at all the portieres and swept through all the corridors in a frenzy, as he smiled at everyone who wanted a drink of vodka. That evening the monk's shadow crept behind me

*"Mrs." in Polish.

wherever I went. *Pan* Romuald could have become a bishop if he had not been a spy.

I drank rum with him. The breath of an alien way of life flickered beneath the ruins of the priest's house, and *Pan* Romuald's ingratiating seduction debilitated me. O crucifixes, tiny as the talismans of a courtesan! O parchment of the Papal Bull and satin of women's love letters moldering in blue silken waistcoats!

I can see you now, you deceptive monk with your purple habit, your puffy, swollen hands, and your soul, tender and merciless like a cat's! I can see the wounds of your God, oozing with the seed, the fragrant poison that intoxicates young maidens.

We drank rum, waiting for the military commissar, but he still hadn't come back from headquarters. Romuald had collapsed in a corner and fallen asleep. He slept and quivered, while beyond the window an alley seeped into the garden beneath the black passion of the sky. Thirsting roses swayed in the darkness. Green lightning bolts blazed over the cupolas. A naked corpse lay on the embankment. And the rays of the moon streamed through the dead legs that are pointing upward.

So this is Poland, this is the arrogant grief of the Rzeczpospolita Polska!* A violent intruder, I unroll a louse-ridden straw mattress in this church abandoned by its clergymen, lay under my head a folio in which a Hosanna has been printed for Jozef Pilsudski,† the illustrious leader of the Polish nobility.

Hordes of beggars are converging on your ancient towns, O Poland! The song of all the enslaved is thundering above them, and woe unto you, Rzeczpospolita Polska, and woe unto you, Prince Radziwill, and you Prince Sapieha,** who have risen for an hour.

My military commissar has still not returned. I go look for him at the headquarters, the garden, the church. The doors of the church are wide open, I enter, and suddenly come face-to-face with two silver skulls flashing up from the lid of a shattered coffin. Aghast, I stumble

---

* Poland's official name after 1918.

† Jozef Klemens Pilsudski, 1867–1935, the first Chief of State of Poland after its independence from Russia in 1918, and commander-in-chief of the Polish army.

** Janusz Radziwill, 1880–1967, politician belonging to an important Polish-Lithuanian princely family; Eustachy Sapieha, 1881–1963, was Polish envoy to London in 1919–20 and Polish Foreign Minister in 1920–21. Later he was a leader of the monarchist movement.

back and fall down into the cellar. The oak staircase leads up to the altar from here, and I see a large number of lights flitting high up, right under the cupola. I see the military commissar, the commander of the special unit, and Cossacks carrying candles. They hear my weak cry and come down to haul me out from the basement.

The skulls turn out to have been carved into the church catafalque and no longer frighten me. I join the others on their search of the premises, because it turned out that *that* was what they were doing in the church, conducting a search, as a large pile of military uniforms had been found in the priest's apartment.*

With wax dripping from our hands, the embroidered gold horse heads on our cuffs glittering, we whisper to one another as we circle with clinking spurs through the echoing building. Virgin Marys, covered with precious stones, watch us with their rosy, mouselike eyes, the flames flicker in our fingers, and rectangular shadows twist over the statues of Saint Peter, Saint Francis, Saint Vincent, and over their crimson cheeks and curly, carmine-painted beards.

We continue circling and searching. We run our fingers over ivory buttons and suddenly icons split open, revealing vaults and caverns blossoming with mold. This church is ancient and filled with secrets. Its lustrous walls hide clandestine passages, niches, and noiseless trapdoors.

You foolish priest, hanging the brassieres of your female parishioners on the nails of the Savior's cross! Behind the holy gates we found a suitcase of gold coins, a morocco-leather sackful of banknotes, and Parisian jewelers' cases filled with emerald rings.

We went and counted the money in the military commissar's room. Columns of gold, carpets of paper money, wind gusts blowing on our candle flames, the raven madness in the eyes of *Pani* Eliza, the thundering laughter of Romuald, and the endless roar of the bells tolled by *Pan* Robacki, the crazed bell ringer.

"I have to get away from here," I said to myself, "away from these winking Madonnas conned by soldiers."

---

*The humorous implication here is that when the narrator first saw the Cossack commanders carrying candles, he had assumed that these hard-line Communist fighters had come to the church to pray.

A LETTER

*H*ere is a letter home dictated to me by Kurdyukov, a boy in our regiment. This letter deserves to be remembered. I wrote it down without embellishing it, and am recording it here word for word as he said it.

Dearest Mama, Evdokiya Fyodorovna,

I hasten in these first lines of my letter to set your mind at rest and to inform you that by the grace of the Lord I am alive and well, and that I hope to hear the same from you. I bow most deepest before you, touching the moist earth with my white forehead. (There follows a list of relatives, godfathers, and godmothers. I am omitting this. Let us proceed to the second paragraph.)

Dearest Mama, Evdokiya Fyodorovna Kurdyukova, I hasten to inform you that I am in Comrade Budyonny's Red Cavalry Regiment, and that my godfather Nikon Vasilich is also here and is at the present time a Red Hero. He took me and put me in his special detachment of the Polit-otdel* in which we hand out books and newspapers to the various positions: the Moscow ZIK *Izvestia,*† the Moscow *Pravda,* and our own merciless newspaper the *Krasny Kavalerist,*** which every fighter on the front wants to read and then

---

* A political organ of the new Soviet government charged with the ideological education of the military during the Russian Civil War and the Russo-Polish War of 1920.

† The newspaper published by the Central Executive Committee, which was the executive branch of the new Bolshevik government.

** *The Red Cavalryman.*

go and heroically hack the damn Poles to pieces, and I am living real marvelous at Nikon Vasilich's.

Dearest Mama, Evdokiya Fyodorovna, send me anything that you possibly in any way can. I beg you to butcher our speckled pig and make a food packet for me, to be sent to Comrade Budyonny's Polit-otdel unit, addressed to Vasily Kurdyukov. All evenings I go to sleep hungry and bitterly cold without any clothes at all. Write to me a letter about my Stepan—is he alive or not, I beg you to look after him and to write to me about him, is he still scratching himself or has he stopped, but also about the scabs on his forelegs, have you had him shod, or not? I beg you dearest Mama, Evdokiya Fyodorovna, to wash without fail his forelegs with the soap. I hid behind the icons, and if Papa has swiped it all then buy some in Krasnodar, and the Lord will smile upon you. I must also describe that the country here is very poor, the muzhiks with their horses hide in the woods from our Red eagles, there's hardly no wheat to be seen, it's all scrawny and we laugh and laugh at it. The people sow rye and they sow oats too. Hops grow on sticks here so they come out very well. They brew home brew with them.

In these second lines of this letter I hasten to write you about Papa, that he hacked my brother Fyodor Timofeyich Kurdyukov to pieces a year ago now. Our Comrade Pavlichenko's Red Brigade attacked the town of Rostov, when there was a betrayal in our ranks. And Papa was with the Whites back then as commander of one of Denikin's companies. All the folks that saw Papa says he was covered in medals like with the old regime. And as we were betrayed, the Whites captured us and threw us all in irons, and Papa caught sight of my brother Fyodor Timofeyich. And Papa began hacking away at Fyodor, saying: you filth you, red dog, son of a bitch, and other things, and hacked away at him until sundown until my brother Fyodor Timofeyich died. I had started writing you a letter then, about how your Fyodor is lying buried without a cross, but Papa caught me and said: you are your mother's bastards, the roots of that whore, I've plowed your mother and I'll keep on plowing her my whole damn life till I don't have a drop of juice left in me, and other things. I had to bear suffering like our Savior Jesus Christ. I managed to run away from Papa in the nick of time and join up with the Reds again, Comrade Pavlichenko's company. And our brigade got the order to go to the town of Voronezh to get more men, and we got more men and horses too, bags, revolvers, and everything we needed.

About Voronezh, beloved Mama Evdokiya Fyodorovna, I can describe that it is indeed a marvelous town, a bit larger I think than Krasnodar, the people in it are very beautiful, the river is brilliant to the point of being able to swim. We were given two pounds of bread a day each, half a pound of meat, and sugar enough so that when you got up you drank sweet tea, and the same in the evenings, forgetting hunger, and for dinner I went to my brother Semyon Timofeyich for blini or goose meat and then lay down to rest. At the time, the whole regiment wanted to have Semyon Timofeyich for a commander because he is a wild one, and that order came from Comrade Budyonny, and Semyon Timofeyich was given two horses, good clothes, a cart specially for rags he's looted, and a Red Flag Medal, and they really looked up to me as I am his brother. Now when some neighbor offends you, then Semyon Timofeyich can completely slash him to pieces. Then we started chasing General Denikin, slashed them down by the thousand and chased them to the Black Sea, but Papa was nowhere to be seen, and Semyon Timofeyich looked for him in all the positions, because he mourned for our brother Fyodor. But only, dearest Mama, since you know Papa and his stubborn character, do you know what he did? He impudently painted his red beard black and was in the town of Maykop in civilian clothes, so that nobody there knew that he is he himself, that very same police constable in the old regime. But truth will always show its head—my godfather Nikon Vasilich saw him by chance in the hut of a townsman, and wrote my brother Semyon Timofeyich a letter. We got on horses and galloped two hundred versts—me, my brother Semyon, and boys which wants to come along from the Cossack village.

And what is it we saw in the town of Maykop? We saw that people away from the front, they don't give a damn about the front, and it's all full of betrayal and Yids like in the old regime. And my brother Semyon Timofeyich in the town of Maykop had a good row with the Yids who would not give Papa up and had thrown him in jail under lock and key, saying that a decree had come not to hack to pieces prisoners, we'll try him ourselves, don't be angry, he'll get what he deserves. But then Semyon Timofeyich spoke and proved that he was the commander of a regiment, and had been given all the medals of the Red Flag by Comrade Budyonny, and threatened to hack to pieces everyone who argued over Papa's person without handing him over, and the boys from the Cossack villages threatened them too. But then, the moment Semyon got hold of Papa, Semyon began whipping him, and lined up all the fighters in the yard as befits military order. And then Semyon splashed water all over Papa's beard and the color flowed from the beard. And Semyon asked our Papa, Timofey Rodyonich, "So, Papa, are you feeling good now that you're in my hands?"

"No," Papa said, "I'm feeling bad."

Then Semyon asked him, "And my brother Fyodor, when you were hacking him to pieces, did he feel good in your hands?"

"No," Papa said, "Fyodor was feeling bad."

Then Semyon asked him, "And did you think, Papa, that someday you might be feeling bad?"

"No," Papa said, "I didn't think that I might be feeling bad."

Then Semyon turned to the people and said, "And I believe, Papa, that if I fell into your hands, I would find no mercy. So now, Papa, we will finish you off!"

Timofey Rodyonich began impudently cursing Semyon, by Mama and the Mother of God, and slapping Semyon in the face, and Semyon sent me out of the yard, so that I cannot, dearest Mama, Evdokiya Fyodorovna, describe to you how they finished off Papa, because I had been sent out of the yard.

After that we stopped at the town of Novorossisk. About that town one can say that there isn't a single bit dry anywhere anymore, just water, the Black Sea, and we stayed there right until May, and then we set off for the Polish Front where we are slapping the Polish masters about in full swing.

I remain your loving son, Vasily Timofeyich Kurdyukov. Mama, look in on Stepan, and the Lord will smile upon you.

This is Kurdyukov's letter, without a single word changed. When I had finished, he took the letter and hid it against the naked flesh of his chest.

"Kurdyukov," I asked the boy, "was your father a bad man?"

"My father was a dog," he answered sullenly.

"And your mother?"

"My mother's good enough. Here's my family, if you want to take a look."

He held out a tattered photograph. In it was Timofey Kurdyukov, a wide-shouldered police constable in a policeman's cap, his beard neatly combed. He was stiff, with wide cheekbones and sparkling, colorless, vacant eyes. Next to him, in a bamboo chair, sat a tiny peasant woman in a loose blouse, with small, bright, timid features. And against this provincial photographer's pitiful backdrop, with its flowers and doves, towered two boys, amazingly big, blunt, broad-faced, goggle-eyed, and frozen as if standing at attention: the Kurdyukov brothers, Fyodor and Semyon.

THE RESERVE CAVALRY
COMMANDER

A wail spreads over the village. The cavalry is trampling the grain and trading in horses. The cavalrymen are exchanging their worn-out nags for the peasants' workhorses. One can't argue with what the cavalrymen are doing—without horses there can be no army.

But this isn't much of a comfort to the peasants. They are stubbornly gathering outside the headquarters, dragging behind them struggling old nags tottering with weakness. The muzhiks' breadwinners have been taken away from them, and with a surge of bitter valor, aware that this valor will not last long, they hurry to rant despairingly at the authorities, at God, and at their bitter lot.

Chief of Staff Z.* is standing on the front porch in full uniform. His inflamed eyelids half closed, he listens to the muzhiks' complaints with evident attention. But his attention is only a ploy. Like all disciplined and weary bureaucrats, he has a knack for shutting down all cerebral activity during empty moments of existence. During these moments of blissful empty-headedness our chief of staff recharges his worn-out instrument.

And this is what he is doing this time too, with the muzhiks.

To the soothing accompaniment of their desperate and disjointed clamor, Chief of Staff Z. cautiously follows his brain's soft wisps, those precursors of clear and energetic thought. He waits for the necessary pause, grasps the final muzhik sob, yells in a commanderial fashion, and returns to his office to work.

* Konstantin Karlovich Zholnarkevich, the staff commander in the *1920 Diary*.

But on this particular occasion even yelling would not have been necessary. Galloping up to the porch on an Anglo-Arabian steed came Dyakov,* a former circus rider and now commander of the Reserve Cavalry—red-faced with a gray mustache, a black cape, and wide red Tatar trousers with silver stripes.

"The Father Superior's blessing on all the honest filth of the earth!" he shouted, reining in his horse in front of the porch, and at that very instant a shabby little horse that had been given in exchange by the Cossacks collapsed in front of him.

"There, you see, Comrade Commander!" a muzhik shouted, slapping his thighs in despair. "There you have what your people are giving our people! Did you see what they've given us? And we're supposed to farm with that?"

"For this horse," Dyakov proclaimed distinctly and momentously, "for this horse, my highly esteemed friend, you have every right to request fifteen thousand rubles from the Reserve Cavalry, and if this horse were a trifle livelier, you, my dearest of friends, would be entitled to twenty thousand rubles. Just because a horse falls does not mean it's *factual*! If a horse falls but then gets up—that is a horse. If, to invert what I am saying, the horse does not get up—then that is not a horse. But I do believe I can make this lively little mare spring to her feet again!"

"Lord in Heaven and Mother of God!" the muzhik cried, throwing his hands up in the air. "How is this poor thing supposed to get up? It's on its last legs!"

"You are insulting this horse, my dear fellow!" Dyakov answered with fierce conviction. "Pure blasphemy, my dear fellow!" And he deftly swung his athlete's body out of his saddle. Splendid and deft as if in the circus ring, he stretched his magnificent legs, his trousers girded by cords around the knees, and walked up to the dying animal. She peered at him dolefully with a severe, penetrating eye, licked some invisible command from his crimson palm, and immediately the feeble mare felt bracing power flow from this sprightly, gray, blossoming Romeo. Her muzzle lolling, her legs skidding under her, feeling the whip tickling her stomach with imperious impatience, the mare slowly and deliber-

* For Dyakov, see *1920 Diary*, entries 7/13/20, and 7/16/20.

ately rose onto her legs. And then we all saw Dyakov's slender hand with its fluttering sleeve run through her dirty mane, and his whining whip swatting her bleeding flanks. Her whole body shivering, the mare stood on all four legs without moving her timid, doglike, lovestruck eyes from Dyakov.

"So you see—this is a horse," Dyakov said to the muzhik, and added softly, "and you were complaining, my dearest of friends!"

Throwing his reins to his orderly, the commander of the Reserve Cavalry jumped the four stairs in a single leap and, swirling off his operatic cloak, disappeared into the headquarters.

PAN APOLEK

*T*he wise and wonderful life of *Pan* Apolek went straight to my head, like an exquisite wine. Among the huddling ruins of Novograd-Volynsk, a town crushed in haste, fate threw at my feet a gospel that had remained hidden from the world. There, surrounded by the guileless shine of halos, I took a solemn oath to follow the example of *Pan* Apolek. The sweetness of dreamy malice, the bitter contempt for the swine and dogs among men, the flame of silent and intoxicating revenge—I sacrificed them all to this oath.

• • •

An icon was hanging high on the wall in the home of the Novograd priest, who had fled. It bore the inscription: "The Death of John the Baptist." There was no doubt about it: in the portrayal of John I saw a man I had seen somewhere before.

I remember the gossamer stillness of a summer morning hung on the bright, straight walls. The sun had cast a ray straight on the foot of the icon. Sparkling dust swarmed in it. The tall figure of John came straight at me from the blue depths of the niche. A black cape hung triumphantly on that inexorable, repulsively thin body. Droplets of blood shone in the cape's round buckles. His head had been hacked diagonally off the flayed neck. It lay on an earthen platter that was held by the large yellow fingers of a warrior. The face of the dead man seemed familiar. I was touched by a mysterious premonition. The hacked-off head on the earthen platter was modeled after *Pan* Romuald, the curate of the priest who had fled. Out of his snarling mouth curled the tiny body of a snake, its scales shining brightly. Its head, a tender pink, was bristling with life, and stood out powerfully against the deep background of the cape.

I was amazed at the painter's artistry, his dark inventiveness. I was even more amazed the following day when I saw the red-cheeked Virgin Mary hanging above the matrimonial bed of *Pani* Eliza, the old priest's housekeeper. Both paintings bore the marks of the same brush. The meaty face of the Virgin Mary was a portrait of *Pani* Eliza. And this is where I found the key to the mystery of the Novograd icons. And the key led me to *Pani* Eliza's kitchen, where on fragrant evenings the shadows of old servile Poland gather, with the holy fool of a painter at their center. But was *Pan* Apolek a holy fool, peopling the local villages with angels, and elevating lame Janek, the Jewish convert, to sainthood?

Pan Apolek had come here thirty years ago on a summer day like any other with blind Gottfried. The two friends, Apolek and Gottfried, had gone to Shmerel's tavern on the Rovno high road, two versts from the edge of the town. In his right hand Apolek was holding a box of paints, and with his left hand leading the blind concertina player. The melodious tread of their reinforced German boots echoed with calmness and hope. A canary-yellow scarf hung from Apolek's thin neck, and three chocolate-brown feathers swung on the blind man's Tyrolean hat.

The newcomers had placed the paints and the concertina on a windowsill in the tavern. The artist unwound his scarf, which was never-ending, like a fairground magician's ribbon. Then he went out into the yard, took off all his clothes, and poured freezing water over his thin, feeble, pink body. Shmerel's wife brought them raisin vodka and a bowl of meat cutlets stuffed with rice. Gottfried ate his fill, and then placed his concertina on his bony knees. He sighed, threw his head back, and flexed his thin fingers. The chords of the Heidelberg songs echoed against the walls of the Jewish tavern. With his scratchy voice Apolek accompanied the blind man. It was as if the organ had been brought from the Church of Saint Indegilda to Shmerel's tavern and the muses, with their quilted scarves and reinforced German boots, had seated themselves in a row upon this organ.

The two men sang till sunset, then they put the concertina and the paints into canvas sacks. *Pan* Apolek bowed deeply and gave Brayna, the taverner's wife, a sheet of paper.

"My dear *Pani* Brayna," he said. "Please accept from the hands of a wandering artist, upon whom the Christian name of Apollinarius has been bestowed, this portrait as a sign of our most humble gratitude for your sumptuous hospitality. If the Lord Jesus Christ sees fit to lengthen my days and give strength to my art, I will come back and add color to this portrait. There shall be pearls in your hair and a necklace of emeralds upon your breast."

Drawn on a small sheet of paper with a red pencil, a pencil red and soft like clay, was *Pani* Brayna's laughing face, surrounded by a mass of copper curls.

"My money!" Shmerel shouted when he saw his wife's portrait. He grabbed a stick and started running after the two men. But as he ran, Shmerel remembered Apolek's pink body with water splashing all over it, the sun in his little courtyard, and the soft sound of the concertina. The taverner's soul drooped, and, putting the stick down, he went back home.

The following morning, Apolek showed the priest of Novograd his diploma from the Munich Academy, and laid out before him twelve paintings with biblical motifs. They had been painted with oil on boards of thin cypress wood. On his table the *Pater* saw the burning purple of cloaks, the emerald sparkle of fields, and blossoming blankets of flowers flung over the plains of Palestine.

Pan Apolek's saints, a multitude of simple, jubilating elders with gray beards and red faces, were encircled by streams of silk and potent evening skies.

That same day, *Pan* Apolek was commissioned to do paintings for the new church. And over Benedictine wine, the *Pater* said to the artist: "Sancta Maria! My dear *Pan* Apollinarius, from what wondrous realms has your joyous grace descended upon us?"

Apolek worked with great zeal, and within a month the new church was filled with the bleating of herds, the dusty gold of setting suns, and straw-colored cow udders. Buffaloes with worn hides struggled under their yokes, dogs with pink muzzles trotted in front of the large flocks of sheep, and plump infants rocked in cradles that hung from the trunks of tall palm trees. The tattered brown habits of

Franciscan monks crowded around a cradle. The group of wise men stood out with their shining bald heads and their wrinkles red like wounds. The small, wrinkled old face of Pope Leo XIII twinkled with its fox-like smile from the group of wise men, and even the priest of Novograd was there, running the fingers of one hand through the carved beads of a Chinese rosary while with his other, free hand, he blessed the infant Jesus.

For five months Apolek inched along the walls, the cupola, and the choir stalls, fastened to the wooden scaffolding.

"You have a predilection for familiar faces, my dear *Pan* Apolek," the priest once said, recognizing himself among the wise men and *Pan* Romuald in the severed head of John the Baptist. The old *Pater* smiled, and sent a tumbler of cognac up to the artist working beneath the cupola.

Apolek finished the Last Supper and the Stoning of Mary Magdalene. Then one Sunday he unveiled the walls. The distinguished citizens the priest had invited recognized Janek the lame convert in the Apostle Paul, and in Mary Magdalene Elka, a Jewish girl of unknown parentage and mother of many of the urchins roaming the streets. The distinguished citizens demanded that the blasphemous images be painted over. The priest showered threats over the blasphemer, but Apolek refused to paint over the walls.

And so an unprecedented war broke out, with the powerful body of the Catholic Church on one side, and the unconcerned icon painter on the other. The war lasted for three decades. The situation almost turned the gentle idler into the founder of a new heresy; in which case he would have been the most whimsical and ludicrous fighter among the many in the slippery and stormy history of the Church of Rome, a fighter roaming the earth in blessed tipsiness with two white mice under his shirt and with a collection of the finest little brushes in his pocket.

"Fifteen zloty for the Virgin Mary, twenty-five zloty for the Holy Family, and fifty zloty for the Last Supper portraying all the client's family. The client's enemy can be portrayed as Judas Iscariot, for which an extra ten zloty will be added to the bill," *Pan* Apolek informed the peasants after he had been thrown out of the Novograd church.

There was no shortage of commissions. And when a year later the archbishop of Zhitomir sent a delegation in response to the frenzied epistles of the Novograd priest, they found the monstrous family portraits, sacrilegious, naive, and flamboyant, in the most impoverished, foul-smelling hovels. Josephs with gray hair neatly parted in the middle, pomaded Jesuses, many-childed village Marys with parted knees. The pictures hung in the icon corners, wreathed with garlands of paper flowers.

"He has bestowed sainthood upon you people during your lifetime!" the bishop of Dubno and Novokonstantinov shouted at the crowd that had come to defend Apolek. "He has endowed you with the ineffable attributes of the saints, you, thrice fallen into the sin of disobedience, furtive moonshiners, ruthless moneylenders, makers of counterfeit weights, and sellers of your daughters' innocence!"

"Your holiness!" lame-footed Witold, the town's cemetery watchman and procurer of stolen goods, then said to the bishop. "Where does our all-forgiving Lord God see truth, and who will explain it to these ignorant villagers? Is there not more truth in the paintings of *Pan* Apolek, who raises our pride, than in your words that are filled with abuse and tyrannical anger?"

The shouts of the crowd sent the bishop running. The agitation in the villages threatened the safety of the clerics. The painter who had taken Apolek's place could not work up the courage to paint over Elka and lame Janek. They can still be seen today above a side altar of the Novograd church: Janek, as Saint Paul, a timorous cripple with the shaggy black beard of a village apostate, and Elka as the whore from Magdala, decrepit and crazed, with dancing body and fallen cheeks.

The battle with the priest lasted three decades. Then the Cossack flood chased the old monk out of his aromatic stone nest, and Apolek— O fickle fortune!—settled into *Pani* Eliza's kitchen. And here I am, a passing guest, imbibing the wine of his conversation in the evenings.

What do we converse about? About the romantic days of the Polish nobility, the fanatical frenzy of women, the art of Luca della Robbia,* and the family of the Bethlehem carpenter.

"There is something I have to tell you, Mr. Clerk," Apolek tells me secretively before supper.

---

* Luca della Robbia, 1399–1482, Florentine sculptor.

"Yes," I answer. "Go ahead, Apolek, I'm listening."

But *Pan* Robacki, the lay brother of the church—stern, gray, bony, and with large ears—is sitting too close. He unfolds a faded screen of silence and animosity before us.

"I have to tell you, *Pan*," Apolek whispers, taking me aside, "that Jesus Christ, the son of Mary, was married to Deborah, a Jerusalem girl of low birth—"

"*O, ten czlowiek!*"* *Pan* Robacki shouts in despair. "This man not dies in his bed! This man the peoples will be killing!"

"After supper," Apolek murmurs in a gloomy voice. "After supper, if that will suit you, Mr. Clerk."

It suits me. Inflamed by the beginning of Apolek's story, I pace up and down the kitchen waiting for the appointed time. And outside the window night stands like a black column. Outside the window the bristling, dark garden has fallen still. The road to the church flows beneath the moon in a sparkling, milky stream. The earth is covered with a dismal sheen, a necklace of shining berries is draped over the bushes. The aroma of lilacs is clean and strong as alcohol. The seething oily breath of the stove drinks in this fresh poison, killing the stuffy resinous heat of the spruce wood lying about the kitchen floor.

Apolek is wearing a pink bow tie and threadbare pink trousers, and is puttering about in his corner like a friendly graceful animal. His table is smeared with glue and paint. He is working in quick small movements. A hushed, melodic drumming comes drifting from his corner: it is old Gottfried tapping with his trembling fingers. The blind man is sitting rigidly in the greasy yellow lamplight. His bald head is drooping as he listens to the incessant music of his blindness and the muttering of Apolek, his eternal friend.

"... And what the priests and the Evangelist Mark and the Evangelist Matthew are telling you, *Pan* Clerk, is not truth. But truth can be revealed to you, *Pan*, for I am prepared for fifty marks to paint your portrait in the form of Saint Francis on a background of green and sky. He was a very simple saint, *Pan* Francis was. And if you have a bride in Russia, *Pan* Clerk, women love Saint Francis, although not all women, *Pan*."

And from his spruce-wood-scented corner he began telling me the

---

* Polish: "Oh, this man!"

tale of the marriage of Jesus to Deborah. According to Apolek, Deborah already had a bridegroom, a young Israelite who traded in ivory. But Deborah's wedding night ended in bewilderment and tears. The woman was grabbed by fear when she saw her husband approach her bed. Hiccups bulged in her throat and she vomited all the food she had eaten at the wedding table. Shame fell upon Deborah, on her father, her mother, and on all her kin. The bridegroom abandoned her with words of ridicule, and called all the guests together. And Jesus, filled with pity at seeing the anguish of the woman who was thirsting for her husband but also fearing him, donned the robes of the newlywed man and united himself with Deborah as she lay in her vomit. Afterward she went out to the wedding guests, loudly exulting like a woman proud of her fall. And only Jesus stood to the side. His body was drenched with mortal sweat, for the bee of sorrow had stung his heart. He left the banquet hall unnoticed, and went into the desert east of Judea, where John the Baptist awaited him. And Deborah gave birth to her first son. . . ."

"So where is that son?" I yelled.

"The priests have hidden him," Apolek said with gravity, raising his thin, cold finger to his drunkard's nose.

"*Pan* Artist!" Robacki suddenly shouted, stepping out of the shadows, his gray ears quaking. "What you saying? But this is outrage!"

"*Tak, tak,*" Apolek said, cringing and grabbing hold of Gottfried. "*Tak, tak, panie.*"*

Apolek pulled the blind man toward the door, but stopped by the doorpost and beckoned me with his finger.

"Saint Francis with a bird on your sleeve," he whispered, winking at me. "A dove or a goldfinch, you can choose, *Pan* Clerk!"

And he disappeared with his blind eternal friend.

"Oh, what foolishness!" Robacki, the church lay brother, said. "This man not dies in his bed!"

Pan Robacki opened his mouth wide and yawned like a cat. I wished him a good night, and went home, to my plundered Jews, to sleep.

The vagrant moon trailed through the town and I tagged along, nurturing within me unfulfillable dreams and dissonant songs.

* Polish: "Yes, yes, gentlemen."

ITALIAN SUN

*Y*esterday I was sitting once more under a heated garland of green spruce twigs in *Pani* Eliza's servants' quarters. I sat by the warm, lively, crackling stove, and then returned to my lodgings late at night. Below, in the ravine, the silent Zbrucz rolled its glassy, dark waves.

The burned-out town—broken columns and the hooks of evil old women's fingers dug into the earth—seemed to me raised into the air, comfortable and unreal like a dream. The naked shine of the moon poured over the town with unquenchable strength. The damp mold of the ruins blossomed like a marble bench on the opera stage. And I waited with anxious soul for Romeo to descend from the clouds, a satin Romeo singing of love, while backstage a dejected electrician waits with his finger on the button to turn off the moon.

Blue roads flowed past me like rivulets of milk trickling from many breasts. On my way back, I had been dreading running into Sidorov, with whom I shared my room, and who at night brought his hairy paw of dejection down upon me. That night, luckily, harrowed by the milk of the moon, Sidorov did not say a single word to me. I found him writing, surrounded by books. On the table a hunchbacked candle was smoking—the sinister bonfire of dreamers. I sat to the side, dozed, dreams pouncing around me like kittens. And it wasn't until late that night that I was awakened by an orderly who had come to take Sidorov to headquarters. They left together. I immediately hurried over to the table where Sidorov had been writing, and leafed through his books.

There was an Italian primer, a print of the Roman Forum, and a street map of Rome. The map was completely marked up with crosses. I leaned over the sheet of paper covered with writing and, with clenched fingers and an expiring heart, read another man's letter. Sidorov, the dejected murderer, tore the pink cotton wool of my imagination to shreds and dragged me into the halls of his judicious insanity. I began reading on the second page, as I did not dare look for the first one:

· · ·

. . . shot through the lungs, and am a little off my head, or, as Sergey always says, flying mad. Well, when you go mad, idiotically mad, you don't go, you fly. Anyway, let's put the horsetail to one side and the jokes to the other. Back to the events of the day, Victoria, my dear friend.

I took part in a three-month Makhno campaign*—the whole thing a grueling swindle, nothing more! Only Volin is still there. Volin is wearing apostolic raiment and clamoring to be the Lenin of anarchism. Terrible. And Makhno listens to him, runs his fingers through his dusty wire curls, and lets the snake of his peasant grin slither across his rotten teeth. And I'm not all that sure anymore if there isn't a seed of anarchy in all this, and if we won't wipe your prosperous noses for you, you self-proclaimed Tsekists from your self-proclaimed Tsekhs,† "made in Kharkov," your self-proclaimed capital.** Your strapping heroes prefer not to remember the sins of their anarchist youth, and now laugh at them from the heights of their governmental wisdom! To hell with them!

Then I ended up in Moscow. How did I end up in Moscow? The boys had treated someone unjustly, something to do with requisitions or something. Well, fool that I am, I defended him. So they let me have it, and rightly so. My wound was not even worth mentioning, but in Moscow, O Victoria, in Moscow I was struck dumb by the misery all around. Every day the hospital nurses would bring me a nibble of kasha. Bridled with reverence, they brought it in on a large tray, and I despised this shock-brigade kasha, this unregimented

---

* Nestor Ivanovich Makhno, 1889–1934, the Ukrainian anarchist leader.
† A pun: the Tsekists are members of the Tseka, the Central Committee of the Bolshevik Party. A "tsekh," however, is a simple guild.
** Today, Kharkiv, a city in northeastern Ukraine. The "self-proclaimed" capital in the sense that Kharkiv replaced Kiev as the capital of the Ukrainian S.S.R from 1917 until 1934.

treatment in regimented Moscow. Then, in the Soviet Council, I ran into a handful of anarchists. All fops and dithering old men! I managed to get all the way to the Kremlin with my plan for some real work. But they patted me on the back and promised to give me a nice deputy position if I changed my ways. I did not change my ways. And what came next? Next came the front, the Red Cavalry, and the damn soldiers stinking of blood and corpses.

Save me, Victoria! Governmental wisdom is driving me insane, boredom is inebriating me. If you won't help me I will die like a dog without a five-year plan! And who wants a worker to die unplanned? Surely not you, Victoria, my bride who will never be my wife. See, I'm becoming maudlin again, damn it to hell!

But let's get to the point now. The army bores me. I cannot ride because of my wound, which means I cannot fight. Use your connections, Victoria, have them send me to Italy! I am studying the language, and I'll be speaking it within two months. The land down there is smoldering, things there are almost ready. All they need is a few shots. One of these shots I shall fire. It is high time that their King be sent to join his ancestors. That is very important. He is a nice old fellow who plays for popularity and has himself photographed with the tamer socialists for family magazines.

But don't say anything about shots or kings at the Tseka or the People's Commissariat for Foreign Affairs. They will pat you on the head and coo: "What a romantic he is!" Just tell them plain and simple: "He's sick, he's angry, he's drunk with depression, he wants some Italian sun and he wants some bananas! Does he deserve it, or doesn't he? He'll recuperate, and *basta*! And if not, then send him to the Odessa Cheka.* They're very sensible there!"

The things I am writing you are so foolish, so unfairly foolish, Victoria, my dear friend.

Italy has seeped into my heart like an obsession. Thinking about that country that I have never seen is as sweet to me as a woman's name, as your name, Victoria. . . .

I read the letter through and then went to lie down on my dirty, crumpled bed, but sleep would not come. On the other side of the wall the pregnant Jewess was crying heartfelt tears, her lanky husband

---

* The Odessa branch of the "Extraordinary Commission" set up in 1917 to investigate counterrevolutionary activities. The Cheka later became the KGB.

answering with mumbling groans. They were lamenting the things that had been stolen, and blaming each other for their bad luck. Then, before daybreak, Sidorov came back. The dwindling candle was expiring on the table. He pulled another candle end out of his boot and pressed it with unusual pensiveness onto the drowned wick. Our room was dark, gloomy, everything in it breathed a damp, nocturnal stench, and only the window, lit up by the fire of the moon, shone like salvation.

He came over, my agonizing neighbor, and hid the letter. Bending forward, he sat down at the table and opened the picture album of Rome. The magnificent book with its gilt-edged pages stood opposite his expressionless, olive-green face. The jagged ruins of the Capitol and the Coliseum, lit by the setting sun, glittered over his hunched back. The photograph of the royal family was also there. He had inserted it between the large, glossy pages. On a piece of paper torn from a calendar was the picture of the pleasant, frail King Victor Emmanuel with his black-haired wife, Crown Prince Umberto, and a whole brood of princesses.

It is night, a night full of distant and painful sounds, with a square of light in the damp darkness, and in this square is Sidorov's deathly face, a lifeless mask hovering over the yellow flame of the candle.

GEDALI

*O*n the eve of the Sabbath I am always tormented by the dense sorrow of memory. In the past on these evenings, my grandfather's yellow beard caressed the volumes of Ibn Ezra. My old grandmother, in her lace bonnet, waved spells over the Sabbath candle with her gnarled fingers, and sobbed sweetly. On those evenings my child's heart was gently rocked, like a little boat on enchanted waves.

I wander through Zhitomir looking for the timid star.* Beside the ancient synagogue, beside its indifferent yellow walls, old Jews, Jews with the beards of prophets, passionate rags hanging from their sunken chests, are selling chalk, bluing, and candle wicks.

Here before me lies the bazaar, and the death of the bazaar. Slaughtered is the fat soul of abundance. Mute padlocks hang on the stores, and the granite of the streets is as clean as a corpse's bald head. The timid star blinks and expires.

Success came to me later, I found the star just before the setting of the sun. Gedali's store lay hidden among the tightly shut market stalls. Dickens, where was your shadow that evening?† In this old junk store you would have found gilded slippers and ship's ropes, an antique compass and a stuffed eagle, a Winchester hunting rifle with the date "1810" engraved on it, and a broken stewpot.

Old Gedali is circling around his treasures in the rosy emptiness of

---

* The Star of David.
† A reference to Charles Dickens's novel *The Old Curiosity Shop*.

the evening, a small shopkeeper with smoky spectacles and a green coat that reaches all the way to the ground. He rubs his small white hands, tugs at his gray beard, lowers his head, and listens to invisible voices that come wafting to him.

This store is like the box of an intent and inquisitive little boy who will one day become a professor of botany. This store has everything from buttons to dead butterflies, and its little owner is called Gedali. Everyone has left the bazaar, but Gedali has remained. He roams through his labyrinth of globes, skulls, and dead flowers, waving his cockerel-feather duster, swishing away the dust from the dead flowers.

We sit down on some empty beer barrels. Gedali winds and unwinds his narrow beard. His top hat rocks above us like a little black tower. Warm air flows past us. The sky changes color—tender blood pouring from an overturned bottle—and a gentle aroma of decay envelops me.

"So let's say we say 'yes' to the Revolution. But does that mean that we're supposed to say 'no' to the Sabbath?" Gedali begins, enmeshing me in the silken cords of his smoky eyes. "Yes to the Revolution! Yes! But the Revolution keeps hiding from Gedali and sending gunfire ahead of itself."

"The sun cannot enter eyes that are squeezed shut," I say to the old man, "but we shall rip open those closed eyes!"

"The Pole has closed my eyes," the old man whispers almost inaudibly. "The Pole, that evil dog! He grabs the Jew and rips out his beard, *oy*, the hound! But now they are beating him, the evil dog! This is marvelous, this is the Revolution! But then the same man who beat the Pole says to me, 'Gedali, we are requisitioning your gramophone!' 'But gentlemen,' I tell the Revolution, 'I love music!' And what does the Revolution answer me? 'You don't know what you love, Gedali! I am going to shoot you, and then you'll know, and I cannot *not* shoot, because I am the Revolution!' "

"The Revolution cannot *not* shoot, Gedali," I tell the old man, "because it is the Revolution."

"But my dear *Pan*! The Pole did shoot, because he is the counter-revolution. And you shoot because you are the Revolution. But Revolution is happiness. And happiness does not like orphans in its house. A good man does good deeds. The Revolution is the good deed done by good men. But good men do not kill. Hence the Revolution is done by bad men. But the Poles are also bad men. Who is going to tell Gedali which is the Revolution and which the counterrevolution? I have studied the Talmud. I love the commentaries of Rashi and the books of Maimonides. And there are also other people in Zhitomir who understand. And so all of us learned men fall to the floor and shout with a single voice, 'Woe unto us, where is the sweet Revolution?' "

The old man fell silent. And we saw the first star breaking through and meandering along the Milky Way.

"The Sabbath is beginning," Gedali pronounced solemnly. "Jews must go to the synagogue."

"*Pan* Comrade," he said, getting up, his top hat swaying on his head like a little black tower. "Bring a few good men to Zhitomir. *Oy*, they are lacking in our town, *oy*, how they are lacking! Bring good men and we shall give them all our gramophones. We are not simpletons. The International,* we know what the International is. And I want the International of good people, I want every soul to be accounted for and given first-class rations. Here, soul, eat, go ahead, go and find happiness in your life. The International, *Pan* Comrade, you have no idea how to swallow it!"

"With gunpowder," I tell the old man, "and seasoned with the best blood."

And then from the blue darkness young Sabbath climbed onto her throne.

"Gedali," I say to him, "today is Friday, and night has already fallen. Where can I find some Jewish biscuits, a Jewish glass of tea, and a piece of that retired God in the glass of tea?"

"You can't," Gedali answers, hanging a lock on his box, "you can't find any. There's a tavern next door, and good people used to run it, but people don't eat there anymore, they weep."

He fastened the three bone buttons of his green coat. He dusted himself with the cockerel feathers, sprinkled a little water on the soft palms of his hands, and walked off, tiny, lonely, dreamy, with his black top hat, and a large prayer book under his arm.

The Sabbath begins. Gedali, the founder of an unattainable International, went to the synagogue to pray.

* The Third Communist International, 1919–1943, an organization founded in Moscow by the delegates of twelve countries to promote Communism worldwide.

MY FIRST GOOSE

*S*avitsky, the commander of the Sixth Division, rose when he saw me, and I was taken aback by the beauty of his gigantic body. He rose—his breeches purple, his crimson cap cocked to the side, his medals pinned to his chest—splitting the hut in two like a banner splitting the sky. He smelled of perfume and the nauseating coolness of soap. His long legs looked like two girls wedged to their shoulders in riding boots.

He smiled at me, smacked the table with his whip, and picked up the order which the chief of staff had just dictated. It was an order for Ivan Chesnokov to advance to Chugunov-Dobryvodka with the regiment he had been entrusted with, and, on encountering the enemy, to proceed immediately with its destruction.

"... the destruction of which," Savitsky began writing, filling the whole sheet, "I hold the selfsame Chesnokov completely responsible for. Noncompliance will incur the severest punitive measures, in other words I will gun him down on the spot, a fact that I am sure that you, Comrade Chesnokov, will not doubt, as it's been quite a while now that you have worked with me on the front. . . ."

The commander of the Sixth Division signed the order with a flourish, threw it at the orderlies, and turned his gray eyes, dancing with merriment, toward me.

I handed him the document concerning my assignment to the divisional staff.

"See to the paperwork!" the division commander said. "See to the paperwork, and have this man sign up for all the amusements except for those of the frontal kind.* Can you read and write?"

"Yes, I can," I answered, bristling with envy at the steel and bloom of his youth. "I graduated in law from the University of Petersburg."

"So you're one of those little powder puffs!" he yelled, laughing. "With spectacles on your nose! Ha, you lousy little fellow, you! They send you to us, no one even asks us if we want you here! Here you get hacked to pieces just for wearing glasses! So, you think you can live with us, huh?"

"Yes, I do," I answered, and went to the village with the quartermaster to look for a place to stay.

The quartermaster carried my little suitcase on his shoulder. The village street lay before us, and the dying sun in the sky, round and yellow as a pumpkin, breathed its last rosy breath.

We came to a hut with garlands painted on it. The quartermaster stopped, and suddenly, smiling guiltily, said, "You see we have a thing about spectacles here, there ain't nothing you can do! A man of high distinguishings they'll chew up and spit out—but ruin a lady, yes, the most cleanest lady, and you're the darling of the fighters!"

He hesitated for a moment, my suitcase still on his shoulder, came up very close to me, but suddenly lunged away in despair, rushing into the nearest courtyard. Cossacks were sitting there on bundles of hay, shaving each other.

"Fighters!" the quartermaster began, putting my suitcase on the ground. "According to an order issued by Comrade Savitsky, you are required to accept this man to lodge among you. And no funny business, please, because this man has suffered on the fields of learning!"

The quartermaster flushed and marched off without looking back. I lifted my hand to my cap and saluted the Cossacks. A young fellow with long, flaxen hair and a wonderful Ryazan face walked up to my suitcase and threw it out into the street. Then he turned his backside toward me, and with uncommon dexterity began emitting shameless sounds.

"That was a zero-zero caliber!" an older Cossack yelled, laughing out loud. "Rapid-fire!"

* The division commander is punning, substituting the word *udovolstvie,* "amusements," for *prodovolstvie,* "provisions."

The young man walked off, having exhausted the limited resources of his artistry. I went down on my hands and knees and gathered up the manuscripts and the old, tattered clothes that had fallen out of my suitcase. I took them and carried them to the other end of the yard. A large pot of boiling pork stood on some bricks in front of the hut. Smoke rose from it as distant smoke rises from the village hut of one's childhood, mixing hunger with intense loneliness inside me. I covered my broken little suitcase with hay, turning it into a pillow, and lay down on the ground to read Lenin's speech at the Second Congress of the Comintern,* which *Pravda* had printed. The sun fell on me through the jagged hills, the Cossacks kept stepping over my legs, the young fellow incessantly made fun of me, the beloved sentences struggled toward me over thorny paths, but could not reach me. I put away the newspaper and went to the mistress of the house, who was spinning yarn on the porch.

"Mistress," I said, "I need some grub!"

The old woman raised the dripping whites of her half-blind eyes to me and lowered them again.

"Comrade," she said, after a short silence. "All of this makes me want to hang myself!"

"Goddammit!" I muttered in frustration, shoving her back with my hand. "I'm in no mood to start debating with you!"

And, turning around, I saw someone's saber lying nearby. A haughty goose was waddling through the yard, placidly grooming its feathers. I caught the goose and forced it to the ground, its head cracking beneath my boot, cracking and bleeding. Its white neck lay stretched out in the dung, and the wings folded down over the slaughtered bird.

"Goddammit!" I said, poking at the goose with the saber. "Roast it for me, mistress!"

The old woman, her blindness and her spectacles flashing, picked up the bird, wrapped it in her apron, and hauled it to the kitchen.

"Comrade," she said after a short silence. "This makes me want to hang myself." And she pulled the door shut behind her.

* The Third Communist International, 1919–1943, an organization founded in Moscow by the delegates of twelve countries to promote Communism worldwide.

In the yard the Cossacks were already sitting around their pot. They sat motionless, straight-backed like heathen priests, not once having looked at the goose.

"This fellow'll fit in here well enough," one of them said, winked, and scooped up some cabbage soup with his spoon.

The Cossacks began eating with the restrained grace of muzhiks who respect one another. I cleaned the saber with sand, went out of the courtyard, and came back again, feeling anguished. The moon hung over the yard like a cheap earring.

"Hey, brother!" Surovkov, the oldest of the Cossacks, suddenly said to me. "Sit with us and have some of this till your goose is ready!"

He fished an extra spoon out of his boot and handed it to me. We slurped the cabbage soup and ate the pork.

"So, what are they writing in the newspaper?" the young fellow with the flaxen hair asked me, and moved aside to make room for me.

"In the newspaper, Lenin writes," I said, picking up my *Pravda*, "Lenin writes that right now there is a shortage of everything."

And in a loud voice, like a triumphant deaf man, I read Lenin's speech to the Cossacks.

The evening wrapped me in the soothing dampness of her twilight sheets, the evening placed her motherly palms on my burning brow.

I read, and rejoiced, waiting for the effect, rejoicing in the mysterious curve of Lenin's straight line.

"Truth tickles all and sundry in the nose,"* Surovkov said when I had finished. "It isn't all that easy to wheedle it out of the pile of rubbish, but Lenin picks it up right away, like a hen pecks up a grain of corn."

That is what Surovkov, the squadron commander, said about Lenin, and then we went to sleep in the hayloft. Six of us slept there warming each other, our legs tangled, under the holes in the roof which let in the stars.

I dreamed and saw women in my dreams, and only my heart, crimson with murder, screeched and bled.

---

* A pun on "truth," *Pravda*, which is also the name of the Russian daily that the narrator is reading to the Cossacks.

THE RABBI

"All things are mortal. Only a mother is accorded eternal life. And when a mother is not among the living, she leaves behind a memory that no one has yet dared to defile. The memory of a mother nourishes compassion within us, just as the ocean, the boundless ocean, nourishes the rivers that cut through the universe."

These were Gedali's words. He uttered them gravely. The dying evening wrapped him in the rosy haze of its sadness.

"In the ardent house of Hasidism," the old man said, "the windows and doors have been torn out, but it is as immortal as a mother's soul. Even with blinded eyes, Hasidism still stands at the crossroads of the winds of history."

That is what Gedali said, and, after having prayed in the synagogue, he took me to Rabbi Motale, the last rabbi of the Chernobyl dynasty.

Gedali and I walked up the main street. White churches glittered in the distance like fields of buckwheat. A gun cart moaned around the corner. Two pregnant Ukrainian women came out through the gates of a house, their coin necklaces jingling, and sat down on a bench. A timid star flashed in the orange battles of the sunset, and peace, a Sabbath peace, descended on the slanted roofs of the Zhitomir ghetto.

"Here," Gedali whispered, pointing at a long house with a shattered facade.

We went into a room, a stone room, empty as a morgue. Rabbi Motale sat at a table surrounded by liars and men possessed. He was wearing a sable hat and a white robe, with a rope for a belt. The rabbi was sitting, his eyes closed, his thin fingers digging through the yellow fluff of his beard.

"Where have you come from, Jew?" he asked me, lifting his eyelids.

"From Odessa," I answered.

"A devout town," the rabbi said. "The star of our exile, the reluctant well of our afflictions! What is the Jew's trade?"

"I am putting the adventures of Hershele of Ostropol* into verse."

"A great task," the rabbi whispered, and closed his eyelids. "The jackal moans when it is hungry, every fool has foolishness enough for despondency, and only the sage shreds the veil of existence with laughter . . . What did the Jew study?"

"The Bible."

"What is the Jew looking for?"

"Merriment."

"Reb Mordkhe," the rabbi said, and shook his beard. "Let the young man seat himself at the table, let him eat on the Sabbath evening with other Jews, let him rejoice that he is alive and not dead, let him clap his hands as his neighbors dance, let him drink wine if he is given wine!"

And Reb Mordkhe came bouncing toward me, an ancient fool with inflamed eyelids, a hunchbacked little old man, no bigger than a ten-year-old boy.

"*Oy*, my dear and so very young man!" ragged Reb Mordkhe said, winking at me. "*Oy*, how many rich fools have I known in Odessa, how many wise paupers have I known in Odessa! Sit down at the table, young man, and drink the wine that you will not be given!"

We all sat down, one next to the other—the possessed, the liars, the unhinged. In the corner, broad-shouldered Jews who looked like fishermen and apostles were moaning over prayer books. Gedali in his green coat dozed by the wall like a bright bird. And suddenly I saw a youth behind Gedali, a youth with the face of Spinoza, with the powerful forehead of Spinoza, with the sickly face of a nun. He was smoking and twitching like an escaped convict who has been tracked down and brought back to his jail. Ragged Reb Mordkhe sneaked up on him

---

* In Yiddish folklore, a trickster. See Babel's story "Shabos-Nakhamu."

from behind, snatched the cigarette from his mouth, and came running over to me.

"That is Ilya, the rabbi's son," Mordkhe wheezed, turning the bloody flesh of his inflamed eyelids to me, "the damned son, the worst son, the disobedient son!"

And Mordkhe threatened the youth with his little fist and spat in his face.

"Blessed is the Lord," the voice of Rabbi Motale Bratslavsky rang out, and he broke the bread with his monastic fingers. "Blessed is the God of Israel, who has chosen us among all the peoples of the world."

The rabbi blessed the food, and we sat down at the table. Outside the window horses neighed and Cossacks shouted. The wasteland of war yawned outside. The rabbi's son smoked one cigarette after another during the silent prayer. When the dinner was over, I was the first to rise.

"My dear and so very young man," Mordkhe muttered behind me, tugging at my belt. "If there was no one in the world except for evil rich men and destitute tramps, how would holy men live?"

I gave the old man some money and went out into the street. Gedali and I parted, and I went back to the railroad station. There at the station, on the propaganda train of the First Cavalry, I was greeted by the sparkle of hundreds of lights, the enchanted glitter of the radio transmitter, the stubborn rolling of the printing presses, and my unfinished article for the *Krasny Kavalerist.**

* The newspaper *The Red Cavalryman.*

THE ROAD TO BRODY

I mourn for the bees. They have been destroyed by warring armies. There are no longer any bees in Volhynia.

We desecrated the hives. We fumigated them with sulfur and detonated them with gunpowder. Smoldering rags have spread a foul stench over the holy republics of the bees. Dying, they flew slowly, their buzzing barely audible. Deprived of bread, we procured honey with our sabers. There are no longer any bees in Volhynia.

The chronicle of our everyday crimes oppresses me as relentlessly as a bad heart. Yesterday was the first day of the battle for Brody. Lost on the blue earth, we suspected nothing—neither I, nor my friend Afonka Bida. The horses had been fed grain in the morning. The rye stood tall, the sun was beautiful, and our souls, which did not deserve these shining, soaring skies, thirsted for lingering pain.

"In our Cossack villages the womenfolk tell tales of the bee and its kind nature," my friend began. "The womenfolk tell all sorts of things. If men wronged Christ, or if no wrong was done, other people will have to figure out for themselves. But if you listen to what the womenfolk of the Cossack villages tell, Christ is hanging tormented on the cross, when suddenly all kinds of gnats come flying over to plague him! And he takes a good look at the gnats and his spirits fall. But the thousands of little gnats can't see his eyes. At that moment a bee flies around Christ. 'Sting him!' a gnat yells at the bee. 'Sting him for us!'—'That I cannot do,' the bee says, covering Christ with her wings. 'That I cannot do, he belongs to the carpenter class.' One has to understand the bees," Afonka, my platoon commander, concluded. "I hope the bees hold out. We're fighting for them too!"

Afonka waved dismissively and started to sing. It was a song about a light bay stallion. Eight Cossacks in Afonka's platoon joined in the song.

The light bay stallion, Dzhigit was his name, belonged to a junior Cossack captain who got drunk on vodka the day of his beheading, sang Afonka sleepily, his voice taut like a string. Dzhigit had been a loyal horse, but on feast days the Cossack's carousing knew no bounds. He had five jugs of vodka on the day of his beheading. After the fourth jug, the junior Cossack captain mounted his steed and rode up to heaven. The climb was long, but Dzhigit was a true horse. They rode into heaven, and the Cossack reached for his fifth jug. But the last jug had been left back on earth. He broke down and wept, for all his efforts had been in vain. He wept, and Dzhigit pointed his ears, and turned to look at his master. Afonka sang, clinking and dozing.

The song drifted like smoke. We rode toward the sunset, its boiling rivers pouring over the embroidered napkins of the peasants' fields. The silence turned rosy. The earth lay like a cat's back, covered with a thick, gleaming coat of grain. The mud hamlet of Klekotov crouched on a little hill. Beyond the pass, the vision of deadly, craggy Brody awaited us. But in Klekotov a loud shot exploded in our faces. Two Polish soldiers peered out from behind a hut. Their horses were tied to a post. A light enemy battery came riding up the hill. Bullets unfurled like string along the road.

"Run for it!" Afonka yelled.

And we fled.

Brody! The mummies of your trampled passions have breathed their irresistible poison upon me. I had felt the fatal chill of your eye sockets filled with frozen tears. And now, in a tumbling gallop, I am being carried away from the smashed stones of your synagogues. . . .

THE *TACHANKA** THEORY

*H*eadquarters sent me a coachman, or, as we generally say here, a vehicular driver. His name is Grishchuk. He is thirty-nine years old.

He had spent five years in a German prison camp, escaped a few months ago, walked across Lithuania and northwest Russia, reached Volhynia, only, in Byelov, to fall into the hands of what must be the world's most brainless draft commission, which reconscripted him into active service. He had been a mere fifty versts from his home in the Kremenec District. He has a wife and children in the Kremenec District. He hasn't been home for five years and two months. The Draft Commission made him my vehicular driver, and now I am no longer a pariah among the Cossacks.

I have a *tachanka* and a driver for it. *Tachanka!* That word has become the base of the triangle on which our way of fighting rests: hack to pieces—*tachanka*—blood.

The simplest little open carriage, the *britzka*, the kind you would see some cleric or petty official riding in, has, through a whim of all the civil strife, become a terrible and fast-moving war machine, creating new strategies and tactics, twisting the traditional face of war, spawning *tachanka* heroes and geniuses. Such was Makhno,[†] who had made the *tachanka* the crux of his secretive and cunning strategy, abolishing infantry, artillery, even cavalry, and replaced that clumsy hodgepodge by

* An open carriage or buggy with a machine gun mounted on the back.
† The Ukrainian anarchist leader.

mounting three hundred machine guns onto *britzkas*. Such was Makhno, as innovative as nature: hay carts lined up in military formation to conquer towns. A wedding procession rolls up to the headquarters of a provincial executive committee, opens fire, and a frail little cleric, waving the black flag of anarchy, demands that the authorities immediately hand over the bourgeois, hand over the proletariat, hand over music and wine.

An army of *tachankas* is capable of unprecedented mobility.

Budyonny was just as adept at demonstrating this as Makhno was. To hack away at such an army is difficult, to corner it impossible. A machine gun buried under a stack of hay, a *tachanka* hidden in a peasant's shed, cease to be military targets. These hidden specks—the hypothetically existing but imperceptible components of a whole—when added up result in the new essence of the Ukrainian village: savage, rebellious, and self-seeking. Makhno can bring an army like this, its ammunition concealed in all its nooks and crannies, into military readiness within an hour, and can demobilize it even faster.

Here, in Budyonny's Red Cavalry, the *tachanka* does not rule so exclusively. But all our machine gun detachments travel only in *britzkas*. Cossack fantasy distinguishes two kinds of *tachanka*, "German settler" and "petty official," which is not fantasy but a real distinction.

The petty official *britzkas*, those rickety little carts built without love or imagination, had rattled through the wheat steppes of Kuban carrying the wretched, red-nosed civil servants, a sleep-starved herd of men hurrying to autopsies and inquests, while the settler *tachankas* came to us from the fat German settlements of the Volga regions of Samara and the Urals. The broad oaken seat backs of the settler *tachankas* are covered with simple paintings, plump garlands of rosy German flowers. The sturdy cart decks are reinforced with steel. The frame rests on soft, unforgettable springs. I can feel the ardor of many generations in these springs, now bouncing over the torn-up high roads of Volhynia.

I am experiencing the delight of first possession. Every day after we eat, we put on the harnesses. Grishchuk leads the horses out of the stable. They are becoming stronger with every passing day. With proud joy I notice a dull sheen on their groomed flanks. We rub the horses' swollen legs, trim their manes, throw Cossack harnesses—a tangled, withered mesh of thin straps—over their backs, and drive out of the yard at a fast trot. Grishchuk is sitting sideways on the box. My seat is covered with a bright sackcloth and hay smelling of perfume and tranquillity. The high wheels creak in the white, granular sand. Patches of blooming poppies color the earth, ruined churches glow on the hills. High above the road, in a niche wrecked by shells, stands the brown statue of Saint Ursula with bare round arms. And narrow, ancient letters form an uneven chain on the blackened gold of her pediment: "Glory Be to Jesus and the Mother of God."

Lifeless Jewish shtetls cluster around the foot of the Polish nobles' estates. The prophetic peacock, a passionless apparition in the blue vastness, glitters on brick walls. The synagogue, enmeshed in a tangle of huts, crouches eyeless and battered, round as a Hasidic hat, on the barren earth. Narrow-shouldered Jews hover sadly at crossroads. And the image of southern Jews flares up in my memory—jovial, potbellied, sparkling like cheap wine. There is no comparison between them and the bitter aloofness of these long bony backs, these tragic yellow beards. In their fervent features, carved by torture, there is no fat or warm pulse of blood. The movements of the Galician and the Volhynian Jew are abrupt, brusque, and offensive to good taste, but the power of their grief is filled with dark grandeur, and their secret contempt for the Polish masters is boundless. Looking at them, I understood the fiery history of these faraway hinterlands, the stories of Talmudists who leased out taverns, of rabbis who dabbled in moneylending, of girls who were raped by Polish mercenaries and for whom Polish magnates shot themselves.

DOLGUSHOV'S DEATH

*T*he veils of battle swept toward the town. At midday, Korotchaev, the disgraced commander of the Fourth Division, who fought alone and rode out seeking death, flew past us in his black Caucasian cloak. As he came galloping by, he shouted over to me, "Our communications have been cut, Radzivillov and Brody are in flames!"

And off he charged—fluttering, black, with eyes of coal.

On the plain, flat as a board, the brigades were regrouping. The sun rolled through the crimson dust. Wounded men sat in ditches, eating. Nurses lay on the grass and sang in hushed voices. Afonka's scouts roamed over the field, looking for dead soldiers and ammunition. Afonka rode by two paces from me and, without turning his head, said, "We got a real kick in the teeth! Big time! They're saying things about our division commander—it looks like he's out. Our fighters don't know what's what!"

The Poles had advanced to the forest about three versts away from us, and set up their machine guns somewhere nearby. Flying bullets whimper and yelp; their lament has reached an unbearable pitch. The bullets plunge into the earth and writhe, quaking with impatience. Vytyagaichenko, the commander of the regiment, snoring in the hot sun, cried out in his sleep and woke up. He mounted his horse and rode over to the lead squadron. His face was creased with red stripes from his uncomfortable sleep, and his pockets were filled with plums.

"Son of a bitch!" he said angrily, spitting out a plum stone. "A damn waste of time! Timoshka, hoist the flag!"

"Oh, so we're going for it?" Timoshka asked, pulling the flagpole out of the stirrup, and unrolling the flag on which a star had been painted, along with something about the Third International.*

"We'll see what happens," Vytyagaichenko said, and suddenly shouted wildly, "Come on, girls, onto your horses! Gather your men, squadron leaders!".

The buglers sounded the alarm. The squadrons lined up in a column. A wounded man crawled out of a ditch and, shading his eyes with his hand, said to Vytyagaichenko, "Taras Grigorevich, I represent the others here. It looks like you're leaving us behind."

"Don't worry, you'll manage to fight them off," Vytyagaichenko muttered, and reared his horse.

"We sort of think we won't be able to fight them off, Taras Grigorevich," the wounded man called after Vytyagaichenko as he rode off.

Vytyagaichenko turned back his horse. "Stop whimpering! Of course I won't leave you!" And he ordered the carts to be harnessed.

At that very moment the whining, high-pitched voice of my friend Afonka Bida burst out, "Let's not set off at full trot, Taras Grigorevich! It's five versts. How are we supposed to hack them down if our horses are worn out? Why the rush? You'll be there in time for the pear pruning on St. Mary's Day!"

"Slow trot!" Vytyagaichenko ordered, without raising his eyes.

The regiment rode off.

"If what they're saying about the division commander is true," Afonka whispered, reining in his horse, "and they're getting rid of him, well then thank you very much—we might as well kill off the cattle and burn down the barn!"

Tears flowed from his eyes. I looked at him in amazement. He spun like a top, held his cap down, wheezed, and then charged off with a loud whoop.

Grishchuk, with his ridiculous *tachanka*,† and I stayed behind, rushing back and forth among walls of fire until the evening. Our divisional staff had disappeared. Other units wouldn't take us in. The reg-

---

* The Third Communist International, 1919–1943, an organization founded in Moscow by the delegates of twelve countries to promote Communism worldwide.
† An open carriage or buggy with a machine gun mounted on the back.

iments pushed forward into Brody but were repelled. We rode to the town cemetery. A Polish patrol jumped up from behind the graves, put their rifles to their shoulders, and started firing at us. Grishchuk spun his *tachanka* around. It shrieked with all its four wheels.

"Grishchuk!" I yelled through the whistling and the wind.

"What damn stupidity!" he shouted back morosely.

"We're done for!" I hollered, seized by the exhilaration of disaster. "We're finished!"

"All the trouble our womenfolk go to!" he said even more morosely. "What's the point of all the matchmaking, marrying, and in-laws dancing at weddings?"

A rosy tail lit up in the sky and expired. The Milky Way surfaced from under the stars.

"It makes me want to laugh!" Grishchuk said sadly, and pointed his whip at a man sitting at the side of the road. "It makes me want to laugh that women go to such trouble!"

The man sitting by the roadside was Dolgushov, one of the telephonists. He stared at us, his legs stretched out in front of him.

"Here, look," Dolgushov said, as we pulled up to him. "I'm finished . . . know what I mean?"

"I know," Grishchuk answered, reining in the horses.

"You'll have to waste a bullet on me," Dolgushov said.

He was sitting propped up against a tree. He lay with his legs splayed far apart, his boots pointing in opposite directions. Without lowering his eyes from me, he carefully lifted his shirt. His stomach was torn open, his intestines spilling to his knees, and we could see his heart beating.

"When the Poles turn up, they'll have fun kicking me around. Here's my papers. Write my mother where, what, why."

"No," I replied, and spurred my horse.

Dolgushov placed his blue palms on the ground and looked at his hands in disbelief.

"Running away?" he muttered, slumping down. "Then run, you bastard!"

Sweat slithered over my body. The machine guns hammered faster and faster with hysterical tenacity. Afonka Bida came galloping toward us, encircled by the halo of the sunset.

"We're kicking their asses!" he shouted merrily. "What're you up to here, fun and games?"

I pointed at Dolgushov and moved my horse to the side.

They spoke a few words, I couldn't hear what they said. Dolgushov held out his papers. Afonka slipped them into his boot and shot Dolgushov in the mouth.

"Afonka," I said, riding up to him with a pitiful smile. "*I* couldn't have done that."

"Get lost, or I'll shoot you!" he said to me, his face turning white. "You spectacled idiots have as much pity for us as a cat has for a mouse!"

And he cocked his trigger.

I rode off slowly, without looking back, a feeling of cold and death in my spine.

"Hey! Hey!" Grishchuk shouted behind me, and grabbed Afonka's hand. "Cut the crap!"

"You damn lackey bastard!" Afonka yelled at Grishchuk. "Wait till I get my hands on him!"

Grishchuk caught up with me at the bend in the road. Afonka was not with him. He had ridden off in the opposite direction.

"Well, there you have it, Grishchuk," I said to him. "Today I lost Afonka, my first real friend."

Grishchuk took out a wrinkled apple from under the cart seat.

"Eat it," he told me, "please, eat it."

THE COMMANDER OF
THE SECOND BRIGADE

*G*eneral Budyonny, in his red trousers with the silver stripes, stood by a tree. The commander of the Second Brigade had just been killed. The general had appointed Kolesnikov to replace him.

Only an hour ago, Kolesnikov had been a regimental captain. A week ago Kolesnikov had been a squadron leader.

The new brigade commander was summoned to General Budyonny. The general waited for him, standing by the tree. Kolesnikov came with Almazov, his commissar.

"The bastards are closing in on us," the general said with his dazzling grin. "We win, or we die like dogs. No other options. Understood?"

"Understood," Kolesnikov answered, his eyes bulging from their sockets.

"You run for it, I'll have you shot," the general said with a smile, and he turned and looked at the commander of the special unit.

"Yes, General!" the commander of the special unit said.

"So start rolling, Koleso!"* one of the Cossacks standing nearby shouted cheerfully.

Budyonny swiftly turned on his heel and saluted his new brigade commander. The latter lifted five young red fingers to his cap, broke into a sweat, and walked along the plowed field. The horses were waiting for him fifty yards away. He hung his head, placing one long and

---

*A pun: Koleso, short for Kolesnikov, means "wheel."

crooked leg in front of the other with agonizing slowness. The fire of the sunset swept over him, as crimson and implausible as impending doom.

And suddenly, on the outstretched earth, on the yellow, harrowed nakedness of the fields, we saw nothing but Kolesnikov's narrow back, his dangling arms, and his hanging head with its gray cap.

His orderly brought him his horse.

He jumped into the saddle and galloped to his brigade without looking back. The squadrons were waiting for him on the main road, the high road to Brody.

A moaning hurrah, shredded by the wind, drifted over to us.

Aiming my binoculars, I saw the brigade commander on his horse circling through columns of thick dust.

"Kolesnikov has taken over the brigade," said our lookout, who was sitting in a tree above our heads.

"So he has," Budyonny answered, lighting a cigarette and closing his eyes.

The hurrahs faded. The cannonade died down. Pointless shrapnel burst above the forest. And we heard the great, silent skirmish.

"He's a good boy," Budyonny said, getting up. "Wants honors. Looks like he'll make it." And Budyonny had the horses brought over, and rode off to the battlefield. His Staff followed him.

As it happened, I was to see Kolesnikov again that very night, about an hour after the Poles had been finished off. He was riding in front of his brigade, alone, on a brown stallion, dozing. His right arm was hanging in a sling. A cavalry Cossack was carrying the unfurled flag about ten paces behind him. The men at the head of the squadron lazily sang bawdy ditties. The brigade stretched dusty and endless, like peasant carts heading to a market fair. At the rear, tired bands were gasping.

That evening, as Kolesnikov rode, I saw in his bearing the despotic indifference of a Tatar khan and saw in him a devotee of the glorified Kniga, the willful Pavlichenko, and the captivating Savitsky.

SASHKA CHRIST

*S*ashka, that was his real name, and Christ is what we called him because he was so gentle. He had been one of the shepherds of his Cossack village and had not done any heavy work since he was fourteen, when he had caught the evil disease.

This is what had happened. Tarakanich, Sashka's stepfather, had gone to the town of Grozny for the winter, and had joined a guild there. The guild was working well—it was made up of Ryazan muzhiks. Tarakanich did carpentry for them, and his income increased. When he realized that he could not manage the work alone anymore, he sent home for the boy to come and be his assistant—the village could survive the winter well enough without him. Sashka worked with his stepfather for a week. Then Saturday came, and they put their tools away and sat down to drink some tea. Outside it was October, but the air was mild. They opened the window, and put on a second samovar. A beggar woman was loitering near the windows. She knocked on the frame and said, "A good day to you! I see you're not from these parts. You can see what state I'm in, no?"

"What is it about your state?" Tarakanich said. "Come in, you old cripple!"

The beggar woman scrambled up and clambered into the room. She came over to the table and bowed deeply. Tarakanich grabbed her by her kerchief, pulled it off, and ruffled her hair. The beggar woman's hair was gray, ashy, and hanging in dusty tatters.

"Ooh, will you stop that, you naughty handsome man you!" she said. "You're a joke a minute, you are! But please, don't be disgusted by me just because I'm a little old woman," she quickly whispered, scampering onto the bench.

Tarakanich lay with her. The beggar woman turned her head to the side and laughed.

"Ooh, luck is raining on this little old woman's field!" she laughed. "I'll be harvesting two hundred *pood* of grain an acre!"

And she suddenly noticed Sashka, who was drinking his tea at the table, not looking up as if his life depended on it.

"Your boy?" she asked Tarakanich.

"More or less mine," Tarakanich answered. "My wife's."

"Ooh, look at him staring at us," the old woman said. "Hey, come over here!"

Sashka went over to her—and he caught the evil disease. But the evil disease had been the last thing on their minds. Tarakanich gave the beggar woman some leftover bones and a silver fiver, a very shiny one.

"Polish the fiver nicely with sand, holy sister," Tarakanich said to her, "and it'll look even better. If you lend it to the Almighty on a dark night, it will shine instead of the moon."

The old cripple tied her kerchief, took the bones, and left. And within two weeks the muzhiks realized what had happened. The evil disease made them suffer. They tried to cure themselves all winter long, dousing themselves with herbs. And in spring they returned to the Cossack village and their peasant work.

The village was about nine versts from the railroad. Tarakanich and Sashka crossed the fields. The earth lay in its April wetness. Emeralds glittered in the black ditches. Green shoots hemmed the soil with cunning stitches. A sour odor rose from the ground, as from a soldier's wife at dawn. The first herds trickled down from the hills, the foals played in the blue expanse of the horizon.

Tarakanich and Sashka walked along barely visible paths.

"Let me be one of the shepherds, Tarakanich," Sashka said.

"What for?"

"I can't bear that the shepherds have such a wonderful life."

"I won't allow it."

"Let me be one, Tarakanich, for the love of God!" Sashka repeated. "All the saints came from shepherds."

"Sashka the Saint!" the stepfather laughed. "He caught syphilis from the Mother of God!"

They passed the bend in the road by Red Bridge, then the grove and the pasture, and saw the cross on the village church.

The women were still puttering around in their vegetable gardens, and Cossacks were sitting among the lilacs, drinking vodka and singing. It was another half verst to Tarakanich's hut.

"Let us pray that everything is fine," Tarakanich said, crossing himself.

They walked over to the hut and peeked in the little window. Nobody was there. Sashka's mother was in the shed milking the cow. They crept over to her silently. Tarakanich came up behind her and laughed out loud.

"Motya, Your Excellency," he shouted, "how about some food for your guests!"

The woman turned around, began to shake, and rushed out of the shed and ran circling around the yard. Then she came back into the shed and, trembling, pressed her head on Tarakanich's chest.

"How silly and ugly you look," Tarakanich said, gently pushing her away. "Where are the children?"

"The children have left the yard," the woman said, her face ashen, and ran out again, throwing herself onto the ground.

"Oh, Aleshonka!" she shrieked wildly. "Our babies have gone, feet first!"

Tarakanich waved at her dismissively and went over to the neighbors. The neighbors told him that a week ago the Lord had taken the boy and the girl with typhus. Motya had written him a letter, but he probably hadn't gotten it. Tarakanich went back to the hut. The woman was stoking the oven.

"You got rid of them quite nicely, Motya," Tarakanich said. "Rip you to pieces, that's what I should do!"

He sat down at the table and fell into deep grief—and grieved till he fell asleep. He ate meat and drank vodka, and did not see to his work around the farm. He snored at the table, woke up, and snored again. Motya prepared a bed for herself and her husband, and another for Sashka to the side. She blew out the light, and lay down next to her husband. Sashka tossed and turned on the hay in his corner. His eyes were open, he did not sleep, but saw, as if in a dream, the hut, a star shining through the window, the edge of the table, and the horse collars under his mother's bed. A violent vision took hold of him; he surrendered to it and rejoiced in his waking dream. It was as if two silver strings hung from the sky, entwined into a thick rope to which a cradle was fastened, a rosewood cradle with carvings. It swung high above the earth but far from the sky, and the silver rope swayed and glittered. Sashka was lying in this cradle, fanned by the air. The air, loud as music, rose from the fields, and the rainbow blossomed above the unripe wheat.

Sashka rejoiced in his waking sleep, and closed his eyes so as not to see the horse collars under his mother's bed. Then he heard panting from the bed, and thought that Tarakanich must be pawing his mother.

"Tarakanich," he said loudly. "There's something I need to talk to you about."

"In the middle of the night?" Tarakanich yelled angrily. "Sleep, you fleabag!"

"I swear by the Holy Cross that there's something I need to talk to you about," Sashka said. "Come out into the yard!"

And in the yard, beneath the unfading stars, Sashka said to his stepfather, "Don't wrong my mother, Tarakanich, you're tainted."

"You should know better than to cross me, boy!" Tarakanich said.

"I know, but have you seen my mother's body? She has legs that are clean, and a breast that is clean. Don't wrong her, Tarakanich. We're tainted."

"Boy!" his stepfather said. "Avoid my blood and my wrath! Here are twenty kopeks, go to sleep and your head will be clearer in the morning."

"I don't need the twenty kopeks," Sashka muttered. "Let me go join the shepherds."

"I won't allow that," Tarakanich said.

"Let me join the shepherds," Sashka muttered, "or I'll tell Mother what we are. Why should she suffer with such a body?"

Tarakanich turned around and went into the shed to get an axe.

"Saint Sashka," he said in a whisper, "you wait and see, I'll hack you to pieces!"

"You'd hack me to pieces on account of a woman?" the boy said, barely audibly, and leaned closer to his stepfather. "Take pity on me and let me join the shepherds."

"Damn you!" Tarakanich said, and threw away the axe. "So go join the shepherds!"

And Tarakanich went back into the hut and slept with his wife.

That same morning Sashka went to the Cossacks to be hired, and from that day on he lived as a village shepherd. He became known throughout the whole area for his simple heart, and the people of the village gave him the nickname Sashka Christ, and he lived as a shepherd until he was drafted. The old men, who had nothing better to do, came out to the pasture to chat with him, and the women came running to Sashka for respite from their husbands' rough ways, and were not put off by Sashka's love for them or by his illness. Sashka's draft call came in the first year of the war. He fought for four years, and then returned to the village, where the Whites were running the show. Sashka was urged to go to the village of Platovskaya, where a detachment was being formed to fight the Whites. A former cavalry sergeant-major—Semyon Mikhailovich Budyonny—was running things in that detachment, and he had his three brothers with him: Emelian, Lukian, and Denis. Sashka went to Platovskaya, and there his fate was sealed. He joined Budyonny's regiment, his brigade, his division, and finally his First Cavalry Army. He rode to the aid of heroic Tsaritsyn,* joined with Voroshilov's Tenth Army, and fought at Voronezh, Kastornaya, and at the Generalsky Bridge on the Donets. In the Polish Campaign, Sashka joined the cavalry transport unit, because he had been wounded and was considered an invalid.

So that's how everything had come about. I had recently met Sashka Christ, and took my little suitcase and moved over to his cart. Many times we watched the sunrise and rode into the sunset. And whenever the obdurate will of war brought us together, we sat in the evenings on a sparkling earth mound,† or boiled tea in our sooty kettle in the woods, or slept next to each other on harvested fields, our hungry horses tied to our legs.

---

* Renamed Stalingrad in 1925 in honor of Joseph Stalin, who had played a major role in the defense of the city against General Denikin's White Russian Army. Today Volgograd.

† *Zavalinka:* a mound of earth around a Russian peasant hut that protects it from the weather and is often used for sitting outside.

THE LIFE OF MATVEY
RODIONOVICH PAVLICHENKO

*D*ear comrades, brothers, fellow countrymen! Hear in the name of mankind the life story of Red General Matvey Pavlichenko. This general had been a mere swineherd, a swineherd on the estate of Lidino of which Nikitinsky was master, and, until life gave him battle stripes, this swineherd tended his master's pigs, and then with those battle stripes our little Matvey was given cattle to herd. Who knows—had he been born in Australia, my friends, our Matvey, son of Rodion, might well have worked his way up to elephants, yes, our Matyushka would have herded elephants, but unfortunately there are no elephants to be found in our district of Stavropol. To be perfectly honest, there is no animal larger than a buffalo in all the lands of Stavropol. And the poor fellow would not have had any fun with buffaloes—Russians don't enjoy taunting buffaloes. Give us poor orphans a mare on Judgment Day, and I guarantee you we will know how to taunt her till her soul goes tearing out of her sides.

So here I am, herding my cattle, cows crowding me from all sides, I'm doused in milk, I stink like a slit udder, all around me calves and mouse-gray bullocks roam. Freedom lies all around me in the fields, the grass of all the world rustles, the skies above me open up like a many-buttoned concertina, and the skies, my brothers, the skies we have in the district of Stavropol, can be very blue. So there I am, herding the beasts and playing my flute to the winds with nothing better to do, when an old man comes up to me and tells me, "Go, Matvey," he says to me, "go to Nastya."

"What for?" I ask him. "Or are you maybe pulling my leg, old man?"

"Go to her," he says. "She wants you."

So I go to her.

"Nastya!" I say to her, and all my blood runs dark. "Nastya," I say to her, "or are you making fun of me?"

But she does not speak a word, runs straight past me, running as fast as her legs can carry her, and she and I run together until we're out on the meadow, dead tired, flushed, and out of breath.

"Matvey," Nastya says to me at this point. "On the third Sunday before this one, when the spring fishing season began and the fishermen came back to shore, you were walking with them, and you let your head hang. Why did you let your head hang, or is it that a thought is squeezing down on your heart? Answer me!"

And I answer her.

"Nastya," I say to her. "I have nothing to tell you, my head is not a gun, it has neither a fore-sight nor back-sight, and you know my heart full well, Nastya, it is empty, completely empty, except perhaps for being doused in milk—it's a terrible thing how I stink of milk!"

And I can see that Nastya is about to burst into laughter at my words.

"I swear by the Holy Cross," she says, bursting into laughter, laughing loudly, laughing with all her might, her laughter booming across the steppes as if she were pounding a drum, "I swear by the Holy Cross, you sure know how to sweet-talk a girl!"

So we exchange a few foolish words, and soon enough we're married. Nastya and me began living together as best we could, and we did our best. We felt hot all night, we felt hot all winter, all night we went naked and tore the hide off each other. We lived it up like devils, until the day the old man came to me again.

"Matvey," he says. "The other day the master touched your wife in all those places, and the master is going to have her."

And I say to him, "No," I say to him, "it cannot be, and please excuse me, old man, or I shall kill you right here and now."

The old man rushed off without another word, and I must have marched a good twenty versts over land that day, yes, that day a good chunk of earth passed beneath my feet, and by evening I sprouted up in the estate of Lidino, in the house of my merry master Nikitinsky. The old man was sitting in his drawing room busy taking apart three saddles, an English, a dragoon, and a Cossack saddle, and I stood rooted by his door like a burdock, I stood rooted there for a good hour. Then he finally clapped eyes on me.

"What do you want?"

"I want to quit."

"You have a grudge against me?"

"I don't have a grudge, but I want to quit."

At this point he turned his eyes away, leaving the high road for the field path, put the red saddlecloths on the floor—they were redder than the Czar's banners, his saddlecloths were—and old Nikitinsky stepped on them, puffing himself up.

"Freedom to the free," he tells me, all puffed up. "Your mothers, all Orthodox Christian women, I gave the lot of them a good plowing! You can quit, my dear little Matvey, but isn't there one tiny little thing you owe me first?"

"Ho, ho!" I answer. "What a joker! May the Lord strike me dead if you're not a joker! It is *you* who still owes *me* my wage!"

"Your wage!" my master thunders, shoving me down onto my knees, kicking me and yelling in my ear, cursing the Father, the Son, and the Holy Ghost. "You want your wage, but the bull's yoke you ruined seems to have slipped your mind! Where is my bull's yoke? Give me back my bull's yoke!"

"I will give you back your bull's yoke," I tell my master, raising my foolish eyes up at him as I kneel there, lower than the lowest of living creatures. "I'll give you back your bull's yoke, but don't strangle me with debts, master, just wait awhile!"

So, my dear friends, my Stavropol compatriots, fellow countrymen, my comrades, my very own brothers: for five years the master waited with my debts, five years I lost, until, lost soul that I was, finally the year '18 came!* It rode in on merry stallions, on Kabardinian steeds! It brought big armies with it and many songs. O, my sweet year '18! O, for us to dance in each other's arms just one more time, my sweet darling year '18! We sang your songs, drank your wine, proclaimed your

*1918, the year following the Bolshevik Revolution.

truth, but all that's left of you now is a few scribblers! Yet, ah, my love, it was not the scribblers back then who came flying through Kuban, shooting the souls of generals to Kingdom Come! No! It was me, Matvey Rodionovich, who lay outside Prikumsk in a pool of my own blood, and from where I, Matvey Rodionovich, lay to the estate of Lidino was a mere five versts. And I rode to Lidino alone, without my regiment, and as I entered the drawing room, I entered peacefully. People from the local authorities were sitting there in the drawing room, Nikitinsky was serving them tea, groveling all over them. When he saw me his face tumbled to pieces, but I lifted my fur hat to him.

"Greetings," I said to the people there. "Greetings. May I come in, your lordship, or how shall we handle this?"

"Let's handle this nicely, correctly," one of the men says, who, judging by the way he speaks, must be a land surveyor. "Let us handle things nicely, correctly, but from what I see, Comrade Pavlichenko, it seems you have ridden quite a distance, and dirt has crossed your face from side to side. We, the local authorities, are frightened of such faces. Why is your face like that?"

"Because you are the local cold-blooded authorities," I answer. "Because in my face one cheek has been burning for five years now, burning when I'm in a trench, burning when I'm with a woman, and it will be burning at my final judgment! At my final judgment!" I tell him, and look at Nikitinsky with fake cheerfulness. But he no longer has any eyes—there are now two cannonballs in the middle of his face, ready and in position under his forehead, and with these crystal balls he winks at me, also with fake cheerfulness, but so abominably.

"My dear Matyusha," he says to me, "we've known each other so long now, and my wife Nadyezhda Vasilevna, whose mind has come unhinged on account of the times we're living in, she was always kind to you, Nadyezhda Vasilevna was, and you, my dear Matyusha, always looked up to her above all others! Wouldn't you like to at least see her, even though her mind has come unhinged?"

"Fine," I tell him, and follow him into another room, and there he started clasping my hands, the right one, then the left.

"Matyusha!" he says. "Are you my fate or are you not?"

"No," I tell him. "And stop using such words! God has dropped us lackeys and run. Our fate is a chicken with its head cut off, our life is not worth a kopeck! Stop using such words and let me read you Lenin's letter!"

"Lenin wrote me, Nikitinsky, a letter?"

"Yes, he wrote you a letter," I tell him, and take out the book of decrees, open it to an empty page, and read—though I'm illiterate to the bottom of my soul. "In the name of the people," I read, "for the establishment of a future radiant life, I order Pavlichenko—Matvey Rodionovich—to deprive, at his discretion, various persons of their lives."

"There we are," I tell him. "That is Lenin's letter to you!"

And he says to me, "No!"

"No," he says, "my dear Matyusha, even if life has gone tumbling to the devil, and blood has become cheap in Holy Mother Russia! But regardless of how much blood you want, you'll get it anyway, and you'll even forget my last dying look, so wouldn't it be better if I just show you my secret hideaway?"

"Show me," I tell him. "Maybe it'll be for the better."

And again we went through the rooms, climbed down into the wine cellar, where he pulled out a brick, and behind this brick lay a little case. In it, in this case, were rings, necklaces, medals, and a pearl-studded icon. He threw the case over to me and stood there rigidly.

"Take it!" he says. "Take what is most holy to the Nikitinskys, and go off to your den in Prikumsk!"

And here I grabbed him by the neck, by the hair.

"And what about my cheek?" I tell Nikitinsky. "How am I supposed to live with my cheek this way?"

And he burst out laughing for all he was worth, and stopped struggling to get away.

"A jackal's conscience," he says, and does not struggle. "I speak to you as to an officer of the Russian Empire, and you, you scum, were suckled by a she-wolf. Shoot me, you son of a bitch!"

But shoot him I did not—I did not owe him a shot. I just dragged him up to the sitting room. There in the sitting room Nadyezhda Vasilevna was wandering about completely mad, with a drawn saber in her hand, looking at herself in the mirror. And when I dragged Nikitinsky into the sitting room, Nadyezhda Vasilevna runs to sit in the chair, and she is wearing a velvet crown and feathers on her head. She sat in the chair and saluted me with the saber. Then I started kicking Nikitinsky, my master, I kicked him for an hour, maybe even more than an hour, and I really understood what life actually is. With one shot, let me tell you, you can only get rid of a person. A shot would have been a pardon for him and too horribly easy for me, with a shot you cannot get to a man's soul, to where the soul hides and what it looks like. But there are times when I don't spare myself and spend a good hour, maybe even more than an hour, kicking the enemy. I want to understand life, to see what it actually is.

THE CEMETERY IN
KOZIN

*T*he cemetery in a shtetl. Assyria and the mysterious decay of the East on the overgrown, weed-covered fields of Volhynia.

Gray, abraded stones with letters three hundred years old. The rough contours of the reliefs cut into the granite. The image of a fish and a sheep above a dead man's head. Images of rabbis wearing fur hats. Rabbis, their narrow hips girded with belts. Beneath their eyeless faces the wavy stone ripple of curly beards. To one side, below an oak tree cleft in two by lightning, stands the vault of Rabbi Asriil, slaughtered by Bogdan Khmelnitsky's Cossacks. Four generations lie in this sepulcher, as poor as the hovel of a water carrier, and tablets, moss-green tablets, sing of them in Bedouin prayer:

"*Azriil, son of Anania, mouth of Jehovah.*
Elijah, son of Azriil, mind that fought oblivion hand to hand.
Wolf, son of Elijah, prince taken from his Torah in his nineteenth spring.
Judah, son of Wolf, Rabbi of Krakow and Prague.
O death, O mercenary, O covetous thief, why did you not, albeit one single
time, have mercy upon us?"

PRISHCHEPA

I'm making my way to Leshniov, where the divisional staff has set up quarters. My traveling companion, as usual, is Prishchepa, a young Cossack from Kuban, a tireless roughneck, a Communist whom the party kicked out, a future rag looter, a devil-may-care syphilitic, an unflappable liar. He wears a crimson Circassian jacket made of fine cloth, with a ruffled hood trailing down his back. As we rode, he told me about himself.

A year ago Prishchepa had run away from the Whites. As a reprisal, they took his parents hostage and killed them at the interrogation. The neighbors ransacked everything they had. When the Whites were driven out of Kuban, Prishchepa returned to his Cossack village.

It was morning, daybreak, peasant sleep sighed in the rancid stuffiness. Prishchepa hired a communal cart and went through the village picking up his gramophone, kvas jugs, and the napkins that his mother had embroidered. He went down the street in his black cloak, his curved dagger in his belt. The cart rattled behind him. Prishchepa went from one neighbor's house to the next, the bloody prints of his boots trailing behind him. In huts where he found his mother's things or his father's pipe, he left hacked-up old women, dogs hung over wells, icons soiled with dung. The people of the village smoked their pipes and followed him sullenly with their eyes. Young Cossacks had gathered on the steppes outside the village and were keeping count. The count rose and the village fell silent. When he had finished, Prishchepa returned to his ransacked home. He arranged his reclaimed furniture the way he remembered it from his childhood, and ordered vodka to be brought to him. He locked himself in the hut and for two days drank, sang, cried, and hacked tables to pieces with his saber.

On the third night, the village saw smoke rising above Prishchepa's hut. Seared and gashed, he came staggering out of the shed pulling the cow behind him, stuck his revolver in her mouth, and shot her. The earth smoked beneath his feet, a blue ring of flame flew out of the chimney and melted away, the abandoned calf began wailing. The fire was as bright as a holy day. Prishchepa untied his horse, jumped into the saddle, threw a lock of his hair into the flames, and vanished.

THE STORY OF
A HORSE

*O*ne day Savitsky, our division commander, took for himself a
white stallion belonging to Khlebnikov, the commander of the
First Squadron. It was a horse of imposing stature, but with a somewhat raw build, which always seemed a little heavy to me. Khlebnikov
was given a black mare of pretty good stock and good trot. But he mis-
treated the mare, hankered for revenge, waited for an opportunity, and
when it came, pounced on it.

After the unsuccessful battles of July, when Savitsky was dismissed
from his duties and sent to the command personnel reserves,
Khlebnikov wrote to army headquarters requesting that his horse be
returned to him. On the letter, the chief of staff penned the decision:
"Aforementioned stallion is to be returned to primordial owner." And
Khlebnikov, rejoicing, rode a hundred versts to find Savitsky, who was
living at the time in Radzivillov, a mangled little town that looked like
a tattered old whore. The dismissed division commander was living
alone, the fawning lackeys at headquarters no longer knew him. The
fawning lackeys at headquarters were busy angling for roasted chickens
in the army commander's smiles, and, vying to outgrovel each other,
had turned their backs on the glorious division commander.

Drenched in perfume, looking like Peter the Great, he had fallen
out of favor. He lived with a Cossack woman by the name of Pavla,
whom he had snatched away from a Jewish quartermaster, and twenty
thoroughbreds which, word had it, were his own. In his yard, the sun
was tense and tortured with the blindness of its rays. The foals were

wildly suckling on their mothers, and stableboys with drenched backs were sifting oats on faded winnowing floors. Khlebnikov, wounded by the injustice and fired by revenge, marched straight over to the barricaded yard.

"Are you familiar with my person?" he asked Savitsky, who was lying on some hay.

"Something tells me I've seen you somewhere before," Savitsky said to him with a yawn.

"In that case, here is the chief of staff's decision," Khlebnikov said gruffly. "And I would be obliged, Comrade of the reserve, if you would look at me with an official eye!"

"Why not?" Savitsky mumbled appeasingly. He took the document and began reading it for an unusually long time. He suddenly called over the Cossack woman, who was combing her hair in the coolness under the awning.

"Pavla!" he yelled. "As the Lord's my witness, you've been combing your hair since this morning! How about heating a samovar for us!"

The Cossack woman put down her comb, took her hair in both hands, and flung it behind her back.

"You've done nothing but bicker all day, Konstantin Vasilevich," she said with a lazy, condescending smile. "First you want this, then you want that!"

And she came over to Savitsky; her breasts, bobbing on her high heels, squirmed like an animal in a sack.

"You've done nothing but bicker all day," the woman repeated, beaming, and she buttoned up the division commander's shirt.

"First I want this, then I want that," the division commander said, laughing, and he got up, clasped Pavla's acquiescing shoulders, and suddenly turned his face, deathly white, to Khlebnikov.

"I am still alive, Khlebnikov," he said, embracing the Cossack woman tighter. "My legs can still walk, my horses can still gallop, my hands can still get hold of you, and my gun is warming next to my skin."

He drew his revolver, which had lain against his bare stomach, and stepped closer to the commander of the First Squadron.

The commander turned on his heels, his spurs yelped, he left the yard like an orderly who has received an urgent dispatch, and once again rode a hundred versts to find the chief of staff—but the chief of staff sent him packing.

"I have already dealt with your matter, Commander!" the chief of staff said. "I ordered that your stallion be returned to you, and I have quite a few other things to deal with!"

The chief of staff refused to listen, and finally ordered the errant commander back to his squadron. Khlebnikov had been away a whole week. During that time we had been transferred to the Dubno forest to set up camp. We had pitched our tents and were living it up. Khlebnikov, from what I remember, returned on the twelfth, a Sunday morning. He asked me for some paper, a good thirty sheets, and for some ink. The Cossacks planed a tree stump smooth for him, he placed his revolver and the paper on it, and wrote till sundown, filling many sheets with his smudgy scrawl.

"You're a real Karl Marx, you are!" the squadron's military commissar said to him in the evening. "What the hell are you writing there?"

"I am describing various thoughts in accordance with the oath I have taken," Khlebnikov answered, and handed the military commissar his petition to withdraw from the Communist Party of the Bolsheviks.

• • •

"The Communist Party," his petition went, "was, it is my belief, founded for the promotioning of happiness and true justice with no restrictings, and thus must also keep an eye out for the rights of the little man. Here I would like to touch on the matter of the white stallion who I seized from some indescribably counterrevolutionary peasants, and who was in a horrifying condition, and many comrades laughed brazenly at that condition, but I was strong enough to withstand that laughing of theirs, and gritting my teeth for the Common Cause, I nursed the stallion back to the desired shape, because, let it be said, Comrades, I am a white-stallion enthusiast and have dedicated to white stallions the little energy that the Imperial War and the Civil War have left me with, and all these stallions respond to my touch as I respond to his silent wants and needs! But that unjust black mare I can neither respond to, nor do I need her, nor can I stand her, and, as all my comrades will testify, there's bound to be trouble! And yet the Party is unable to return to me, according to the chief of staff's decision, that which is my very own, handing me no option but to write this here petition with tears that do not befit a fighter, but which flow endlessly, ripping my blood-drenched heart to pieces!"

• • •

This and much more was written in Khlebnikov's petition. He spent the whole day writing it, and it was very long. It took me and the military commissar more than an hour to struggle through it.

"What a fool you are!" the military commissar said to him, and tore it up. "Come back after dinner and you and I will have a little talk."

"I don't need your little talk!" Khlebnikov answered, trembling. "You and I are finished!"

He stood at attention, shivering, not moving, his eyes darting from one side to the other as if he were desperately trying to decide which way to run. The military commissar came up to him but couldn't grab hold of him in time. Khlebnikov lunged forward and ran with all his might.

"We're finished!" he yelled wildly, jumped onto the tree stump, and began ripping his jacket and tearing at his chest.

"Go on, Savitsky!" he shouted, throwing himself onto the ground. "Kill me!"

We dragged him to a tent, the Cossacks helped us. We boiled some tea for him, and rolled him some cigarettes. He smoked, his whole body shivering. And it was only late in the evening that our commander calmed down. He no longer spoke about his deranged petition, but within a week he went to Rovno, presented himself for an examination by the Medical Commission, and was discharged from the army as an invalid on account of having six wounds.

That's how we lost Khlebnikov. I was very upset about this because Khlebnikov had been a quiet man, very similar to me in character. He was the only one in the squadron who owned a samovar. On days when there was a break in the fighting, the two of us drank hot tea. We were rattled by the same passions. Both of us looked upon the world as a meadow in May over which women and horses wander.

KONKIN

So there we were making mincemeat of the Poles at Belaya Tserkov. So much so that the trees were rattling. I'd been hit in the morning, but managed to keep on buzzing, more or less. The day, from what I remember, was toppling toward evening. I got cut off from the brigade commander, and was left with only a bunch of five proletarian Cossacks tagging along after me. All around me everyone's hugging each other with hatchets, like priests from two villages, the sap's slowly trickling out of me, my horse has pissed all over itself. Need I say more?

Me and Spirka Zabuty ended up riding off a ways from the forest. We look—and yes, two and two does make four!—no less than a hundred and fifty paces away, we see a dust cloud which is either the staff or the cavalry transport. If it's the staff—that's great, if it's the cavalry transport—that's even better! The boys' tattered clothes hung in rags, their shirts barely covering their manhood.

"Zabuty!" I yell over to Spirka, telling him he's a son of a whore, that his mother is a you-know-what, or whatever (I leave this part up to you, as you're the official orator here). "Isn't that *their* staff that's riding off there?"

"You can bet your life it's their staff!" Spirka yells back. "The only thing is, we're two and they're eight!"

"Let's go for it, Spirka!" I shout. "Either way, I'm going to hurl some mud at their chasubles! Let's go die for a pickle and World Revolution!"

And off we rode. They were eight sabers. Two of them we felled with our rifles. I spot Spirka dragging a third to Dukhonin's headquarters to get his papers checked. And me, I take aim at the big King of Aces. Yes, brothers, a big, red-faced King of Aces, with a chain and a gold pocket watch. I squeezed him back toward a farm. The farm was full of apple and cherry trees. The horse that the Big Ace was riding was nice and plump like a merchant's daughter, but it was tired. So the general drops his reins, aims his Mauser at me, and puts a hole in my leg.

"Ha, fine, sweetheart!" I think to myself. "I'll have you on your back with your legs spread wide in no time!"

I got my wheels rolling and put two bullets in his horse. I felt bad about the horse. What a Bolshevik of a stallion, a true Bolshevik! Copper-brown like a coin, tail like a bullet, leg like a bowstring. I wanted to present him alive to Lenin, but nothing came of it. I liquidated that sweet little horse. It tumbled like a bride, and my King of Aces fell out of his saddle. He dashed to one side, then turned back again and put another little loophole in my body. So, in other words, I had already gotten myself three decorations for fighting the enemy.

"Jesus!" I think to myself. "Just watch him finish me off by mistake!"

I went galloping toward him, he'd already pulled his saber, and tears are running down his cheeks, white tears, the milk of man.

"You'll get me a Red Flag Medal!" I yell. "Give yourself up while I'm still alive, Your Excellency!"

"I can't do that, *Pan*!" the old man answers. "Kill me!"

And suddenly Spirka is standing before me like a leaf before a blade of grass.* His face all lathered up with sweat, his eyes as if they're dangling on strings from his ugly mug.

"Konkin!" he yells at me. "God knows how many I've finished off! But you have a general here, he's got embroidery on him, I'd like to finish him off myself!"

"Go to the Turk!" I tell Zabuty, and get furious. "It's my blood that's on his embroidery!"

---

* From the Russian folktale *The Little Humpbacked Horse*, in which the hero summons his magic horse with, "Appear before me like a leaf before a blade of grass!"

And with my mare I edge the general into the barn, where there was hay or something. It was silent in there, dark, cool.

"*Pan*, think of your old age!" I tell him. "Give yourself up to me, for God's sake, and we can both have a rest."

And he's against the wall, panting with his whole chest, rubbing his forehead with a red finger.

"I can't," he says. "Kill me, I will only hand my saber to Budyonny!"

He wants me to bring him Budyonny! O, Lord in Heaven! And I can tell the old man's on his last legs.

"*Pan!*" I shout at him, sobbing and gnashing my teeth. "On my proletarian honor, I myself am the commander-in-chief. Don't go looking for embroidery on me, but the title's mine. You want my title? I am the musical eccentric and salon ventriloquist of Nizhny . . . Nizhny, a town on the Volga!"

Then the devil got into me. The general's eyes were blinking like lanterns in front of me. The Red Sea parted before me. His snub enters my wound like salt, because I see that the old man doesn't believe me. So, my friends, what I did is, I closed my mouth, pulled in my stomach, took a deep breath, and demonstrated, in the proper way, our way, the fighter's way, the Nizhny way—demonstrated to this Polish nobleman my ventriloquy.

The old man went white in the face, clutched his heart, and sat on the ground.

"Do you now believe Konkin the Eccentric, commissar of the Third Invincible Cavalry Brigade?"

"A commissar?" he shouts.

"A commissar," I tell him.

"A Communist?" he shouts.

"A Communist," I tell him.

"At my hour of death," he shouts, "at my last breath, tell me, my dear Cossack friend, are you a Communist, or are you lying to me?"

"I am a Communist," I tell him.

So there's grandpa, sitting on the ground, kissing some kind of amulet or something, breaks his saber in half, and in his eyes two sparks flare up, two lanterns above the dark steppes.

"Forgive me," he says, "but I cannot give myself up to a Communist."

And he shakes my hand. "Forgive me," he says, "and finish me off like a soldier."

Konkin, the political commissar of the N. Cavalry Brigade and three-time Knight of the Order of the Red Flag, told us this story with his typical antics during a rest stop one day.

"So, Konkin, did you and the *Pan* come to some sort of an agreement in the end?"

"Can you come to an agreement with someone like that? He was too proud. I begged him again, but he wouldn't give in. So we took his papers, those he had with him, we took his Mauser, and the old fool's saddle, the one I'm sitting on right now. Then I see all my life flowing out of me in drops, a terrible tiredness grabs hold of me, my boots are full of blood, I lost interest in him."

"So you put the old man out of his misery?"

"Well, I guess I did."

BERESTECHKO

*W*e were advancing from Khotin to Berestechko. Our fighters were dozing in their saddles. A song rustled like a stream running dry. Horrifying corpses lay on thousand-year-old burial mounds. Muzhiks in white shirts raised their caps and bowed as we passed. The cloak of Division Commander Pavlichenko was fluttering ahead of the staff officers like a gloomy banner. His ruffled hood hung over his cloak, his curved saber at his side.

We rode past the Cossack burial mounds and the tomb of Bogdan Khmelnitsky. An old man with a mandolin came creeping out from behind a gravestone and with a child's voice sang of past Cossack glory. We listened to the song in silence, then unfurled the standards, and burst into Berestechko to the beat of a thundering march. The inhabitants had put iron bars over their shutters, and silence, a despotic silence, had ascended to the shtetl throne.

I happened to be billeted in the house of a redheaded widow, who was doused with the scent of widow's grief. I washed off the dirt of the road and went out into the street. An announcement was already nailed up on telegraph poles that Divisional Military Commissar Vinogradov would be giving a speech on the Second Congress of the Comintern.* Right outside the house a couple of Cossacks were getting ready to shoot an old silver-bearded Jew for espionage. The old man was screeching, and tried to break free. Kudrya from the machine gun

* The Third Communist International, 1919–1943, an organization founded in Moscow by the delegates of twelve countries to promote Communism worldwide.

detachment grabbed his head and held it wedged under his arm. The Jew fell silent and spread his legs. Kudrya pulled out his dagger with his right hand and carefully slit the old man's throat without spattering himself. Then he knocked on one of the closed windows.

"If anyone's interested," he said, "they can come get him. It's no problem."

And the Cossacks disappeared around the corner. I followed them, and then wandered through Berestechko. Most of the people here are Jewish, and only on the outskirts have a few Russian townspeople, mainly tanners, settled. The Russians live cleanly, in little white houses behind green shutters. Instead of vodka, they drink beer or mead, and in their front gardens grow tobacco which, like Galician peasants, they smoke in long curved pipes. That they are three diligent and entrepreneurial races living next to each other awakened in all of them an obstinate industriousness that is sometimes inherent in a Russian man, if he hasn't become louse-ridden, desperate, and besotted with drink.

Everyday life, which once flourished, has blown away. Little sprouts that had survived for three centuries still managed to blossom in Volhynia's sultry hotbed of ancient times. Here, with the ropes of profit, the Jews had bound the Russian muzhiks to the Polish *Pans* and the Czech settlers to the factory in Lodz. These were smugglers, the best on the frontier, and almost always warriors of the faith. Hasidism kept this lively population of taverners, peddlers, and brokers in a stifling grip. Boys in long coats still trod the ancient path to the Hasidic cheder, and old women still brought daughters-in-law to the *tsaddik* with impassioned prayers for fertility.

The Jews live here in large houses painted white or a watery blue. The traditional austerity of this architecture goes back centuries. Behind the houses are sheds that are two, sometimes three stories high. The sun never enters these sheds. They are indescribably gloomy and replace our yards. Secret passages lead to cellars and stables. In times of war, people hide in these catacombs from bullets and plunder. Over many days, human refuse and animal dung pile up. Despair and dismay fill the catacombs with an acrid stench and the rotting sourness of excrement.

Berestechko stinks inviolably to this day. The smell of rotten herring emanates from everyone. The shtetl reeks in expectation of a new era, and, instead of people, fading reflections of frontier misfortune wander through it. I had had enough of them by the end of the day, went beyond the edge of the town, climbed the mountain, and reached the abandoned castle of the Counts Raciborski, the recent owners of Berestechko.

The silence of the sunset turned the grass around the castle blue. The moon rose green as a lizard above the pond. Looking out the window, I could see the estate of the Raciborskis—meadows and fields of hops hidden beneath the crepe ribbons of dusk.

A ninety-year-old countess and her son had lived in the castle. She had tormented him for not having given the dying clan any heirs, and—the muzhiks told me this—she used to beat him with the coachman's whip.

A rally was gathering on the square below. Peasants, Jews, and tanners from the outlying areas had come together. Above them flared Vinogradov's ecstatic voice and the clanking of his spurs. He gave a speech about the Second Congress of the Comintern, and I roamed along the walls where nymphs with gouged eyes danced their ancient round dance. Then on the trampled floor, in a corner, I found the torn fragment of a yellowed letter. On it was written in faded ink:

Berestechko, 1820, Paul, mon bien aimé, on dit que l'empereur Napoléon est mort, est-ce vrai? Moi, je me sens bien, les couches ont été faciles, notre petit héros achève sept semaines. . . .

Below me, the voice of the divisional military commissar is droning on. He is passionately haranguing the bewildered townspeople and the plundered Jews: "You are the power. Everything here belongs to you. There are no masters. I shall now conduct an election for the Revolutionary Committee."

---

* Berestechko, 1820, my beloved Paul, I hear that Emperor Napoleon is dead. Is it true? I feel well; it was an easy birth, our little hero is already seven weeks old.

SALT

*D*ear Comrade Editor,

I want to tell you of some ignorant women who are harmful to us. I set my hopes on you, that you who travel around our nation's fronts, have not overlooked the far-flung station of Fastov, lying afar beyond the mountains grand, in a distant province of a distant land, where many a jug of home-brewed beer we drank with merriment and cheer. About this aforementioned station, there is much you can write about, but as we say back home: you can shovel till the cows come home, but the master's dung heap never gets no smaller. So I will only describe what my eyes have seen in person.

It was a quiet, glorious night seven days ago when our well-deserved Red Cavalry transport train, loaded with fighters, stopped at that station. We were all burning to promote the Common Cause and were heading to Berdichev. Only, we notice that our train isn't moving in any way at all, our Gavrilka is not beginning to roll, and the fighters begin mistrusting and asking each other: "Why are we stopping here?" And truly, the stop turned out to be mighty for the Common Cause, because the peddlers, those evil fiends among whom there was a count-less force of the female species, were all behaving very impertinently with the railroad authorities. Recklessly they grabbed the handrails, those evil fiends, they scampered over the steel roofs, frolicked, made trouble, clutching in each hand sacks of contraband salt, up to five *pood* in a sack. But the triumph of the capitalist peddlers did not last long. The initiative showed by the fighters who jumped out of the train made it possible for the struggling railroad authorities to emit sighs from their breasts. Only the female species with their bags of salt stayed around. Taking pity, the soldiers let some of the women come into the railroad cars, but others they didn't. In our own railroad car of the Second Platoon two girls popped up, and after the first bell there comes an imposing woman with a baby in her arms: "Let me in, my dear Cossacks," she says. "I have been suffering through the whole war at train stations with a suckling baby in my arms, and now I want to meet my husband, but the way the railroad is, it is impossible to get through! Don't I deserve some help from you Cossacks?"

"By the way, woman," I tell her, "whichever way the platoon decides will be your fate." And, turning to the platoon, I tell them that here we have a woman who is requesting to travel to her husband at an appointed place and that she does, in fact, have a child with her, so what will your decision be? Let her in or not?

"Let her in," the boys yell. "Once we're done with her, she won't be wanting that husband of hers no more!"

"No," I tell the boys quite politely, "I bow to your words, platoon, but I am astonished to hear such horse talk. Recall, platoon, your lives and how you yourselves were children with your mothers, and therefore, as a result, you should not talk that way!"

And the Cossacks said, "How persuasive he is, this Balmashov!" And they let the woman into the railroad car, and she climbs aboard thankfully. And each of the fighters, saying how right I am, tumble all over each other telling her, "Sit down, woman, there in the corner, rock your child the way mothers do, no one will touch you in the corner, so you can travel untouched to your husband, as you want, and we depend upon your conscience to raise a new change of guard for us, because what is old grows older, and when you need youth, it's never around! We saw our share of sorrow, woman, both when we were drafted and then later in the extra service, we were crushed by hunger, burned by cold. So just sit here, woman, and don't be frightened!"

The third bell rang and the train pulled out of the station. The glorious night pitched its tent. And in that tent hung star lanterns. And the fighters remembered the nights of Kuban and the green star of Kuban. And thoughts flew like birds. And the wheels clattered and clattered.

With the passing of time, when night was relieved of its watch and the red drummers drummed in the dawn on their red drums, then the Cossacks came to me, seeing that I am sitting sleepless and am unhappy to the fullest.

"Balmashov," the Cossacks say to me, "why are you so horribly unhappy and sitting sleepless?"

"I bow to you deeply, O fighters, and would like to ask you the small favor of letting me speak a few words with this citizen."

And trembling from head to toe, I rise from my bunk from which sleep had run like a wolf from a pack of depraved dogs, and walk up to her, take the baby from her arms, rip off the rags it's swaddled in and its diaper, and out from the diaper comes a nice fat forty-pound sack of salt.

"What an interesting little baby, Comrades! It does not ask Mommy for titty, doesn't peepee on mommy's skirty, and doesn't wake people from their sleep!"

"Forgive me, my dear Cossacks," the woman cut into our conversation very coolly, "it wasn't me who tricked you, it was my hard life."

"I, Balmashov, forgive your hard life," I tell the woman. "It doesn't cost Balmashov much. What Balmashov pays for something, that is the price he sells it for! But address yourself to the Cossacks, woman, who elevated you as a toiling mother of the republic. Address yourself to these two girls, who are now crying for having suffered under us last night. Address yourself to our women on the wheat fields of Kuban, who are wearing out their womanly strength without husbands, and to their husbands, who are lonely too, and so are forced against their will to rape girls who cross their paths! And you they didn't touch, you improper woman, although you should have been the first to be touched! Address yourself to Russia, crushed by pain!"

And she says to me, "As it is I've lost my salt, so I'm not afraid of calling things by their real name! Don't give me that about saving Russia—all you care about is saving those Yids, Lenin and Trotsky!"

"Right now our topic of conversation is not the Yids, you evil citizen! And by the way, about Lenin I don't really know, but Trotsky is the dashing son of the Governor of Tambov who, turning his back on his high social rank, joined the working classes. Like prisoners sentenced to hard labor, Lenin and Trotsky are dragging us to life's road of freedom, while you, foul citizen, are a worse counterrevolutionary than that

White general waving his sharp saber at us from his thousand-ruble horse. You can see him, that general, from every road, and the worker has only one dream—to kill him! While you, you dishonest citizen, with your bogus children who don't ask for bread and don't run out into the wind, you one doesn't see. You're just like a flea, you bite and bite and bite!"

And I truthfully admit that I threw that citizen off the moving train and onto the embankment, but she, being brawny as she was, sat up, shook out her skirts, and went on her deceitful way. Seeing this uninjured woman and Russia all around her, the peasant fields without an ear of corn, the raped girls, and the comrades, many of whom were heading for the front but few of whom would ever return, I wanted to jump from the train and either kill myself or kill her. But the Cossacks took pity on me and said, "Just shoot her with that rifle."

And I took the loyal rifle from the wall and wiped that blot off the face of the working land and the republic.

And we, the fighters of the Second Platoon, swear before you, dear Comrade Editor, and before you, dear Comrades of the editorial office, that we will deal relentlessly with all the traitors who pull us into the pit and want to turn back the stream and cover Russia with corpses and dead grass.

In the name of all the fighters of the Second Platoon,

Nikita Balmashov, Fighter of the Revolution.

EVENING

O statutes of the RCP!* You have laid impetuous rails across the rancid dough of Russian prose. You have transformed three bachelors, their hearts filled with the passion of Ryazan Jesuses, into editors of the *Krasny Kavalerist*.† You have transformed them so that day after day they can churn out a rambunctious newspaper filled with courage and rough-and-ready mirth.

Galin with his cataract, consumptive Slinkin, and Sychev with his withered intestines shuffle through the barren soil of the rear lines, spreading the revolt and fire of their news sheet through the ranks of dashing, pensioned-off Cossacks, reserve cheats who have registered as Polish translators, and girls sent out to our Polit-otdel train** from Moscow for recuperation.

By evening the newspaper is ready—a dynamite fuse placed under the cavalry. The cross-eyed lantern of the provincial sun expires in the sky, the lights of the printing press scatter in all directions and burn uncontrollably like the passion of a machine. And then, toward midnight, Galin comes out of the railroad car shuddering from the bite of his unrequited love for Irina, our train's washerwoman.

"Last time," Galin says, pale and blind, his shoulders narrow, "last

---

* The Russian Communist Party
† *The Red Cavalryman*, the newspaper distributed to the Red Cavalry forces and for which Babel also wrote pieces. See *The Red Cavalryman:* Articles, Part V in this book.
** The train belonging to the Polit-otdel, the political organ of the new Soviet government charged with the ideological education of the military.

time, Irina, we discussed the shooting of Nicholas the Bloody, executed by the proletariat of Ekaterinburg. Now we will proceed to the other tyrants who died like dogs. Peter III was strangled by Orlov, his wife's lover. Paul was torn to pieces by his courtiers and his own son. Nikolai Palkin poisoned himself, his son perished March first, his grandson drank himself to death. It is important for you to know all this, Irina!"

And raising his blank eye, filled with adoration, to the washerwoman, Galin rummages relentlessly through the crypts of murdered emperors. He is standing stoop-shouldered, bathed in the rays of the moon hovering high above like a nagging splinter, the printing presses are hammering somewhere nearby, and the radio station is shining with clear light. Irina nestles against the shoulder of Vasily the cook as she stands listening to Galin's dull and nonsensical mutterings of love. Above her, the stars are dragging themselves through the black seaweed of the sky. The washerwoman yawns, makes the sign of the cross over her puffy lips, and stares wide-eyed at Galin.

Next to Irina, rough-faced Vasily yawns. Like all cooks he scorns mankind. Cooks: they constantly have to handle the meat of dead animals and the greed of the living, which is why, when it comes to politics, a cook always seeks things that have nothing to do with him. This goes for Vasily too. Hiking his pants up to his nipples, he asks Galin about the civil lists of various kings, the dowries of Czars' daughters. Then he yawns and says, "It's night, Irina, another day will be rolling in tomorrow. Let's go crush some fleas."

They closed the kitchen door, leaving Galin alone, with the moon hovering high above like a nagging splinter. I sat opposite the moon on the embankment by the sleeping pond, wearing my spectacles, with boils on my neck, my legs bandaged. My confused poetic brain was digesting the class struggle when Galin came up to me with his twinkling cataracts.

"Galin," I said, overcome with self-pity and loneliness, "I am sick, my end is near, I am tired of life in the Red Cavalry!"

"You're a wimp!" Galin said, and the watch on his bony wrist showed one in the morning. "You're a wimp, and we end up having to put up with wimps like you! We're cracking the nut for you, and soon enough you will be able to see the meat inside, at which point you'll take your thumb out of your mouth and sing the glories of the new life in striking prose—but for the time being, just sit where you are, nice and quiet, you wimp, and stop getting in the way with all your whimpering!"

He came closer to me, fixed the bandages which had slipped off my itching sores, and let his head loll onto his pigeon breast. The night comforted us in our anguish; a light breeze rustled over us like a mother's skirt, and the weeds below us glittered with freshness and moisture.

The roaring machines of the train's printing press screeched and fell silent. Dawn drew a line across the edge of the earth, the kitchen door creaked and opened a crack. Four feet with fat heels came thrusting out into the coolness, and we saw Irina's loving calves and Vasily's big toe with its crooked black nail.

"Vasilyok," the woman whispered in a throaty, expiring voice. "Get out of my bed, you troublemaker!"

But Vasily only jerked his heel and moved closer to her.

"The Red Cavalry," Galin said to me, "the Red Cavalry is a public conjuring trick pulled off by our Party's Central Committee. The curve of the Revolution has thrown the Cossack marauders, saddled with all kinds of prejudices, into the forefront, but the Central Committee is going to weed them out with its iron rake."

Then Galin began talking about the political education of the First Cavalry. He spoke long, in a dull voice, with complete clarity. His eyelid fluttered over his cataract.

AFONKA BIDA

*W*e were fighting by Leshniov. A wall of enemy cavalry rose all around us. The new Polish strategy was uncoiling like a spring, with an ominous whistle. We were being pushed back. It was the first time in our campaign that we felt on our own backs the devilish sharpness of flank attacks and breaches in the rear lines—slashes from the very weapons that had served us so well.

The front at Leshniov was being held by the infantry. Blond and barefoot, Volhynian muzhiks shuffled along crooked trenches. This infantry had been plucked from behind its plows the day before to form the Red Cavalry's infantry reserve. The peasants had come along eagerly. They fought with the greatest zeal. Their hoarse peasant ferocity amazed even the Budyonny fighters. Their hatred for the Polish landowners was built of invisible but sturdy material.

In the second phase of the war, when our whooping had lost its effect on the enemy's imagination, and cavalry attacks on our opponents, burrowed in their trenches, had become impossible, this ragtag infantry could have proved extremely useful to the Red Cavalry. But our poverty got the upper hand: there were three muzhiks to every rifle, and the cartridges that were issued didn't fit. The venture had to be dropped, and this true peasant home guard was sent back to its villages.

But back to the fighting at Leshniov. Our foot soldiers had dug themselves in three versts from the shtetl. A hunched youth with spectacles was walking up and down in front of them, a saber dangling at his side. He moved along in little hops, with a piqued look on his face, as if his boots were pinching him. This peasant *ataman*,* chosen and cherished by the muzhiks, was a Jew, a half-blind Jewish youth, with the sickly, intent face of a Talmudist. In battle, he showed circumspect and coolheaded courage that reflected the absentmindedness of a dreamer.

It was after two o'clock on a crystalline July day. A gossamer rainbow of heat glittered in the air. A festive stripe of uniforms and horse manes braided with ribbons came sparkling from behind the hills. The youth gave the signal for the men to take their positions. The muzhiks, shuffling in their bast sandals, ran to their posts and took aim. But it turned out to be a false alarm. It was Maslak's† colorful squadrons that came riding up the Leshniov high road, their emaciated but spirited horses trotting at a steady pace. In fiery pillars of dust, magnificent banners were fluttering on gilded poles weighed down by velvet tassels. The horsemen rode with majestic and insolent haughtiness. The tattered foot soldiers came crawling out of their trenches and, their mouths hanging open, watched the light-footed elegance of the unruffled stream.

In front of the regiment, riding a bowlegged steppe horse, was Brigade Commander Maslak, filled with drunken blood and the putridness of his fatty juices. His stomach lay like a big cat on the silver-studded pommel of his saddle. When Maslak saw the muzhik foot soldiers, his face turned a merry purple, and he beckoned Platoon Commander Afonka Bida to come over. We had given the platoon commander the nickname "Makhno"** because he looked so much like him. Maslak and Bida whispered for about a minute. Then Bida turned toward the First Squadron, leaned forward, and in a low voice ordered, "Charge!" The Cossacks, one platoon after another, broke into a trot. They spurred their horses and went galloping toward the trenches from which the muzhik foot soldiers were peering, dazzled by the sight.

"Prepare to engage!" sang Afonka's voice, dismal and as if he were calling from far away.

Maslak, wheezing and coughing, relishing the spectacle, rode off to

* Term for Cossack leader.
† Maslakov, commander of the First Brigade of the Fourth Division, a relentless partisan who was soon to betray the Soviet regime. [Footnote by Isaac Babel.]
** The Ukrainian anarchist leader.

the side, and the Cossacks charged. The poor muzhik foot soldiers ran, but it was too late. The Cossack lashes were already cutting across their tattered jackets as the horsemen circled the field, twirling their whips with exquisite artistry.

"What's all this nonsense about?" I shouted over to Afonka.

"Just a bit of fun," he shouted back, fidgeting in his saddle, and he dragged a young man out of the bushes in which he was hiding.

"Just a bit of fun!" he yelled, clobbering away at the terrified young man.

The fun ended when Maslak, tired and majestic, waved his plump hand.

"Foot soldiers! Stop gawking!" Afonka yelled, haughtily straightening his frail body. "Go catch some fleas!"

The Cossacks grinned at each other and gathered into formation. The foot soldiers vanished without a trace. The trenches were empty. And only the hunched Jewish youth stood in the same spot as before, eyeing the Cossacks haughtily through his spectacles.

The gunfire from the direction of Leshniov did not let up. The Poles were encircling us. We could see the single figures of their mounted scouts through our binoculars. They came galloping from the shtetl and disappeared again like jack-in-the-boxes. Maslak gathered together a squadron and divided it on either side of the high road. A sparkling sky hung above Leshniov, indescribably void as always in hours of danger. The Jew threw his head back and blew mournfully and loud on his metallic pipe. And the foot soldiers, the battered foot soldiers, returned to their positions.

Bullets flew thickly in our direction. Our brigade staff came under machine gun fire. We rushed into the forest and fought our way through the bushes on the right side of the high road. Branches, hit, cracked heavily above us. By the time we had managed to cut our way through the bushes, the Cossacks were no longer positioned where they had been. The division commander had ordered them to retreat toward Brody. Only the muzhiks sent a few snarling shots out of their trenches, and Afonka, trailing behind, went chasing after his platoon.

He was riding on the outermost edge of the road, looking around him and sniffing at the air. The shooting died down for a few moments. Afonka decided to take advantage of the lapse and began galloping at full speed. At that moment a bullet plunged into his horse's neck. Afonka galloped on another hundred paces or so, and then, right in front of our line, his horse abruptly bent its forelegs and sank to the ground.

Afonka casually pulled his wedged foot out of the stirrup. He sat on his haunches and poked about in the wound with his copper-brown finger. Then he stood up again and ran his agonized eyes over the glittering horizon.

"Farewell, Stepan," he said in a wooden voice, and, taking a step away from the dying horse, bowed deeply to it. "How will I return to my quiet village without you? Who am I to throw your embroidered saddle on? Farewell, Stepan!" he repeated more loudly, then choked, squeaked like a mouse in a trap, and began wailing. His gurgling howls reached our ears, and we saw Afonka frantically bowing like a possessed woman in a church. "But you'll see! I won't give in to goddamn fate!" he yelled, lifting his hands from his ashen face. "You'll see! From now on I'm going to hack those cursed Poles to pieces with no mercy at all! Right down to their gasping hearts, right down to their very last gasp, and the Mother of God's blood! I swear this to you, Stepan, before my dear brothers back home!"

Afonka lay down with his face on the horse's wound and fell silent. The horse turned its deep, sparkling, violet eye to its master, and listened to his convulsive wheezing. In tender oblivion it dragged its fallen muzzle over the ground, and streams of blood, like two ruby-red harness straps, trickled over its chest covered in white muscles.

Afonka lay there without moving. Maslak walked over to the horse, treading daintily on his fat legs, slid his revolver into its ear, and fired. Afonka jumped up and swung his pockmarked face to Maslak.

"Take the harness off, Afanasi, and go back to your unit," Maslak said to him gently.

And from our slope we saw Afonka, bent under the weight of the saddle, his face raw and red like sliced meat, tottering toward his squadron, boundlessly alone in the dusty, blazing desert of the fields.

Late that evening I saw him at the cavalry transport. He was sleeping on a cart which held all his "possessions"—sabers, uniform jackets, and pierced gold coins. His blood-caked head with its wrenched, dead mouth, lay as if crucified on the saddle's bow. Next to him lay the harness of the dead horse, the inventive and whimsical raiment of a Cossack racer: breastplates with black tassels, pliant tail cruppers studded with colored stones, and the bridle embossed with silver.

Darkness thickened around us. The cavalry transport crawled heavily along the Brody high road. Simple stars rolled through Milky Ways in the sky, and distant villages burned in the cool depths of the night. Orlov, the squadron subcommander, and big-mustached Bitsenko were sitting right there on Afonka's cart discussing his grief.

"He brought the horse all the way from home," long-mustached Bitsenko said. "Where's one to find another horse like that?"

"A horse—that's a friend," Orlov answered.

"A horse—that's a father," Bitsenko sighed. "The horse saves your life more times than you can count. Bida is finished without his horse."

In the morning Afonka was gone. The skirmishes near Brody began and ended. Defeat was replaced by fleeting victory, we had a change of division commander, but Afonka was still nowhere to be seen. And only a terrible rumbling from the villages, the evil and rapacious trail of Afonka's marauding, showed us his difficult path.

"He's off somewhere getting a horse," the men of the squadron said about him, and on the endless evenings of our wanderings I heard quite a few tales of this grim, savage pillaging.

Fighters from other units ran into Afonka about ten versts from our position. He lay in wait for Polish cavalrymen who had fallen behind, or scoured the forests looking for herds hidden by the peasants. He set villages on fire and shot Polish elders for hiding horses. Echoes of the frenzied one-man battle, the furtive ransacking robbery of a lone wolf attacking a herd, reached our ears.

Another week passed. The bitter events of the day crowded out the tales of Afonka's sinister bravado, and we began to forget our "Makhno." Then the rumor went round that Galician peasants had slaughtered him somewhere in the woods. And on the day we entered Berestechko, Yemelyan Budyak from the First Squadron went to the division commander to ask if he could have Afonka's saddle and the yellow saddlecloths. Yemelyan wanted to ride in the parade on a new saddle, but it was not to be.

We entered Berestechko on August 6. Fluttering in front of our division was our new division commander's Asiatic quilted jacket and his red Cossack coat. Lyovka, the division commander's brutal lackey, walked behind him leading his stud mare. A military march filled with protracted menace resounded through the pretentious, destitute streets. The town was a colorful forest of dead-end alleys and decrepit and convulsive planks and boards. The shtetl's heart, corroded by time, breathed its despondent decay upon us. Smugglers and philistines hid in their large, shadowy huts. Only *Pan* Ludomirski, a bell ringer in a green frock coat, met us at the church.

We crossed the river and entered deeper into the petit-bourgeois settlement. We were nearing the priest's house when Afonka suddenly came riding around the corner on a large stallion.

"Greetings," he called out in a barking voice, and, pushing the fighters apart, took his old position in the ranks.

Maslak stared into the colorless distance.

"Where did you get that horse?" he wheezed, without turning around.

"It's my own," Afonka answered, and rolled himself a cigarette, wetting the paper with a quick dart of his tongue.

One after the other, the Cossacks rode up to greet him. A monstrous pink pustule shone repugnantly in his charred face where his left eye had been.

The following morning Bida went carousing. He smashed Saint Valentine's shrine in the church and tried to play the organ. He was wearing a jacket that had been cut from a blue carpet and had an embroidered lily on its back, and he had combed his sweat-drenched forelock* over his gouged-out eye.

After lunch he saddled his horse and fired his rifle at the knocked-out windows of the castle of the Count Raciborski. Cossacks stood around him in a semicircle. They tugged at the stallion's tail, prodded its legs, and counted its teeth.

"A fine figure of a horse!" Orlov, the squadron subcommander, said.

"An exemplary horse," big-mustached Bitsenko confirmed.

---

* Ukrainian Cossacks shaved their heads, leaving only a forelock, known as a *chub*.

AT SAINT VALENTINE'S

*O*ur division occupied Berestechko yesterday evening. The head-quarters have been set up in the house of Father Tuzynkiewicz. Dressed as a woman, Tuzynkiewicz had fled Berestechko before our troops entered the town. All I know about him is that he had dealt with God in Berestechko for forty-five years, and that he had been a good priest. The townspeople make a point of this, telling us he was even loved by the Jews. Under Tuzynkiewicz, the old church had been renovated. The renovations had been completed on the day of the church's three-hundredth anniversary, and the bishop had come from Zhitomir. Prelates in silk cassocks had held a service in front of the church. Potbellied and beatific, they stood like bells on the dewy grass. Faithful streams flowed in from the surrounding villages. The muzhiks bent their knees, kissed priestly hands, and on that day clouds never before seen flamed in the sky. Heavenly banners fluttered in honor of the church. The bishop himself kissed Tuzynkiewicz on the forehead and called him the Father of Berestechko, *Pater Berestechkae.*

I heard this tale in the morning at the headquarters, where I was checking over the report of our scout column that was on a reconnaissance mission near Lvov in the district of Radziekhov. I read the documents. The snoring of the orderlies behind me bespoke our never-ending homelessness. The clerks, sodden with sleeplessness, wrote orders to the division, ate pickles, and sneezed. It wasn't until midday that I got away, went to the window, and saw the church of Berestechko, powerful and white. It shone in the mild sun like a porcelain tower. Flashes of midday lightning sparkled on its shining flanks. The lightning's arcs began at the ancient green cupolas and ran lightly downward. Pink veins glimmered in the white stone of the portal, and above it were columns as thin as candles.

Then organ music came pouring into my ears, and that instant an old woman with disheveled yellow hair appeared outside the doors of the headquarters. She moved like a dog with a broken paw, hobbling in circles, her legs tottering. The pupils of her eyes, filled with the white liquid of blindness, oozed tears. The sounds of the organ, now drawn-out, now rapid, came fluttering over to us. Their flight was difficult, their wake reverberated plaintive and long. The old woman wiped her eyes with her yellow hair, sat on the floor, and began kissing the tops of my boots. The organ fell silent and then burst into a laughter of bass notes. I took the old woman by the arm and looked around. The clerks were pounding their typewriters and the orderlies snored ever louder, the spurs on their boots ripping the felt under the velvet upholstery of the sofas. The old woman kissed my boots tenderly, hugging them as she would an infant. I led her to the door and locked it behind me. The church towered strikingly before us, like a stage set. Its side doors were open, and on the graves of Polish officers lay horses' skulls.

We hurried into the churchyard, went through a dark corridor, and arrived in a square-shaped room, which had been built as an extension to the chancel. Sashka, the nurse of the Thirty-first Regiment, was puttering about in there, rummaging through a pile of silk that somebody had thrown on the floor. The cadaverous aroma of brocade, scattered flowers, and fragrant decay seeped into her nostrils, tickling and poisonous. Then Cossacks entered the room. They burst into guffaws, grabbed Sashka by the arms, and flung her with gusto onto a pile of cloth and books. Sashka's body, blossoming and reeking like the meat of a freshly slaughtered cow, was laid bare, her raised skirts revealing the legs of a squadron woman, slim, cast-iron legs, and dim-witted Kurdyukov, the silly fool, sat on top of Sashka, bouncing as if he were in a saddle, pretending to be in the grip of passion. She pushed him off and rushed out the door. We passed the altar, and only then did we enter the nave of the church.

The church was filled with light, filled with dancing rays, columns of air, and an almost cool exultation. How can I ever forget Apolek's painting, hanging over the right side-altar? In this painting twelve rosy *Paters* are rocking a cradle girdled with ribbons, with a plump infant Jesus in it. His toes are stretched out, his body lacquered with hot morning sweat. The child is writhing on his fat, wrinkly back, and twelve apostles in cardinals' miters are bending over the cradle. Their faces are meticulously shaven, flaming cloaks are billowing over their bellies. The eyes of the Apostles sparkle with wisdom, resolution, and cheer. Faint grins flit over the corners of their mouths, and fiery warts have been planted on their double chins—crimson warts, like radishes in May.

This church of Berestechko had its private and beguiling approach to the death agonies of the sons of man. In this church the saints marched to their deaths with the flair of Italian opera singers, and the black hair of the executioners shone like the beard of Holofernes. Here, above the altar, I saw the sacrilegious painting of John the Baptist, which had also sprung from Apolek's heretical, intoxicating brush. In this painting the Baptist was beautiful in the ambiguous and reticent way that drives the concubines of kings to shed their half-lost honor and their blossoming lives.

At first I did not notice the signs of destruction in the church, or didn't think they looked too bad. Only the shrine of Saint Valentine had been smashed. Lying around it were shreds of decayed wadding and the saint's ridiculous bones, which, if they resembled anything, looked like chicken bones. And Afonka Bida was still playing the organ. Afonka was drunk, wild, his body was lacerated. He had come back to us only yesterday with the horse he had seized from local farmers. Afonka was obstinately trying to play a march, and someone was badgering him in a sleepy voice, "Enough, Afonka, enough, let's go eat!" But Afonka wouldn't give up. Many more of Afonka's songs followed. Each sound was a song, and one sound was torn from the other. The song's dense tune lasted for a moment and then crossed over into another. I listened, looked around—the signs of destruction didn't look too bad. But *Pan* Ludomirski, the bell ringer of the Church of Saint Valentine and husband of the old blind woman, thought otherwise.

Ludomirsky had suddenly appeared out of nowhere. He walked through the church with measured steps, his head lowered. The old man could not bring himself to cover the scattered relics because a simple man, a lay person, may not touch what is holy. The bell ringer threw himself on the blue slabs of the floor, lifted his head, his blue nose jutting up above him like a flag above a corpse. His blue nose quivered above him and at that moment a velvet curtain by the altar swayed, rustled, and fell open. In the depths of the niche, against the backdrop of a sky furrowed with clouds, ran a bearded little figure wearing an orange Polish caftan—barefoot, his mouth lacerated and bleeding. A hoarse wail assailed our ears. The man in the orange caftan was being pursued by hatred, and his pursuer had caught up with him. The man lifted his arm to ward off the blow, and blood poured from it in a purple stream. The young Cossack standing next to me yelled out and, ducking, started to run, even though there was nothing to run from, because the figure in the niche was only Jesus Christ—the most unusual portrayal of the Son of God I have ever seen in my life.

Pan Ludomirski's Savior was a curly-headed Jew with a scraggly little beard and a low, wrinkled forehead. His sunken cheeks were tinted with carmine, and thin, red-brown eyebrows curved over eyes that were closed in pain.

His mouth was wrenched open, like a horse's mouth, his Polish caftan fastened with a precious girdle, and from under the caftan jutted crooked little porcelain feet, painted, bare, pierced by silver nails.

Pan Ludomirski stood under the statue in his green frock coat. He stretched his withered arm toward us and cursed us. The Cossacks stared at him with wide eyes and let their straw-colored forelocks hang. In a thundering voice, the bell ringer of the Church of Saint Valentine cursed us in the purest Latin. Then he turned away, fell to his knees, and clasped the feet of the Savior.

Back at the headquarters, I wrote a report to the division commander about the insult to the religious feelings of the local population. A decree was issued that the church be closed, and the guilty parties were charged with a breach of discipline and sent before the military tribunal.

SQUADRON COMMANDER
TRUNOV

*A*t noon we brought the bullet-ridden body of Trunov, our squadron commander, back to Sokal. He had been killed that morning in a battle with enemy airplanes. All the hits had caught Trunov in the face; his cheeks were riddled with wounds, his tongue torn out. We washed the dead man's face as best we could so that he would look less horrifying, placed his Caucasian saddle at the head of his coffin, and dug him a grave in a stately spot—in the public park in the middle of the town, right by the fence. Our squadron rode there on horseback. The regimental staff and the divisional military commissar were also present. And at two in the afternoon, by the cathedral clock, our rickety little cannon fired the first shot. The cannon saluted Squadron Commander Trunov with its timeworn three-inch bore, did a full salute, and we carried the coffin to the open pit. The coffin was open, the clean midday sun lit the lanky corpse, lit his mouth filled with smashed teeth and his carefully polished boots, their heels placed together as at a drill.

"Fighters!" Regimental Captain Pugachov said, as he eyed the dead man and walked up to the edge of the pit. "Fighters!" he said, standing at attention, shaking with emotion. "We are burying Pashka Trunov, an international hero! We are according Pashka the final honor!"

Pugachov raised his eyes, burning with sleeplessness, to the sky and shouted out his speech about the dead fighters of the First Cavalry, that proud phalanx which pounds the anvil of future centuries with the hammer of history. Pugachov shouted out his speech loudly, clenched

the hilt of his curved Chechen saber, and scuffed the earth with his tattered boots and their silver spurs. After his speech the orchestra played
the "Internationale," and the Cossacks took leave of Pashka Trunov.
The whole squadron leaped onto their horses and fired a volley into the
air, our three-inch cannon hissed toothlessly a second time, and we sent
three Cossacks to find a wreath. They whirled off at full gallop, firing
as they rode and plunging from their saddles in a display of acrobatics,
and brought back armfuls of red flowers. Pugachov scattered the flowers around the grave, and we stepped up to Trunov for the last kiss. I
touched my lips on an unblemished patch of forehead crowned by his
saddle, and then left to go for a walk through the town, through gothic Sokal, which lay in its blue dust and in Galicia's dejection.

A large square stretched to the left of the park, a square surrounded by ancient synagogues. Jews in long, torn coats were cursing and
shoving each other on this square. Some of them, the Orthodox, were
extolling the teachings of Adassia, the Rabbi of Belz, which led the
Hasidim of the moderate school, students of Rabbi Iuda of Husyatyn,
to attack them. The Jews were arguing about the Kabbala, and in their
quarrel shouted the name of Elijah, Gaon of Vilna, the persecutor of
the Hasidim.

Ignoring war and gunfire, the Hasidim were cursing the name of
Elijah, the Grand Rabbi of Vilna, and I, immersed in my sorrow over
Trunov, joined in the jostling and yelled along with them to ease my
pain, until I suddenly saw a Galician before me, sepulchral and gaunt
as Don Quixote.

This Galician was wearing a white linen garment that reached
down to his ankles. He was dressed as for burial or as for the
Eucharist, and led a bedraggled little cow tied to a rope. Over its wide
back darted the tiny wriggling head of a snake. On the snake's head
was a teetering wide-brimmed hat made of village straw. The pitiful
little cow tagged along behind the Galician. He led her with importance, and his lanky body cut into the hot brilliance of the sky like a
gallows.

He crossed the square with a stately stride and went into a crooked
little alley seasoned with sickeningly thick smoke. In the charred little
hovels, in beggarly kitchens, were Jewesses who looked like old Negro
women, Jewesses with boundless breasts. The Galician walked past

them and stopped at the end of the alley before the pediment of a shattered building.

There by the pediment, near a crooked white column, sat a gypsy blacksmith shoeing horses. The gypsy was pounding the horses' hooves with a hammer, shaking his greasy hair, whistling, and smiling. A few Cossacks with horses were standing around him. My Galician walked up to the blacksmith, gave him a dozen or so baked potatoes without a word, and turned and walked off, not looking up at anyone. I was about to follow him, but one of the Cossacks, waiting for his horse to be shod, stopped me. This Cossack's name was Seliverstov. He had left Makhno* some time ago and was serving in the Thirty-third Cavalry Regiment.

"Lyutov," he said, shaking my hand, "you can't keep from picking quarrels with everyone! You've got the devil in you! Why did you finish off Trunov this morning?"

And from the scraps of gossip he had heard, Seliverstov yelled foolish gibberish at me, about how that very morning I had given Trunov, my squadron commander, a good beating. Seliverstov hurled all kinds of reproaches at me, reproached me in front of all the Cossacks, but there wasn't a grain of truth in what he said. It was true that Trunov and I had argued that morning, because Trunov wasted so much time dawdling with the prisoners. He and I had argued, but Pashka Trunov is dead, he will no longer be judged in this world, and I would be the last to do so. I will tell you why we quarreled.

We had taken some men prisoner at dawn today near the train station. There were ten of them. They were in their underwear when we took them. A pile of clothes lay next to the Poles—it was a trick, so that we couldn't tell the officers from the regular men by their uniforms. They had taken off their clothes themselves, but this time Trunov decided to find out the truth.

"All officers, step forward!" he commanded, walking up to the prisoners and pulling out his revolver.

Trunov had already been wounded in the head that morning. His head was bandaged with a rag, and blood trickled from it like rain from a haystack.

---

* The Ukrainian anarchist leader.

"Officers! Own up!" he repeated, and began prodding the Poles with the butt of his revolver.

Suddenly a thin old man with yellow cheekbones, a drooping mustache, and a large, bare bony back, came forward.

"End of this war!" the old man said with incomprehensible delight. "All officers run away, end of this war!"

And the Pole held out his blue hands to Trunov.

"Five fingers," he said, sobbing, twisting his large, wilted hands from side to side. "I raising with these five fingers my family!"

The old man gasped, swayed, and broke into tears of delight. He fell on his knees before Trunov, but Trunov pushed him back with his saber.

"Your officers are dogs!" Trunov said. "Your officers threw their uniforms here, but I'm going to finish off whoever they fit! We're going to have a little fitting!"

And Trunov picked out an officer's cap from the pile of rags and put it on the old man's head.

"It fits," Trunov murmured, stepping up closer to him, "it fits." And he plunged his saber into the prisoner's gullet.

The old man fell, his legs twitching, and a foamy, coral-red stream poured from his neck. Then Andryushka Vosmiletov, with his sparkling earring and his round villager's neck, sidled up to the dying man. Andryushka unbuttoned the dying Pole's trousers, shook him lightly, and pulled the trousers off. He flung them onto his saddle, grabbed another two uniforms from the pile, and then trotted off, brandishing his whip. At that moment the sun came out from behind the clouds. It nimbly enveloped Andryushka's horse, its cheerful trot, the carefree swish of its docked tail. Andryushka rode along the path to the forest— our cavalry transport was in the forest, the carters of the transport yelling and whistling, and making signs to Vosmiletov like to a deaf man.

The Cossack was already halfway there when Trunov, suddenly falling to his knees, hoarsely yelled after him.

"Andrei!" he shouted, lowering his eyes to the ground. "Andrei!" he repeated without looking up. "Our Soviet Republic is still alive, it's too early to be dealing out her property! Bring back those rags, Andrei!"

But Vosmiletov didn't even turn around. He rode at his amazing Cossack trot, his horse pertly swatting its tail, as if to shoo us away.

"Treason!" Trunov mumbled in disbelief. "Treason!" he said, quickly shouldering his gun and shooting, missing in his haste. This time Andrei stopped. He turned his horse toward us, bouncing on his saddle like a woman, his face red and angry, his legs jerking.

"Listen, countryman!" he yelled, riding closer, and immediately calming down at the sound of his own deep and powerful voice. "I should knock you to Kingdom Come to where your you-know-what mother is! Here you've caught a dozen Poles, and make a big song-and-dance of it! We've taken hundreds and didn't come running for your help! If you're a worker, then do your job!"

Andryushka threw the trousers and the two uniforms off his saddle, snorted, turned away from the squadron commander, and came over to help me draw up a list of the remaining prisoners. He loafed about and snorted unusually loudly. The prisoners howled and ran away from him. He ran after them and gathered them under his arms, the way a hunter grips an armful of reeds and pushes them back to see a flock of birds flying to the river at dawn.

Dealing with the prisoners, I exhausted my repertoire of curses, and somehow managed to write up eight of the men, the numbers of their units, the type of gun they carried, and moved on to the ninth prisoner. The ninth was a young man who looked like a German acrobat from a good circus, a young man with a white, German chest, sideburns, a tricot undershirt, and a pair of long woolen drawers. He turned the nipples on his high chest toward me, threw back his sweaty blond hair, and told me the number of his unit. Andryushka grabbed him by his drawers and sternly asked him, "Where did you get those?"

"My mama knitted them," the prisoner answered, suddenly tottering.

"She's a great knitter, that mama of yours," Andryushka said, looking more closely at the drawers, and ran his fingertips over the Pole's neat nails. "Yes, a great knitter—us, we never got to wear nothing like that."

He felt the woolen drawers again and took the ninth man by the hand in order to take him over to the other prisoners who were already on my list. But at that moment I saw Trunov creeping out from behind a mound. Blood was trickling from his head like rain from a haystack and the dirty rag had come undone and was hanging down. He crawled on his stomach holding his carbine in his hands. It was a Japanese carbine, lacquered and with a powerful shot. From a distance of twenty paces, Pashka shot the young Pole's skull to pieces and his brains spattered onto my hands. Trunov ejected the empty cartridges from his carbine and came over to me.

"Cross that one off," he said, pointing at my list.

"I'm not crossing him off," I answered, quaking. "From what I see, Trotsky's orders don't apply to you!"

"Cross that one off the list!" Trunov repeated, pressing his black finger down onto the paper.

"I'm not crossing him off!" I yelled with all my might. "There were ten of them, now there are eight—back at headquarters, Trunov, they're not going to let you get away with this!"

"At headquarters they'll chalk it up to the rotten life we live," Trunov said, coming up to me, all tattered, hoarse, and covered in soot. But then he stopped, raised his blood-drenched face to the sky, and said with bitter reproach, "Buzz, buzz! And there comes another one buzzing!"

And Trunov pointed to four dots in the sky, four bombers that came floating out from behind the shining, swanlike clouds. These were machines from the air squadron of Major Fauntleroy, large, armored machines.

"To horse!" the platoon commanders yelled when they saw the airplanes, and took the squadron at a fast trot into the woods. But Trunov did not ride with his squadron. He stayed back at the station building, huddled silently against the wall. Andryushka Vosmiletov and two machine-gunners, two barefoot fellows in crimson breeches, stood next to him, increasingly anxious.

"Run for it, boys!" Trunov said to them, and the blood began to drain from his face. "Here's a message to Pugachov from me."

And Trunov scrawled gigantic peasant letters on a crookedly torn piece of paper.

"As I have to perish today," he wrote, "I see it my duty to add two dead toward my possible shooting down of the enemy, and at the same time I am handing over my command to Platoon Commander Semyon Golov."

He sealed the letter, sat down on the ground, and took off his boots with great difficulty.

"For you," he said, handing the machine-gunners the message and his boots. "These boots are new."

"Good luck to you, Commander," the machine-gunners muttered back to him, shifting from one foot to the other, hesitating to leave.

"And good luck to you too," Trunov said, "whatever happens." And he went over to the machine guns that stood on a mound by the station hut. Andryushka Vosmiletov, the rag looter, was waiting for him there.

"Yes, whatever happens," Trunov said to him, and aimed his machine gun. "So you're staying with me, Andryushka?"

"Jesus Christ!" Andryushka answered, terrified, started sobbing, went white, and burst out laughing. "Damned Mother of Lord Jesus Christ!"

And he aimed the second machine gun at the airplanes.

The airplanes came flying over the station in tighter circles, rattled fussily high in the air, plunged, drew arcs, and the sun rested its pink rays on the sparkle of their wings.

In the meantime we, the Fourth Squadron, sat in the forest. There, in the forest, we awaited the outcome of the unequal battle between Pashka Trunov and Major Reginald Fauntleroy of the American forces. The major and three of his bombers proved their ability in this battle. They descended to three hundred meters, and first shot Andryushka and then Trunov. None of the rounds our men fired did the Americans any harm. The airplanes turned and flew away without even noticing our squadron hidden in the forest. And that was why, after waiting for half an hour, we were able to go pick up the bodies. Andryushka Vosmiletov's body was taken by two of his kinsmen who were serving in our squadron, and we took Trunov, our deceased squadron commander, to the gothic town of Sokal and buried him there in a stately spot—in a flower bed, in the public park in the middle of the town.

IVAN AND IVAN

*D*eacon Aggeyev had deserted from the front twice. For this he had been sent to Moscow's "regiment of the branded." Sergei Sergeyevich Kamenev,* the commander in chief, had inspected this regiment at Mozhaysk before it was to be sent to the front.

"I have no use for them," the commander in chief had said. "Send them back to Moscow to clean latrines."

In Moscow the branded regiment was somehow absorbed into an infantry company. The deacon also ended up in it. He arrived at the Polish front, where he claimed to be deaf. Barsutsky, the medical assistant from the first-aid detachment, after going back and forth with him for a week, was amazed at the deacon's obstinacy.

"To hell with that deaf man!" Barsutsky said to Soychenko, the medical orderly. "Go see if you can get a cart from the cavalry transport, we'll send the deacon to Rovno for a checkup."

Soychenko went to the transport and got three carts. Akinfiev was the driver of the first cart.

"Ivan," Soychenko said to him, "you're going to take the deaf man to Rovno."

"Take him I can," Akinfiev answered.

"Be sure to get me a receipt."

"Will do," Akinfiev said. "And what was it that caused it, this deafness of his?"

* Sergei Sergeyevich Kamenev, 1881–1963, was the commander in chief of the Eastern Front.

"To save his own goods and chattels a man will gladly set fire to another man's hide," Soychenko, the medical orderly, said. "That's what caused it. He's a damn freemason, that's what he is, not deaf!"

"Take him I can," Akinfiev repeated, and drove off after the other carts.

Three carts pulled up in front of the first-aid station. In the first cart sat a nurse who was being transferred to the rear lines, the second cart had been brought for a Cossack with an inflamed kidney, and in the third cart sat Ivan Aggeyev, the deacon.

Having arranged everything, Soychenko called the medical assistant.

"There goes that damn freemason," he said. "I'm putting him on the Revolutionary Tribunal cart* against receipt. They'll be off any minute now."

Barsutsky looked out the window, saw the carts, and went running out of the house, red-faced and hatless.

"Hey, I know you're going to cut his throat!" he yelled to Ivan Akinfiev. "I want the deacon in another cart!"

"Wherever you put him," the Cossacks standing nearby said, laughing, "our Ivan's going to get him."

Ivan Akinfiev, whip in hand, was also standing there next to his horses.

"Greetings, Comrade Medical Assistant," he said politely, taking off his cap.

"Greetings, my friend," Barsutsky answered. "You're going to have to put the deacon in another cart, you wild beast!"

"It would interest me to know," Akinfiev began in a whiny voice, and his upper lip shivered, slid up, and began quivering over his dazzling teeth, "it would interest me to know, if this is right behavior or behavior that is not right, that when the enemy is tormenting us unbelievably, when the enemy is pounding our last breath out of us, when the enemy is clinging to our legs like a lead weight and tying our hands with snakes, is it correct behavior for us to clog our ears at such a deadly hour?"

---

* The Revolutionary Tribunals were set up by the Bolsheviks after the October Revolution in 1918 to combat counterrevolutionary elements, abuse of power, speculation, and desertion from the Soviet army. The Revolutionary Tribunal carts were used to transport any personnel, prisoners, and supplies that connected with the tribunals' military work.

"Our Ivan thinks like a commissar!" Korotkov, the driver of the first cart, shouted.

"So what if he thinks like a commissar!" Barsutsky muttered, and turned away. "We all do. But we have to stick to the rules."

"But our deaf friend, he can hear perfectly well!" Akinfiev suddenly interrupted. He twirled his whip with his fat fingers, laughed, and winked at the deacon. The deacon sat on the cart, his large shoulders drooping, his head trembling.

"Well then, go with God!" the medical assistant yelled in desperation. "I hold you responsible, Ivan!"

"I'll gladly be held responsible," Ivan Akinfiev said slowly, and lowered his head. "Make yourself comfortable," he said to the deacon, without looking back at him. "Make yourself even more comfortable," he repeated, and took the reins in his hands.

The carts formed a line and hurried off one after the other along the high road. Korotkov drove in front and Akinfiev at the back, whistling a tune and waving the reins. They rode this way some fifteen versts, but as evening fell they came up against a sudden enemy attack.

On that day, July 22, the Poles in a swift maneuver had mangled the rear lines of our army, stormed the shtetl of Kozin, and had taken prisoner many of our fighters of the Eleventh Division. The squadrons of the Sixth Division rushed off to Kozin to counterattack the enemy. The lightning maneuvers of the units threw the cavalry transport into turmoil, and the Revolutionary Tribunal carts rolled through the raging throes of battle for two days and nights, and it was only on the third night that they came out onto the road along which the rearguard staff was retreating. It was on this road at midnight where I ran into the three carts.

Numb with despair, I ran into them after the battle at Khotin. In the battle at Khotin my horse had been killed. After I lost him, I climbed onto an ambulance cart, and gathered up wounded men until evening. Then all the able-bodied men were kicked off the ambulance cart, and I was left behind near a destroyed hut. Night came galloping toward me on swift steeds. The wailing of the transport carts deafened the universe; on the earth enveloped by screams the roads faded away. Stars slithered out of the cool gut of the sky, and on the horizon abandoned villages flared up. With my saddle on my shoulders I walked along a torn-up field path, stopping by a bend to answer the call of nature. Relieved, I buttoned myself up, but suddenly felt droplets falling on my hand. I switched on my flashlight, turned around, and saw lying on the ground the body of a Pole, drenched in my urine. A notebook and scraps of Pilsudski's proclamation* lay next to the corpse. The Pole's notebook had a list of his expenses, a schedule of performances at the Krakow Dramatic Theater, and an entry indicating the birthday of a woman by the name of Marie-Louisa. I picked up Pilsudski's proclamation, wiped the stinking liquid from my unknown brother's skull, and walked on, bent under the weight of my saddle.

At that moment, there was a groaning of wheels close by.

"Halt!" I yelled. "Who goes there?"

Night came galloping toward me on swift steeds, flames danced on the horizon.

"We're from the Revolutionary Tribunal," a voice smothered by darkness called back.

I rushed forward and ran right into the cart.

"They killed my horse!" I said loudly. "His name was Lavrik."

No one answered. I climbed onto the cart, put the saddle under my head, fell asleep, and slept till dawn, warmed by the rotting hay and the body of Ivan Akinfiev, my chance neighbor. In the morning, the Cossack woke up later than I did.

"Thank God it's light enough to see again," he said, took his revolver out from under his little trunk, and fired a shot next to the deacon's ear. The deacon was sitting right in front of us, driving the horses. Airy gray hair fluttered over his large, balding skull. Akinfiev fired another shot next to the deacon's other ear, and slipped the revolver back into its holster.

"Good day to you, Ivan!" he said to the deacon, grunting as he pulled on his boots. "So we'll grab a bite, huh?"

"Hey!" I yelled. "What the hell d'you think you're doing?"

"Not enough, that's what I'm doing!" Akinfiev answered, unpacking the food. "It's the third day now he's been pretending."

Then Korotkov, who I knew from the Thirty-first Regiment, yelled back from the first cart, telling me the whole story of the deacon from

* Jozef Klemens Pilsudski, 1867–1935, the first Chief of State of Poland after its independence from Russia in 1918, and commander in chief of the Polish army.

the beginning. Akinfiev listened carefully, cupping his ear, and then from under his saddle pulled out a roasted leg of ox. It was wrapped in a sackcloth and had straw all over it.

The deacon climbed over to us from the box, carved off a slice of green meat with his knife, and gave everyone a piece. After breakfast, Akinfiev wrapped the leg of ox in the sackcloth and slid it into the hay.

"Ivan," he said to Deacon Aggeyev, "let's drive out the devil. We have to stop anyway, since the horses need water."

He took a medicine bottle out of his pocket and a Tarnovsky syringe,* and gave them to the deacon. They climbed off the cart and walked about twenty paces into the field.

"Nurse!" Korotkov yelled from the first cart. "Adjust your eyes for distance, and you'll be dazzled by Akinfiev's endowment!"

"I you-know-what you and your endowments," the woman muttered, and turned away.

Akinfiev pulled up his shirt. The deacon knelt in front of him and gave him his injection. Then he wiped the syringe with a rag and held it up to the light. Akinfiev pulled his trousers up. He waited a moment, went behind the deacon, and fired another shot right next to his ear.

"My humblest thanks, Ivan," he said, buttoning up his trousers.

The deacon laid the medicine bottle on the grass and got up from his knees. His airy hair flew up.

"I will answer to a higher judge," he said dully. "You are not above me, Ivan."

"Nowadays everyone judges everyone else," the driver of the second cart, who looked like a boisterous little hunchback, interrupted. "They even sentence you to death, just like that!"

"Or even better," Deacon Aggeyev said, straightening up, "kill me, Ivan."

"Don't talk nonsense, Deacon!" Korotkov, whom I knew from before, said, coming up to him. "You should realize what kind of man you're riding with here. A lesser man would have shot you down like a duck, you wouldn't have had time to quack, yet he's trying to fish the truth out of you, and teach you a thing or two, you defrocked cleric!"

---

* A device for treating syphilis.

"Or even better," the deacon repeated obstinately, stepping forward, "kill me, Ivan."

"As it is, you'll kill yourself, you bastard," Akinfiev answered, going white and breaking into a lisp. "You're digging your own pit and burying yourself in it!"

Akinfiev waved his arms, tore his collar open, and fell down on the ground in a fit.

"O my dear little sweetheart!" he yelled wildly, and threw sand into his face. "O my bittersweet darling, my sweet darling Soviet power!"

"Ivan," Korotkov said, coming up to him, tenderly laying his hand on his shoulder. "Don't beat yourself, my dear friend, don't be sad. Come, we have to go now."

Korotkov filled his mouth with water and spat it into Akinfiev's face, and then carried him over to the cart. The deacon sat on the box again, and we drove off.

There were no more than two versts left to the shtetl of Verba. Countless transport carts had crowded into the town that morning. They were from the Eleventh, the Fourteenth, and the Fourth Divisions. Jews in waistcoats, with raised shoulders, stood in their doorways like bedraggled birds. Cossacks went from yard to yard collecting rags and eating unripe plums. The moment we arrived, Akinfiev curled up on the hay and fell asleep, and I took a blanket from his cart and went to look for some shade to lie down in. But the fields on both sides of the road were covered with excrement. A bearded muzhik in copper-rimmed spectacles and a Tyrolean hat was sitting by the wayside reading a newspaper. He waved to me and said, "We call ourselves human, but we make more filth than the jackals! One is ashamed to face the earth!"

And he turned away and went back to reading his newspaper through his large spectacles.

I headed for the forest to the left, and saw the deacon approaching me.

"Where are you off to, countryman?" Korotkov yelled to him from the first cart.

"To relieve myself," the deacon mumbled. He grabbed my hand, and kissed it. "You are a fine gentleman," he whispered with a grimace, shuddering and gasping for air. "I beg you, whenever you have a free moment, to write a letter to the town of Kasimov, so my wife can mourn for me."

"Are you deaf, Father Deacon, or not?" I shouted into his face.

"Excuse me?" he said. "Excuse me?" And he cupped his ear.

"Are you deaf, Aggeyev, or not?"

"That's exactly it, deaf!" he quickly said. "Three days ago I could hear perfectly well, but Comrade Akinfiev crippled my hearing with a shot. He was supposed to deliver me to Rovno, Comrade Akinfiev was, but I really doubt he'll deliver me there."

And the deacon fell to his knees and crawled headfirst between the carts, completely entangled in his disheveled, priestly hair. Then he got up from his knees, pulled himself free from in between the carts, and went over to Korotkov, who gave him some tobacco. They rolled cigarettes and lit them for each other.

"That's better," Korotkov said, and made some space next to him.

The deacon sat down, and both were silent.

Then Akinfiev woke up. He rolled the leg of ox out of the sackcloth, carved off a slice of green meat with his knife, and gave everyone a piece. At the sight of the festering meat I felt overcome by weakness and desperation, and gave my piece back.

"Farewell, boys!" I said. "Good luck to you all!"

"Farewell," Korotkov said.

I took my saddle from the cart and left. As I walked off, I heard the endless muttering of Akinfiev.

"Ivan, you made a big mistake, my friend," he was saying to the deacon. "You should have trembled at my name, but you just got into my cart without a second thought. You could still have escaped before you ran into me, but now I'm going to hurt you, Ivan, you can bet on it, I'm really going to hurt you!"

THE CONTINUATION
OF THE STORY OF
A HORSE

*F*our months ago, Savitsky, our former division commander, took away the white stallion belonging to Khlebnikov, commander of the First Squadron. Khlebnikov had left the army shortly after, and today Savitsky received a letter from him.

Khlebnikov to Savitsky

And no anger upon the Budyonny army can I have longer, my sufferings in that army I understand and keep within my heart purer than anything holy. But to you, Comrade Savitsky, as an international hero, the working masses of Vitebsk, where I am the chairman of the District Revolutionary Committee, send the proletarian cry: "Give us World Revolution!" And we hope that that white stallion will trot beneath you on soft paths for many a year to come in aid of Freedom so beloved by all, and the Brother Republics in which we must keep a sharp eye out for the provincial authorities and the district units in an administrative respect. . . .

Savitsky to Khlebnikov

My true and dear Comrade Khlebnikov,
    Which letter you wrote me is very commendable for the Common Cause, all the more after your foolishness when the good of your own hide made your eyes blind and you de-joined our Communist Party of the Bolsheviks. Our Communist Party, Comrade Khlebnikov, is an iron column of fighters sacrificing their blood in the front lines, and when blood flows from iron, then it is no joke, Comrade, but victory

or death. The same goes for the Common Cause, the dawn of which I do not expect to see because the fighting is heavy and I have to change commanding officers every two weeks. Thirty days I have been fighting in the rear guard, covering the retreat of the invincible First Red Cavalry, and finding myself facing powerful gunfire from airplanes and artillery. Tardy was killed, Likhmanikov was killed, Gulevoy was killed, Trunov was killed, and the white stallion is no longer under me, so with the change in our fortunes of war, Comrade Khlebnikov, do not expect to see your beloved Division Commander Savitsky ever again. To tell you the truth, we shall meet again in the Kingdom of Heaven, although, from what people say, the old man up there in heaven isn't running a kingdom, but an all-out whorehouse, and as it is we have enough clap down here on earth—so, who knows, we might not get to see each other after all. Farewell, Comrade Khlebnikov.

THE WIDOW

Shevelyov, the regimental captain, is dying in an ambulance cart. A woman is sitting at his feet. Night, pierced by the flashes of the cannonade, is stooping over the dying man. Lyovka, the division commander's driver, is warming up food in a pot. Lyovka's forelock is hanging over the fire, the hobbled horses are crackling in the bushes. Lyovka is stirring the pot with a twig and talking to Shevelyov, who is stretched out in the ambulance cart.

"I worked in the town of Temryuk, Comrade, as a circus rider and also as a lightweight wrestler. The women in a small town like that get very bored, so when the little ladies saw me, all the walls came tumbling down. 'Lev Gavrilich,' they'd say to me, 'surely you won't turn down a little à la carte appetizer—you won't find it a waste of your time.' So I went with one of them to a tavern. We order two portions of veal, we order a jug of vodka, we sit there nice and quiet, we drink, I look, and what do I see? Some sort of gentleman bustling over toward me, nicely dressed, clean, but I notice that he is full of himself, not to mention that he was two sheets to the wind.

" 'If you will pardon me,' he says to me, 'what, if I may ask, is your nationality?'

" 'For what reason are you touching me about my nationality when I am in the company of a lady?' I ask him.

"And he: 'You? You are an athlete?' he says. 'In French wrestling they'd finish you off in the twinkle of an eye. Show me your nationali—'
Yet I, believe it or not, still don't catch what's going on.

"So I ask him, 'Why do you—I don't even know your name—why do you try to provoke the kind of misunderstanding where one man or the other will have to lose his life, in other words, lie flat on his back awaiting his last breath?'"

"Lie flat on his back awaiting his last breath!" Lyovka repeats enthusiastically, stretching his arms up to the sky, letting the night envelop him like an aura. The tireless wind, the clean wind of the night, sings, fills itself with sound, and gently rocks the soul. The stars, blazing in the darkness like wedding rings, fall on Lyovka, become entangled in his hair, and expire on his tousled head.

"Lyovka, come here," Shevelyov suddenly whispers to him with blue lips. "The gold I have is for Sashka," the wounded man whispers. "The rings, the harness—everything's hers. We did our best to get by, I want to reward her. My clothes, my underwear, my medal for selfless heroism, are for my mother on the Terek. Send them to her with a letter and write in the letter: The regimental captain sends his regards, and don't cry. The house is yours, old woman, enjoy it. If anyone lays a finger on you, go straight to Budyonny and tell him, 'I'm Shevelyov's mama!' My horse, Abramka, I offer to the regiment, I am offering the horse in memory of my soul."

"Don't worry, I'll see to the horse," Lyovka mumbles. "Sashka!" he yells to the woman, waving to her. "You heard what he said? Swear before him—will you be sure to give the old woman what's hers or won't you?"

"I you-know-what the old woman!" Sashka says, and walks off into the bushes, holding her head high like a blind woman.

"Will you give her her miserable share?" Lyovka asks, catching up with her and grabbing her by the throat. "Say it here in front of him!"

"I'll give it to her, let me go!"

And then, having forced the declaration out of her, Lyovka grabbed the pot from the fire and began pouring soup into the dying man's rigid mouth. Cabbage soup trickled down Shevelyov's face, the spoon clanked against his sparkling, dead teeth, and bullets sang with growing mournfulness and force through the dense expanses of the night.

"They're shooting with rifles, the bastards," Lyovka said.

"The damn lackeys!" Shevelyov answered. "They're ripping open our right flank with their machine guns."

And Shevelyov, closing his eyes, stately as a corpse on a slab, listened to the battle with his large, waxen ears. Next to him, Lyovka was chewing meat, crunching and panting. When he had finished, Lyovka licked his lips and pulled Sashka into a ditch.

"Sash," he said, trembling, burping, his hands fidgeting. "Sash, as the Lord is my witness, we're covered in vice like yard dogs with lice. You only live once and then you die! Let me have you, Sash—I'll serve you, even if it's with my blood! His time's up, Sash, but the Lord has plenty more days in store for us!"

They sat down in the tall grass. The wavering moon crept from behind the clouds and stopped over Sashka's bare knee.

"You're warming each other," Shevelyov mumbled, "but it looks like the Fourteenth Division has been routed."

Lyovka crunched and panted in the bushes. The misty moon loitered in the sky like a beggar woman. Distant gunfire floated in the air. Feather grass rustled on the troubled earth onto which August stars fell.

Then Sashka returned to her previous place. She changed the wounded man's bandages and raised the flashlight over the festering wound.

"By tomorrow you'll be gone," Sashka said, wiping the cold sweat off Shevelyov. "By tomorrow you'll be gone. Death's already in your guts."

At that moment a heavy, many-voiced blast hit the earth. Four fresh enemy brigades, sent into battle under a unified command, had fired their first shell at Busk, lighting up the Bug watershed and severing our communications. Obedient blazes rose on the horizon, and heavy birds of cannon fire soared up from the flames. Busk was burning and Lyovka sped through the forest with the rattling cart of the commander of Division Six. He gripped the red reins tightly; the lacquered wheels banged against tree stumps. Shevelyov's ambulance cart came flying behind, Sashka checking the horses, which were straining at their harnesses.

They came to a clearing in the forest where there was a first-aid station. Lyovka unharnessed the horses and set out for the medical officer to ask for a horse blanket. He walked through the forest, which was filled with carts. Nurses' bodies jutted out from under their carts, timid dawn trudged over the soldiers' sheepskins. The sleeping men's boots lolled in a jumble, their pupils pointed to the sky, the black pits of their mouths askew.

The medical officer did have a horse blanket. Lyovka returned to Shevelyov, kissed his forehead, and pulled the blanket over his head. Then Sashka came up to the cart. She had knotted her kerchief under her chin and shaken the straw out of her dress.

"Pavlik," she said. "Jesus Christ in Heaven." And she lay herself against the dead man, covering him with her massive body.

"Her grief's killing her," Lyovka said. "Say what you want, she had it good with him. Now she'll have to take on the whole squadron again. It's tough."

And he drove off to Busk, where the headquarters of the Sixth Cavalry Division had been set up.

There, about ten versts from town, the battle against the Savinkov Cossacks was raging. The traitors were fighting us under the command of Cossack Captain Yakovlev, who had gone over to the Poles. They fought with courage. It was the second day our division commander was out with the troops, and as Lyovka did not find him at the headquarters, he went back to his hut, cleaned his horses, poured water over the wheels of his cart, and lay down to sleep on the threshing floor in the shed. The shed was filled with fresh hay, as arousing as perfume. Lyovka slept himself out, and then sat down to eat. His landlady boiled him some potatoes, which she doused in buttermilk. Lyovka was still sitting at the table when the funereal wail of trumpets and the clatter of many hooves resounded in the street. A squadron with bugles and banners rode along the winding Galician street. Shevelyov's body, covered with flags, was lying on a gun carriage. Sashka was riding behind the coffin on Shevelyov's stallion. A Cossack song came drifting from the back rows.

The squadron marched along the main street and turned toward the river. Lyovka, barefoot and without a cap, ran after the marching detachment and grabbed the reins of the squadron commander's horse.

Neither the division commander, who had stopped by the crossroads to salute the dead commander, nor his staff could hear what Lyovka was saying to the squadron commander.

"Drawers . . . mother on the Terek . . ." came wafting over to us in fragments on the breeze. Lyovka was shouting incoherently.

The squadron commander, without listening any further, freed his reins and pointed at Sashka. The woman shook her head and rode on. Lyovka jumped onto her horse behind her, grabbed her by the hair, pulled her head back, and slammed his fist into her face. Sashka wiped the blood away with the hem of her skirt and rode on. Lyovka slipped off her saddle, shook his forelock out of his face, and tied his red scarf around his hips. And the howling bugles led the squadron to the sparkling shore of the River Bug.

Lyovka came back to us later that day, his eyes glittering, and shouted, "I gave it to her! 'When the time comes,' she says, 'I'll send it to his mother. I won't forget him,' she says, 'I'll remember him.' 'You'd better remember him, you evil snake! If you forget, we'll come around and remind you! And if you forget a second time, we'll come around and remind you a second time!' "

ZAMOSC

*T*he division commander and his staff were lying on a harvested field about three versts from Zamosc. The troops were going to attack the town that evening. Our orders were that we were to spend the night in Zamosc, and the division commander was waiting for a report of victory.

It was raining. Wind and darkness blew over the sodden earth. Stars were extinguished in the swelling ink of the clouds. Exhausted horses sighed and stamped their hooves in the darkness. We had nothing to give them to eat. I tied my horse's reins to my foot, wrapped myself in my cloak, and lay down in a waterlogged pit. The wet earth wrapped me in its comforting sepulchral embrace. The mare tugged at her reins, pulling at my leg. She found a tuft of grass and began nibbling at it. I fell asleep and dreamed of a threshing floor covered with hay. The dusty gold of threshed corn droned over it. Sheaves of wheat flew into the sky, the July day turned into evening, and the thickets of the sunset arched back over the village.

I lay stretched out on my silent bed of hay, and the hay caressing the nape of my neck drove me out of my mind. Then the barn doors opened with a whistle. A woman in a ball gown came up to me. She released one of her breasts from the black lace of her bodice and carefully offered it to me, like a wet nurse about to suckle an infant. She laid her breast on mine. An agonizing warmth shook the foundations of my soul, and drops of sweat—living, flowing sweat—seethed between our nipples.

"Margot!" I wanted to shout. "The earth is dragging me away with the rope of its wretchedness like a stubborn dog, and yet I have managed to see you again!"

I wanted to shout these words, but my jaws, clamped shut by a sudden frost, would not unclench.

Then the woman moved away from me and fell to her knees.

"Lord Jesus," she said, "take unto Thee the soul of Thy departed slave!"

She pressed two worn five-kopeck coins onto my lids and stuffed fragrant hay into the opening of my mouth. A moan tried in vain to flutter through my clenched jaws; my expiring pupils slowly rolled beneath the copper coins; I could not unclasp my hands, and . . . I awoke.

A muzhik with a tangled beard was lying in front of me. He held a rifle in his hands. My horse's back cut the sky like a black crossbeam. The reins gripped my foot in a tight noose, pulling it upward.

"You fell asleep, countryman," the muzhik said, and smiled with nocturnal, sleepless eyes. "That horse has dragged you a good half verst!"

I untied the reins and got up. Blood was trickling down my face, slashed by thistles.

Right there, not two paces away from me, lay the front line. I could see the chimneys of Zamosc, the thievish lights in the ravines of its ghetto, and the watchtower with its shattered lantern. The damp sunrise poured down on us like waves of chloroform. Green rockets soared over the Polish camp. They flashed in the air, came showering down like roses beneath the moon, and expired.

And in the silence I heard the distant breath of a moan. The smoke of a furtive murder encircled us.

"They're killing someone," I said. "Who is it they're killing?"

"The Pole's on a rampage," the muzhik told me. "The Pole is slashing the Yids' throats."

The muzhik moved the rifle from his right hand to his left. His beard had slid completely to one side. He looked at me fondly. "These nights on the front line are long," he said. "There's no end to these nights. One itches all over to talk to someone, but where d'you find this someone?"

The muzhik passed me his cigarette for me to light mine.

"It's all the fault of those Yids," he said. "They try to please every-body. After the war there'll be hardly any of them left. How many Yids you reckon there's in the world?"

"Around ten million," I answered, and began to bridle my horse.

"There'll be two hundred thousand of them left!" the muzhik yelled, grabbing me by the arm, afraid that I was about to leave. But I climbed onto my saddle and galloped off in the direction of our head-quarters.

The division commander was preparing to ride off. The orderlies were standing at attention before him, dozing on their feet. Squadrons of dismounted horsemen crept over wet hillocks.

"They've turned the screws on us," the division commander whis-pered, and rode off.

We followed him along the road to Sitaniec.

It began raining again. Dead mice floated down the roads. Autumn surrounded our hearts with traps. Trees, upright naked corpses, stood swaying at crossroads.

We arrived in Sitaniec in the morning. I was with Volkov, the staff quartermaster. He found us a hut at the edge of the village.

"Wine," I told the mistress of the house. "Wine, meat, and bread!"

The old woman sat down on the floor and fed the calf she had hid-den under her bed.

"*Nic niema*,"* she answered indifferently, "and I don't remember a time when there ever was anything."

I sat at the table, took off my revolver, and fell asleep. A quarter of an hour later I opened my eyes and saw Volkov hunched over the win-dowsill. He was writing a letter to his bride.

"Highly esteemed Valya," he wrote. "Do you remember me?"

I read the first line, and then took some matches out of my pocket and lit a pile of straw lying on the floor. Unfettered flames flashed up and came moving toward me. The old woman hurled herself chest-first onto the fire and extinguished it.

"What you doing, *Pan?*" the old woman gasped, staggering back in horror.

---

* Polish: "There's nothing."

Volkov turned around and stared at her with his empty eyes, and went back to writing his letter.

"I'm going to burn you, old woman," I muttered, drowsily. "I'm going to burn you and that stolen calf of yours."

"*Czekaj!*"* she shouted in a high-pitched voice. She ran out into the hall and came back with a jug of milk and some bread.

We had barely eaten half the bread when we heard shots rattling outside in the yard. There were many shots. They went on rattling and got on our nerves. We finished the milk, and Volkov went out into the yard to see what was going on.

"I've saddled your horse," he called through the window. "They've shot mine full of holes. The Poles have set up their machine guns less than a hundred paces from here!"

So the two of us ended up with one horse. She barely managed to take us out of Sitaniec. I sat in the saddle, and Volkov climbed on behind.

Transport carts rolled, roared, and sank in the mud. The morning seeped out of us like chloroform seeping over a hospital table.

"You married, Lyutov?" Volkov suddenly said, sitting behind me.

"My wife left me," I answered, dozing off for a few seconds, and I dreamed that I was sleeping in a bed.

Silence.

Our horse totters.

"Two more versts and this mare will be finished," Volkov says, sitting behind me.

Silence.

"We've lost the campaign," Volkov mutters, and begins to snore.

"Yes," I say.

* Polish: "Wait."

TREASON

*C*omrade Investigator Burdenko. Answering your question, my
Party Membership Number is twenty-four zero-zero, issued to
Nikita Balmashov by the Krasnodar Party Committee. My life history
I would describe as domestic until 1914, as I worked on my father's
fields, and I went from the fields into the ranks of the imperialists to
defend Citizen Poincaré and the butchers of the German Revolution
Ebert-Noske,* who, it looks like, were fast asleep one day and in their
dreams saw how they could help St. Ivan, my Cossack village in the
District of Kuban. And so the string kept unraveling all the way until
Comrade Lenin, together with Comrade Trotsky, turned my beast of a
bayonet to point it at new and better guts and paunches. From that
time on I've been carrying number twenty-four zero-zero on the
watchful tip of my bayonet, and I find it shameful and laughable to hear
your words, Comrade Investigator Burdenko, this impossible sham
about some unknown hospital in N. I neither fired at this hospital nor
attacked it—I couldn't have. We were wounded, the three of us, in
other words, Fighter Golovitsyn, Fighter Kustov, and me, not to mention that we had a fever in our bones and so didn't attack, but were crying, standing there in our hospital shirts out on the square among the
free people of Jewish nationality! And as for the destruction of the three
windowpanes, which we destroyed with an officer's revolver, I declare

*Raymond Poincaré, 1860–1932, president of France, supported the Imperialist Russian forces
against the Bolsheviks in the Russian Civil War. Ebert and Noske were held responsible for the
suppression of the Spartacus Rebellion in Germany.

from the bottom of my heart that these windowpanes did not corre-
spond to their purpose, as they were in the storeroom, which did not
need them. And Dr. Yaveyn, seeing our bitter gunshot, only laughed
with lots of chuckles, standing by the window of his hospital, and this
too can be corroborated by the aforementioned free Jews of the shtetl
of Kozin. As to Dr. Yaveyn, I also submit the following material,
Comrade Investigator, that he laughed when we, the three wounded
men, in other words Fighter Golovitsyn, Fighter Kustov, and me, ini-
tially presented ourselves for cure, and from his very first words, he
informed us far too roughly, 'You, fighters, will each take a bath in the
tub, and this very instant remove your weapons and clothes, as I'm worried they might be infectious—I want them out of here and dropped off
at the storeroom!' And as Fighter Kustov saw a beast before him and
not a man, he stepped forward with his broken leg and expressed himself, that the only people who need fear an infection from his sharp
Kuban saber are the enemies of our Revolution, and Fighter Kustov
also expressed an interest in knowing if at the storeroom one would find
among the things there a Party Fighter or, on the contrary, someone
from the partyless masses. And here Dr. Yaveyn obviously saw that we
were well able to recognize treason. He turned his back and without
another word and—again with lots of chuckles—sent us to the ward
where we also went, limping with broken legs, waving our crippled
arms, holding each other up, as the three of us are from the same
Cossack village of St. Ivan, in other words Fighter Golovitsyn, Fighter
Kustov, and me, we have the selfsame fate, and he who has a ripped-off
leg, he holds on to his comrade's arm, and he who is missing an arm,
he leans on his comrade's shoulder! Following the order issued, we went
to the ward where we expected to encounter Cultural and Educational
Work and devotion to the Cause, but what did we see in the ward? We
saw Red Army soldiers, only infantrymen, sitting on neat beds, playing
checkers, and with them nurses of tall build, smooth, standing by the
windows, fluttering their eyelashes. When we saw this, we stood there
as if lightning had struck us.

"You're done with fighting, boys?" I shout to the wounded.

"We're done with fighting," the wounded answer, and they move
their checkers made of bread pellets.

"Too soon," I tell the wounded, "too soon have you finished fighting, infantry, when the enemy walks on soft paws not fifteen versts from this town, and when you can read of our international situation in the *Krasny Kavalerist* newspaper, that it's one big disaster and that the horizon is full of black clouds!" But my words bounced off the heroic infantry like sheep dung from a regimental drum, and instead of a discussion the sisters of mercy led us off to some bunks and started all that drivel again about how we should hand in our weapons as if we had already been defeated! They agitated Kustov beyond words, and he began tearing at the wound on his left shoulder above his bleeding heart of a fighter and proletarian. Seeing his struggle, the nurses were quiet, but they only were quiet for the shortest time, and then again the partyless masses began making fun, and in the night the nurses sent volunteers ready to rip our clothes off us as we slept, or force us for Cultural and Educational Work to play theater roles in women's clothes, which is unseemly.

Unmerciful sisters! They tried more than once to trick us out of our clothes with sleeping powders, so that we started sleeping in shifts with one eye open, and we even went to the latrine in full uniform and with our revolvers. And suffering like this for a week and a day, so that we were already ranting and seeing visions, finally, waking on the accused morning of August 4, we noted on ourselves the following change: that we are lying there in shirts with numbers on them, like prisoners, without weapons and without the clothes sewn by our mothers, poor doddering old women from Kuban. And the sun, we see, is shining nice and bright, but the trench infantry, among who we three Red Cavalrymen are suffering, is hooliganizing us! And along with them the unmerciful sisters, who the night before gave us sleeping powders and now are wiggling their fresh breasts, bringing us trays with cococoa to drink, and milk enough in this cococoa to drown in! This whole frolicking merry-go-round makes the infantry bang their crutches on the ground so loud it's dreadful, and they pinch our bottoms like we're buyable females, yelling that Budyonny's First Cavalry has also finished fighting. But no, my curly-headed Comrades, you who have stuffed yourselves with such splendid paunches that rattle like machine guns in the night! Budyonny's First Cavalry has not yet finished fighting! So what we did was we excused ourselves as if we had to go answer a call of nature. Then the three of us went down into the courtyard and from the courtyard we went with our fevers and blue boils to Citizen Boyderman, the chairman of the Revolutionary Committee, without whom, Comrade Investigator Burdenko, it would never have come to this misunderstanding with the shooting—in other words, if it hadn't been for him, I mean if it hadn't been for the chairman of the Revolutionary Committee, who made us lose our senses completely. And even though we cannot present hard evidence about Citizen Boyderman, when we came in to the office of the chairman of the Revolutionary Committee, we noticed that he was a citizen of advanced years in a sheepskin coat, of Jewish nationality, sitting at the table, and the table is so full of papers that it is a terrible sight to see. And Citizen Boyderman's eyes dart first to one side, then to the other, and it is clear he has no idea what these papers are. These papers are a misery to him, even more so when unknown but deserving fighters come threatening, demanding rations, while one after the other local workers interrupt, informing him of the counterrevolution in the surrounding villages. And also regular workers suddenly appear who wish to get married at the Revolutionary Committee as soon as possible and without red tape. And we too announced with loud voices the incidents of treason at the hospital, but Citizen Boyderman only stared at us and his eyes darted again first to one side and then to the other, and he patted us on the shoulder, which already is not an Authority, and unworthy of an Authority! He didn't issue any resolution at all, and only announced, "Comrade Fighters, if you have compassion for the Soviet State, then leave these premises!" But we would not agree to do this, in other words, leave the premises, but demanded a full verification of his person, which, when he would not do that, we lost consciousness. And having lost consciousness, we went out onto the square in front of the hospital, where we disarmed the militia which was made up of one cavalry individual, and with tears in our eyes destroyed the three poor-quality windowpanes in the aforementioned storeroom. Dr. Yaveyn, during this unallowable action, made faces and chuckled, and all that at the very moment when four days later Comrade Kustov was to die of his illness!

In his short Red life, Comrade Kustov was endlessly distressed about treason, which one moment is winking at us from the window, the next is making fun of the coarse proletariat. But the proletariat,

Comrades, knows full well how coarse treason is, and we are pained by that, our soul is burning, and its fire tears our bodily prison to pieces.

Treason, I tell you, Comrade Investigator Burdenko, grins at us from the window, treason creeps in its socks through our house, treason has flung its boots over its shoulders, so that the floorboards of the house it is about to ransack will not creak.

CZESNIKI

*T*he Sixth Division had gathered in the forest near the village of Czesniki and waited for the signal to attack. But Pavlichenko, commander of the Sixth Division, was waiting for the Second Brigade, and would not give the signal. So Voroshilov* rode up to the division commander and prodded his chest with the muzzle of his horse.

"We're dawdling, Division Commander," he said, "we're dawdling!"

"The Second Brigade is proceeding as you ordered at full trot to the place of engagement," Pavlichenko answered in a hollow voice.

"We're dawdling, Division Commander, we're dawdling!" Voroshilov repeated, tugging at his reins.

Pavlichenko took a step back.

"In the name of conscience," he shouted, wringing his clammy fingers, "in the name of conscience, do not rush me, Comrade Voroshilov."

"Do not rush me?" hissed Klim Voroshilov, the political representative of the Revolutionary War Council, closing his eyes. He sat on his horse, silent, his eyes closed, his lips moving. A Cossack wearing bast sandals and a bowler hat stared at him in amazement. The galloping squadrons went crashing through branches, roaring through the forest like the wind. Voroshilov combed his horse's mane with his Mauser.

"Army Commander!" he yelled, turning to Budyonny. "Say a few words to your troops before we ride! There he is, the Pole, standing on top of the hill like a pretty picture, laughing at you!"

* Kliment Yefremovich Voroshilov, 1881–1969, was a close friend and colleague of Stalin's, and cofounder with Budyonny of the Red Cavalry.

As a matter of fact, we could see the Poles through our binoculars. The army staff jumped onto their horses and the Cossacks streamed toward Budyonny from all sides.

Ivan Akinfiev, the former vehicular driver of the Revolutionary Tribunal, rode past sitting sidesaddle, and prodded me with his stirrup.

"What? You're with the troops now, Ivan?" I called out to him. "You've got no ribs left!"

"I you-know-what these ribs," Akinfiev called back. "Let's hear what the man has to say!"

He rode on and pushed his way through right up to Budyonny.

Budyonny shuddered, and said in a quiet voice: "Men! Our situations . . . well, it's . . . bad. A bit more liveliness, men!"

"To Warsaw!" the Cossack in the bast sandals and the bowler hat yelled, his eyes wild, and he slashed the air with his saber.

"To Warsaw!" Voroshilov shouted, rearing his horse and vaulting into the center of the squadrons.

"Fighters and Commanders!" he shouted passionately. "In Moscow, our ancient capital, there rages a power never before seen! A government of workers and peasants, the first in the world, orders you, fighters and commanders, to attack the enemy and bring back victory!"

"Draw your sabers!" Pavlichenko sang out from far behind the army commander, and his fat crimson lips glistened foam-speckled through the ranks. Pavlichenko's red Cossack coat hung in tatters, his repulsive, meaty face was twisted. He saluted Voroshilov with the blade of his precious saber.

"In accordance with my duty to the revolutionary pledge," said the commander of Division Six, wheezing, his eyes darting around, "I hereby report to the Revolutionary War Council that the Second Invincible Cavalry Brigade is at the present time moving at a fast trot to the place of engagement!"

"Well, get on with it," Voroshilov answered, waving him away. He tugged at his reins and rode off, with Budyonny at his side. On their long-limbed chestnut mares they rode next to each other in identical military jackets and glittering silver-embroidered trousers. The fighters, whooping, flocked after them, and pale steel gleamed in the purulence of the autumn sun. But I did not hear solidarity in the howls of the Cossacks, and, waiting for the attack, I went into the forest, into its heart, to our provision station.

A wounded Red Army soldier lay there in a delirium, and Styopka Duplishchev, a young, dim-witted Cossack, was rubbing down Hurricane, the division commander's thoroughbred stallion, which was descended from Lyulyusha, the Rostov record holder. The wounded man was rambling, reminiscing about Shuya, about a heifer and some sort of flax strands. Duplishchev, to drown out the pitiful muttering, was singing a song about an orderly and a fat general's wife. He sang louder and louder, waving his currycomb and patting the horse. But he was interrupted by Sashka, puffy Sashka, the lady of all the squadrons. She rode up to Duplishchev and jumped off her horse.

"So we'll do it, or what?" Sashka said to him.

"Get out of here," the young Cossack answered, turning his back to her, and began plaiting ribbons into Hurricane's mane.

"You stick to your word, Styopka!" Sashka told him. "Or are you just a lump of boot wax?"

"Get out of here!" Styopka answered. "I stick to my word."

He plaited all the ribbons into the horse's mane, and suddenly turned to me in despair. "Just look at that! See how she tortures me, Kiril Vasilich? For a whole month already you wouldn't believe what I've had to put up with! Wherever I turn to, she's there, wherever I run to, she blocks my path, always wanting me to let the stallion have a go. But the division commander tells me every day, 'Styopka,' he tells me, 'with a stallion like this one, many will be coming to ask you to let the stallion have a go, but don't let him, not before he's four!'"

"I bet you you won't be letting anyone before he's fifteen," Sashka muttered, and turned away. "And when he's fifteen, you'll be drooling bubbles, for all I know!"

She went over to her mare, tightened the saddle strap, and was about to ride off.

The spurs on her boots clattered, her lace stockings were full of straw and spattered with dirt, her monstrous breasts went swinging toward her back.

"And to think I brought a ruble with me," Sashka said to herself, shoving her spurred boot into the stirrup. "I brought it with me but now I'll have to take it away again."

She took out two fifty-kopeck coins, jingled them in her palm, and hid them again in her cleavage.

"So we'll do it, or what?" Duplishchev said, his eyes fixed on the silver, and he brought over the stallion.

Sashka went to a sloping place in the clearing and had her mare stand there.

"You'd be amazed, but you're the only one in these mudfields who's got a stallion," she said to Styopka, pushing Hurricane into position. "My mare's a frontline war horse, two years now she hasn't been humped, so I says to myself—why not get her some good blood?"

Sashka finished with the stallion, and then led her horse to the side.

"So, sweetie, we got our stuffing now," she whispered, kissing her mare's wet, skewbald lips from which slobbering strands of spittle hung. She rubbed her cheek against the mare's muzzle, and suddenly noticed the noise thudding through the forest.

"The Second Brigade's coming back," Sashka said sternly, turning to me. "We must go, Lyutov!"

"Coming back, not coming back, I don't give a damn!" Duplishchev shouted, the words getting stuck in his throat. "You've had your feast, now pay the priest!"

"My money's nice and fine where it is!" Sashka muttered, and leaped onto her mare.

I dashed after her, and we rode off in full gallop. Duplishchev's howl and the light thud of a gunshot rang out behind us.

"Just look at that!" the Cossack boy yelled as loudly as he could, running through the forest.

The wind hopped through the branches like a crazed rabbit, the Second Brigade went flying through the Galician oak trees, the placid dust of the cannonade rose above the earth as above a peaceful hut. And at a sign from the division commander, we launched our attack, the unforgettable attack on Czesniki.

AFTER THE BATTLE

*T*he story of my fight with Akinfiev is as follows:
On the thirty-first came the attack on Czesniki. The squadrons had gathered in the forest next to the village, and hurled themselves at the enemy at six in the evening. The enemy was waiting for us on a hill three versts away. We galloped the three versts on our totally exhausted horses, and when we got to the hill we saw a deadly wall of black uniforms and pale faces. They were Cossacks who had betrayed us at the beginning of the Polish Campaign and had been rounded up into a brigade by Cossack Captain Yakovlev. The Cossack captain formed his horsemen into a square formation, and waited with his saber unsheathed. A gold tooth flashed in his mouth and his black beard lay on his chest like an icon on the chest of a corpse. The enemy's machine guns fired at twenty paces; wounded men fell in our lines. We went trampling over them and hurled ourselves at the enemy, but his square formation did not waver, and we turned and ran.

So the Savinkov Cossacks gained a short-lived victory over the Sixth Division. They gained the victory because they did not turn their faces from the lava flow of our oncoming squadrons. The Cossack captain stood firm that time, and we ran without reddening our sabers with the traitors' contemptible blood.

Five thousand men, our whole division, poured down the slope with no one in pursuit. The enemy stayed on the hill, unable to believe their illogical victory and muster their wits to set out in pursuit after us. That is why we survived and went bounding into the valley unharmed, where we were met by Vinogradov, our military commissar. Vinogradov was dashing about on his crazed horse trying to send the fleeing Cossacks back into battle.

"Lyutov!" he yelled when he saw me. "Get those fighters to turn around or I'll rip your soul out!"

Vinogradov pounded his tottering stallion with the butt of his Mauser, howled, and tried rounding up the men. I got away from him and rode up to Gulimov, a Kirghiz, who was galloping past.

"Gulimov! Get back up there!" I yelled to him. "Turn back your horse!"

"Turn back your own damn horse!" Gulimov yelled back. His eyes darted about thievishly and he fired a shot, singeing the hair above my ear.

"Turn your own horse back," Gulimov hissed, grabbed my shoulder with one hand, and tried unsheathing his saber with the other. The saber was jammed in its sheath, the Kirghiz shuddered and looked around. He held my shoulder tightly and brought his head closer and closer.

"Yours first," he whispered almost inaudibly, "and mine will follow." And he tapped me lightly on the chest with the blade of his saber, which he had managed to unsheathe.

I felt a wave of nausea from death's closeness and its tight grip. With the palm of my hand I pushed away the Kirghiz's face, hot as a stone in the sun, and scratched it with all my might. Warm blood rippled under my nails, tickling them. I rode away from Gulimov, out of breath as after a long journey. My horse, my tormented friend, trotted slowly. I rode without looking where I was going, I rode without turning around, until I came across Vorobyov, the commander of the First Squadron. Vorobyov was looking for his quartermasters and couldn't find them. He and I made our way to Czesniki and sat down on a bench along with Akinfiev, the former vehicular driver of the Revolutionary Tribunal. Sashka, the nurse of the Thirty-first Cavalry Regiment, came by, and two commanders sat down on the bench with us. The commanders sat there in silence, dozing. One of them was shell-shocked, shaking his head uncontrollably and winking with one bloated eye. Sashka went to tell the people at the field hospital about him, and then came back to us, dragging her horse behind her by the reins. Her mare resisted, her hooves skidding in the wet mud.

"So where are you sailing off to?" Vorobyov asked the nurse. "Sit down here with us, Sash!"

"I'm not sitting with you!" Sashka answered, and slapped her mare on the belly. "No way!"

"What d'you mean?" Vorobyov shouted, laughing. "Or have you had second thoughts about drinking tea with men?"

"It's you that I've had second thoughts about!" she told the commander, hurling away the reins. "Yes, I've had second thoughts about drinking tea with you, after I saw you all today and saw what heroes you all are, and how disgusting you are, Commander!"

"So when you saw it," Vorobyov muttered, "how come you didn't join in the shooting?"

"Join in the shooting?" Sashka shouted in desperation, tearing off her nurse's band. "What am I supposed to shoot with? This?"

Here Akinfiev, the former vehicular driver of the Revolutionary Tribunal, with whom I still had some unfinished business to settle, came up to us.

"You've got nothing to shoot with, Sash," he said soothingly. "No one's blaming you for that! I blame those who get all mixed up in battle and forget to load cartridges in their revolvers!" A spasm suddenly shot over his face. "You rode in the attack!" he shouted at me. "You rode but didn't put any cartridges in! Why?"

"Back off, Ivan," I said to Akinfiev. But he wouldn't back off, and kept coming closer to me, an epileptic with a twisted spine and no ribs.

"The Pole shot at you, yes, but you didn't shoot at him!" he muttered, twisting and turning with his shattered hip. "Why?"

"The Pole did shoot at me," I told him brusquely, "but I didn't shoot at the Pole!"

"So you're a wimp, right?" Akinfiev whispered, stepping back.

"So I'm a wimp!" I said, louder than before. "What do you want?"

"What I want is for you to be aware," Akinfiev yelled in wild triumph, "aware that you're a wimp, because in my books all wimps should be shot dead, they believe in God!"

A crowd gathered, and Akinfiev yelled on about wimps without stopping. I wanted to walk away, but he ran after me, and caught up with me, and punched me in the back with his fist.

"You didn't put any cartridges in!" Akinfiev whispered in a breathless voice right next to my ear, and with his large thumbs began trying to wrench my mouth open. "You believe in God, you traitor!"

He tugged and tore at my mouth. I pushed the epileptic back and hit him in the face. He keeled over onto his side, hit the ground, and began to bleed.

Sashka went over to him with her dangling breasts. She poured water over him, and pulled out of his mouth a long tooth which was swaying in the blackness like a birch tree on a bare country road.

"These bantams know just one thing," Sashka said, "and that's how to belt each other in the mouth. With a day like this and everything, I just want to shut my eyes!"

There was anguish in her voice, and she took wounded Akinfiev with her, while I staggered off into the village of Czesniki, which was sliding around in the relentless Galician rain.

The village floated and bulged, crimson clay oozing from its gloomy wounds. The first star flashed above me and tumbled into the clouds. The rain whipped the willow trees and dwindled. The evening soared into the sky like a flock of birds and darkness laid its wet garland upon me. I was exhausted, and, crouching beneath the crown of death, walked on, begging fate for the simplest ability—the ability to kill a man.

THE SONG

*W*hen we were quartered in the village of Budziatycze, it was my lot to end up with an evil landlady. She was a widow, she was poor. I broke many locks on her storerooms, but found no provisions.

All I could do was to try and outsmart her, and one fine day, coming home early before dusk, I caught her closing the door of the stove, which was still warm. The hut smelled of cabbage soup, and there might well have been some meat in that soup. I did smell meat in her soup and laid my revolver on the table, but the old woman denied everything. Her face and black fingers were gripped by spasms, she glowered at me with fear and extraordinary hatred. Nothing would have saved her—I would have made her own up with my revolver if Sashka Konyayev, in other words Sashka Christ, hadn't suddenly turned up.

He came into the hut with his concertina under his arm, his exquisite legs shuffling in battered boots.

"How about a song?" Sashka said, looking at me, his eyes filled with blue and dreamy ice crystals. "How about a song?" he said, and sat down on the bench and played a prelude.

The pensive prelude came as if from far away. He stopped, and his blue eyes filled with longing. He turned away, and, knowing what I liked, started off on a song from Kuban.

"Star of the fields," he sang, "star of the fields over my native hut, and my mother's hand, so sorrowful. . . ."

I loved that song. Sashka knew this, because both of us, both he

---

and I, had first heard this song back in '19 in the shallows of the Don in the Cossack village of Kagalnitskaya.

A hunter who poached in the protected waters there had taught it to us. There, in the protected waters, fish spawn and countless flocks of birds nest. The fish multiply in the shallows in incredible numbers, you can scoop them up with a ladle or even with your bare hands, and if you dip your oar in the water, it just stands there upright—a fish will have grabbed it and will carry it away. We saw this with our own eyes, we will never forget the protected waters of Kagalnitskaya. Every government has banned hunting there—a good ban—but back in '19 a war was raging in the shallows, and Yakov the hunter, who plied his forbidden trade right before our eyes, gave Sashka Christ, our squadron singer, a concertina as a present so that we would look the other way. He taught Sashka his songs. Many of them were soulful, old songs. So we forgave the roguish hunter, for we needed his songs: back then, no one could see the war ever ending, and Sashka covered our arduous paths with melody and tears. A bloody trail followed our paths. The songs soared over this trail. That is how it was in Kuban and on our campaigns against the Greens,* and that is how it was in the Urals and in the Caucasian foothills, and that is how it is to this very day. We need these songs, no one can see this war ever ending, and Sashka Christ, our squadron singer, is too young to die.

And this evening too, cheated of my landlady's cabbage soup, Sashka calmed me with his soft, wavering voice.

"Star of the fields," he sang, "star of the fields over my native hut, and my mother's hand, so sorrowful. . . ."

And I listened, stretched out in a corner on my rotting bedding. A dream broke my bones, the dream shook the putrid hay beneath me, and through the dream's burning torrent I could barely make out the old woman, who was standing by the wall, her withered cheek propped on her hand. She hung her ravaged head and stood fixed by the wall, not moving even after Sashka had finished playing. Sashka finished and put down his concertina, yawned, and burst out laughing as after a long

---

*Defectors from the Imperial army and later also from the new Soviet army, who banded together in guerrilla groups. They were called "Greens" because they hid in forests. Both the Whites and the Reds tried to organize them under their influence, creating bands of Red Greens and White Greens.

sleep, and then, noticing the chaos in the widow's hut, he wiped the debris from the bench and brought in a bucket of water.

"You see, deary, what your boss is up to?" the landlady said to him, pointing at me and rubbing her back against the door. "Your boss came in here, yelled at me, stamped his foot, broke all the locks in my house, and shoved his gun at me. It is a sin before the Lord to shove a gun at me—I'm a woman, after all!"

She rubbed her back against the door again and threw a sheepskin coat over her son. Her son lay snoring beneath an icon on a large bed covered with rags. He was a deaf-mute boy with a white, water-swollen head and gigantic feet, like those of a grown muzhik. His mother wiped the snot from his nose and came back to the table.

"Mistress," Sashka said to her, caressing her shoulder, "if you wish, I could be really nice to you."

But it was as if the woman hadn't heard what he had said.

"I didn't see no cabbage soup at all," she said, her cheek propped on her hand. "It ran away, my cabbage soup, and people shove their guns at me, so that even when a nice man comes along and I get a chance to tumble a little, I've ended up feeling so drab, I can't even enjoy sinning!"

She dragged out her mournful lament and, mumbling, rolled her deaf-mute son to the wall. Sashka lay with her on the rag-covered bed while I tried to sleep, conjuring up dreams so that I would doze off with pleasant thoughts.

THE RABBI'S SON

*D*o you remember Zhitomir, Vasily? Do you remember the River Teterev, Vasily, and that night in which the Sabbath, the young Sabbath, crept along the sunset crushing the stars with the heel of her red slipper?

The thin horn of the moon dipped its arrows in the black waters of the Teterev. Little, funny Gedali, the founder of the Fourth International,* who took us to Rabbi Motale Bratslavsky for evening prayer. Little, funny Gedali, shaking the cockerel feathers of his top hat in the red smoke of the evening. The candles' predatory pupils twinkled in the rabbi's room. Broad-shouldered Jews crouched moaning over prayer books, and the old jester of the Chernobyl line of *tsaddiks* jingled copper coins in his frayed pocket.

You remember that night, Vasily? Outside the window horses neighed and Cossacks shouted. The wasteland of war yawned outside and Rabbi Motale Bratslavsky, clutching his tallith with his withered fingers, prayed at the eastern wall. Then the curtains of the cabinet fell open, and in the funerary shine of the candles we saw the Torah scrolls wrapped in coverings of purple velvet and blue silk, and above the Torah scrolls hovered the humble, beautiful, lifeless face of Ilya, the rabbi's son, the last prince of the dynasty.

And then, Vasily, two days ago the regiments of the Twelfth Army

* See the story "Gedali," in which Gedali envisions an ideal International that would supplant the Third Communist International founded in Moscow in 1919 to promote Communism worldwide.

opened the front at Kovel. The victors' haughty cannonade thundered through the town. Our troops were shaken and thrown into disarray. The Polit-otdel train* crept along the dead spine of the fields. The typhoid-ridden muzhik horde rolled the gigantic ball of rampant soldier death before it. The horde scampered onto the steps of our train and fell off again, beaten back by rifle butts. It panted, scrambled, ran, was silent. And after twelve versts, when I no longer had any potatoes to throw to them, I threw a bundle of Trotsky leaflets at them. But only one of them stretched out a dirty, dead hand to grab a leaflet. And I recognized Ilya, the son of the Zhitomir rabbi. I recognized him straightaway, Vasily! It was so painful to see the prince, who had lost his trousers, his back snapped in two by the weight of his soldier's rucksack, that we broke the rules and dragged him up into the railroad car. His naked knees, clumsy like the knees of an old woman, knocked against the rusty iron of the steps. Two fat-breasted typists in sailor blouses dragged the dying man's timid, lanky body along the floor. We laid him out in the corner of the train's editorial compartment. Cossacks in red Tatar trousers fixed his slipped clothing. The girls, their bandy bovine legs firmly planted on the floor, stared coolly at his sexual organs, the withered, curly manhood of the emaciated Semite. And I, who had met him during one of my nights of wandering, packed the scattered belongings of Red Army soldier Ilya Bratslavsky into my suitcase.

I threw everything together in a jumble, the mandates of the political agitator and the mementos of a Jewish poet. Portraits of Lenin and Maimonides lay side by side—the gnarled steel of Lenin's skull and the listless silk of the Maimonides portrait. A lock of woman's hair lay in a book of the resolutions of the Sixth Party Congress, and crooked lines of Ancient Hebrew verse huddled in the margins of Communist pamphlets. Pages of *The Song of Songs* and revolver cartridges drizzled on me in a sad, sparse rain. The sad rain of the sunset washed the dust from my hair, and I said to the young man, who was dying on a ripped mattress in the corner, "Four months ago, on a Friday evening, Gedali the junk dealer took me to your father, Rabbi Motale, but back then, Bratslavsky, you were not in the Party."

* The train sent out by the Polit-otdel, the political organ of the new Soviet government charged with the ideological education of the military.

"I was in the Party back then," the young man answered, scratching his chest and twisting in his fever. "But I couldn't leave my mother behind."

"What about now, Ilya?"

"My mother is just an episode of the Revolution," he whispered, his voice becoming fainter. "Then my letter came up, the letter 'B,' and the organization sent me off to the front. . . ."

"So you ended up in Kovel?"

"I ended up in Kovel!" he shouted in despair. "The damn kulaks opened the front. I took over a mixed regiment, but it was too late. I didn't have enough artillery."

He died before we reached Rovno. He died, the last prince, amid poems, phylacteries, and foot bindings. We buried him at a desolate train station. And I, who can barely harness the storms of fantasy raging through my ancient body, I received my brother's last breath.

The Red Cavalry Cycle: Additional Stories

T he seven additional RED CAVALRY stories in this section were not
   included in Babel's book KONARMIA (RED CAVALRY), published
in 1926. Most of them appeared in magazines in the late 1920s and
1930s after the book had come out, while "And Then There Were Nine" and
the fragment "And Then There Were Ten" were not published during Babel's
lifetime. The last piece, "A Letter to the Editor," appeared in the magazine
OKTYABR in October 1924. It was a response to General Budyonny's
vitriolic article with the punning title "Babism Bablya" ("Babel's woman-
ishness"), in which he condemned Babel's RED CAVALRY stories and their
portrayal of himself and other real commanders.

MAKHNO'S BOYS

The previous night, six Makhno* fighters raped a maid. When I heard this the following morning, I decided to find out what a woman looks like after being raped six times. I found her in the kitchen. She stood bent over a tub, washing clothes. She was a fat girl with blooming cheeks. Only a tranquil life on fertile Ukrainian soil can douse a Jewish girl in such bovine juices, lend her face such a lusty gloss. The girl's legs, fat, brick-red, bulging like globes, gave off the luscious stench of freshly carved meat, and it seemed to me that all that remained of yesterday's virginity were her cheeks, more flushed than usual, and her lowered eyes.

Young Kikin, the errand boy at Makhno's headquarters, was also in the kitchen. He was known at the headquarters as something of a simpleton—he had a tendency to walk about on his hands at the most unsuitable moments. More than once I found him in front of the mirror, stretching out his leg in his tattered trousers. He would wink at himself, slap himself on his bare, boyish stomach, sing marching tunes, and make triumphant grimaces which made even him guffaw. This boy's imagination worked with incredible vigor. Today I again found him busy on one of his special projects—he was sticking strips of gold paper on a German helmet.

"How many of them did you accommodate yesterday, Ruhlya?" he asked the girl, narrowing his eyes as he eyed the decorated helmet.

She remained silent.

* Nestor Ivanovich Makhno, 1889–1934, the Ukrainian anarchist leader.

"You accommodated six of them," he continued, "but there are girls who can accommodate up to twenty. Our boys did a Krapivno housewife and they kept pounding and pounding away at her till they ran out of steam. But she was a good deal fatter than you are."

"Go get me some water," the girl said.

Kikin brought a bucket of water from the yard. He shuffled over to the mirror in his bare feet, put the helmet with the gold ribbons on his head, and carefully peered at his reflection. His image in the mirror fascinated him. He stuck his fingers in his nose and avidly watched it change shape under the pressure from within.

"I'll be going out on a mission," he said to the Jewess. "Don't you say a word to no one! Stetsenko's taking me into his squadron. At least they give you a real uniform, people respect you, and I'll have some real fighter pals, not like here, where we're just some dinky little flea-ridden outfit. Yesterday, when they grabbed you and I was holding you down by the head, I said to Matvey Vasilich, Hey, Matvey Vasilich, I said to him, four have already had a go, and I still get to keep holding and holding her down! You've already had her twice, Matvey Vasilich, and just because I'm underage and not in your gang, everyone can just push me around! And you yourself, Ruhlya, must have heard what he said to me—We, he said to me, don't push you around, Kikin! Once all my orderlies have had a go, it'll be your turn. He did say I could, and then, when they were already dragging you out into the woods, Matvey Vasilich tells me, You can do her now, Kikin, if you wish!—No way do I wish, Matvey Vasilich! I tell him, not after Vaska has had her, I'd never get over it till I die!"

Kikin grunted and fell silent. Barefoot, lanky, sad, his stomach bare, the glittering helmet on his straw-colored head, he lay down on the floor and stared into the distance.

"The whole world reckons the Makhno gang is all heroic and everything!" he said morosely. "But when you start hanging out with them, you soon see that they all harbor some grudge or other!"

The Jewess lifted her flushed face from the tub, glanced over at the boy, and left the kitchen with the heavy gait of a cavalryman whose numb legs have just touched the ground after a very long ride. Left alone, the boy looked dully around the kitchen, sighed, rested his palms on the floor, swung his legs in the air, and, with his heels together, quickly walked around on his hands.

A HARDWORKING
WOMAN

*T*hree Makhno fighters—Gniloshkurov and two others—had come to an agreement with a woman about her love services. For two pounds of sugar, she agreed to take on the three of them, but when the third one's turn came, she couldn't hold out and went reeling around the room. The woman scrambled out into the yard, where she ran straight into Makhno.* He lashed her with his whip, tearing her upper lip, and Gniloshkurov got it too.

This happened in the morning, at nine o'clock. After that the day went by with much activity, and now it's night, the rain is drizzling, whispering and unyielding. It is rustling beyond the wall. In front of me, outside the window, hangs a single star. The town of Kamenka has drowned in the haze—the teeming ghetto is filled with teeming darkness and the inexorable bustling of the Makhno fighters. Someone's horse neighs softly like a pining woman; beyond the edge of the shtetl sleepless *tachankas*† creak, and the cannonade, falling silent, lies down to sleep on the black, wet earth.

Only Makhno's window is ablaze in a faraway street. It cuts through the gloom of the autumn night like an exhilarated searchlight, flashing, drenched with rain. There, in Makhno's headquarters, a brass band is playing in honor of Antonina Vasilevna, a nurse who was spending her first night with Makhno. The thick, melancholy trumpets blow louder and louder, and the partisans, huddled together beneath

---

* The anarchist leader.
† An open carriage or buggy with a machine gun mounted on the back.

my window, listen to the thundering of old marches. Three partisans are sitting beneath my window—Gniloshkurov and his comrades—and then Kikin, a crazed Cossack, comes rushing over to join them. He kicks his legs up in the air, does a handstand, chirps and sings, and has difficulty calming down, like an epileptic after a fit.

"Oat-head!" Gniloshkurov suddenly whispers to Kikin. "Oat-head," he repeats morosely. "How can it be that she let two more have a go after me without so much as batting an eyelash? There I was, putting my belt back on, and she looks at me and says to me, '*Merci* for spending some time with me, Papa, you are so charming! My name is Anelya—that's what I'm called, Anelya.' So you see, Oat-head, I think to myself she must have been chewing some bitter herbs since the morning, and then Petka wanted to have a go at her too!"

"Then Petka wanted to have a go at her too," fifteen-year-old Kikin chimes in, sitting down and lighting a cigarette. " 'Young man,' she tells Petka, 'would you please be kind enough, I'm at the end of my rope!' And she jumps up and starts spinning like a top, and the boys spread their arms and won't let her out the door, and she keeps begging and begging." Kikin stands up, his eyes flash, and he begins to laugh. "She escapes," Kikin continues, "and then right there at the door, who does she run into? Makhno himself. 'Halt!' he yells. 'I bet you have the clap! I'm going to hack you up here and now!' And he starts lashing her, and she—she still wants to give him some lip!"

"It must also be said," Petka Orlov's pensive and tender voice interrupts Kikin, "it must also be said, that there is greed among people, ruthless greed! I told her—'There's three of us, Anelya! Bring a girlfriend along, share the sugar with her, she'll help you!' 'No,' she says, 'I can cope well enough, I have three children to feed, it's not like I'm a virgin or something.' "

"A hardworking woman!" Gniloshkurov, still sitting beneath my window, assures Petka. "Hardworking to the last!"

And he falls silent. I can still hear the sound of water. The rain is continuing to stutter, bubble, and moan on the roofs. The wind grabs the rain and shoves it to the side. The triumphant blowing of the trumpets falls silent in Makhno's courtyard. The light in his room has dimmed by half. Gniloshkurov rises from the bench, splicing the dim glimmer of the moon. He yawns, tugs his shirt up, and scratches his remarkably white stomach, and then goes over to the shed to sleep. Petka Orlov's tender voice floats after him.

"In Gulya-Polye there was this out-of-town muzhik called Ivan Golub," Petka says. "He was a quiet muzhik—no drinking, he was cheerful when he worked, lifted too much of a load, got himself a rupture, and died. The people of Gulya-Polye mourned him and the whole village walked behind his coffin. They walked, even though he was a stranger."

And at the door of the shed, Petka begins muttering the story of the late Ivan, muttering more and more softly and tenderly.

"There is ruthlessness among people," Gniloshkurov says to him, yawning, "there really is, I tell you."

Gniloshkurov falls asleep, and the two others with him, and I remain alone by the window. My eyes explore the soundless dark, the beast of memory tears at me, and sleep will not come.

. . . She had sat in the main street selling berries since the morning. The Makhno fighters had paid her in abolished banknotes. She had the plump, airy body of a blonde. Gniloshkurov, his stomach jutting out, was sunning himself on a bench. He dozed, waited, and the woman, anxious to sell off her wares, gazed at him with her blue eyes, and blushed slowly and tenderly.

"Anelya," I whisper her name. "Anelya."

GRISHCHUK

*O*ur second trip to the shtetl ended badly. We had set out in the cart to find some fodder, and were heading back around midday. Grishchuk's back was bobbing gently up and down before my eyes. Right outside the village, he laid his reins carefully together, sighed, and slipped down from the box, crawled over my knees, and sprawled out across the cart. His cooling head rocked gently, the horses trotted on slowly, and a yellowing fabric of peace settled on his face like a shroud.

"Didn't eat nothing," he politely answered my cry of alarm, and wearily closed his eyelids.

That was how we rolled into the village—the coachman sprawled out across the cart.

At our lodgings I gave him some bread and a potato to eat. He ate sluggishly, dozing and shaking himself awake. Then he went out into the middle of the yard and lay down on his back, his arms spread wide.

"If you never tell me anything, Grishchuk," I said to him in exasperation, "how am I supposed to understand your pain?"

He said nothing and turned away. It was only that night, as we lay warming each other in the hay, that he shared with me a chapter from his mute novel.

Russian prisoners of war had worked building German fortifications along the North Sea coast. During the harvest season they were herded together and sent into the heart of Germany. A lone, crazed farmer took on Grishchuk. His madness consisted in his never speaking. He beat and starved Grishchuk until Grishchuk learned to communicate with him by hand signals. They lived together peacefully and in silence for four years. Grishchuk didn't learn the language because he never heard it spoken. After the German Revolution* he returned to Russia. His master had walked him to the edge of the village. They stopped at the side of the high road. The German pointed at the church, at his heart, at the boundless and empty blue of the horizon. He laid his gray, tousled head on Grishchuk's shoulder. They stood in a silent embrace. And then the German, throwing up his arms, ran back to his house with quick, faltering, stumbling steps.

*The abortive German November Revolution of 1918.

ARGAMAK

I decided to join the ranks at the front. The division commander grimaced when he heard this.

"Why the hell d'you want to go there? If you let your mouth hang open for a second, they shoot you point-blank!"

I held my ground. And that wasn't all. My choice fell on the most active division, the Sixth. I was assigned to the Fourth Squadron of the Twenty-third Cavalry Regiment. The squadron was commanded by Baulin, a Bryansk factory metalworker, who was a mere boy. He had grown a beard to inspire respect. Ash-blond tufts covered his chin. In his twenty-two years, Baulin had let nothing ruffle him. This quality, found in thousands of Baulins, proved an important element in the victory of the Revolution. Baulin was hard, taciturn, and headstrong. The path of his life had been decided. He had no doubts about the rightness of this path. Deprivation came easy to him. He could sleep sitting up. He slept pressing one arm against the other, and when he woke, his path from oblivion to full alertness was seamless.

One could expect no mercy under Baulin's command. My service started with an unusual omen of success—I was given a horse. There weren't any horses in the reserve stables or with the peasants. Chance helped. The Cossack Tikhomolov had killed two captured officers without authorization. He had been instructed to take them to the brigade headquarters, as enemy officers could give important information. Tikhomolov did not take them there. It was decided that he would be tried before the Revolutionary Tribunal,* but then they changed their minds. Squadron Commander Baulin came up with a punishment much harsher than anything the tribunal could have inflicted—he took Tikhomolov's stallion Argamak away from him, and sent Tikhomolov off to the transport carts.

The agony I had to suffer with Argamak was beyond what a man can endure. Tikhomolov had brought his horse from the Terek, where he was from. The stallion had been trained in the Cossack trot, that specific Cossack hard trot—dry, violent, sudden. Argamak's stride was long, extended, obstinate. With this devilish stride he carried me off, out of the lines, separating me from the squadron. I lost my sense of direction, roamed for days on end looking for my unit, ended up in enemy territory, slept in ravines, tried to tag along with other regiments but was chased away by them. My horsemanship was limited to the fact that in the Great War I had served with an artillery unit in the Fifteenth Infantry Division. Most of the time we had spent sitting on ammunition carts; we rarely rode out on raids. I didn't have an opportunity to get used to Argamak's cruel, bounding trot. Tikhomolov had bestowed on his horse all the devils of his downfall. I shook like a sack on the stallion's long, dry spine. I rode his back to pieces. Sores appeared on it. Metallic flies preyed upon these sores. Hoops of baked black blood girded the horse's flanks. Bad shoeing made Argamak trip, his hind legs became swollen at the breeching strap and turned elephantine. Argamak grew thin. His eyes filled with the fire one sees in tortured horses, the fire of hysteria and obstinacy. He no longer let me saddle him.

"You've liquidated that horse, four-eyes!" my platoon commander said.

The Cossacks said nothing in my presence, but behind my back plotted like plunderers in drowsy treachery. They didn't even ask me to write letters for them anymore.

The cavalry took Novograd-Volynsk. In a single day we had to cover seventy, eighty versts. We were getting close to Rovno. Rest days

---

* The Revolutionary Tribunals were the organs of military justice representing the Revolutionary Military Council. They investigated crimes committed by military personnel and dealt with prisoners of war. Revolutionary Tribunal detachments were present in each army division and brigade.

were annulled. Night after night I had the same dream: I am riding Argamak at full trot. Campfires are burning by the roadside. The Cossacks are cooking food. I ride past them, they don't even look up. A few call out a greeting, others don't even turn around, they're not interested in me. What does this mean? Their indifference indicates that there is nothing unusual in my horsemanship, I ride like everyone else, there's no reason for them to look at me. I gallop off and am happy. My thirst for peace and happiness was never quenched in my waking hours, which is why I dreamed these dreams.

There was no sign of Pashka Tikhomolov. He was watching me from somewhere on the fringes of the march, in the bumbling tail of carts crammed full with looted rags.

"Pashka keeps asking what's with you," my platoon commander said to me one day.

"Why, he has a problem with me?"

"It looks like he does."

"I reckon he feels I've done him wrong."

"Why, you reckon you didn't do him wrong?"

Pashka's hatred followed me through forests and over rivers. I felt it on my hide and shuddered. He nailed his bloodshot eyes on my path.

"Why did you saddle me with an enemy?" I asked Baulin.

Baulin rode past, yawning.

"Not my problem," he answered without looking back. "It's your problem."

Argamak's back healed a little, then his wounds opened up again. I put three saddlecloths under his saddle, but I could not really ride him, the wounds weren't healing. The knowledge that I was sitting on an open wound made me cringe.

A Cossack from our platoon, his name was Bizyukov, was Tikhomolov's countryman from the Terek, and he knew Pashka's father.

"His father, Pashka's father, he breeds horses for fun," Bizyukov told me one day. "A rough rider, sturdy. He comes to a herd, he picks out a horse on the spot, and they bring it to him. He stands face-to-face with the horse, his legs planted firm, glares at it. What does he want? This is what he wants: he waves his fist and punches the horse right between the eyes—the horse is dead. 'Why did you finish off the horse, Kalistrat?'—'I had a terrible desire for this horse, but I wasn't fated to ride it. The horse didn't take to me, but my desire for this horse was deadly!' He's a rough rider, let me tell you!"

And then Argamak, who had survived Pashka's father, who had been chosen by him, fell into my hands. How was this to end? I weighed many plans in my mind. The war had released me from other worries. The cavalry attacked Rovno. The town was taken. We stayed there for two days. The following night the Poles pushed us out. They engaged us in a skirmish to get their retreating units through. Their maneuver worked. The Poles were covered by a storm, lashing rain, a violent summer storm that tumbled onto the world in floods of black water. We cleared out of Rovno for a day. During the nocturnal battle we lost Dundic, the Serb, one of our bravest men. Pashka Tikhomolov also fought in this battle. The Poles attacked his transport carts. The area there was flat, without any cover. Pashka lined up his carts in a bat-tle formation known only to him. It was, doubtless, how the Romans lined up their chariots. Pashka had a machine gun. He had probably stolen it and hidden it, for an emergency. With this machine gun he repelled the attack, saved his possessions, and led the whole transport to safety, except for two carts whose horses had been shot.

"What do you intend to do with your best fighters, marinate them?" they asked Baulin at headquarters a few days after the battle.

"If I'm letting them marinate, there must be a reason, right?"

"Careful, you'll run into trouble."

No amnesty was proclaimed for Pashka, but we knew that he was coming back. He came wearing galoshes on his bare feet. His toes had been hacked off, ribbons of black gauze hung from them. The ribbons dragged behind him like a train. In the village of Budziatycze, Pashka appeared at the square in front of the church where our horses stood tied to the hitching post. Squadron Commander Baulin was sitting on the church, steps, his feet soaking in a steaming bucket. His toes were rotting. They were pink, the way steel is pink before it is forged. Tufts of young straw-blond hair tumbled over Baulin's forehead. The sun burned on the bricks and tiles of the church. Bizyukov, standing next to Baulin, popped a cigarette into Baulin's mouth and lit it. Tikhomolov, dragging his tattered train behind him, went up to the hitching post. His galoshes shuffled. Argamak stretched his long neck and neighed to his master in greeting, a quiet, rasping neigh, like that of a horse in a desert. Pus coiled like lace between the strips of torn flesh on the horse's back. Pashka stood next to the horse. The dirty ribbons lay still on the ground.

"So that's how things stand," the Cossack said, barely audibly.

I stepped forward.

"Let's make peace, Pashka. I'm glad the horse is going back to you. I can't handle him. Let's make peace?"

"It's not Easter yet, for people to make peace," the platoon commander said from behind me, rolling a cigarette. His Tatar trousers loose, his shirt open over his copper chest, he was resting on the church steps.

"Kiss him three times, Pashka,"* mumbled Bizyukov, Tikhomolov's countryman, who knew Kalistrat, Pashka's father. "He wants to kiss three times."

I was alone among these men whose friendship I had not managed to win.

Pashka stood in front of the horse as if rooted there. Argamak, breathing strong and free, stretched his muzzle to him.

"So that's how things stand," the Cossack repeated. He turned to me sharply, and said emphatically, "I will not make peace with you."

He walked away, dragging his galoshes down the chalk-white, heat-baked street, his bandages sweeping the dust of the village square. Argamak walked behind him like a dog. The reins swung beneath his muzzle, his long neck hung low. Baulin continued soaking the reddish steel of his feet's rotting flesh in the tub.

"Why did you saddle me with an enemy?" I said to him. "None of this is my fault."

The squadron commander raised his head.

"I can see right through you!" he said. "Right through you! What you want is to live without enemies, you'll do anything not to have enemies."

"Kiss him three times," Bizyukov muttered, turning away.

A fiery spot burned on Baulin's forehead. His cheek twitched.

"You know what you end up with like that?" he said in a gasping voice. "You end up being bored! To goddamn hell with you!"

* A manifestation of friendship symbolizing the Holy Trinity.

It was obvious I had to leave. I got myself transferred to the Sixth Squadron. Things went better there. The long and the short of it was that Argamak had taught me some of Tikhomolov's horsemanship. Months passed. My dream had become a reality. The Cossacks' eyes stopped following me and my horse.

THE KISS

At the beginning of August, headquarters sent us to Budziatycze to regroup. The Poles had occupied it at the beginning of the war, but we had been quick to win it back. Our brigade entered the shtetl at dawn. I arrived later in the day. The best billets had already been taken, and I ended up at the schoolmaster's house. He was a paralyzed old man sitting in an armchair in a low-ceilinged room, among buckets with fruit-bearing lemon trees. On his head was a Tyrolean hat with a feather. His gray beard lay on his chest, which was covered with cigarette ash. Babbling, his eyes fluttering, he seemed to be asking me for something. I washed, went to the headquarters, and didn't come back until night. My orderly, Mishka Surovtsev, a cunning Cossack from Orenburg, gave me a full report: besides the paralyzed old man, there was also a daughter present, Elizaveta Alekseyevna Tomilina, and her five-year-old son who was also called Mishka, like Surovtsev. The daughter, the widow of an officer who had fallen in the Great War, was a respectable woman but, according to Surovtsev's information, would be willing to make herself available to a proper gentleman.

"I can arrange things," he told me, and went off to the kitchen, where he began clattering about with plates. The schoolmaster's daughter helped him. As they cooked, Surovtsev told her of my brave feats, how I had knocked two Polish officers out of their saddles in a battle, and how much the Soviet authorities respected me. He was answered by the restrained, soft voice of Tomilina.

"Where d'you sleep?" Surovtsev asked her as he left the kitchen. "You should come sleep closer to us, we're living, breathing people."

He brought me some fried eggs in a gigantic frying pan, and put it on the table.

"She's up for it," he said, sitting down. "She just hasn't come out and said it yet."

At that very instant we heard whispering, rattling, and heavy, careful steps. We didn't have time to finish eating our war meal, when some old men on crutches and old women with kerchiefs on their heads came hobbling through the house. They dragged little Mishka's bed into the dining room, into the lemon-tree forest, next to his grandfather's armchair. The feeble guests, readying themselves to defend Elizaveta Alekseyevna's honor, huddled together in a flock, like sheep in a storm, and, barricading the door, spent the whole night silently playing cards, whispering, "My trick," and falling silent at every sound. I was so mortified, so embarrassed, that I simply could not fall asleep behind that door, and could barely wait for the sun to rise.

"For your information," I told Tomilina when I ran into her in the hall, "for your information, I have a law degree and am a member of the so-called intelligentsia!"

Rigid, her arms dangling, she stood there in her old-fashioned housedress, which clung tightly to her slim body. Without blinking, she looked straight at me with widening blue eyes sparkling with tears.

Within two days we were friends. The schoolmaster's family, a family of kind, weak people, lived in boundless fear and uncertainty. Polish officials had convinced them that Russia had fallen in fire and barbarity, like Rome. They were overcome with a childlike, fearful joy when I told them of Lenin, the Moscow Arts Theater, of a Moscow in which the future was raging. In the evenings, twenty-two-year-old Bolshevik generals with scraggly red beards came to visit us. We smoked Moscow cigarettes, we ate meals that Elizaveta Alekseyevna prepared with army provisions, and sang student songs. Leaning forward in his armchair, the paralyzed old man listened avidly, his Tyrolean hat bobbing to the rhythm of our songs. Through all these days the old man was in the clutches of a sudden, stormy, vague hope, and, in order not to let anything darken his happiness, he did his best to overlook the foppish bloodthirstiness and loudmouthed simplicity with which in those days we solved all the problems of the world.

After our victory over the Poles—the family counsel decided—the Tomilins would move to Moscow. We would have a celebrated professor cure the old man, Elizaveta Alekseyevna would take classes, and we would put Mishka in the selfsame school that his mother had once gone to at Patriarkhy Prudy. The future seemed incontestably ours, and war was merely a stormy prelude to happiness, happiness, the core of our being. The only things that remained unresolved were the specific details, and nights passed in discussing these details, mighty nights, in which the candle end was mirrored in the dull bottle of our home-brewed vodka. Elizaveta Alekseyevna, blossoming, was our silent listener. I have never met a more impulsive, free, or timorous being. In the evenings, cunning Surovtsev, in the wicker cart he had requisitioned back in Kuban, drove us up the hill to where the abandoned house of the Counts Gasiorowski shone in the flames of the sunset. The horses, thin but long-bodied and thoroughbred, were running in step in their red reins. A carefree earring swayed on Surovtsev's ear. Round towers rose up from a pit that was overgrown with a yellow tablecloth of flowers. The ruined walls drew a crooked line flooded with ruby-red blood across the sky. A dog-rose bush hid its berries, and blue steps, the remains of the flight of stairs that Polish kings had once mounted, shone in the thickets. Once, as I sat there, I pulled Elizaveta Alekseyevna's head toward me and kissed her. She slowly pulled away, got up, and leaned against the wall, holding on to it with both hands. She stood there motionless, and around her, around her dazzled head, swirled a fiery dusty ray. Shuddering, as if she had just heard something, Tomilina raised her head and let go of the wall. She ran down the hill, her uncertain steps becoming faster. I called out to her, she didn't answer. Below, red-cheeked Surovtsev lay sprawled out in his wicker cart.

At night, when everyone was asleep, I crept to Elizaveta Alekseyevna's room. She sat reading, holding her book at arm's length. Her hand, lying on the table, seemed lifeless. She turned when I knocked, and rose.

"No," she said, looking me in the eyes, "please, dearest, no." And, embracing my head with her long, bare arms, she gave me an increasingly violent, never-ending, silent kiss.

The shrill ring of the telephone in the next room pushed us apart. An orderly was calling from headquarters.

"We're pulling out!" he said over the phone. "You are to report to the brigade commander now!"

I rushed out of the house without even putting on my hat, stuffing my papers into my bag as I ran. Horses were being brought out of yards, horsemen galloped yelling through the darkness. The brigade commander, tying his cloak, told us that the Poles had broken through our lines near Lublin, and that we had been ordered to execute a bypass maneuver. Both regiments pulled out an hour later. The old man, awoken from his sleep, anxiously followed me with his eyes through the leaves of a lemon tree.

"Promise me you will return," he kept saying, his head wagging.

Elizaveta Alekseyevna, a fur jacket over her batiste nightdress, accompanied us out onto the street. An invisible squadron raced past violently. At the curve in the road by the field I turned to look back— Elizaveta Alekseyevna was bending down to fix the jacket of little Mishka, who was standing in front of her, and the erratic light of the lamp burning on the windowsill streamed over the tender bones of her nape.

After riding a hundred kilometers without rest, we joined forces with the Fourteenth Cavalry Division and, fighting, we began our retreat. We slept in our saddles. At rest stops, we fell to the ground overwhelmed with exhaustion, and our horses, pulling at their reins, dragged us fast asleep through the harvested fields. It was the beginning of autumn and the soundless, drizzling Galician rain. Huddled together in a bristling silent herd, we dodged and circled, fell into the Poles' waiting net, but managed to slip out again just before they could close it. We lost all sense of time. When we were quartered in the church in Toszcza, it did not even occur to me that we were only nine versts from Budziatycze. Surovtsev reminded me, we exchanged glances.

"The problem is that the horses are exhausted," he said cheerfully. "Otherwise we could go."

"We couldn't anyway," I replied. "They'd notice if we left in the middle of the night."

And we went. We tied gifts to our saddles—a clump of sugar, a fox-fur wrap, and a live, two-week-old goat kid. The road went through a swaying wet forest, a metallic star strayed through the crowns of the oaks. In less than an hour we arrived at the shtetl, its burned-out center filled with trucks, pale with flour dust, and with machine-gun-cart harnesses and broken shafts. Without dismounting, I knocked on the familiar window. A white cloud flitted through the room. Wearing the same batiste nightdress with its hanging lace, Tomilina came rushing out onto the porch. She took my hand in her hot hand and led me into the house. Men's underclothes were hanging out to dry on the broken branches of the lemon trees, and unknown men were sleeping in camp beds lined up in tight rows like in a field hospital. With crooked, hardened mouths they yelled out hoarsely in their sleep, breathing greedily and loud, their dirty feet jutting out. The house was occupied by our War Spoils Commission, and the Tomilins had been bundled off into a single room.

"When will you take us away from here?" Elizaveta Alekseyevna asked, clasping my hand.

The old man woke, his head wagging. Little Mishka cuddled the goat kid, and brimmed over with happy, soundless laughter. Above him stood Surovtsev, puffing himself up. Out of the pockets of his Cossack trousers he shook spurs, shot-through coins, and a whistle hanging on a yellow string. In this house occupied by the War Spoils Commission there was nowhere to hide, and Tomilina and I went to the wooden shed where the potatoes and beehive frames were kept in winter. There, in the shed, I saw what an inevitably pernicious path that kiss had been, the path that had begun by the castle of the Counts Gasiorowski.

Surovtsev came knocking shortly before dawn.

"When will you take us from here?" Elizaveta Alekseyevna asked, turning her head away.

I stood there silently, and then walked over to the house to say good-bye to the old man.

"The problem is we're running out of time," Surovtsev said, blocking my way. "Get on your horse, we've got to go!"

He jostled me out onto the street and brought me my horse. Elizaveta Alekseyevna gave me her chilled hand. As always, she held her head high. The horses, well rested overnight, carried us off at a brisk trot. The flaming sun rose through the black tangle of the oak trees. The rejoicing morning filled my whole being.

A glade in the forest opened up before us. I directed my horse toward it, and, turning back to Surovtsev, called out to him, "We could have stayed a bit longer. You came for me too early!"

"Too early?" he said, riding up closer to me, pushing away the wet branches that dropped their sparkling raindrops. "If it wasn't for the old man, I'd have come for you even earlier. He was trying to tell me something and suddenly was all nerves, started squawking, and keeled over. I rush to him, I look, he's dead, dead as a doornail!"

The forest came to an end. We rode over a plowed field without paths. Standing up in his stirrups, looking all around, whistling, Surovtsev sniffed out the right direction and, breathing it in with the air, hunched forward and went galloping toward it.

We arrived in time. The men of the squadron were just being awakened. The sun shone warmly, promising a hot day. That morning our brigade crossed the former border of the Kingdom of Poland.

AND THEN
THERE WERE NINE

*This story is an earlier variation of
"Squadron Commander Trunov."*

Nine prisoners of war are no longer alive. I know that in my heart. When Golov, a platoon commander from the Sormov workers,* killed the gangly Pole, I said to the chief of staff, "The example the platoon commander is setting is demoralizing our fighters. We must draw up a list of prisoners and then send them to headquarters for interrogation."

The chief of staff agreed. I took pencil and paper out of my bag and called Golov over.

"You look at the world through your spectacles," he told me, looking at me with hatred.

"Yes, through my spectacles," I said to him. "And what about you, Golov? How do you look at the world?"

"I look at it through the miserable life of a worker," he said, and went over to the prisoner who was holding a Polish uniform with dangling sleeves. The uniform had been too small for him. The sleeves had barely reached his elbows. Golov examined the prisoner's woolen drawers.

"You an officer?" Golov asked him, shielding his eyes from the sun.

"No," the Pole answered firmly.

"We never got to wear nothing like that!" Golov muttered, and fell silent. He stood there without saying a word, shuddered, looked at the prisoner, and his eyes paled and widened.

* The Sormov Steelworks (19,839 workers in 1917) played a key role in the Revolution and the Civil War.

"My mama knitted them," the prisoner said firmly. I turned around and looked at him. He was a slender young man. Long sideburns curled over his yellowish cheeks.

"My mama knitted them," he repeated, and lowered his eyes.

"She's a great knitter, that mama of yours," Andryushka Burak cut in. He was a young red-cheeked Cossack with silky hair, who earlier had dragged the trousers off a dying Pole. The trousers now lay thrown over his saddle. Laughing, Andryushka rode over to Golov, carefully scooped the uniform out of his hands, threw it over the trousers on his saddle, and, tapping his horse lightly with his whip, rode off.

At that moment the sun came pouring out from behind a cloud, enveloping with dazzling light Andryushka's horse, its lively trot, the carefree swish of its docked tail. In a daze, Golov watched the Cossack ride off. He turned and saw me drawing up the list of prisoners. He saw the young Pole with the curly sideburns. The Pole raised calm eyes filled with youthful arrogance and smiled at Golov's dismay. Golov cupped his hands to his mouth and yelled, "Our Republic is still alive, Andrei! It's too early to be dealing out her property! Bring back those rags!"

Andrei turned a deaf ear. He rode on at a trot, his horse pertly swatting its tail, as if it were shooing us away.

"Treason!" Golov mumbled, morose and rigid, pronouncing the word syllable by syllable. He kneeled, took aim, and fired, but missed. Andrei swerved his horse around and came galloping back toward Golov. His red-cheeked, blossoming face was filled with anger.

"Listen, countryman!" he yelled loudly, suddenly rejoicing in the sound of his powerful voice. "I should knock you to Kingdom Come, Platoon Commander! I should knock you to where your you-know-what mother is! You've got a dozen Poles on your hands, and you're making a big fuss! We've taken hundreds, and didn't come running for your help! If you're a worker, then do your job!"

And, glancing at us triumphantly, Andryushka rode off at a gallop. Platoon Commander Golov did not look up at him. He clutched his forehead. Blood was trickling from his head like rain from a haystack. He lay down on his stomach, crawled toward the stream, and for a long time held his smashed, blood-drenched head in the shallow water.

Nine prisoners of war are no longer alive. I know that in my heart.

Sitting on my horse, I made a list of them arranged in neat columns. In the first column I entered a row of numbers, in the second their names and surnames, and in the third column the units to which they had belonged. All in all there were nine names. The fourth name was Adolf Shulmeister, a clerk from Lodz, a Jew. He kept snuggling up to my horse and caressing my boots with tender, trembling fingers. His leg had been shattered by a rifle butt, and he left behind him a thin track, like a lame, wounded dog. The sun boiled the sparkling sweat on his orange, pockmarked, bald pate.

"You *Jude, Pane*,"* he whispered, frantically caressing my stirrup. "You Jude!" he whimpered, dribbling spittle, writhing with joy.

"Get back in line, Shulmeister," I yelled at the Jew, and suddenly, seized by deathly numbness, slipped off my saddle.

"How come you know?" I asked him breathlessly.

"Your eyes, their sweet Jewish look," he yelped, hopping on one leg, leaving his thin dog's track behind him. "Your sweet Jewish look, *Pane!*"

I barely managed to extricate myself from his condemned man's frenzy. I came back to my senses slowly, as after a concussion.

The chief of staff ordered me to take care of the details and rode off to the units.

The machine guns were dragged up onto the hill like calves on halters. They moved up side by side, like a well-ordered herd, clanking reassuringly. The sun played on their dusty muzzles. And I saw a rainbow on their steel. The Polish youth with the curly sideburns stared at them with village curiosity. He leaned his whole body forward, revealing a view of Golov, who was crawling out of a ditch pale and intent, his smashed head and his rifle raised. I stretched my hands out to Golov and yelled, but the sound choked and bulged in my throat. Golov quickly shot the prisoner in the back of the neck and jumped up to his feet. The surprised Pole turned to him, executing a half spin on his heel, as in a military exercise. With the slow movements of a woman giving herself to a man, he lifted both hands to his nape, slumped to the ground, and died instantly.

A smile of peace and relief flitted over Golov's face. A light flush returned to his cheeks.

*"You are a Jew, sir"—Shulmeister uses *vy*, the Russian polite form for "you," *Jude*, the German word for "Jew," and *Pane*, the Polish word for "sir."

"Our mothers don't knit drawers like that for us," he told me slyly. "Cross that one off, and give me a list for eight."

I gave him the list.

"You'll answer for that, Golov!" I said in desperation.

"I will answer for that!" he yelled in unbridled triumph. "But not to you, four-eyes, I'll answer to my own people from the Sormov factory. They know what's what!"

Nine prisoners of war are no longer alive. I know that in my heart. This morning I decided to hold a memorial service for the murdered men. In the Red Cavalry there is no one but me who can do it. Our unit stopped to rest on a ravaged Polish estate. I took out my diary and went into the flower garden, which had remained untouched. Hyacinths and blue roses were growing there.

I began writing about the platoon commander and the nine dead men, but a noise, a familiar noise, interrupted me. Cherkashin, the headquarters lackey, had launched a raid against the beehives. Mitya, a red-cheeked youth from Oryol, was following him, holding a smoking torch in his hand. Their heads were wrapped in their army coats. The slits of their eyes glowed. Swarms of bees charged their conquerors and died by their hives. And I put down my pen. I was horrified at the great number of memorial services awaiting me.

AND THEN
THERE WERE TEN

The following story fragment is an earlier variation of the two stories "Squadron Commander Trunov" and "And Then There Were Nine."

Zavadi Station. This happened yesterday. About thirty Poles were sitting tight in the stone building by the junction of the railroad tracks. The chief of staff himself got involved in this serious business. He strutted in front of our line of men with a revolver in his hand.

"How pointless it is to die at Zavady Station," I thought, and went over to the chief of staff.

The Poles ran [and broke through] our line of men. We brought back ten of them alive. We took them to the field. They looked like a striped blanket laid out on the ground. In front of them, Platoon Commander Golov, mounted, was standing in his stirrups.

"Officers! Own up!" he said, shaking his reins. Blood trickled from his head like rain from a haystack. He had been wounded on the forehead.

"All officers, step forward!" he repeated in a thicker voice, getting off his horse.

Suddenly a lanky man with a drooping little mustache stepped forward from the group.

"End of this war!" the man said with delight, and began crying. "All officers run away, end of this war!"

And the lanky man held out his blue hand to the squadron commander. On his face was an incomprehensible bliss.

"Five fingers," he muttered, sobbing, "I raising with these five fingers my family!"

And, with burning eyes, he slowly waved his large, wilted hand. Golov pushed it back with his saber.

"Your officers threw their uniforms here!" he yelled. "But we're going to have a little fitting now, and whoever the uniforms fit, I'm going to finish off!"

He picked out a cap without a brim from the pile of rags and put it on the lanky man's head.

"It fits," Golov whispered. He stepped up closer to the prisoner, looked him in the eyes, and plunged his saber into his gullet. The lanky man fell, shivered, his legs twitching in a frenzy. A foamy, coral-red stream poured from his neck. A young red-cheeked Cossack with silky hair knelt before the dying man. He unbuttoned the man's [trousers].

A LETTER TO THE EDITOR

This letter from Babel was published in 1924 in the literary magazine Oktyabr, issue no. 4, in answer to an article by General Budyonny, in which Budyonny attacked Babel for his portrayal of the Red Cavalry and its fighters in his stories, accusing Babel, among other things, of character assassination and "counterrevolutionary lies."

*I*n 1920, I served in the First Cavalry's Sixth Division, of which Comrade Timoshenko was commander at the time. I witnessed his heroic, military, and revolutionary work with much admiration. This wonderful and pristine image of my beloved division commander long ruled my imagination, and when I set about to write my memoirs of the Polish Campaign, my thoughts often returned to him. But in the process of writing, my aim of keeping within the parameters of historical truth began to shift, and I decided instead to express my thoughts in a literary form. All that remained from my initial outline were a few authentic surnames. Through an unforgivable oversight, however, I did not undertake to remove these surnames, and, to my great consternation, these names have now appeared by mistake in print, as for instance in the piece "Timoshenko and Melnikov,"* published in the third volume of *Krasnaya Nov,* 1924. This oversight came about because I was late handing in the materials for that volume, and the editorial office, not to mention the typesetting department, had put me under extreme pressure, and in this last-minute rush, I overlooked the vital task of changing the original surnames in the final proofs. I need not stress that Comrade Timoshenko has nothing whatsoever in common with the character in that piece, a fact clear to anyone who has ever crossed paths with the former commander of Division Six, one of the most courageous and selfless of our Red Commanders.

I. Babel

---

* In later editions of *Red Cavalry,* this piece was renamed "The Story of a Horse."

Stories, 1925-1938

By 1925, Isaac Babel was beginning to gain fame and notoriety throughout the Soviet Union. In the previous two years, his RED CAVALRY stories had appeared in quick succession in newspapers and literary magazines, and had been received with great enthusiasm by readers and critics. But they were received with outrage by the powerful commanders who found themselves appearing in the stories in a most unfavorable light. General Budyonny, Division Commander Timoshenko, and Squadron Commander Melnikov (who had been portrayed in the "The Story of a Horse" as having a breakdown that prompted him to leave the cavalry and to resign his membership in the Communist Party), wrote outraged letters and articles that were printed in major newspapers and magazines.* This added greatly to Babel's mystique, and after the RED CAVALRY stories came out as a book in 1926, it was reprinted eight times over the next few years.

In the stories in this section, Babel broadened his range of subject matter, dealing more directly than before with autobiographical material and

---

*In reaction to the protests, Babel changed some of the names in later editions of the stories. Timoshenko, for instance, became Savitsky, and Melnikov became Khlebnikov.

writing in longer forms. He intended to collect the stories he wrote based on his childhood in a single volume under the title THE STORY OF MY DOVECOTE, and began working on a novel, VELIKAYA KRINITSA, named after a Ukrainian village (*Velikaya Staritsa*) that he visited in the spring of 1930. The novel was to be about the effects of enforced collectivization on farmers, a dangerous subject for a book during the Stalin era. Two chapters of this novel have survived as separate stories, "Gapa Guzhva," which was to be the first chapter, and "Kolyvushka," which was not published during Babel's lifetime.

Some of Babel's most celebrated stories are from this period. As Maxim Gorky wrote to Romain Rolland in 1928, "Babel is the great hope of Russian literature."

THE STORY OF
MY DOVECOTE

For Maxim Gorky

*A*s a child I wanted a dovecote very badly. In all my life I have never desired anything more intensely. I was nine years old when my father promised to give me the money to buy some planks and three pairs of doves. The year was 1904. I was getting ready for the examinations for the preparatory class of the Nikolayev Lycée. My family lived in Nikolayev, in the province of Kherson. This province no longer exists; our town was absorbed into the district of Odessa.

I was only nine years old, and was frightened of the examinations. In both Russian and mathematics I could not afford to get less than five, the highest grade. The Jewish entry quota for our lycée was harsh, only five percent. Out of forty boys, only two Jews could be admitted into the preparatory class. The teachers would come up with the most cunning questions for these two boys; nobody was given the kind of complicated questions we were. So my father promised to buy me doves on condition that I manage to get two five-pluses. He tormented me more than I can say, I tumbled into a never-ending daydream—the long, desperate dream of a child—and though I went to the examination immersed in that dream, I still fared better than the rest.

I was good at learning. The teachers, though they tried every trick, did not manage to waylay my mind and my sharp memory. I was good at learning, and so got two fives. But then the situation changed. Khariton Efrussi,* the grain merchant who exported wheat to

---

*The Efrussi family was one of the oldest and wealthiest Jewish merchant families in Odessa.

Marseilles, proffered a five-hundred-ruble bribe for his son, I was given a five-minus instead of a five, and the lycée admitted Efrussi Junior in my place. My father was deeply pained by this. From the time I was six, he had taught me all the subjects you could imagine. That minus drove him to desperation. He wanted to beat Efrussi up, or to hire two dock-workers to beat him up, but mother talked him out of it, and I began preparing myself for the examination next year for the following grade. Behind my back, my family talked my tutor into going over the lessons for both the preparatory class and the first class within one year, and, as we were completely desperate, I ended up learning three books by heart. These books were Smirnovsky's grammar, Yevtushevsky's book of mathematical problems, and Putsikovich's introduction to Russian history. Children no longer study these books, but I learned them by heart, line by line, and the following year Karavayev, the schoolmaster, gave me those unattainable five-pluses in my Russian language examination.

Karavayev was a ruddy-faced, indignant man who had been a student in Moscow. He was barely thirty. His manly cheeks blossomed with the flush seen on the cheeks of peasant children. He had a wart on his face from which a tuft of ashen, feline hair sprouted. Also present at the examination besides Karavayev was the deputy warden, who was considered an important figure not only in the lycée but in the whole province. The deputy warden asked me about Peter I, and a blankness came over me, a feeling that the end, the abyss, was near, a dry abyss surrounded by delight and despair.

I knew by heart the passage about Peter the Great in Putsikovich's book and Pushkin's poems. I recited the poems in sobs. Faces swarmed into my eyes, mixing and shuffling deep inside like a fresh deck of cards, while I, shivering, straight-backed, shouted out Pushkin's verses with all my might, as fast as I could. I went on shouting the verses for a long time, nobody interrupting my crazed rambling. Across my crimson blindness, across the freedom that had taken hold of me, I only saw Pyatnitsky's old face leaning forward with its silvery beard. He did not interrupt me, but turned to Karavayev, who was rejoicing in Pushkin and me, and whispered, "What a nation! The devil is in these Yids!"

When I finished he said, "Very good, off you go now, my little friend."

I left the classroom and went out into the corridor, and there, leaning against the unpainted wall, I woke from the convulsions of my dreams. Russian boys were playing all around me, the school bell hung nearby over the official-looking flight of stairs, a watchman was dozing on a broken chair. I gazed at him and began to come back to my senses. Children came creeping toward me from all sides. They wanted to poke me and get me to play with them, but suddenly Pyatnitsky appeared in the corridor. Passing by me, he stopped for an instant, his frock coat undulating in a heavy slow wave over his back. I saw emotion in his large, fleshy, gentlemanly back, and I went up to him.

"Children," he told the schoolboys. "Leave this boy alone!" And he laid his fat, tender hand on my shoulder. "My little friend," Pyatnitsky said, turning to me. "You can go and tell your father that you have been accepted into the first class."

A magnificent star shone on his chest, medals tinkled by his lapel, and hemmed in by the murky walls, moving between them like a barge moves through a deep canal, his large, black, uniformed body marched off on rigid legs and disappeared through the doors of the headmaster's office. A little attendant brought him tea with solemn ceremony, and I ran home to our store.

In our store a muzhik customer sat scratching his head in the grip of indecision. When my father saw me, he abandoned the muzhik and drank in my story without a moment's doubt. He shouted to his sales clerk to close the store, and rushed over to Sobornaya Street to buy me a cap with the school emblem on it. My poor mother barely managed to wrest me away from my delirious father. She stood there, pale, trying to foresee my fate. She kept caressing me and then pushing me away in disgust. She said that a list of all the children admitted into the lycée was always published in the newspapers, and that God would punish us and that people would laugh at us, if we bought a school uniform ahead of time. My mother was pale, she was trying to foresee my fate in my eyes, and looked at me with bitter pity, as if I were a little cripple, for she was the only one who fully realized how luckless our family was.

All the men of our clan had been too trusting of others and too quick to take unconsidered action. We had never had any luck in anything. My grandfather had once been a rabbi in Belaya Tserkov, had been chased out of town for blasphemy, and then lived in scandal and poverty for another forty years, learned foreign languages, and started going insane in his eightieth year. My Uncle Lev, my father's brother, studied at the Yeshiva in Volozhin, evaded conscription in 1892, and abducted the daughter of a quartermaster serving in the Kiev military district. Uncle Lev took this woman to California, to Los Angeles, where he abandoned her, and he died in a madhouse among Negroes and Malays. After his death, the American police sent us his belongings—a large trunk reinforced with brown iron hoops—from Los Angeles. In this trunk were dumbbells, locks of a woman's hair, Uncle's *tallith*, whips with gilded tips, and herbal tea in little boxes trimmed with cheap pearls. The only men left in the family were mad Uncle Simon, who lived in Odessa, my father, and me. But my father was too trusting of others, he offended people with his exhilarating welcome of first love. They did not forgive him for this, and so cheated him. This was why my father believed that his life was governed by a malevolent fate, an inscrutable being that pursued him and that was unlike him in every way. So in our family I was my mother's only hope. Like all Jews, I was short in stature, weak, and plagued by headaches from too much study. My mother could see this clearly. She had never been blinded by her husband's destitute pride and his incomprehensible belief that our family would one day be stronger and richer than other people in this world. She did not foresee any success for us, was frightened of buying a school uniform ahead of time, and only acceded to my having my picture taken by a portrait photographer.

On September 20, 1905, a list of all those who had managed to enter the first class was posted outside the lycée. My name was on that list. My whole family went to look at this piece of paper—even Grandpa Shoyl, my great-uncle, went to the lycée. I loved this braggart of an old man because he sold fish in the market. His fat hands were moist, covered with fish scales, and reeked of wonderful, cold worlds. Shoyl was also different from other people because of his fabricated stories about the Polish uprising of 1861. In the distant past, he had been an innkeeper in Skvira. He had witnessed the soldiers of Nicholas I shoot Count Godlewski and other Polish insurgents. But then again, maybe he hadn't witnessed this. Now I know that Shoyl was no more than an old fool and a naive teller of tall tales, but I have not forgotten those little tales of his, they were good tales. So even foolish Shoyl went over to the lycée to read the list that had my name on it, and in the evening he danced and stamped his feet at our beggarly feast.

My father organized a feast of celebration and invited his comrades—grain merchants, estate brokers, and itinerant salesmen who sold agricultural machines in our region. These itinerant salesmen sold machines to everyone. Both muzhiks and landowners were afraid of them, as they could not get rid of them without buying something. Of all the Jews, the itinerant salesmen are the most worldly and cheerful. At our feast they sang drawn-out Hasidic songs made up of only three words, but with many funny intonations. Only those who have celebrated Passover with the Hasidim, or who have visited their boisterous synagogues in Volhynia, know the charm of these intonations. Old Liberman, who taught me Hebrew and the Torah, also came to our house that evening. My family always addressed him as Monsieur Liberman. He drank more Bessarabian wine than he should have, the traditional silk strings slipped out from under his red vest, and he called out a toast in my honor in Hebrew. In this toast the old man congratulated my parents, and said that by passing this examination I had won a victory over all my foes, I had won a victory over the fat-cheeked Russian boys and the sons of our roughneck rich. Thus in ancient times had David, the King of the Jews, won a victory over Goliath, and just as I had triumphed over Goliath, so too would our people, through its sheer power of mind, triumph over the foes that surround us, eager for our blood. Monsieur Liberman wept, pronounced these words weeping, drank some more wine, and yelled, "*Vivat!*" The dancing guests took him into the circle and danced with him the ancient quadrille, as at a shtetl wedding. Everyone was joyful at our feast, even my mother took a little sip of wine, though she did not like vodka and did not understand how anyone could. Which is why she thought all Russians were mad, and why she could not understand how women could live with Russian husbands.

But our happy days were to begin later. For my mother they began when she started making me sandwiches in the morning before I left for school, when we went from store to store buying festive supplies—a pencil box, a piggybank, a schoolbag, new books with hard covers, and notebooks with glossy covers. No one in the world has a stronger response to new things than children. They shudder at the smell that new things give off, like dogs at the scent of a rabbit, and experience a madness, which later, when one is an adult, is called inspiration. And this clean, childish feeling of ownership of new things infected my mother too. It took us a whole month to get used to the pencil box and the morning twilight, when I would drink tea at the edge of the large, brightly lit table and gather my books into my schoolbag. It took us a whole month to get used to our happy life, and it was only after the first school term that I remembered the doves.

I had gotten everything ready for them—the one and a half rubles and the dovecote made out of a box by Grandpa Shoyl. The dovecote was given a coat of brown paint. It had nests for twelve pairs of doves, a series of little slats on its roof, and special grating I had invented so that it would be easier for other doves to come in too. Everything was ready. On Sunday, October 22, I set off to the wild game market, but I ran into unexpected obstacles along the way.

The story I am relating here, in other words my entry into the first class of the lycée, took place in the autumn of 1905. Czar Nicholas was in the process of giving the Russian people a constitution, and orators in threadbare coats were clambering onto podiums outside the buildings of the town councils and giving speeches to the people. On the streets at night shots were fired, and my mother did not want to let me go to the wild game market. Early in the morning on October 20, the boys from next door were flying a kite right outside the police station, and our water carrier, abandoning all his duties, strolled pomaded and red-faced along the street. Then we saw the sons of Kalistov, the baker, drag a leather vaulting horse out onto the street and start to do their exercises right in the middle of the road. Nobody tried to stop them. Semernikov, the constable, was even egging them on to jump higher. Semernikov was wearing a homemade silk waistband, and his boots that day had been polished to a shine they had never before achieved. An out-of-uniform constable frightened my mother more than anything else, and it was because of him that she would not let me go out. But I crept out onto the street through backyards, and ran all the way to the wild game market, which lay behind the train station.

Ivan Nikodimich, the dove seller, was sitting at his usual place in the market. Besides doves, he was also selling rabbits and a peacock. The peacock, its tail fanned out, sat on a perch, darting its dispassionate head from one side to the other. Its foot was tied with a twisted string, the other end of the string lay wedged under Ivan Nikodimich's wicker chair. The moment I got there, I bought from the old man a pair of cherry-red doves with wonderful ruffled tails, and a pair of crested ones, and hid them in a sack under my shirt. I still had forty kopecks after my purchase, but the old man wouldn't give me a male and female Kryukov dove for that price. What I liked about Kryukov doves was their beaks, which were short, mottled, and amiable. Forty kopecks was the right price for them, but the old man overpriced them and turned away his yellow face, harrowed by the unsociable passions of the bird-catcher. As the market started closing, Ivan Nikodimich called me over, seeing that there weren't going to be any other buyers. Things turned out my way, things turned out badly.

Shortly before noon, or a little after, a man in felt boots walked across the square. He walked lightly on swollen feet, his lively eyes twinkling in his haggard face.

"Ivan Nikodimich," he said, as he walked past the bird-catcher. "Gather up your bits and bobs, in town the nobles of Jerusalem are being given a constitution. On Rybnaya Street they've just served Grandpa Babel a helping of death."

He made his way lightly among the cages, like a barefoot plowman walking along a field path.

"This is wrong!" Ivan Nikodimich muttered after him. "This is wrong!" he shouted more adamantly, gathering up the rabbits and the peacock, and pushing the Kryukov doves into my hands for forty kopecks.

I hid them under my shirt and watched the people run from the market. The peacock on Ivan Nikodimich's shoulder was the last to disappear. It sat like the sun in a damp autumn sky, like July on a rosy riverbank, a scorching July in long cold grass. There was no one left at the market, and shots were thundering not too far away. Then I ran to the train station, cut across the little park, which suddenly seemed to turn upside down, and I dashed into a deserted alley tamped with yellow earth. At the end of the alley sat legless Makarenko in a wheelchair, in which he rode around town selling cigarettes from a tray. The boys from our street bought cigarettes from him, the children liked him, I went running toward him in the alley.

"Makarenko," I said, breathless from running, and patted the legless man on the shoulder. "Have you seen Shoyl?"

The cripple didn't answer, his rough face of red fat and fists and iron was shining translucently. He was fidgeting in his chair, his wife, Katyusha, turning her puffed-up backside toward us, was riffling through things that lay scattered on the ground.

"How many have you counted?" the legless man asked her, pitching away from the woman with his whole body, as if he knew in advance that he wouldn't be able to bear her answer.

"Seven pairs of spats," Katyusha said, without straightening up, "six duvet covers, now I'm counting the bonnets."

"Bonnets!" Makarenko shouted, choked, and made a sound as if he were sobbing. "Obviously, God has chosen me to bear the Cross, Katyusha! People are carting off whole bales of cloth—these people get nice and proper things, and what do we get? Bonnets!"

And sure enough, a woman with a beautiful, fiery face went running down the alley. She was holding a bunch of fezzes in one hand and a bolt of cloth in the other. In a happy, desperate voice she was calling out to her children, who had disappeared. A silk dress and a blue jacket trailed after her scuttling body, and she didn't hear Makarenko, who went rushing after her in his wheelchair. The legless man couldn't catch up with her. His wheels rattled, he moved the levers with all his might.

"Madame!" he yelled deafeningly. "Madamochka! Where did you get the calico?"

But the woman with the scuttling dress was no longer to be seen. A rickety cart came flying around the corner where she had just disappeared. A young peasant was standing upright in the cart.

"Where's everyone run off to?" the young man asked, raising the red reins above his nags, who were straining in their collars.

"Everyone's on Sobornaya Street," Makarenko whined in an imploring voice. "Everyone's there, my dearest, my very dearest friend! Whatever you can grab, bring it here to me—I'll buy everything!"

The young man leaned forward over the front of his cart and whipped his skewbald nags. They bounced in their dirty cruppers like colts and went galloping off. The yellow alley was once again left yellow and empty. The legless man glared at me with his dead eyes.

"Well, am I not the man that God singled out?" he said lifelessly. "Am I not the Son of Man, huh?"

And he stretched out a hand flecked with leprosy.

"What've you got there in that bag?" he said, snatching away the sack that had warmed my heart.

The cripple's fat hand turned the sack upside down and he pulled out a cherry-red dove. The bird lay in his palm, its feet sticking up.

"Doves!" Makarenko said, and rolled up to me with squeaking wheels. "Doves!" he repeated, and slapped me across the face.

He hit me hard with the palm of his hand, crushing the bird. Katyusha's puffed-up backside loomed before my eyes, and I fell down in my new overcoat.

"Their seed has to be stamped out!" Katyusha said, getting up from the bonnets. "I cannot abide their seed and their stinking men!"

She also said other things about our seed, but I no longer heard anything. I lay on the ground, the innards of the crushed bird trickling down the side of my face. They trickled, winding and dribbling, down my cheek, blinding me. The dove's tender entrails slithered over my forehead, and I closed my uncaked eye so that I would not see the world unravel before me. This world was small and ugly. A pebble lay in front of my eyes, a pebble dented like the face of an old woman with a large jaw. A piece of string lay near it and a clump of feathers, still breathing. My world was small and ugly. I closed my eyes so I wouldn't see it, and pressed myself against the earth that lay soothing and mute beneath me. This tamped earth did not resemble anything in our lives. Somewhere far away disaster rode across it on a large horse, but the sound of its hooves grew weaker and vanished, and silence, the bitter silence that can descend on children in times of misfortune, dissolved the boundary between my body and the unmoving earth. The earth smelled of damp depths, of tombs, of flowers. I breathed in its scent and cried without the slightest fear. I walked down a foreign street filled with white boxes, walked in my raiment of blood-drenched feathers, alone on sidewalks swept clean as on a Sunday, and I cried more bitterly, more fully and happily than I would ever cry again. Whitened wires hummed above my head, a little mongrel mutt was running in front of me, in a side street a young muzhik in a vest was smashing a window frame in the house of Khariton Efrussi. He was smashing it with a wooden hammer, his whole body steeped in the movement. He breathed in deeply, smiled in all directions the gentle smile of drunkenness, of sweat and hearty strength. The whole street was filled with the crackling, crashing song of shattering wood. All this muzhik wanted was to flex his back, to sweat, and to yell out bizarre words in an unknown, not Russian language. He shouted them and sang, opening his blue eyes wide, until a religious procession appeared on the street, marching from the town council.

Old men with painted beards were carrying the portrait of a neatly combed Czar, banners with sepulchral saints fluttered above the religious procession, inflamed old women were running in front of it. When the muzhik in the vest saw the procession, he pressed the hammer to his chest and went running after the banners, while I, waiting for the procession to pass, carefully made my way to our house. It was empty. Its white doors stood open, the grass by the dovecote was trampled down. Kuzma, our janitor, was the only one who had not left our courtyard. Kuzma was sitting in the shed, laying out Shoyl's dead body.

"The wind brings you in like a bad splinter," the old man said when he saw me. "You were gone for ages! See how the townsfolk have hacked our Grandpa down?"

Kuzma began sniffling, turned away, and pulled a perch out of the fly of Grandpa's trousers. Two perches had been shoved into Grandpa—one into his fly, the other into his mouth—and although Grandpa was dead, one of the perches was still alive and quivering.

"Just our Grandpa's been hacked down, no one else!" Kuzma said, throwing the perches to the cat. "You should have heard him curse their goddamn mothers up and down! What a sweet man he was. You should lay two fivers on his eyes."

But back then, just ten years old, I had no idea what dead people needed fivers for.

"Kuzma," I whispered, "save us!"

And I went over to the janitor, embraced his old, bent back with its crooked shoulders, and peered at Grandpa Shoyl from behind the janitor's back. Grandpa Shoyl was lying there in the sawdust, his chest crushed, his beard pointing up, rugged shoes on his bare feet. His legs, spread apart, were dirty, purple, dead. Kuzma was bustling around them. He bound Grandpa's jaws, and kept looking to see if there was anything else he had to do for the deceased. He was bustling about as if some new object had just been delivered to his house. He only calmed down after he finished combing the dead man's beard.

"He cursed their goddamn mothers," he said, smiling, and looked at the corpse lovingly. "If they had been Tatars attacking him, he'd have fought them off—but it was Russians who came, women too, damn Russians; those damn Russians think it's an insult to forgive someone, I know those Russians well!"

The janitor poured sawdust under the dead man. He took off his carpenter's apron and grabbed hold of my hand.

"Let's go to your father," he mumbled, squeezing my hand harder and harder. "Your father's been looking for you since this morning, he must be half dead with worry!"

And I went with Kuzma to the house of the tax inspector, where my parents had hidden from the pogrom.

FIRST LOVE

*W*hen I was ten years old I fell in love with a woman by the name of Galina Apollonovna. Her surname was Rubtsov. Her husband, an officer in the army, had gone to the Japanese War and returned in October 1905. He brought many trunks back with him. These trunks were full of Chinese things: folding screens, precious weapons—all in all, thirty *poods*. Kuzma told us that Rubtsov had bought them with money he had made serving in the engineering corps of the Manchurian Army. Others said the same thing. People found it hard to gossip about the Rubtsovs, because the Rubtsovs were happy. Their house lay right next to our property. Their glass veranda cut into a piece of our land, but my father had not quarreled with them about it. Old Rubtsov, the tax inspector, was known in our town as a fair man, he counted Jews among his acquaintances. And when his son, the officer, returned from the Japanese War, we all saw how lovingly and happily he and his wife settled down together. For days on end Galina Apollonovna would hold her husband's hand. She didn't take her eyes off him, as she hadn't seen him for a year and a half. But I was horrified at her gaze, and looked away, shivering. In the two of them I was watching the strange and shameful life of all the people in the world, and I wanted to fall into a magic sleep to forget this life that surpassed all my dreams. Sometimes Galina Apollonovna would walk about her room in red shoes and a Chinese dressing gown, her braid hanging loose. Beneath the lace of her low-cut chemise I could see the deepening onset of her pressed-down breasts, white and swollen, and on her dressing gown dragons, birds, and hollow trees embroidered in silk.

All day she trailed about the house, a vague smile on her wet lips, bumping into the trunks that had not yet been unpacked and the exercise ladders that lay around on the floor. Whenever Galina bruised her leg, she would lift her dressing gown above her knees and croon to her husband, "Kiss my little booboo!"

And the officer, bending his long legs in dragoon's breeches, spurs, and tight kidskin boots, got down on the dirty floor, and, smiling, shuffled crawling on his knees to her and kissed the bruised spot, the spot where her garter had left a puffy crease. I saw those kisses from my window. They caused me great suffering, but it is not worth describing because the love and jealousy of a ten-year-old boy resembles in every way the love and jealousy of a grown man. For two weeks I did not go to my window and avoided Galina, until a coincidence threw us together. The coincidence was the pogrom that broke out in 1905 in Nikolayev and other towns inside the Jewish Pale. A crowd of hired killers ransacked my father's store and killed my Grandpa Shoyl. All this happened without me. That morning I had been out buying doves from Ivan Nikodimich, the hunter. For five of my ten years I had dreamed with all the fervor of my soul about having doves, and then, when I finally managed to buy them, Makarenko the cripple smashed the doves against the side of my face. After that Kuzma had taken me to the Rubtsovs. A cross had been drawn in chalk on the Rubtsovs' gate, no one would harm them, and they had hidden my parents. Kuzma took me to their glass veranda. There, in the green rotunda, sat my mother and Galina.

"We're going to have to wash our face," Galina said to me. "We're going to have to wash it, my little rabbi. Our whole little face is covered in feathers, and the feathers are all bloody."

She hugged me and led me along the corridor with its sharp aroma. My head was leaning against Galina's hip, and her hip moved and breathed. We went into the kitchen, and she put my head under the tap. A goose was frying on the tiled oven, flickering kitchenware hung along the walls, and next to the kitchenware, in the cook's corner, hung Czar Nicholas I, decorated with paper flowers. Galina washed off the remains of the dove that were caking my cheeks.

"As handsome as a bridegroom, my pretty little boy," she said, then kissed me on the lips with her puffy mouth and turned away.

"Your Papa," she suddenly whispered, "your Papa is very troubled right now. All day long he has been wandering aimlessly through the streets. Go to the window and call him!"

Outside the window I saw the empty street with the enormous sky above it, and my red-haired father walking along. He wasn't wearing a hat, and his red hair was tousled and wispy. His paper shirtfront was twisted to the side and fastened haphazardly with a button, but not the right one. Vlasov, a haggard workman in patched-up soldier's rags, was doggedly following my father.

"No, we don't need it!" he was saying in a fervent, wheezing voice, patting my father tenderly with both hands. "We don't need freedom just so the Yids can trade freely! Just give a working man a life of bright . . . brightfulness . . . for all his big horrible toil! Give it to him, my friend! You hear me? Give it to him!"

The workman was patting my father, beseeching him. In his face, flashes of pure drunken inspiration alternated with drowsy despondence.

"Like wimps, that's what our lives should be like," he muttered, swaying on unsteady legs. "Our lives should be just like wimps, only without that God of the Old Betrievers*—it's from Him the Jews make a profit, no one else does!"

And Vlasov began shouting desperately about the God of the "Old Betrievers," who took pity on no one but the Jews. Vlasov howled, stumbled, and tried to catch up with his mysterious God, but at that moment a mounted Cossack patrol blocked his path. An officer in striped trousers, wearing a silver parade belt, was riding at the head of the detachment. A tall peaked cap was perched on his head. The officer rode slowly, without looking left or right. He rode as if he were riding through a ravine where one can only look forward.

"Captain," my father whispered, when the Cossack reached his side. "Captain," my father repeated, falling to his knees in the mud and clasping his head.

* Vlasov mispronounces *Staro-Ver* ("Old Believer") as *Stalo-Ver* ("Started-Believing"), and comically identifies the Old Believers with the Jews. The Old Believers were an archconservative Christian sect that had split from the Russian Orthodox Church in the seventeenth century.

"What can I do for you?" the officer answered, still looking forward, lifting his hand in its lemon suede glove to his peaked cap.

Up ahead, at the corner of Rybnaya Street, thugs were smashing our store and throwing out into the street boxes of nails, tools, and also the new portrait photograph of me in my lycée uniform.

"Over there," my father said, without getting up from his knees. "They're smashing everything I've worked for all my life, Captain! Why are they doing this?"

The officer muttered something, tapped his cap with his lemon suede glove, and tugged the reins, but his horse didn't move. My father had crawled on his knees in front of it, brushing against its kindly, short, slightly shaggy legs.

"I will see to it!" the captain said, tugged at the reins, and rode off. The Cossacks followed him.

They sat dispassionately on their high saddles, riding through their imaginary ravine, and disappeared around the corner of Sobornaya Street.

Galina again pushed me toward the window.

"Get your Papa to come home," she said. "He hasn't eaten anything since this morning."

And I leaned out the window.

My father turned around when he heard my voice.

"My darling son," he called out with indescribable tenderness.

He and I went up to the veranda of the Rubtsovs, where mother was lying in the green rotunda. Next to her bed lay dumbbells and an exercise machine.

"Those damn kopecks!" my mother said to us as we came in. "People's lives, and children, and our luckless luck. You gave them everything! Those damn kopecks!" she shouted in a hoarse voice unlike her own. She shuddered convulsively, and lay quiet on the bed.

Then, in the silence, I began to hiccup. I stood by the wall with my cap pulled down and couldn't stop hiccuping.

"Shame on you, my pretty little boy," Galina said, smiling her haughty smile at me, and tapping me with the stiff flap of her dressing gown. She went over to the window in her red shoes and began to hang Chinese curtains on the extraordinary rod. Her bare arms drowned in the silk, the live braid moved over her hip. I looked at her with delight.

Learned boy that I was, I looked at her as at a distant stage lit by many lights. And I imagined I was Miron, the son of the coal merchant who sold coal on our street corner. I imagined myself in the Jewish Self-defense Brigade. I could see myself walking around, just like Miron, in tattered shoes tied together with string. A dingy rifle hangs on a green strap from my shoulder, and I'm kneeling by the old wooden fence, firing shots at the murderers. Beyond the fence lies a vacant lot with heaps of dusty coal. My old rifle shoots badly, the murderers with their beards and white teeth are edging ever closer to me. I feel the proud sensation of impending death, and high, high up, high in the blue heavens, I see Galina. I see an opening cut into the wall of a gigantic fortress built with myriads of bricks. This crimson building looms over the side street with its badly tamped gray earth. On the parapet stands Galina. With her haughty smile she smiles from that inaccessible opening, her husband, the half-dressed officer, standing behind her back, kissing her neck.

In my attempt to stop hiccuping, I imagined all this in order to make my loving her more bitter, hot, and hopeless, and perhaps because so much grief is overwhelming for a ten-year-old boy. These foolish fantasies helped me forget the death of the doves and the death of Shoyl. I would have perhaps forgotten these deaths if Kuzma had not come onto the veranda with that terrible Jew, Aba.

It was twilight when they came. A weak little lamp, hiding in a corner, shone on the veranda—a twinkling lamp, a disciple of misfortune.

"I have prepared Grandfather," Kuzma said as he came in. "Now he's lying nice and pretty—I brought the *shamas* too so he can say some words over the old man."

And Kuzma pointed to *shamas* Aba.

"Let him whine a little," Kuzma said amiably. "Stuff a *shamas'* guts, and the *shamas* will pester God all night."

Kuzma stood on the threshold, his good-natured, broken nose jutting in all directions, and warmly began telling us how he had bound the dead man's jaw. But my father interrupted him.

"I would be thankful, Reb Aba, if you would pray over the deceased, I will pay you," my father said.

"Pay me? But I'm worried you won't pay," Aba answered in a weary voice, laying his squeamish bearded face on the tablecloth. "I am worried that you will take my ruble and run off to Argentina, to Buenos Aires, and open a wholesale business there with that ruble of mine! A wholesale business!" Aba said. He chewed his disdainful lips and picked up the newspaper *Son of the Fatherland*, which was lying on the table. In this newspaper there was an article about the Czar's manifesto of October 17, and about freedom.

"Citizens of free Russia," Aba read haltingly, and chewed his beard, which he had stuffed into his mouth. "Citizens of free Russia, Happy Easter to you all, Christ has risen!" The old *shamas* held the shaking newspaper sideways in front of him. He read it drowsily, in a singsong voice, pronouncing the Russian words he did not know in the strangest way. Aba's pronunciation of these words resembled the muffled babble of a Negro who has just arrived at a Russian port from his native land. It even made my mother laugh.

"I am being sinful," she shouted, leaning out of the rotunda. "You are making me laugh, Aba! You should tell us how you and your family are doing?"

"Ask me about something else," Aba mumbled without releasing his beard from between his teeth, and continued reading the newspaper.

"Ask him something else," my father repeated, walking over to the middle of the room. His eyes, smiling at us through their tears, suddenly began rolling and fixed themselves on a spot invisible to all.

"Oy, Shoyl!" my father uttered in a flat, false, theatrical voice. "*Oy,* beloved Shoyl!"

We saw that he was getting ready to start hollering, and my mother forewarned us.

"Manus!" she shouted, tearing at my father's breast, her hair becoming instantly disheveled. "Look what a state our child is in, can't you hear him hiccuping? Can't you?"

Father fell silent.

"Rakhel," he said timorously, "I cannot tell you how unhappy I am about Shoyl."

Aba went to the kitchen and came back with a glass of water.

"Drink, you little *shlemazl*," he said, coming over to me. "Drink this water, which will help you as much as incense helps a dead man!"

And sure enough, the water did not help me in the least. My hiccups became stronger and stronger. A growl tore out of my chest. A swelling, pleasant to the touch, expanded in my throat. The swelling breathed, widened, covered my gullet, and came bulging out over my collar. Within the swelling gurgled my torn breath. It gurgled like boiling water. By nightfall I was no longer the silly little boy I had been all my life, but had turned into a writhing heap. My mother, now taller and shapelier, wrapped herself in her shawl and went to Galina, who stood watching stiffly.

"My dear Galina," my mother said in a strong, melodious voice. "We are imposing on you and dear Nadyezhda Ivanovna, and all your family so much. My dear Galina, I am so embarrassed!"

With fiery cheeks my mother jostled Galina toward the door, and then came hurrying over to me, stuffing her shawl into my mouth to smother my groans.

"Hold on, my little darling," mother whispered. "Hold on for Mama."

But even if I could have held on, I wouldn't have, because I no longer felt any shame at all.

That was how my illness began. I was ten years old at the time. The following morning I was taken to the doctor. The pogrom continued, but no one touched us. The doctor, a fat man, diagnosed an illness of the nerves.

He told us to go to Odessa as quickly as we could, to the specialists, and to wait there for the warm weather and bathing in the sea.

And that is what we did. A few days later I left for Odessa with my mother to stay with Grandfather Levy-Itskhok and Uncle Simon. We left in the morning on a ship, and by midday the churning waters of the Bug changed to the heavy green waves of the sea. This was the beginning of my life in the house of my crazed Grandfather Levy-Itskhok. And I bade farewell forever to Nikolayev, where I had lived the first ten years of my childhood.

KARL-YANKEL

*I*n the days of my childhood there was a smithy in Peresyp* that belonged to Jonas Brutman. Horse dealers, carters—known as *bindyuzhniks* in Odessa—and butchers from the town slaughterhouses gathered in this smithy. It was on the Balta Road, and it was quite handy as a lookout post for intercepting muzhiks carting oats and Bessarabian wine into town. Jonas was a small, timid man, but he knew his way around wine. In him dwelled the soul of an Odessa Jew.

In my day he had three growing sons. He only came up to their waists. It was on the beach of Peresyp that I first reflected on the power of the forces in nature. The boys, three fattened bulls with crimson shoulders and feet big as shovels, carried shriveled-up little Jonas to the water the way one carries an infant. And yet it had been he, and no one else, who had sired them. There was no doubt about that. The black-smith's wife went to the synagogue twice a week, on Friday evenings and on the morning of the Sabbath. It was a Hasidic synagogue, where on Passover they whirled themselves into an ecstasy like dervishes. Jonas's wife paid tribute to the emissaries sent by the Galician *tsaddiks* to our southern provinces. The blacksmith did not interfere in his wife's relationship with God. After work, he went to a wine shop next to the slaughterhouses, and there, sipping his cheap pink wine, listened meek-ly to what people were talking about—politics and the price of cattle.

His sons resembled their mother in strength and build. As soon as

* Odessa's eastern suburb by the harbor.

they came of age, two of the boys went and joined the partisans. The elder was killed at Voznesensk, the other, Semyon, went over to Primakov* and joined a Red Cossack division. He was chosen to be commander of a Cossack regiment. He and a few other shtetl youths were the first in this unexpected breed of Jewish fighters, horsemen, and partisans.

The third son became a blacksmith like his father. He works at the Ghen plow factory.† He has not married and has not sired anyone.

The children of Semyon, the Cossack commander, tagged along from place to place with his division. But the old woman needed a grandchild to whom she could tell stories about the Baal-Shem. She was expecting a grandchild from her youngest daughter Paulina. Paulina was the only one in the whole family who resembled little old Jonas. She was timid, nearsighted, and had delicate skin. Many came around asking for her hand in marriage. Paulina chose Ofsey Byelotserkovsky. We could not understand why she chose him. Even more surprising was the news that the young couple was happy. A woman runs her household as she wills, an outsider cannot see pots breaking. But in this case it was Ofsey Byelotserkovsky who was to break the pots. A year into their marriage, he dragged Brana Brutman, his mother-in-law, to court. The old woman had taken advantage of Ofsey's being away on a business trip and Paulina's being in the hospital for a breast inflammation to abduct her newborn grandson and take him to the neighborhood charlatan, Naftula Gerchik. And there, in the presence of ten doddering wrecks—ten ancient and impoverished men, denizens of the Hasidic synagogue—the rites of circumcision were performed.

Ofsey Byelotserkovsky did not find out what had happened until after his return. Ofsey had put himself forward as a candidate to join the Party. He decided to seek the advice of Bychach, the secretary of the local cell of the State Trade Committee.

"You've been morally bespattered!" Bychach told him. "You must pursue this matter further."

---

*Vitaly Markovich Primakov, 1897–1937, a Red Commander who had taken part in the storming of the Winter Palace. In 1918, he had formed the first Red Cossack Regiment, and was later both commander and military commissar of the Eighth Cavalry Division.

† One of the largest agricultural machinery factories of the time.

Odessa's public prosecutor's office decided to set up a model public trial at the Petrovsky factory.* Naftula Gerchik, the neighborhood charlatan, and Brana Brutman, sixty-two years of age, found themselves on the defendants' bench.

Naftula was as much an Odessan fixture as the statue of the Duke of Richelieu.† Naftula used to walk past our windows on Dalnitskaya Street carrying his tattered, grease-stained midwife's bag. In that bag he kept his simple instruments. Sometimes he took a little knife out of it, sometimes a bottle of vodka and a piece of honey cake. He'd sniff the honey cake before he drank his vodka, and having drunk it would rattle off some prayers. Naftula was as redheaded as the first redheaded man on earth. When he sliced off what was his due, he did not strain off the blood through a glass funnel, but sucked it with puckered lips. The blood smudged his tousled beard. He appeared tipsy before the guests. His bearlike eyes twinkled cheerfully. Redheaded as the first redheaded man on earth, he whimpered a blessing over the wine. With one hand Naftula pitched his vodka into his mouth's overgrown, crooked, fire-spitting pit, while in the other he held a plate. On this plate lay the little knife, reddened with the infant's blood, and some gauze. As he collected his money, Naftula went from guest to guest with his plate, elbowing his way through the women, falling on them, grabbing their breasts. "Fat mamas!" he howled for the whole street to hear, his little coral eyes glittering. "Go churn out some boys for Naftula, thresh some corn on your bellies! Do your best for Naftula! Go churn out some boys, fat mamas!"

The husbands threw money onto his plate. The women wiped away the blood from his beard. The courtyards of Glukhaya and Gospitalnaya Streets did not lack offspring. They seethed with children, as the mouths of rivers seethe with roe. Naftula went trudging around with his bag, like a tax collector. Orlov, the investigating magistrate, brought Naftula's rounds to an end.

The investigating magistrate thundered from the bench, endeavoring to prove that the neighborhood charlatan was a priest in a cult.

*One of the largest steelworks of the time. Its more than eight thousand workers had played a key role in the Revolution. Holding this trial at the Petrovsky factory indicated that the new Soviet government wanted to make a landmark case out of it.

†A French émigré nobleman, governor general of Odessa from 1803–1814, on whom Lord Byron modeled his Don Juan. The famous bronze statue of him was sculpted by Ivan Martos.

"Do you believe in God?" he asked Naftula.

"Let him who won two thousand believe in God," the old man answered.

"Were you not surprised when Comrade Brana Brutman came to you at such a late hour in the rain, carrying a newborn in her hands?"

"I am surprised when a person does something reasonable," Naftula said. "When a person does idiotic things, then I'm not surprised!"

These answers did not satisfy the investigating magistrate. The matter of the glass funnel came next. He charged that by sucking blood with his lips, the defendant was exposing children to the danger of infection. Naftula's head, that shaggy nut of his, hung almost to the ground. He sighed, closed his eyes, and wiped his drooping mouth with his fist.

"What are you muttering about, Comrade Gerchik?" the judge asked him.

Naftula fixed his extinguished eyes on Orlov, the investigating magistrate.

"The late Monsieur Zusman, your late Papa," Naftula said to him with a sigh, "he had a head the likes of which you can't find nowhere in the world. And praised be God, that your papa did not have an apoplectic fit when he had me come over to perform your *bris*. And we can all see plain enough that you grew into a big man in the Soviet government, and that Naftula did not snip off along with that little piece of *shmokhtes* anything you might have needed later on."

He blinked with his bearlike eyes, shook his red-haired nut, and fell silent. There were volleys of laughter, thunderous guffawing salvos. Orlov, né Zusman, waved his arms in the air and shouted out something that could not be heard in the cannonade. He demanded that the record reflect that . . . Sasha Svetlov, one of the satirists of the *Odessa News*, sent him a note from the press box. "You're a nincompoop, Syoma," the note went. "Finish him off with irony, only what is funny will kill! Your Sasha."

The room quieted down when they brought Byelotserkovsky to the witness box.

Byelotserkovsky reiterated what was in his deposition. He was lanky and wore riding breeches and cavalry jackboots. According to Ofsey, the Tiraspol and Balta Party Committees had been fully cooperative in the business of acquiring livestock feed. In the heat of the negotiations he had received a telegram announcing the birth of his son. After discussing the matter with the Balta Party Committee's head of operations, he decided not to interrupt the transaction and to restrict himself to dispatching a congratulatory telegram. He did not return home for another two weeks. Sixty-four thousand *poods* of livestock feed had been gathered throughout the region. No one was at home, except for the witness Kharchenko—a neighbor and laundress by profession—and his infant son. His wife was away at the hospital, and the witness Kharchenko was rocking the cradle and was engaged in the now-obsolete practice of singing a lullaby. Knowing the witness to be an alcoholic, he did not find it necessary to try making out the words of this song, but he was taken aback to hear her call the boy Yankel, when he had expressly given instructions that his son be named Karl, in honor of our esteemed teacher Karl Marx. Unwrapping the child's swaddling clothes, he came face-to-face with his misfortune.

The investigating magistrate asked a few questions, the defense did not. The bailiff led in the witness Paulina Byelotserkovskaya. She staggered toward the bar. The bluish tremor of recent motherhood twisted her face, and there were drops of sweat on her forehead. She looked over to her father, the little blacksmith, dressed to the nines in a bow tie and new boots as if for a feast, and to her mother's coppery, gray-mustached face. The witness Paulina Byelotserkovskaya did not answer the question as to what she knew about the matter at hand. She said that her father was a poor man, who had worked in the smithy on the road to Balta for forty years. Her mother had given birth to six children, of whom three had died. One brother was a Red commander, the other worked in the Ghen factory. "My mother is very devout, everyone knows that, and she always suffered because her children were not religious. She could not bear the idea that her grandchildren would not be Jews. You must take into consideration in what kind of a family my mother was raised. Everyone knows the shtetl of Medzhibozh,* the women there are still wearing wigs."

"Will the witness please tell us," a sharp voice interrupted her. Paulina fell silent, the drops of sweat darkening on her forehead as if

* A shtetl in Western Ukraine in the District of Khmelnitsky where the founder of Hasidism, Israel ben Eliezer the "Baal Shem Tov," was from.

blood were seeping through her delicate skin. "Will the witness please tell us," repeated the voice of Samuel Lining, a former barrister. Were the Sanhedrin* to exist nowadays, Lining would have been its head. But the Sanhedrin no longer exists, and Lining, who had learned to read and write Russian at twenty-five, had begun in his fourth decade to write appeals to the government indistinguishable from the treatises of the Talmud. The old man had slept throughout the trial. His jacket was covered in cigarette ash. But he had woken up when Paulina Byelotserkovskaya had appeared. "Will the witness please tell us"—his fishlike rows of bobbing blue teeth were clacking—"if you had been aware of your husband's decision to name his son Karl?"

"Yes."

"What name did your mother give him?"

"Yankel."

"And what about you, Comrade Witness? What do you call your son?"

"I call him 'sweetie.'"

"And why 'sweetie,' of all things?"

"I call all children 'sweetie.'"

"Let us proceed," Lining said. His teeth slipped out, but he caught them with his nether lip and slid them back into his mouth. "Let us proceed. In the evening, when the child was taken over to the defendant Gerchik, you were not at home. You were at the hospital. Is my statement in accordance with the facts?"

"I was at the hospital."

"At what hospital were you being treated?"

"The one in Nezhinskaya Street, at Dr. Drizo's."

"Dr. Drizo was treating you?"

"Yes."

"Are you sure of this?"

"Why wouldn't I be?"

"I would like to introduce this here document into evidence." Lining's lifeless face rose over the table. "From this document the court will ascertain that during the period of time in question, Dr. Drizo was away at a congress of pediatricians in Kharkov."

---

* The highest court of the ancient Jewish nation.

The investigating magistrate did not object to the introduction of the document.

"Let us proceed," Lining said, his teeth clacking.

The witness leaned her whole body against the bar. Her whisper was barely audible.

"Maybe it wasn't Dr. Drizo," she said, resting her whole weight against the bar. "I can't remember everything. I am exhausted."

Lining raked his pencil through his yellow beard. He rubbed his stooping back against the bench and joggled his false teeth.

Paulina was asked to produce her official medical report, but she told the court she had misplaced it.

"Let us proceed," the old man said.

Paulina ran her palm over her forehead. Her husband sat at the end of the bench, away from the other witnesses. He sat there stiffly, his long legs in their cavalry boots pulled in under him. The rays of the sun fell on his face, packed with a framework of minute, spiteful bones.

"I will find my medical record," Paulina whispered, and her hands slid off the bar.

At that moment a bawling baby was heard. A child was crying and mewling outside the doors.

"You see, Paulina?" the old woman suddenly yelled out in a hoarse voice. "The child hasn't been fed since this morning! He's shriveling up with hollering!" Startled Red Army fighters snatched up their rifles. Paulina began to slide lower and lower, her head falling back to the floor. Her arms flew up, flailed, and then tumbled down.

"The court is adjourned!" the public prosecutor shouted.

An uproar erupted in the room. Byelotserkovsky stalked over to his wife with cranelike steps, a green sheen on his hollow cheeks.

"Feed the child!" people were shouting from the back rows, cupping their hands like megaphones around their mouths.

"They're already feeding him!" a woman's voice shouted back. "You think they were waiting for you?"

"The daughter's tangled up in all of this," said a worker sitting next to me. "The daughter's got her hand in it."

"It's a family thing," the man sitting next to him said. "One of those dark, nighttime jobs. At night they go tangling up things that in daylight you just can't untangle."

The sun cut through the room with its slanting rays. The crowd stirred heavily, breathing fire and sweat. Elbowing my way through, I reached the corridor. The door to the Red Corner* stood ajar. I could hear Karl-Yankel's mewling and slurping inside. Lenin's portrait hung in the Red Corner, the portrait in which he is giving a speech from the armored car on the square in front of the Finland Station. It was surrounded by multicolored production graphs showing the Petrovsky factory's output. The walls were lined with banners and rifles on wooden mounts. A woman worker with a Kirghiz face, her head bent forward, was feeding Karl-Yankel, a plump little fellow about five months old with knitted socks and a white tuft of hair on his head. Fastened to the Kirghiz woman by his mouth, he gurgled, banging her breast with his little clenched fist.

"What are they shouting for?" the Kirghiz woman said. "There's always someone who'll feed a baby."

There was also a girl of about seventeen puttering about the room in a red kerchief, her cheeks puffed out like pine cones. She was wiping dry Karl-Yankel's changing-mat.

"He's going to be a fighter, he is," the girl said. "Look at those punches he's throwing!"

The Kirghiz woman gently pulled her nipple out of Karl-Yankel's mouth. He began growling, and in desperation threw back his head with its white tuft of hair. The woman took out her other breast and gave it to him. He looked at her nipple with dull eyes that suddenly lit up. The Kirghiz woman looked at Karl-Yankel, squinting her black eyes at him.

"Not a fighter, no," she crooned, fixing the boy's cap. "He'll be an aviator. He will fly through the sky, he will."

In the other room the hearing had resumed.

A battle was now raging between the investigating magistrate and the experts who were giving vague and inconclusive testimony. The public prosecutor got up from his seat and began banging the desk with his fist. I could see the public in the first few rows—Galician *tsaddiks*, their beaver hats resting on their knees. They had come to the Petrovsky factory, where, according to the Warsaw papers, the Jewish

---

* A reading room in public buildings that contained Communist Party literature and the works of Marx and Lenin.

religion was being put on trial. The faces of the rabbis sitting in the first row hovered in the stormy, dusty brightness of the sun.

"Down with them!" shouted a member of the Young Communist League who had managed to fight his way right up to the podium.

The battle raged with growing force.

Karl-Yankel, staring blankly at me, sucked at the Kirghiz woman's breast.

The straight streets that my childhood and youth walked unfurled outside the window—Pushkin Street went to the train station, Malo-Arnautskaya Street jutted out into the park by the sea.

I grew up on these streets. Now it was Karl-Yankel's turn. But nobody had fought over me the way they were fighting over him, nobody had cared much about me.

"I can't believe that you won't be happy, Karl-Yankel," I whispered to myself. "I can't believe you won't be happier than me."

THE AWAKENING

*A*ll the people of our circle—middlemen, storekeepers, clerks in banks and steamship offices—sent their children to music lessons. Our fathers, seeing they had no prospects of their own, set up a lottery for themselves. They built this lottery on the bones of their little children. Odessa was in the grip of this craze more than any other town. And sure enough, over the last few decades our town had sent a number of child prodigies onto the stages of the world. Mischa Elman, Zimbalist, Gawrilowitsch all came from Odessa—Jascha Heifetz started out with us.*

When a boy turned four or five, his mother took the tiny, frail creature to Mr. Zagursky. Zargursky ran a factory that churned out child prodigies, a factory of Jewish dwarfs in lace collars and patent leather shoes. He went hunting for them in the Moldavanka slums and the reeking courtyards of the old bazaar. Zagursky gave them the first push, then the children were sent off to Professor Auer[†] in Petersburg. There was powerful harmony in the souls of these little creatures with their swollen blue heads. They became acclaimed virtuosi. And so—my father decided to keep up with them. I had passed the age of child prodigies—I was almost fourteen—but because of my height and frail-

[*] Mischa Elman, 1891–1967; Efrem Zimbalist, 1890–1985; Ossip Gawrilowitsch, 1878–1936; and Jascha Heifetz, 1901–1987, were among the foremost violinists and conductors of the twentieth century.

[†] Leopold Auer, 1845–1930, world-famous professor of violin at the St. Petersburg Conservatory.

ness I could be mistaken for an eight-year-old. Therein lay all our hopes.

I was brought to Zagursky. Out of respect for my grandfather, he agreed to take me at a ruble a lesson—a low fee. My grandfather was the laughingstock of the town, but also its ornament. He walked the streets in a top hat and tattered shoes, and provided answers to the murkiest questions. People asked him what a Gobelin was, why the Jacobins had betrayed Robespierre, how synthetic silk was made, what a cesarean section was. My grandfather knew the answers to all these questions. It was out of respect for his knowledge and madness that Zagursky charged us only a ruble a lesson. And he put a lot of effort into me, fearing Grandfather, though putting any effort into me was pointless. Sounds scraped out of my violin like iron filings. These sounds cut even into my own heart, but my father would not give up. All anyone talked about at home was Mischa Elman; the Czar himself had absolved him from military service. Zimbalist, from what my father had heard, had been presented to the King of England and had played at Buckingham Palace. Gawrilowitsch's parents had bought two houses in Petersburg. The child prodigies brought wealth to their parents. My father was prepared to resign himself to a life of poverty, but he needed fame.

"It's unthinkable," people who went out dining with my father at his expense assured him, "absolutely unthinkable, that the grandson of a grandfather like his wouldn't become . . ."

But I had other things in my head. Whenever I practiced my violin I placed books by Turgenev or Dumas on my music stand, and, as I scraped away, devoured one page after another. During the day I told stories to the neighborhood boys, at night I put them down on paper. Writing was a hereditary occupation in our family. Grandpa Levy-Itskhok, who had gone mad in his old age, had spent his life writing a novel with the title *The Headless Man*. I followed in his footsteps.

Laden with violin case and music scores, I dragged myself over to Zagursky's on Witte Street, formerly Dvoryanskaya Street.* There, along the walls, Jewesses sat, waiting flushed and hysterical for their

---

* The street had been renamed in honor of Sergei Witte, an Odessan who had been Russia's Minister of Finance.

turn. They pressed to their weak knees violins more magnificent than those destined to play at Buckingham Palace.

The door of the inner sanctum opened. Large-headed, freckled children came bustling out of Zagursky's chamber, their necks thin as flower stalks, a convulsive flush on their cheeks. Then the door closed, swallowing up the next dwarf. In the adjacent room Zagursky, with his red curls, bow tie, and thin legs, sang and conducted in ecstasy. The founder of this freakish lottery filled the Moldavanka and the back alleys of the old bazaar with specters of pizzicato and cantilena. This incantation of his was then fine-tuned to a diabolical brilliancy by old Professor Auer.

I had no business being a member of his sect. I too was a dwarf just as they were, but I heard a different calling in the voice of my ancestors.

This was an arduous apprenticeship for me. One day I set out from home, laden with my music, my violin, its case, and the sum of twelve rubles, the fee for a month of lessons. I walked down Nezhinskaya Street, and should have turned into Dvoryanskaya Street to get to Zagursky's place. Yet I walked down Tiraspolskaya and ended up in the port. My allotted three hours flew past in the Prakticheskaya harbor. That was the beginning of my liberation. Zagursky's waiting room was never to see me again. More important things were occupying my mind. My classmate Nemanov and I got in the habit of going on board the *Kensington* to visit an old sailor called Mr. Trottyburn. Nemanov was a year younger than I, but from the time he was eight years old he had engaged in the most complex trading you could imagine. He was a genius at anything having to do with trade, and always delivered what he promised. Now he is a millionaire in New York, the general manager of General Motors, a company as powerful as Ford. Nemanov took me along because I obeyed his every command. He bought smuggled tobacco pipes from Mr. Trottyburn. These pipes had been carved by the old sailor's brother in Lincoln.

"Mark my words, gentlemen," Mr. Trottyburn said to us. "You have to make your children with your own hands. Smoking a factory-made pipe is like sticking an enema tube in your mouth. Do you know who Benvenuto Cellini was? He was a master! My brother in Lincoln could tell you about him. My brother lives and lets live. The one thing he believes in is that you have to make your children with your own hands, you can't leave that sort of thing to others. And he is right, gentlemen!"

Nemanov sold Trottyburn's pipes to bank managers, foreign consuls, and rich Greeks. He made a hundred percent profit.

The pipes of the Lincoln master exuded poetry. Each and every one of them contained a thought, a drop of eternity. A little yellow eye twinkled from their mouthpieces. Their cases were lined with satin. I tried to imagine how Matthew Trottyburn, the last of the pipe-carving masters, lived in an England of old, defying the winds of change.

"He is right, gentlemen, you have to make your children with your own hands!"

The heavy waves by the harbor wall separated me more and more from a home reeking of onions and Jewish fate. From the Prakticheskaya harbor I moved on to the breakwater. There, on a stretch of sandbar, the boys of Primorskaya Street hung out. They went without pants from morning till night, they dove under fishing boats, stole coconuts for food, and waited for the time when carts carrying watermelons rolled in from Kherson and Kamenki, and they could split these watermelons open on the moorings of the dock.

My dream now was to learn how to swim. I was ashamed of admitting to those bronzed boys that I, though born in Odessa, had not even seen the sea until I was ten, and that I still could not swim at fourteen.

How late I learned the essential things in life! In my childhood, nailed to the Gemara,* I led the life of a sage, and it was only later, when I was older, that I began to climb trees.

It turned out that the ability to swim was beyond my reach. The hydrophobia of my ancestors, the Spanish rabbis and Frankfurt money changers, dragged me to the bottom. Water would not carry me. Battered, doused in salt water, I went back to the shore, to my violin and my music scores. I was attached to my instruments of crime, and dragged them along with me. The battle of the rabbis with the sea lasted until the local water god—Efim Nikitich Smolich, a proofreader for the *Odessa News*—took pity on me. In that athletic chest of his there was a warmth for Jewish boys. Nikitich led crowds of frail little crea-

---

* Part of the Talmud, the Gemara is a rabbinical commentary on the Mishna, the first codification of ancient Jewish oral laws.

tures, gathering them up from the bedbug-ridden hovels of the Moldavanka. He took them to the beach, built sand castles with them, exercised and dived with them, taught them songs, and, baking in the hard rays of the sun, told them tales of fishermen and animals. To grown-ups, Nikitich explained that he was simply a devotee of natural philosophy. Nikitich's stories made the Jewish children collapse with laughter. They squealed and frolicked like puppies. The sun spattered them with creeping freckles, freckles the color of lizards.

Nikitich silently watched me combat the waves single-handed. Seeing that there was no hope I would ever learn to swim on my own, he let me join the other little lodgers of his heart. His cheerful heart was completely devoted to us. It was never disdainful, never miserly, and never agitated. He lay among us by the breakwater, the king of these melon and kerosene waters, with his copper shoulders, his head that of an aging gladiator, and his lightly crooked, bronze legs. I loved him as only a boy afflicted with hysteria and headaches can love an athlete. I didn't leave his side, and tried to please him every way I could.

"Calm down," he told me. "Steady your nerves, and swimming will come of its own accord. . . . What do you mean, the water won't hold you up? Why shouldn't it?"

Seeing how I was reaching out to him, Nikitich made an exception for me among all his pupils, and invited me to come up to his place, a clean, spacious garret covered in mats, and showed me his dogs, his hedgehog, his tortoise, and his doves. In gratitude for his generosity I brought him a tragedy I had written the night before.

"I knew you were a scribbler!" Nikitich said. "You have that look in your eyes. You're no longer looking at things."

He read my play, shrugged his shoulders, ran his fingers through his stiff, gray locks, and paced up and down the garret.

"I believe," he said in a slow drawl, pausing between words, "that there is a divine spark in you."

We went out into the street. The old man stopped, banged his stick hard on the sidewalk, and peered at me.

"There's something lacking in your work, but what is it? That you are young is no problem—that will pass in time. What you lack is a feel for nature."

He pointed his stick at a tree with a reddish trunk and a low crown.

"What kind of tree is that?"

I didn't know.

"What's growing on this bush?"

I didn't know that either. We walked through the little park on Aleksandrovsky Boulevard. The old man poked at all the trees with his stick, grabbed my shoulder whenever a bird flew by, and had me listen to their different calls.

"What bird is that singing?"

I couldn't answer. The names of birds and trees, what families they belonged to, where the birds flew, on which side the sun rose, when the dew was at its heaviest—all this was unknown to me.

"And you have the audacity to write? A man who does not exist in nature the way a stone or an animal exists in it will not write a single worthwhile line in all his life. Your landscapes resemble descriptions of stage sets. Goddamn it! What could your parents have been thinking of these past fourteen years?"

What had they been thinking of? Of contested bills and the mansions of Mischa Elman. I didn't tell Nikitich that, I remained silent.

At home, at the dinner table, I didn't touch my food—it wouldn't go down.

"A feel for nature!" I thought. My God, why hadn't this occurred to me? Where could I find someone to tell me what the different birdcalls and the names of trees were? How much did I know about these things? I could perhaps identify lilacs—that is, if they were in bloom. Lilacs and acacias. Deribasovskaya and Grecheskaya Streets were lined with acacias.

At dinner, Father told us a new story about Jascha Heifetz. On his way to Robyn's, father had run into Mendelson, Jascha's uncle. It turned out that the boy was getting eight hundred rubles a performance: "So go ahead and add up how much that comes to at fifteen concerts a month!"

I added it up. The result was twelve thousand a month. As I multiplied the number, carrying the four in my head, I looked out the window. My music teacher, Mr. Zagursky, wearing a lightly billowing cape, red ringlets jutting out from under his soft hat, and propping himself up with his cane, came marching through our cement yard. It cannot be said that he had been quick to notice my absence: more than three months had already passed since the day my violin had sunk to the sandy bottom off the breakwater.

Zagursky came up to our front door. I rushed off to the back door. It had been boarded up the night before to keep out thieves. So I locked myself in the toilet. Within half an hour my whole family had gathered outside the toilet door. The women were crying. Auntie Bobka, quivering with sobs, was grinding her fat shoulder against the door. My father was silent. He began speaking more quietly and distinctly than ever before in his life.

"I am an officer," my father said. "I have an estate. I ride out on hunts. The muzhiks pay me rent. I sent my son to the Cadet Corps. There is no reason for me to lose any sleep over my son."

He fell silent. The women sniffled. Then a terrible blow came crashing against the toilet door. My father began throwing himself on it with his whole body; he took runs and hurled himself against it.

"I am an officer!" he howled. "I ride out on hunts! I will kill him! That's it!"

The hook went hurtling off the door, but the bolt was still there, held by a single nail. The women threw themselves on the floor, grappling for my father's legs. Raving, he tried to tear himself loose. Hearing the rumpus, my old grandmother, my father's mother, came hurrying in.

"My child," she said to him in Yiddish. "Our sorrow is great, it knows no bounds. The last thing we need in our house is blood. I do not want to see blood in our house!"

My father moaned. I heard his footsteps receding. The latch was hanging on its last nail.

I sat in my fortress till nightfall. When everybody had gone to bed, Auntie Bobka took me to my grandmother's. It was a long walk. The moonlight froze on unknown shrubs, on nameless trees. An invisible bird whistled once and then was quiet, perhaps it had fallen asleep. What kind of bird was it? What was it called? Was there dew in the evenings? Where was the constellation of the Great Bear in the sky? On what side did the sun rise?

We walked along Pochtovaya Street. Auntie Bobka held my hand tightly so that I wouldn't run away. She was right. I was thinking of running away.

IN THE BASEMENT

*I*was a boy who told lies. This came from reading. My imagination was always aroused. I read during class, between classes, on my way home, and under the table at night, hidden by the tablecloth that hung down to the floor. Reading books, I missed out on everything the world around me had to offer: skipping classes to go to the port, the coming of billiards to the coffee shops along Grecheskaya Street, swimming at Langeron.* I had no friends. Who would have wanted to spend time with someone like me?

One day I saw the brightest student in our class, Mark Borgman, with a book about Spinoza. He had just read it and was dying to tell the boys around him about the Spanish Inquisition. What he told them was nothing but scientific prattle. There was no poetry in Borgman's words. I could not stop myself from cutting in. To whoever would listen, I talked about old Amsterdam, about the gloom of the ghetto, about the philosopher diamond cutters. I added quite a lot of spice to what I had read in books. I couldn't resist. My imagination sharpened dramatic scenes, altered endings, steeped the beginnings in more mystery. Spinoza's death, his lonely death in freedom, appeared to me in my imagination as a battle. The Sanhedrin had tried to compel the dying man to repent, but he held fast. It was at this point that I blended in Rubens. I imagined Rubens standing at the head of Spinoza's bed, casting a death mask of the corpse's face.

* A beach in Odessa, named after the French count, Alexander Langeron, who was governor general of Odessa from 1816–1822.

My schoolmates listened to my outlandish tale with open mouths. I told my tale with gusto. When the bell rang we reluctantly dispersed. Borgman came up to me during the following break, took me by the arm, and we went for a walk together. Soon we were seeing eye to eye. Borgman wasn't a bad specimen of top student. To his powerful brain, high school learning was only a scribble in the margin of the book of life. And he sought that book with ardor. Even as foolish little twelve-year-olds, we were all very aware that a wondrous and erudite life lay before him. He didn't even prepare for classes, he just sat there and listened. This reserved, sober boy was drawn to me because of my knack for twisting things, even the simplest things you could imagine.

That year we moved up to the third class. My report card was full of three-minuses.* I was so strange, with all the outlandish gibberish bouncing through my mind, that my teachers, after much deliberation, decided against giving me twos.

At the beginning of summer, Borgman invited me to come to his dacha. His father was the director of the Russian Bank for International Trade. He was one of those men who was turning Odessa into a Marseilles or Naples. The core of the old Odessa merchant was within him. He was one of those pleasant but skeptical bon vivants who avoided speaking Russian, preferring instead the rough, choppy language of the Liverpool ship captains. When an Italian opera came to Odessa in April, Borgman invited the whole cast to dinner. The puffy banker, the last of the Odessa merchants, had a little two-month liaison with the buxom prima donna. She took with her memories that did not burden her conscience along with a necklace chosen with taste but not costing too much.

The old man also held the position of Argentinean consul, and was chairman of the stock exchange committee. And I had been invited to his house. My Auntie Bobka ran out into the courtyard trumpeting the news. She dressed me up as best she could. I took the train to the sixteenth stop at Bolshoy Fontan.† The dacha stood on a low, red cliff right by the shore. A flower garden of fuchsias and clipped thuya shrubs covered the cliff.

---

* The equivalent of a C-minus. Five was the highest grade, one the lowest.
† "Large Fountain" was an elegant beach spa outside Odessa.

I came from a loud, impoverished family. The Borgman dacha filled me with awe. White wicker chairs glittered in walks covered with foliage. The dinner table was filled with flowers, the windows fitted with green casings. A low wooden colonnade opened up before the house.

The bank director came to the dacha in the evenings. After dinner he placed his wicker chair at the very edge of the cliff in front of the shifting plain of the sea, stretched out his legs in his white trousers, lit a cigar, and began to read the *Manchester Guardian*. The guests, Odessa ladies, played poker on the veranda. A narrow samovar with ivory handles was sputtering on the edge of the table.

The women—card-playing gourmands, sluttish coquettes, and furtive debauchees with large hips and perfumed undergarments—fluttered black fans and staked their gold. The sun pierced its way to them through the copse of wild vines. Its fiery globe was immense. Copper sparks weighed down the women's black hair. Flashes of sunset pierced their diamonds—diamonds that hung everywhere: in the deep hollows of breasts pressed apart, from powdered ears, and on plump and bluish female fingers.

Evening fell. A bat rustled by. The sea rolled blacker against the red cliff. My twelve-year-old heart surged with the cheer and ease of others' wealth. My friend and I ambled hand in hand down the long walks. Borgman told me that he would become an aviation engineer. There was a rumor that his father would be appointed the London representative of the Russian Bank for International Trade. Borgman would be educated in England.

At our house, Auntie Bobka's house, no one talked of such things. I had nothing with which I could match this uninterrupted splendor. So I told Borgman that although things back at my place were very different, my grandfather Levy-Itskhok and my uncle had traveled the whole world over and had thousands of adventures under their belts. I described these adventures one after the other. Within seconds, I lost all sense of reality, and took Uncle Volf from the Russian-Turkish War to Alexandria and Egypt.

Night rose in the poplars, stars pressed down on stooping branches. I spoke with wild gesticulations. The fingers of the future aviation engineer trembled in my hand. He emerged with difficulty from the hallucination, and promised to come visit me at my place the following Sunday. Braced by his promise, I took the ferry back home to Auntie Bobka's.

The whole following week I imagined I was a bank director. I brought about millions of transactions with Singapore and Port Said. I acquired a yacht, and sailed it single-handedly. By Sabbath reality struck. Little Borgman was to come visiting the following day. Nothing of what I had told him actually existed. What did exist was far more extraordinary than anything I had invented, but at the age of twelve I had no idea how to grapple with the truth of my world. Grandpa Levy-Itskhok, a rabbi chased out of his shtetl for forging Count Branitsky's signature on promissory notes, was considered a madman by neighbors and street boys alike. Uncle Simon-Volf I could not stand because of his loud eccentricity, full of mad fire, yelling, and harassment. Auntie Bobka was the only one I could count on. She was very proud that the son of a bank director was my friend. She saw this friendship as the beginning of a bright career and baked a fruit strudel and a poppy-seed pie for our guest. Into that pie she put the heart of our tribe, the heart that had withstood so many tribulations. We hid my grandfather, with his tattered top hat and his swollen feet bound in rags, with our neighbors the Apelkhots, and I begged him not to show himself until our guest left. I also dealt with Simon-Volf. He went off with his profiteer pals to drink tea at the Medved Tavern. Tea there was braced with vodka, and it was safe to assume that Simon-Volf would be delayed. It has to be said that my family was not your typical Jewish family. There were drunks in our clan, we had run away with the daughters of generals and then abandoned them before crossing the border, and our grandfather had forged signatures and written blackmailing letters for abandoned wives.

All my efforts went into keeping Simon-Volf away for the whole day. I gave him the three rubles I had managed to save up. Spending three rubles took some doing, Simon-Volf would come back late, and the bank director's son would never know that the tales of my uncle's kindness and strength were all lies. It must, however, be said that were one to appraise things purely with one's heart, then my tale could be seen as true and not a lie at all. But when you first came face-to-face with the loud and dirty Simon-Volf, this intangible truth was not to be discerned.

On Sunday morning, Bobka put on her brown, raw-cloth dress. Her fat, kindly breasts bounced in all directions. She tied on her kerchief with the black floral print, the kind of kerchief worn in the synagogue on Yom Kippur and Rosh Hashanah. Bobka arranged the pies, jam, and pretzels on the table and waited. We lived in the basement. Borgman raised his eyebrows as he walked over the corridor's crooked floor. A barrel of water stood by the entrance. The instant Borgman was inside, I began entertaining him with every conceivable marvel. I showed him the alarm clock which my grandfather had constructed down to the last screw—a lamp was hooked up to the clock, and every time the clock reached a full or half hour, the lamp would light up. I also showed him our little keg of shoe wax. Grandpa Levy-Itskhok had invented that shoe wax recipe, and he would not reveal it to anyone. Then Borgman and I read a few pages from my grandfather's manuscript. He wrote in Yiddish, on square sheets of yellow paper large as maps. The manuscript was called *The Headless Man*. In it was a description of all Levy-Itskhok's neighbors over a period of sixty years—first in Skvira and Belaya Tserkov, then in Odessa. Undertakers, cantors, Jewish drunks, cooks at *bris* feasts, and the charlatans who performed the ritual operation—these were Levy-Itskhok's characters. They were all loud and offensive people, with crude speech and fleshy noses, pimply faces, and twisted backsides.

As we were reading, Bobka appeared in her brown dress. She came floating in, engulfed by her fat, kindly breasts, carrying a tray on which stood a samovar. I introduced them. "Pleased to meet you," Bobka said, reaching out her sweaty, stiff fingers and doing a little scraping bow. I couldn't have wished for things to go better. Our neighbors the Apelkhots wouldn't let Grandfather leave their place. I dragged out all his treasures one by one: grammars of every language you could imagine, and sixty-six volumes of the Talmud. Borgman was dazzled by the keg of shoe wax, the wondrous alarm clock, and the mountain of Talmuds—all things one would never see in any other home.

We each drank two glasses of tea with our strudel. Bobka left, bowing her head and shuffling backward out of the room. I fell into a joyful state of mind, struck a pose, and began declaiming the verses that I loved more than anything in the world. Antony, bending over Caesar's dead body, speaks to the people of Rome.

Friends, Romans, countrymen, lend me your ears;
I come to bury Caesar, not to praise him.

That is how Antony begins his performance. I gasped and pressed
my hand to my heart.

He was my friend, faithful and just to me:
But Brutus says he was ambitious;
And Brutus is an honorable man.
He hath brought many captives home to Rome
Whose ransoms did the general coffers fill:
Did this in Caesar seem ambitious?
When that the poor have cried, Caesar hath wept:
Ambition should be made of sterner stuff:
Yet Brutus says he was ambitious;
And Brutus is an honorable man.

Brutus's face hovered before my eyes, in the mists of the universe.
His face turned whiter than chalk. The people of Rome began closing
in on me menacingly. I raised my arm—Borgman's eyes obediently followed it—my clenched fist was quaking, I raised my arm, and through
the window saw Uncle Simon-Volf walk through the yard with
Leykakh the junk dealer. They were carrying a rack made of antlers,
and a red trunk with handles in the form of lions' jaws. Bobka also saw
them from the window. Forgetting my guest, she came running into the
room and grabbed hold of me with trembling hands.

"Oy, Bubele! He's been buying furniture again!"

Borgman rose in his school uniform, and bowed to Auntie Bobka
in bewilderment. They were pounding on the door. The thud of boots
and the clatter of the trunk being dragged across the floor came rumbling from the corridor. The thundering voices of Simon-Volf and redheaded Leykakh were deafening. Both were tipsy.

"Bobka!" Simon-Volf yelled. "Guess how much I paid for these horns!"

He blared like a trumpet, but there was a hint of uncertainty in his
voice. Drunk though he was, he knew how much we hated redheaded
Leykakh, who spurred him on to keep buying things, flooding our place
with useless and ridiculous furniture.

Bobka stood there in silence. Leykakh said something to Simon-Volf in his wheezing voice. To drown out his snakelike hissing and my anxiety, I started shouting Anthony's words.

> *But yesterday the word of Caesar might*
> *Have stood against the world; now lies he there.*
> *And none so poor to do him reverence.*
> *O masters, if I were disposed to stir*
> *Your hearts and minds to mutiny and rage,*
> *I should do Brutus wrong, and Cassius wrong,*
> *Who, you all know, are honorable men . . .*

Suddenly there was a thud. Bobka had fallen down, knocked off her feet by her husband's blow. She must have made a sharp remark about the antlers. The daily ritual began. Simon-Volf's brassy voice thundered to high heaven.

"You are squeezing the last drop out of me!" my uncle roared. "You are squeezing out of me the last drop so you can stuff those damn pig snouts of yours! My soul's been crushed by work, I've nothing left to work with, no hands, no legs, nothing! You've hung a millstone around my neck, a goddamn millstone!"

He heaped Yiddish curses on Bobka and me, he wished that our eyes would fall out, that our children would rot and wither in their mothers' wombs, that we would not live to bury each other, and that we would be dragged by our hair to a pauper's grave.

Little Borgman stood up. He looked around the room, his face pale. He did not understand the ins and outs of Jewish blasphemy, but he was familiar enough with Russian swearing. And Simon-Volf did not refrain from slipping into Russian. The bank director's son stood there kneading his cap. My eyes saw him double as I struggled to shout away all the evil in the world. My mortal agony and Caesar's death became one. I was dead and I was shouting. A wheeze rose from the depths of my being.

> *If you have tears, prepare to shed them now.*
> *You all do know this mantle: I remember*
> *The first time ever Caesar put it on;*

'Twas on a summer's evening, in his tent,
That day he overcame the Nervii:
Look, in this place ran Cassius' dagger through:
See what a rent the envious Casca made:
Through this the well-beloved Brutus stabb'd;
And as he pluck'd his cursed steel away,
Mark how the blood of Caesar follow'd it . . .

No one would have had the power to drown out Simon-Volf.
Bobka sat on the floor, sobbing and blowing her nose. Leykakh, unruffled, was dragging the trunk along behind the partition. And it was at
this very moment that my crazed grandfather got it into his head to
come to my rescue. He tore himself loose from the Apelkhots next
door, crawled over to the window, and began sawing away at his violin,
most probably so that people wouldn't hear Simon-Volf's cursing.
Borgman looked out the window, which was at ground level, and stumbled back in horror. My poor grandfather was twisting his rigid blue
mouth into wild grimaces. He had on his crooked top hat and his black
quilted cloak with its bone buttons; the remnants of what had been
shoes clung to his elephantine feet. His sooty beard hung in tatters and
blew into the window. Borgman ran for the door.

"Please don't worry," he muttered, as he ran for freedom. "Please
don't worry."

His uniform and his cap with the raised brim flashed through the
yard.

With Borgman's departure my agitation began to subside. I waited
for evening to come. After Grandfather lay down in his cot and went
to sleep, having filled a sheet of paper with Yiddish scribbles (describing the Apelkhots, at whose house, through my ministrations, he had
spent the whole day), I went out into the corridor. It had a dirt floor. I
moved through the darkness, barefoot, in my long, patched-up nightshirt. The cobblestones shimmered like blades of light through the
cracks in the boards. The barrel of water stood as always in the corner.
I lowered myself into it. The water cut me in two. I plunged my head
under, choked, and came up for air. Our cat gazed at me sleepily from
high up on a shelf. The second time I held out longer. The water
swished around me, swallowing my moan. I opened my eyes and saw

my billowing shirt and my legs pressed against each other. Again I didn't have enough strength. I came up. My grandfather was standing next to the barrel in his nightshirt. His single tooth jiggled in his mouth.

"My grandson." He spoke these words distinctly and with contempt. "I shall go and drink some castor oil so that I will have something to dump on your grave."

I started shouting and thrashing, plunging into the water with all my might. I was pulled up by my grandfather's weak hand. I cried for the first time that day, and the world of tears was so immense and beautiful that everything except my tears disappeared from before my eyes.

When I regained consciousness, I was lying wrapped in blankets in my bed. Grandfather was pacing up and down the room, whistling. Fat Bobka was warming my hands on her breasts.

"Oy, how he is shivering, our silly little boy!" Bobka said. "And how does he have the strength to shiver like that?"

Grandfather tugged at his beard, whistled, and began walking up and down the room again. In the next room Simon-Volf was snoring with tormented breath. He always yelled himself out during the day, and so never woke in the night.

GAPA GUZHVA

Gapa Guzhva is the first chapter of the novel Velikaya Krinitsa *that Babel worked on in the early 1930s. Although friends of Babel's report-ed that they knew of subsequent chapters that he had completed, only two chapters, this and "Kolyvushka," have survived. Both this story and "Kolyvushka" (which was unpublished during Babel's lifetime) dealt with the devastating effects of Stalin's enforced collectivization—a dangerous subject matter for a novel at the time.*

*S*ix weddings were held in Velikaya Krinitsa on Shrovetide in 1930. They were celebrated with a wild abandon, the likes of which had not been seen for a long time. Old customs were reborn. The father of one of the bridegrooms got drunk and demanded that he be allowed to try out the bride, a custom that had been discontinued some twenty years back. The father-in-law had already taken off his sash and thrown it to the ground. The bride, shaking with laughter, was tugging at the old man's beard. He puffed out his chest closer and closer to her, guffawed, and stamped his boots. And yet there was not much for the old man to be worried about. Of the six sheets that were hung up over the huts after the wedding night, only two were stained with virginal blood. As for the other brides, they had gone on late-night walks and come back soiled. One of the sheets was grabbed by a Red Army sol-dier who was home on leave, and Gapa Guzhva climbed up for the other one. She jumped onto the roof, kicking away the men behind her, and clambered up the pole, which bent and swayed under her weight. She tore down the reddened rag and came sliding down the pole. A table and a stool stood on the gable of the roof, and on the table was a half liter bottle of vodka and slices of cold meat. Gapa tipped the bot-tle into her mouth, and with her free hand waved the sheet. The crowd down below roared and danced. The stool slid out from under her, shook, and fell apart. Berezan herdsmen, driving their oxen to Kiev, stared at the woman drinking vodka on the roof under the sky.

"She's no woman, that one!" the villagers told them. "Our widow's the devil, she is!"

Gapa threw bread, twigs, and plates from the roof. She finished the vodka and smashed the bottle against the chimney ledge. The muzhiks who had gathered below roared. The widow jumped off the roof, untied her shaggy-bellied mare who stood dozing by the wooden fence, and rode off to get some wine. She came back weighed down with flasks, as a Circassian tribesman is weighed down with ammunition. Her horse was panting heavily and tossing its muzzle. Its belly, heavy with foal, surged and bulged, and equine madness quivered in its eyes.

At the weddings, the villagers danced holding handkerchiefs, with lowered eyes, their boots shuffling in one spot. Only Gapa whirled around, as they do in the towns. She danced with Grishka Savchenko, her lover. They held each other as if they were wrestling. They tugged at each other's shoulders with headstrong anger. They drummed the ground with their boots, and tumbled down as if they had been knocked off their feet.

The third day of the wedding feasts began. The couples' best men wore their sheepskin coats inside out and ran smeared with soot through the village, banging on oven doors. Bonfires were lit in the streets. People jumped through them, horns painted on their foreheads. Horses were harnessed to troughs that were dragged hurtling through the flames over clods of grass. Men fell to the ground, overpowered by sleep. Housewives threw broken pots and pans into their yards. The newlyweds washed their feet and climbed into tall beds, and only Gapa was still dancing alone in an empty shed. She whirled in circles, holding a tarred boat pole in her hand, her hair untied. She pounded the pole against the walls, leaving sticky black wounds, the thuds jolting the shed.

"We bring fire and death," Gapa whispered, waving the pole over her head.

Planks and straw rained down on her as the walls caved in.

She danced with loose hair among the ruins, in the din and dust of the crumbling wattle and the flying splinters of the breaking planks. Her delicate red-rimmed boots whirled through the rubble, drumming the ground.

Night fell. The bonfires were dying out in the thawing snow pits.

The shed lay in a tangled heap on the hill. A light began to flicker in the village council hut across the street. Gapa threw away her pole and ran over to the hut.

"Ivashko!" she yelled, as she rushed into the room. "Come have some fun with us, let's drink our life away!"

Ivashko was the representative of the Regional Commission for Collectivization. For two months now he had been trying to talk the villagers into collectivizing. He was sitting in front of a pile of crumpled, tattered papers, his hands resting on the table. The skin on either side of his forehead was wrinkled, and in his eyes hung the pupils of an ailing cat. Above them bulged the arches of his bare pink eye sockets.

"Are you sneering at our peasants?" Gapa yelled, stamping her foot.

"I'm not sneering," Ivashko said gloomily. "But it would be inappropriate for me to join you all."

Gapa danced past him, tapping her feet and waving her arms.

"Come break bread with us," she said to him. "And then tomorrow we'll do exactly as you say, Comrade Representist! We will tomorrow, not today!"

Ivashko shook his head.

"It would be inappropriate for me to break bread with you," he said. "You people aren't human—you bark like dogs! I've lost fifteen pounds since I came here!"

He chewed his lip and closed his eyes. He stretched out his hand, groped for his canvas bag, got up, staggered forward, and made his way toward the door with dragging feet, as if he were walking in his sleep.

"Comrade Ivashko is pure gold," Kharchenko, the council secretary, said after he had left. "He's a kind fellow, but our village has been too rough on him."

An ash-blond forelock* hung over Kharchenko's button nose and pimples. He was reading a newspaper, his feet resting on the bench.

"Just wait till the judge from Voronkov† comes over," Kharchenko said, turning a page of his newspaper. "Then you'll all sit up straight."

Gapa slipped a bag of sunflower seeds out of her cleavage.

"How come all you think about's your duties, Comrade Secretary?"

---

* It was a custom among Ukrainian villagers to shave their heads except for a forelock.
† A town southeast of Kiev.

she asked. "Why are you afraid of death? Who ever heard of a muzhik turning away from death?"

Outside, a swollen black sky was seething around the village belfry, and wet huts crouched and slithered away. The stars struggled to ignite above them, and the wind crept along the ground.

Gapa heard the dull murmur of an unfamiliar, husky voice in the front room of her hut. A woman pilgrim had come to spend the night and was sitting on the bench above the stove with her legs pulled in under her. The icon lamp's crimson threads of flame threw a net on the wall. A stillness hung over the clean hut. An odor of apple liquor seeped from the walls and partitions. Gapa's fat-lipped daughters, craning their necks, were staring at the beggar woman. Short horsy hair covered their heads, and their lips were large and puffed out. A dead, greasy sheen lay on their narrow foreheads.

"Keep up your lies, Grandma Rakhivna," Gapa said, leaning against the wall. "I love it when you tell your lies."

Rakhivna sat on the bench above the stove with her head against the low ceiling, plaiting her hair into braids, which she then coiled in rows over her little head. Her washed, misshapen feet rested on the edge of the stove.

"There's three patriarchs in this world," the old woman said, lowering her wrinkled face. "Our government has imprisoned the Patriarch of Moscow, the Jerusalem Patriarch is living among Turks. It is the Antioch Patriarch who now rules all of Christianity. He sent forty Greek priests onto Ukrainian soil to curse the churches from which our government took down the bells. The Greek priests passed Kholodny Yar, they've already been seen at Ostrogradsk, and come next Sunday they'll be here in Velikaya Krinitsa!"

Rakhivna closed her eyes and fell silent. The light of the icon lamps flickered over the hollows of her feet.

"The judge from Voronkov," the old woman suddenly said. "He collectivized the whole of Voronkov in a single day! He stuck nine squires in a cold cell, and on the following day they were to march in the chain gangs to Sakhalin. I tell you, daughter, there's people everywhere, Christ is gloried everywhere! The squires were kept in a cold cell all night—then in come the guards to take them, the guards open the dungeon door, and what do their eyes behold in the full light of the morning? Nine squires dangling from the rafters on their belts!"

Before she lay down, Rakhivna fussed about for a long time, sorting through her rags, whispering to her God as she would have whispered to her old man lying next to her. Then her breathing suddenly became light. Grishka Savchenko, the husband of one of the village women, was lying on a bench by the wall. He lay curled up, right on the edge as if he had been crushed, his back twisted, his vest bunched up over it, and his head sunk in pillows.

"A man's love," Gapa said, prodding and shaking him. "I know all there is to know about a man's love. They turn their snouts away from their wives and shuffle off, like this one here! *He* didn't go home to his wife Odarka, no, he didn't!"

Half the night they rolled on the bench in the darkness, their lips tightly clenched, their arms stretching out in the darkness. Gapa's braid went flying over the pillow. At dawn Grishka started up, moaned, and fell asleep with a snarl on his lips. Gapa gazed at her daughters' brown shoulders, low foreheads, thick lips, and dark breasts.

"What camels!" she said to herself. "How could they have come from me?"

Darkness receded from the oak-framed window. Dawn opened a violet streak in the clouds. Gapa went out into the yard. The wind enveloped her like cold river water. She harnessed her sledge and loaded it with sacks of wheat—during the wedding celebrations everyone had run out of flour. The road slithered through the fog and mist of dawn.

It snowed all day. At the mill they couldn't start grinding till the following evening. At the edge of the village, short-legged Yushko Trofim, wearing a soaked cap, came out from inside a sheet of snow to meet Gapa. His shoulders, covered in a sea of flakes, were surging and falling.

"Well, they finally got up," he muttered. He came up to her sledge and raised his bony black face up to her.

"What's that supposed to mean?" Gapa asked him. She pulled at her reins.

"All the big men came to our village last night," Trofim said. "They've already dragged off that old biddy staying with you and arrested her. The head of the Collectivization Commission and the secretary of the District Party Committee. They've nabbed Ivashko and now the Voronkov judge is stepping in."

Trofim walked off, his walrus whiskers bobbing, snowflakes slithering down them. Gapa shook the reins but then tugged at them again.

"Trofim! What did they drag the old biddy off for?"

Trofim stopped and yelled back from far away through the whirling, flying snow.

"They said it was because of her propaganda campaign about the world coming to an end!"

He walked on, limping on one foot, and in an instant his wide back was swallowed up by the sky that melted into the earth.

Gapa rode up to her hut and tapped on the window with her whip. Her daughters were lounging around the table dressed in shawls and shoes as if they were at a feast.

"Mama," the oldest said. "Odarka came over while you were out and took her husband back home."

The daughters set the table and lit the samovar. Gapa ate, and then went to the village council, where she found the elders of Velikaya Krinitsa sitting in silence along the walls. The window, smashed some time back during a debate, was boarded up, the glass of the lamps had worn thin, and a sign saying "No Smoking" had been nailed to the pockmarked walls. The judge from Voronkov, his shoulders hunched, sat at the table reading. He was reading through the record ledger of the village council of Velikaya Krinitsa. He had raised the collar of his shabby little coat. Kharchenko, the council secretary, was sitting next to him, drawing up a formal charge against his own village. On columned sheets of paper he was entering all the crimes, arrears, and fines—all the wounds, visible and invisible. When Judge Osmolovsky from Voronkov had arrived in the village, he had refused to call a general meeting of the citizens, as the representatives before him had done. He did not give speeches, but simply asked for a list of quota dodgers and former merchants, an inventory of their property, crops, and farmsteads.

The elders of Velikaya Krinitsa sat quietly on the benches, while Kharchenko's bustling, whistling pen crackled through the silence. There was a flurry of movement when Gapa came into the room. Evdokim Nazarenko's face lit up when he saw her.

"Here's our number one activist, Comrade Judge!" Evdokim said, guffawing and rubbing his palms together. "Our widow here has been actively ruining all our village youths."

Gapa stopped by the door and narrowed her eyes. A sneer flitted over Judge Osmolovsky's lips, and he crinkled his thin nose.

"Good morning," he said, nodding to her.

"She was the first one to sign up for the collective farm," Evdokim said, trying to chase away the brewing storm with a gush of words. "But then the good people of the village had a chat with her, and she designed up."

Gapa didn't move. Her face flushed brick red.

"The good people of the village say that in the collective farm everyone is to sleep under the same blanket!" she said in her sonorous voice.

Her eyes twinkled in her fixed face.

"Well, I for one am against sleeping wholesale! *We* like sleeping in twos, and we like our home-brewed vodka, goddamn it!"

The muzhiks burst out laughing, but immediately fell silent. Gapa peered at the judge. He raised his inflamed eyes and nodded to her. Then he slumped even lower, took his head in his thin, red-haired hands, and once again immersed himself in the record ledger of Velikaya Krinitsa. Gapa turned around, and her stately back flashed out of the room.

In the yard, Grandpa Abram, overgrown with raw flesh, was sitting on some wet planks with his knees pulled up. A yellow mane of hair hung to his shoulders.

"What's wrong?" Gapa asked him.

"I'm sad," the old man said.

Back at home, her daughters were already in bed. Late at night, a little slanting flame, its mercurial tongue flickering, hovered across the road in the hut of Nestor Tyagay, a member of the Young Communist League. Judge Osmolovsky was lodging there. A sheepskin coat had been laid out on a bench, and his supper was waiting for him. A bowl of yogurt, an onion, and a thick slice of bread. The judge took off his spectacles and covered his aching eyes with his palms. He was known throughout the district as Comrade Two-Hundred-and-Sixteen-Percent—that had been the percentage of grain which he had managed to exact from the renegade town of Voronkov. Osmolovsky's percentage had given rise to tales, songs, and folk legends.

He chewed the bread and the onion, and spread out in front of him

Pravda, the instructions of the District Committee, and the collectivization reports of the People's Commissariat for Agriculture. It was late, after one in the morning, when the door opened and Gapa, her shawl tied across her chest, came in.

"Judge," she said to him, "what's going to happen to the whores?"

Osmolovsky raised his eyes, his face covered in rippled light.

"They will no longer exist."

"Won't the whores be allowed to earn their living?"

"They will," the judge said. "But in a different, better way."

Gapa stared into a corner of the room with unseeing eyes. She fingered the necklace that hung across her chest.

"I'm glad to hear that!"

Her necklace clinked. Gapa left, closing the door behind her.

The piercing, frenzied night hurled itself down on her with thickets of low-hanging clouds—twisted ice floes lit up by black sparks. Silence spread over Velikaya Krinitsa, over the flat, sepulchral, frozen desert of the village night.

KOLYVUSHKA

*F*our men entered Ivan Kolyvushka's courtyard: Ivashko, the representative of the Regional Commission for Collectivization, Evdokim Nazarenko, the head of the village council, Zhitnyak, the chairman of the newly formed kolkhoz,* and Adrian Morinets. Adrian walked like a tower that had uprooted itself and was on the march. Ivashko had hurried past the barns, pressing his canvas briefcase to his side, and came bursting into Kolyvushka's house. Kolyvushka's wife and two daughters were sitting by the window spinning yarn on blackened spindles. They looked like nuns, with their kerchiefs, their long bodices, and their small, clean, bare feet. Photographs of Czarist ensigns, schoolmistresses, and townsfolk at their dachas hung on the walls between embroidered towels and cheap mirrors. Ivan Kolyvushka came into the house after his guests, and took off his hat.

"How much tax does Kolyvushka pay?" Ivashko asked, turning to face the others.

Evdokim, the village council head, watched the whirling wheels of the spindles with his hands in his pockets.

Ivashko snorted when he was told that Kolyvushka paid two hundred and sixteen rubles.

"Surely he can swing more than that!"

"It looks like he can't."

Zhitnyak stretched his dry lips in a thin line. Evdokim continued

---

* Collective farm.

watching the spindles. Ivan Kolyvushka stood in the doorway and winked at his wife, who went and pulled a receipt out from behind an icon and handed it to Ivashko, the representative of the Collectivization Commission.

"And what about the seed fund?" Ivashko asked abruptly, impatiently digging his foot into the floorboards.

Evdokim raised his eyes and looked around the room.

"This household has already been cleaned out, Comrade Representative," Evdokim said. "This isn't the kind of household that doesn't pay its share."

The whitewashed walls curved up into a low, warm cupola over the guests' heads. The flowers in glass jars, the plain cupboards, the polished benches, all sparkled with an oppressive cleanliness. Ivashko jumped up and hurried out the door, his briefcase swinging.

"Comrade Representative!" Kolyvushka called out, hurrying after him. "So will instructions be sent to me, or what?"

"You'll be notified!" Ivashko shouted, his arms dangling, and rushed off.

Adrian Morinets, inhumanly large, rushed after him. Timish, the cheerful bailiff, bobbed past the gate close at Ivashko's heel, wading with his long legs through the mud of the village street.

"What's this all about?" Kolyvushka called out, waving him over and grabbing him by the sleeve. The bailiff, a long cheerful stick, bent forward and opened his mouth, which was packed with a purple tongue and set with rows of pearls.

"They are about to confiscate your house."

"What about me?"

"You'll be sent off for resettlement."

And Timish rushed after Ivashko and the others with cranelike steps.

A horse harnessed to a sledge was standing in Kolyvushka's courtyard, and the red reins had been thrown over some sacks of wheat piled up in the sledge. There was a tree stump with an axe stuck in it in the middle of the yard by a stooping lime tree. Kolyvushka ran his fingers over his hat, pushed it back, and sat down. The mare came over to him, dragging the sledge behind her. She hung out her tongue and then curled it up. She was with foal, and her belly was heavily swollen. She playfully nudged and nuzzled her master's shoulder. Kolyvushka looked down at his feet. The trampled snow lay in ripples around the tree stump. Hunching over, Kolyvushka grabbed the axe, held it up high in the air for an instant, and brought it down on the horse's forehead. One of her ears lunged back, the other fluttered and then slumped down. She moaned and bolted to the side, the sledge toppling over, the wheat flying in curved ribbons over the snow. She reared her forelegs into the air, tossing back her muzzle, and got caught in the spikes of a harrow by the shed. Her eyes peered out from under a streaming curtain of blood. She sang out in lament. The foal turned within her. A vein puffed up on her belly.

"Forgive me!" Ivan said, stretching out his hand to her. "Forgive me, my one and only!"

He held out his palm to her. The mare's ear hung limply, her eyes rolled, rings of blood sparked around them, her muzzle lay in a straight line with her neck. She curled back her upper lip in despair. She stretched out her neck and scuttled forward, pulling the jumping harrow behind her. Ivan raised the axe over his head. The blow hit her between the eyes, her foal again turned inside her tumbling belly. Ivan walked across the yard to the shed and dragged out the winnowing fan. He swung the axe down with wide, slow blows, smashing the machine, dragging the axe into the drum and the delicate grid of the wheels. His wife came out onto the stoop in her long bodice.

"Mother!" Kolyvushka heard her faraway voice. "Mother! He's smashing everything up!"

The door opened. Out of the house came an old woman in canvas trousers, steadying herself on a stick. Yellow hair hung over the hollows of her cheeks, and her shirt clung to her thin body like a shroud. The old woman stepped into the snow with her shaggy stockings.

"Murderer!" she said to her son, grabbing the axe out of his hand. "Do you remember your father? Do you remember your brothers in the labor camps?"

The neighbors began to gather in the yard. The muzhiks stood in a semicircle and looked away. A woman lunged forward and began to shriek.

"Shut up, you foolish cow!" her husband told her.

Kolyvushka stood leaning against the wall. His rasping breath echoed through the courtyard. It was as if he were working strenuously, panting heavily.

Kolyvushka's Uncle Terenti was shuffling about the gate, trying to lock it.

"I am a man!" Kolyvushka suddenly said to the people around him. "I am a man, a villager like you! Have you never seen a man before?"

Terenti hustled the villagers out of the yard. The gates creaked and fell shut. They swung open again in the evening, and a sledge piled high with possessions came sweeping out of the yard, the women perched on bales like frozen birds. A cow, tethered by her horn, came trotting behind. The sledge passed the outskirts of the village and disappeared into the flat, snowy desert. The wind spiraled in this desert, pummeling and moaning, scattering its blue waves behind which stretched the metallic sky, through which a mesh of diamonds wound sparkling.

Kolyvushka walked down the street to the village council, his eyes fixed straight ahead. A meeting of the new kolkhoz named "Renaissance" was under way. Hunchbacked Zhitnyak sat slouching behind the desk.

"The great change in our lives—what's this great change all about?" he said.

The hunchback's hands pressed against his torso, and then went flying up.

"Fellow villagers! We are redirecting ourselves into dairy production and market gardening! This is of momentous importance! Our fathers and grandfathers trudged over great treasures with their boots, and the time has now come for us to dig these treasures up! Is it not a disgrace, is it not an outrage that though we are only some sixty versts from our regional capital, we haven't developed our farming according to scientific methods? Our eyes were closed, my fellow villagers, we've been running away from ourselves! What does sixty versts mean? Does anyone here know? In our country that is equal to an hour—but even that one hour belongs to us! It is worth its weight in gold!"

The door of the village council opened. Kolyvushka came in and walked over to the wall in his voluminous fur jacket and tall sheepskin hat. Ivashko's fingers jumped and went scuttling into the pile of papers in front of him.

"I must ask all individuals without a voting right to immediately leave this meeting," he said, looking down at the papers.

Outside the window, beyond the dirty glass, the sunset was spilling out in green emerald streams. In the twilight of the village hut, sparks glittered faintly in the raw clouds of rough tobacco. Ivan Kolyvushka took off his hat, and his mop of black hair came pouring forth.

He walked up to the table around which the committee was sitting: Ivga Movchan, a woman who worked as a farmhand, Evdokim, the head of the village council, and silent Adrian Morinets.

"My people!" Ivan Kolyvushka said, stretching out his hand and laying a bunch of keys on the table. "My people, I am cutting all ties with you!"

The iron keys clanked and lay on the blackened boards. Adrian's haggard face appeared from within the darkness.

"Where will you go, Ivan?"

"My people won't have me, maybe the earth will!"

Kolyvushka walked out quietly, his head lowered.

"It's a trick!" Ivashko yelled the moment the door fell shut. "It's a provocation! He's gone to get his rifle, that's what! He's gone to get his rifle!"

Ivashko banged his fist on the table. Words about panic and the need to keep calm tried to struggle through his lips.

Adrian's face again retreated into its dark corner. "No, Comrade Chairman," he said from within the darkness. "I don't think he went to get his rifle."

"I have a proposal to make!" Ivashko shouted.

The proposal was that a guard be set up outside Kolyvushka's place. Timish the bailiff was voted to be the guard. Grimacing, he took a bentwood chair out onto the stoop, slumped down on it, and laid his shotgun and his truncheon by his feet. From the heights of the stoop, from the heights of his village throne, Timish bantered with the girls, whistled, shouted, and thumped his shotgun on the ground. The night was lilac and heavy, like a bright mountain crystal. Veins of frozen rivulets lay across it. A star sank into a well of black clouds.

The following morning Timish reported that there had been no incidents. Kolyvushka had spent the night at Grandpa Abram's, an old man overgrown with raw flesh.

In the evening Abram had hobbled off to the well.

"Why go there, Grandpa Abram?" Kolyvushka asked.

"I'm going to put on a samovar," Grandpa said.

They slept late. Smoke rose above the hut. Their door remained shut.

"He's run for it!" Ivashko said at the kolkhoz meeting. "Are we going to cry tears over him? What d'you think, villagers?"

Zhitnyak sat at the table, his sharp, quivering elbows spread wide, entering the particulars of the confiscated horses. The hump on his back cast a moving shadow.

"How much more are we going to stuff down our throats?" Zhitnyak pronounced philosophically as he wrote. "Now we suddenly need everything in the world! We need crop sprinklers, we need plows, tractors, pumps! Gluttony, that's what this is! Our whole country has been seized by gluttony!"

The horses that Zhitnyak entered in the book were all bay or skewbald, with names like "Boy" and "Little Miss." Zhitnyak had the owners sign against their surnames.

He was interrupted by a noise, a faraway, muffled clatter of hooves. A tidal wave was rolling toward Velikaya Staritsa* and came crashing over it. A crowd poured over the ravished street, legless cripples hobbling in front. An invisible banner was fluttering above their heads. They slowed as they arrived at the village council and drew into formation. A circle opened in their midst, a circle of ruffled-up snow, a gap as for a priest during a church procession. Kolyvushka was standing in the circle, his shirt hanging loose beneath his vest, his head completely white. The night had silvered his gypsy locks, not a black hair was left. Flakes of snow, weak birds carried by the wind, drifted across the warming sky. An old man with broken legs jostled his way forward and peered avidly at Kolyvushka's white hair.

"Tell us, Ivan," the old man said, raising his arms. "Tell us what is in your soul!"

"Where will you chase me to, my fellow villagers?" Kolyvushka whispered, looking around. "Where shall I go? I was born here among you."

---

* The actual village that Babel visited in the spring of 1930 and decided to base his novel on. In the novel's first chapter, "Gapa Guzhva," the same village appears as Velikaya Krinitsa. Babel had decided to change the name of the village so as not offend the inhabitants.

The crowd began to rumble. Morinets elbowed his way to the front.

"Let him be," he said in a low, trembling voice, the cry trapped in his powerful chest. "Let him be! Whose share will he grab?"

"Mine!" Zhitnyak said, and burst out laughing. He walked up to Kolyvushka, shuffling his feet, and winked at him.

"I slept with a woman last night!" the hunchback said. "When we got up she made pancakes, and me and her, we gobbled them down like we was hogs—ha, we blew more farts than you could shake a stick at—"

The hunchback stopped in midsentence, his guffaws broke off, and the blood drained from his face.

"So you've come to line us up against the wall?" he asked in a lower voice. "You've come to bully us with that white head of yours, to turn the thumbscrews on us? But we won't let you, the time for thumbscrews has passed!"

The hunchback came nearer on his thin, bowed legs. Something whistled inside him like a bird.

"You should be killed," he whispered, an idea flitting through his mind. "I'll go get my gun and finish you off."

His face brightened. He gave Kolyvushka's hand a spirited tap and hurried off into the house to get Timish's gun. Kolyvushka wavered for a moment, and then walked off. His silver head disappeared in the tangled mesh of houses. He stumbled as he walked, but then his strides grew firmer. He took the road to Ksenevka.

No one ever saw him again in Velikaya Staritsa.

THE ROAD

I left the crumbling front in November 1917. At home my mother packed underwear and dried bread for me. I arrived in Kiev the day before Muravyov began shelling the city.* I was trying to get to Petersburg. For twelve days and nights I hid with Chaim Tsiryulnik in the basement of his Hotel Bessarabka. The commander of Soviet Kiev issued me a pass to leave the city.

In all the world there is no more cheerless sight than the Kiev train station. For many years makeshift wooden barracks have defaced the town outskirts. Lice crackled on wet planks. Deserters, smugglers, and gypsies were all crowded together in the station. Old Galician women urinated standing on the platform. The low sky was furrowed with clouds full of rain and gloom.

Three days went by before the first train left. At first it stopped every verst; then it gathered speed, its wheels rattling faster, singing a powerful song. This filled everyone in our transport car with joy. Fast travel filled people with joy in 1918. At night, the train gave a jolt and stopped. The door of our car opened, and we saw the green glimmer of snow before us. A station telegrapher in soft Caucasian boots and a fur coat tied with a strap climbed aboard. The telegrapher stretched out his hand and tapped his finger on his open palm. "Put all travel permits here!"

Right by the door an old woman lay quietly curled up on some

---

* Mikhail Artemevich Muravyov, 1880–1918, was the commander in chief of the Southern Revolutionary Front. He was shelling Kiev in order to occupy it for the Bolsheviks.

bundles. She was heading for Lyuban to her son, who was a railroad worker. Dozing next to me was a schoolmaster, Yehuda Veynberg, and his wife. The schoolmaster had married a few days earlier, and was taking his young wife to Petersburg. They had been whispering throughout the journey about new structured methods in teaching, and then dozed off. Their hands were clasped even in sleep.

The telegrapher read their permit signed by Lunacharsky,* pulled a Mauser with a thin, dirty muzzle from under his coat, and shot the schoolmaster in the face.

A big, hunchbacked muzhik in a fur cap with dangling earflaps was standing behind the telegrapher. The telegrapher winked at him, and the muzhik put his lamp on the floor, unbuttoned the dead man's trousers, sliced off his sexual organs with a pocketknife, and stuffed them into the wife's mouth.

"*Tref†* wasn't good enough for you!" the muzhik said. "So now eat something kosher!"

The woman's soft throat swelled. She remained silent. The train was standing on the steppes. The furrowed snows swarmed with polar brilliance. Jews were being thrown out of the cars onto the rails. Shots rang out unevenly, like shouts. The muzhik in the fur cap with the dangling earflaps took me behind a pile of logs and began to search me. The darkened moon shone down on us. Smoke rose from the forest's lilac wall. Frozen wooden fingers crept stiffly over my body.

"A Yid or a Russian?" the telegrapher yelled from the car platform.

"Yeah, a Russian! So much so, he'd make a first-rate rabbi!" the muzhik muttered as he searched me.

He brought his wrinkled, anxious face close to mine, ripped out the four golden ten-ruble coins which my mother had sewn into my underwear for the journey, took my boots and my coat, and then, turning me around, hit me on the back of my neck with the edge of his palm and said in Yiddish, "*Antloyf, Chaim!*"**

I ran, my bare feet sinking in the snow. I felt him mark a target on my back, the nip of his aim cutting through my ribs. But the muzhik

---

*Anatoly Lunacharsky, 1875–1933, Marxist critic and playwright, was the USSR's first Commissar of Education.

† Food that is not kosher, and so is unfit to eat according to Jewish dietary laws.

** Yiddish: "Run away, Chaim."

did not shoot. A light was quavering within a garland of smoke among the columns of pine trees, within the covered cellar of the forest. I ran toward the hut. The smoke of burning dung patties rose from it. The forester groaned when I burst into his hut. Huddled in strips cut from furs and coats, he was sitting on a finely wrought bamboo armchair with velvet cushions, crumbling tobacco on his knees. Enveloped in smoke, the forester groaned again, got up, and bowed deeply.

"You mustn't come in here, my dearest friend! You mustn't come in here, dearest Comrade!"

He led me to a path and gave me some rags to wrap my feet in. By late next morning I had reached a shtetl. There was no doctor at the hospital to amputate my frostbitten feet. The medical orderly was running the ward. Every morning he came galloping over to the hospital on his short black stallion, tied it to the hitching post, and came over to us full of fire, sparks burning in his eyes.

"Friedrich Engels teaches us that there should be no nations," the medical orderly said, bending over the head of my bed, his pupils fiery coals. "And yet we say the opposite—nations have to exist."*

Ripping the bandages off my feet, he straightened his back, and, gnashing his teeth asked me in a low voice, "So where is it taking you, this nation of yours? Where? Why doesn't it stay in one place? Why is it stirring up trouble, making waves?"

The Soviets moved us out on a cart in the night: patients who had not seen eye to eye with the medical orderly and old Jewesses in wigs, the mothers of the shtetl commissars.

My feet healed. I continued along the destitute road to Zhlobin, Orsha, and Vitebsk. The muzzle of a howitzer acted as my shelter from Novosokolniki to Loknya.† We were riding on the uncovered cannon platform. Fedyukha, my chance traveling companion, a storyteller and witty jokester, was undertaking the great journey of the deserters. We slept beneath the powerful, short, upward-pointing muzzle, and warmed each other in the canvas pit, covered with hay like the den of

---

* The medical orderly is confusing Engels's concept of the nation state with nationality, in this case Russian versus Jewish nationality.

† Zhlobin, Orsha, and Vitebsk are towns, today in Belarus, that the narrator would have passed through on his way north from Kiev to Petersburg. Novosokolniki and Loknya are in Russia on the other side of the Belarus border.

an animal. After Loknya, Fedyukha stole my suitcase and disappeared. The shtetl soviet had issued me the suitcase along with two pairs of soldier's underwear, dried bread, and some money. Two days went by without food as we approached Petersburg. At the station in Tsarskoe Selo* I witnessed the last of the shooting. The defense detachment fired shots into the air as our train pulled in. The smugglers were led out onto the platform and their clothes were ripped off, and rubber suits filled with vodka came tumbling off of them onto the asphalt.

Shortly after eight in the evening, the Petersburg station hurled me from its howling bedlam onto the Zagorodny Boulevard. A thermometer on the wall of a boarded-up pharmacy across the street showed −24 degrees Celsius. The wind roared through the tunnel of Gorokhovaya Street; jets of gaslight faded over the canals. This frozen, basalt Venice stood transfixed. I entered Gorokhovaya Street, which lay there like a field of ice cluttered with rocks.

The Cheka† had installed itself at number 2, the former office of the governor. Two machine guns, iron dogs with raised muzzles, stood in the entrance hall. I showed the commandant the letter from Vanya Kalugin, my sergeant in the Shuysky Regiment. Kalugin had become an investigator in the Cheka, and had sent me a letter to come see him.

"Go to Anichkov Palace," the commandant told me. "He's there now."

"I'll never make it," I thought, and smiled at him.

The Nevsky Prospekt flowed into the distance like the Milky Way. Dead horses lay along it like milestones. Their legs, pointing upward, supported the descending sky. Their bare bellies were clean and shiny. An old man who resembled an Imperial guardsman trudged past me, dragging a wooden toy sledge behind him, driving his boots with difficulty into the ice. A Tyrolean hat was perched on his head, and he had tied his beard with a piece of string and stuck it into his shawl.

"I'll never make it," I said to the old man.

He stopped. His furrowed leonine face was filled with calm. He hesitated for a moment, but then continued dragging the sledge along the street.

---

* Today the city of Pushkin, fourteen miles south of St. Petersburg.

† The "Extraordinary Commission," formed in 1917 to investigate counterrevolutionary activities.

"Thus falls away the need to conquer Petersburg," I said to myself, and tried to remember the name of the man who had been crushed by the hooves of Arab stallions at the very end of his journey. It was Yehuda Halevi.*

Two Chinese men in bowler hats stood on the corner of Sadovaya Street with loaves of bread under their arms. They showed them to passing prostitutes, and with frozen fingernails drew lines across the crust. The women walked past them in a silent parade.

At Anichkov Bridge I sat on the base of the statue by Klodt's horses.†

I lay down on the polished flagstone, my elbow under my head, but the freezing granite blistered me, and drove, pushed, propelled me forward to the palace.

The portal of the raspberry-red side wing stood open. Blue gaslight shone above a lackey, who had fallen asleep in an armchair. His lower lip was hanging from an inky, moribund face filled with wrinkles, and his military tunic, flooded with light, hung beltless over livery trousers trimmed with gold lace. A splotchy arrow, drawn in ink, pointed the way to the commandant. I went up the stairs and passed through low, empty chambers. Women painted in somber black danced rounds on ceilings and walls. Iron grates covered the windows, their broken latches hung on the frames. At the end of the suite of chambers Kalugin was sitting at a table, lit as if on stage, his head framed by straw-colored muzhik hair. On the table in front of him was a heap of toys, colorful rags, and torn picture books.

"So here you are!" Kalugin said, raising his head. "Great! We need you here."

I brushed aside the toys piled on the table, lay down on the shining tabletop, and . . . woke up on a low sofa—perhaps a few minutes, perhaps a few hours later. The lights of a chandelier danced above me in a waterfall of glass. The wet rags that had been cut off me lay on the floor in a puddle.

"You need a bath," Kalugin told me, standing above the sofa. He lifted me up and carried me to a bathtub. It was an old-fashioned tub,

---

*Yehuda Halevi, 1075–1141, was a Jewish poet and religious philosopher from Toledo, who embarked on a pilgrimage to Palestine at the end of his life. He died in Egypt, slain, according to legend, by a hostile Muslim on the threshold of Palestine.
†A sculpture of a group of horses by Peter Karlovich Klodt, 1805–1867.

with low sides. The water didn't flow from taps. Kalugin poured water over me with a bucket. Clothes were laid out on yellowish satin pouffes, on wicker stools—a robe with buckles, a shirt and socks of double-woven silk. The long underpants went all the way up to my head, the robe had been tailored for a giant, the sleeves were so long I tripped over them.

"So you're making fun of old Alexander Alexandrovich?" Kalugin said as he rolled up my sleeves. "The old boy weighed a good nine *pood!*"*

We somehow managed to tie Czar Alexander III's robe, and went back to the room we had been in before. It was the library of Maria Fyodorovna,† a perfumed box, its walls lined with gilded bookcases filled with crimson spines.

I told Kalugin which of our men in the Shuysky Regiment had been killed, who had become a commissar, who had gone to Kuban. We drank tea, and stars streamed over the crystal walls of our glasses. We chased our tea down with horsemeat sausages, which were black and somewhat raw. The thick, airy silk of a curtain separated us from the world. The sun, fixed to the ceiling, reflected and shone, and the steam pipes from the central heating gave off a stifling heat.

"You only live once," he said, after we had finished our horsemeat. He left the room and came back with two boxes—a gift from Sultan Abdul Hamid** to the Russian sovereign. One was made of zinc, the other was a cigar box sealed with tape and paper emblems. "*A sa majesté, l'Empererur de toutes les Russies,*" was engraved on the zinc lid, "from his well-wishing cousin."

Maria Fyodorovna's library was flooded with an aroma she had known a quarter of a century ago. Cigars twenty centimeters long and thick as a finger were wrapped in pink paper. I do not know if anyone besides the autocrat of all the Russias had ever smoked such cigars, but nevertheless I chose one. Kalugin looked at me and smiled.

"You only live once," he said. "Let's hope they've not been counted. The lackeys told me that Alexander III was an inveterate smoker. He loved tobacco, kvass, and champagne. But on his table—take a

---

* Czar Alexander III, 1845–94 lived in the Anichkov Palace. Nine *pood* is 325 pounds.
† Empress Maria Fyodorovna, 1847–1928, wife of Czar Alexander III.
** Abdul Hamid II, 1842–1918, the Sultan of the Ottoman Empire.

look!—there are five-kopeck clay ashtrays, and there are patches on his trousers!"

And sure enough, the robe I had been arrayed in was stained, shiny, and had been mended many times.

We passed the rest of the night going through Nicholas II's toys, his drums and locomotives, his christening shirt, and his notebooks with their childish scribbles. Pictures of grand dukes who had died in infancy, locks of their hair, the diaries of the Danish Princess Dagmar,* the letters of her sister, the Queen of England, breathing perfume and decay, crumbling in our fingers. On the title pages of the Bible and Lamartine,† her friends and governesses—the daughters of burgomasters and state councilors—bade farewell in laborious slanting lines to the princess leaving for Russia. Her mother, Louisa, queen of a small kingdom, had put much effort into seeing her children well settled. She gave one of her daughters to Edward VII, the Emperor of India and King of England, and the other to a Romanov. Her son George was made King of Greece. Princess Dagmar turned into Maria in Russia. The canals of Copenhagen and the chocolate sideburns of King Christian faded in the distance. Bearing the last of the sovereigns, Maria, a tiny woman with the fierceness of a fox, hurried through the palisades of the Preobrazhensky Grenadiers. But her maternal blood was to spill on Russia's implacable, unforgiving granite earth.

We could not tear ourselves from the dull, fatal chronicle till dawn. I had finished smoking Abdul-Hamid's cigar. In the morning, Kalugin took me to the Cheka, to Gorokhovaya Street, number two. He had a word with Uritsky.** I stood behind a heavy curtain that hung to the ground in cloth waves. Fragments of words made their way through to me.

"He's one of us," Kalugin said. "His father is a storekeeper, a merchant, but he's washed his hands of them. . . . He knows languages."

Uritsky came out of his office with a tottering gait. His swollen eyelids, burned by sleeplessness, bulged behind the glass of his pince-nez.

---

* Later Empress Maria Fyodorovna, wife of Czar Alexander III.

† Alphonse de Lamartine, 1790–1869, was a French Romantic poet and statesman.

** Mikhail (Mosey) Solomonovich Uritsky, 1873–1918, the son of a Jewish merchant, was the commissar of internal affairs for the northern district and the chairman of the Petrograd (Petersburg) Cheka.

They made me a translator in the Foreign Division. I was issued a military uniform and food coupons. In a corner of the Petersburg City Hall that was allocated to me I set about translating depositions of diplomats, agents provocateurs, and spies.

Within a single day I had everything: clothes, food, work, and comrades true in friendship and death, comrades the likes of which you will not find anywhere in the world, except in our country.

That is how, thirteen years ago, a wonderful life filled with thought and joy began for me.

THE *IVAN AND MARIA*

*I*n the summer of 1918 Sergei Vasilevich Malishev,* who was to become the chairman of the Nizhny-Novgorod Fair Committee, organized our nation's first produce expedition. With Lenin's approval, he loaded a series of trains with goods useful to peasants, and sent these trains to the Volga region to exchange the goods for wheat.

I ended up in the clerical department of this expedition. We chose the Novo-Nikolayev district in the province of Samara as our field of operation. According to the specialists, this province, if properly cultivated, was capable of feeding the whole Moscow region.

Near Saratov,† the goods were reloaded onto a barge at the river docks of Uvek. The hold of this barge became a makeshift department store. We pinned up portraits of Lenin and Marx between the curved ribs of our floating warehouse and framed the portraits with ears of corn, and we arranged bales of calico, scythes, nails, and leather goods on the shelves, even concertinas and balalaikas.

At Uvek we had been given a tugboat, the *Ivan Tupitsin,* named after a Volga merchant who had been its previous owner. The "staff," Malishev with his assistants and cashiers, made themselves at home on the tugboat, while the guards and sales clerks slept on the barge, under the counters.

It took a week to load the goods onto the barge. On a July morn-

---

* Sergei Vasilevich Malishev, 1877–1938, nicknamed "The Red Merchant," was one of the chief trade administrators during the early years of Soviet rule.
† Saratov, a city in western Russia, lies along the middle course of the Volga River.

ing the *Ivan Tupitsin*, gushing fat puffs of smoke, began to pull us up the Volga to Baronsk.* The local German settlers call it Katarinenstadt. It is now the capital of the Volga German Province, a wonderful region settled by hardy, taciturn folk.

The steppes outside Baronsk are covered with heavy, golden wheat, such as you can only find in Canada. They are filled with sunflowers and black oily clumps of earth. We had traveled from a Petersburg licked clean by granite flames to a California that was Russian through and through, and therefore even more outlandish. In our own California a pound of grain cost sixty kopecks, and not ten rubles as it did back in the north. We threw ourselves onto the loaves of bread with a savagery that nowadays is impossible to understand. We plunged our canine teeth, sharpened by hunger, into the bread's gossamer core. For two weeks we languished in a blissful drunkenness of indigestion. To me, the blood flowing through our veins had the taste and color of raspberry jam.

Malishev's calculations had been right: sales went well. Slow streams of carts flowed to the riverbank from all corners of the steppes. The sun crept over the backs of well-fed horses. The sun shone on the tops of the wheat-covered hills. Carts in a thousand dots descended to the Volga. Giants in woolen jerseys, descendants of the Dutch farmers who had settled in the Volga regions in the days of Catherine, strode beside the horses. Their faces looked just as they had back in Zaandam† and Haarlem. Drops of sparkling turquoise shone from within a mesh of leathery wrinkles beneath patriarchal mossy eyebrows. Smoke from tobacco pipes melted into the bluish lightning that flashed over the steppes. The settlers slowly climbed the gangplank onto the barge. Their wooden shoes clanged like bells heralding strength and peace. The goods were chosen by old women in starched bonnets and brown bodices. Their purchases were carried to the carts. Village painters had strewn armfuls of wildflowers and pink bull muzzles along the sides of the carts—the outer sides were usually painted a deep blue, within which waxen apples and plums gleamed, touched by the rays of the sun.

---

* Renamed Marks (Marx).
† Today Zaanstadt.

People from far away rode in on camels. These animals lay on the riverbank, their collapsed humps cutting into the horizon. Our trading always ended toward evening. We locked our store. The guards—war invalids—and the sales clerks undressed and jumped off the barges into the Volga burning in the sunset. On the distant steppes the wheat rolled in red waves. The walls of the sunset were collapsing in the sky. The swimming workers of the Samara Province Produce Expedition (that is what we were called in official documents) were an unusual spectacle. The cripples spouted silty pink streams from the river. Some of the guards were one-legged, others were missing an arm or an eye. They hooked themselves up in twos so they could swim. Two men would then have two legs, thrashing the water with their stumps, silty streams rushing in whirls between their bodies. Growling and snorting, the cripples rolled out onto the riverbank, frolicking, shaking their stumps at the flowing skies, covering themselves with sand, and wrestling, grabbing hold of each other's chopped extremities. After swimming, we went to the tavern of Karl Biedermayer. Our day was crowned by supper there. Two girls with brick-red hands, Augusta and Anna, served us meat patties—red flagstones quivering under whorls of seething butter and heaped with haystacks of fried potatoes. They spiced this mountain of village fare with onions and garlic. They placed jars of sour pickles in front of us. The smoke of the sunset wafted in from the marketplace through little round windows high up near the ceiling. The pickles smoldered in the crimson smoke and smelled of the seashore. We washed down the meat with cider. Every evening we, the residents of Peski and Okhta, men of the Petersburg suburbs that were frozen over with yellow urine, once again felt like conquerors. The little windows, cut into black walls centuries old, resembled portholes. Through them shone a courtyard, blissfully clean, a little German courtyard with rosebushes and wisteria, and the violet precipice of an open stable. Old women in bodices sat on stoops, knitting stockings for Gulliver. Herds were coming back from the pastures. Augusta and Anna sat down on stools beside the cows. Radiant bovine eyes glittered in the twilight. It was as if there had never been war on earth. And yet the front of the Ural Cossacks was only twenty versts from Baronsk.*

* The Red Army was fighting the White counterrevolutionary troops made up of Ural Cossacks and Czech divisions.

Karl Biedermayer had no idea that the Civil War was rolling toward his home.

At night I returned to our hold in the barge with Seletsky, who was a clerk, just as I was. He sang as we walked. Heads in nightcaps peered out of lancet windows. The moonlight flowed down the roof tiles' red canals. The muffled barking of dogs rose above this Russian Zaandam. Riveted Augustas and Annas listened to Seletsky's song. His deep bass carried us to the steppes, to the gothic enclosure of the wheat barns. Crossbeams of moonlight flickered on the river, and the breezy darkness swept over the sand of the riverbanks. Iridescent worms writhed in a torn sweep net.

Seletsky's voice was unnaturally powerful. He was an enormous fellow who belonged to that race of provincial Chaliapins,* of which so many, to our great fortune, have arisen throughout Russia. He even had the same kind of face as Chaliapin, part Scottish coachman, part grandee from the era of Catherine the Great. Seletsky was a simple man, unlike his divine prototype, but his voice resounded boundlessly, fatally, filled one's soul with the sweetness of self-destruction and gypsy oblivion. Seletsky preferred the songs of convicts to Italian arias. It was from him that I first heard Grechaninov's† song "Death." It resounded, menacing, relentless, passionate, over the dark water through the night.

> *She will not forget, she will come to you,*
> *Caress, embrace, and love you for all eternity.*
> *But a bridal wreath of thorns shall crown her head.*

This song flows within man's ephemeral shell like the waters of eternity. It washes away everything, it gives birth to everything.

The front was twenty versts away. The Ural Cossacks, joined by Major Vozenilek's Czech battalion, were trying to drive the dispersed Red detachments out of Nikolayevsk. Farther north, the troops of Komchuk—the Committee of the Members of the Constituent

---

* Fyodor Ivanovich Chaliapin, 1873–1938, a legendary bass, one of the most renowned opera singers of the early twentieth century.
† Alexander Tichonovich Grechaninov, 1864–1956, Russian composer and songwriter, noted for his religious works and children's music.

Assembly—were advancing from Samara.* Our scattered, untrained units regrouped on the left bank. Muravyov had just betrayed us. Vatsetis was appointed the Soviet commander in chief.†

Weapons for the front were brought from Saratov. Once or twice a week the pink and white paddle steamer *Ivan and Maria* docked at Baronsk. It carried rifles and shells. Its deck was full of boxes with skulls stenciled on them, under which the word "lethal" was written.

The ship's captain, Korostelyov, was a man ravished by drink, with lifeless flaxen hair. He was an adventurer, a restless soul, and a vagabond. He had traveled the White Sea on sailing vessels, walked the length and breadth of Russia, had done time in jail and penance in a monastery.

We always dropped by to see him on our way back from Biedermayer's if there were still lights on board the *Ivan and Maria*. One night, as we passed the wheat barns with their enchanted blue and brown castle silhouettes, we saw a torch blazing high in the sky. Seletsky and I were heading back to our barge in that warm, passionate state of mind that can only be spawned by this wondrous land, youth, night, and the melting rings of fire on the river.

The Volga was rolling on silently. There were no lights on the *Ivan and Maria*, and the hulk of the ship lay dark and dead, with only the torch burning above it. The flame was flaring and fuming above the mast. Seletsky was singing, his face pale, his head thrown back. He stopped when we came to the edge of the river. We walked up the unguarded gangplank. Boxes and gun wheels lay about the deck. I knocked on the door of the captain's cabin, and it fell open. A tin lamp without a glass cover was burning on the table, which was covered with spilled liquor. The metallic ring around the wick was melting. The windows had been boarded up with crooked planks. The sulfuric aroma of home-brewed vodka rose from cans under the table. Captain Korostelyov was sitting on the floor in a canvas shirt among green streams of vomit. His clotted, monastic hair stood around his head. He

* The Komchuk was a government formed in Samara by the anti-Soviet Social Revolutionary Party on June 18, 1918.
† Mikhail Artemevich Muravyov, 1880–1918, had been the commander in chief of the Southern Revolutionary Front, but began an anti-Soviet uprising in Simbirsk on July 10, 1918. He was killed the following day. Ioachim Ioachimovich Vatsetis, 1883–1938, took over from Muravyov immediately after his defection.

was staring fixedly up at Larson, his Latvian commissar, who was sitting, holding a *Pravda* in a yellowish cardboard folder open in front of him, reading it in the light of the melting kerosene flicker.

"You're showing your true colors!" Captain Korostelyov said from the floor. "Go on with what you were saying . . . go on torturing us if you have to."

"Why should I do the talking?" Larson answered, turning his back and fencing himself off with his *Pravda*. "I'd rather listen to you."

A redheaded muzhik, his legs dangling, was sitting on a velvet sofa. "Lisyei! Vodka!" the captain said to him.

"None left," Lisyei said. "And nowhere to get none."

Larson put down his paper and burst out laughing, as if he were pounding a drum.

"A Russian man needs his drink, the Russian man's soul wants to carouse, but there's not a drop to be found anywhere around here!" the Latvian said in his thick accent. "And it still calls itself the Volga!"

Captain Korostelyov stretched out his thin, boyish neck, and his legs in their canvas trousers sprawled out across the floor. There was pitiful bewilderment in his eyes, and then they flashed. "Torture us," he said to the Latvian, barely audibly, stretching out his neck. "Torture us, Karl."

Lisyei clasped his plump hands together and peered at the Latvian. "Ha! He's trumping the Volga! No, Comrade, you will not trump our Volga, you will not bad-mouth her! Don't you know the song we sing: Mother Volga, Czarina of all rivers?"

Seletsky and I were still standing by the door. I kept thinking of retreating.

"Well, this is simply beyond my grasp!" Larson said, turning to us, but clearly continuing the argument. "Maybe these comrades here can explain to me why reinforced concrete is worse than birches and aspens, and airships worse than Kaluga dung?"

Lisyei's head twisted in his quilted collar. His legs didn't reach the floor. His plump fingers, pressed to his stomach, were knotting an invisible net.

"Ha! And what is it you know about Kaluga, my friend?" Lisyei asked in a pacifying tone. "I'll have you know there's famous folk that lives in Kaluga! Yes, fabulous folk!"

"Some vodka," Captain Korostelyov muttered from the floor.

Larson again threw back his piggish head and laughed out loud. "You win some, you lose some, " he muttered, pulling the *Pravda* closer. "Yes, you win some, you lose some."

Sweat was seething on his forehead, and oily streams of fire were dancing in his clotted, dirt-crusted hair.

"You win some, you lose some," Larson snorted again. "Yes, you win some, you lose some."

Captain Korostelyov patted the floor around him with his fingers. He began crawling forward, hauling himself along with his hands, dragging his skeletal body in its sackcloth shirt behind him.

"Don't you dare bait Russia, Karl," he whispered, crawling toward the Latvian, hitting him in the face with his clenched fist, and then, with a sudden shriek, beginning to flail at him. The Latvian puffed himself up and looked at us over his skewed glasses. Then he wound a silken rivulet of Korostelyov's hair around his finger and banged Korostelyov's head on the floor. He yanked his head up and banged it down again.

"There!" Larson said curtly, flinging the bony body to the side. "And there's more where that came from!"

The captain propped himself up on his hands and got on all fours like a dog. Blood was flowing from his nostrils, and his eyes were crossed, darting about. Suddenly he flung himself up and hurled himself with a howl under the table.

"Russia!" he mumbled from under the table, and started kicking and flailing. "Russia!"

The shovels of his bare feet thrashed about. Only one whistling, moaning word could be heard in his screeching.

"Russia!" he moaned, stretching out his hands, beating his head against the floor.

Redheaded Lisyei was still sitting on the velvet sofa.

"This has been going on since noon," he said, turning to Seletsky and me. "Fighting for Russia, feeling sorry for Russia."

"Vodka!" Korostelyov said harshly from under the table. He crawled out and stood up. His hair, dripping with blood, hung down on his cheeks.

"Where's the vodka, Lisyei?"

"The vodka, my friend, is forty versts away, in Voznesenskoe—forty versts by water or by land. There's a church there now, so there must be home brew to be had. Whatever you do, the Germans don't have none!"*

Captain Korostelyov turned around and walked out on rigid heron's legs.

"We're Kalugans!" Larson yelled out unexpectedly.

"He has no respect for Kaluga," Lisyei sighed, "whichever way you look at it. But me, I've been there in Kaluga! Proper folk live there, famous—"

Outside, someone yelled an order, and the clanking of the anchor was heard—the anchor was being weighed. Lisyei raised his eyebrows.

"We're not off to Voznesenskoe, are we?"

Larson burst out laughing, throwing his head back. I ran out of the cabin. Korostelyov stood barefoot on the bridge. The copper rays of the moon lay on his gashed face. The gangplanks fell onto the riverbank. Whirling sailors unwound the moorings.

"Dimitri Alekseyevich," Seletsky shouted up to Korostelyov. "At least let us get off! What do you need us along for?"

The engines erupted into erratic hammering. The paddlewheel dug into the river. A rotten plank on the pier creaked softly. The *Ivan and Maria* swung its bow around.

"So we're off," Lisyei said, coming out of the cabin. "So we're off to Voznesenskoe to get some home brew."

The *Ivan and Maria*'s uncoiling paddlewheel was gaining speed. The engine's oily clanking, rustling, and whistling grew. We flew through the darkness, forging straight ahead, plowing through buoys, beacons, and red signals. The water foamed beneath the paddles and went flashing back like the golden wings of a bird. The moon plunged into swirls of black water. "The Volga's waterway is full of bends" was a phrase I remembered from a schoolbook. "It abounds in sandbanks." Captain Korostelyov was shuffling about on the bridge. Blue shining skin stretched over his cheekbones.

* Lisyei is saying that the Volga German settlement of Wosnesenka, called Voznesenskoe by the Russians, now has a Russian community—hence the Orthodox church. And where there are Russians, there is home-brewed vodka, which one could not get from the Germans, who were mainly Mennonites.

"Full steam ahead!" he said into the tube.

"Full steam ahead it is!" a muffled invisible voice answered.

"I want even more steam!"

There was silence from the engine room.

"The engine will blow," the voice said, after a moment of silence. The signal torch toppled off the mast and streamed over the rolling waves. The steamer rocked. An explosion shuddered through the hull. We flew through the darkness, straight ahead. A rocket went soaring up from the riverbank, a three-inch gun started pounding us. A shell went whistling between the masts. The galley boy, dragging a samovar across the deck, raised his head. The samovar went skidding out of his hands and rolled down the stairs, split open, and a glittering stream poured down the dirty steps. The galley boy snarled, tottered over to the stairs, and fell asleep. The deadly aroma of home-brewed vodka came pouring from his mouth. Belowdecks, among the oily cylinders, the stokers, stripped to the waist, were roaring, waving their arms, and rolling on the floor. Their twisted faces shone in the pearly gleam of the pistons. The crew of the *Ivan and Maria* was drunk. Only the helmsman stood firmly at his wheel. He turned and looked at me.

"Hey, Yid!" he called out to me. "What's going to become of the children?"

"What children?"

"The children aren't going to school," the helmsman shouted, turning the wheel. "The children will turn into thieves!"

He brought his leaden, blue cheekbones close to my face and gnashed his teeth. His jaws grated like millstones. It was as if his teeth were being ground to sand.

"I'll rip you to pieces!"

I edged away from him. Lisyei came walking across the deck.

"What's going on here, Lisyei!"

"I guess he'll get us there," the redheaded muzhik said, and sat down on a bench.

When we got to Voznesenskoe, we sent him ashore. There was no "church" to be found, no lights, no carousel. The sloping riverbank was dark, covered by a low-hanging sky. Lisyei sank into darkness. He had been away for more than an hour when he resurfaced right by the water, hauling some large cans. A pockmarked woman, as well built as a horse, was following him. The child's blouse she was wearing was much too small and stretched tightly over her breasts. A dwarf in a pointed hat and tiny little boots was standing nearby, openmouthed, watching us haul the cans on deck.

"Plum liquor," Lisyei said, putting the cans on the table. "The plummiest home brew!"

And the race of our spectral ship began once more. We arrived in Baronsk toward daybreak. The river spread out boundlessly. Water trickled off the riverbanks, leaving a blue satin shadow. A pink ray struck the mist hanging on the ragged bushes. The bleak, painted walls of the barns and their thin steeples slowly turned and floated toward us. We steamed toward Baronsk among peals of song. Seletsky had cleared his throat with a bottle of the plummiest home brew, and was singing his heart out. Mussorgsky's *Flea* was in his song, Mephistopheles' booming laughter, and the aria of the crazed miller, "I am a raven, no miller am I."

The barefoot captain lay slumped over the railing of the bridge. His head was lolling, his eyelids shut tight, and his gashed face, a vague childish smile wandering over it, was flung up toward the sky. He regained consciousness when the boat began slowing down.

"Alyosha!" he shouted into the tube. "Full steam ahead!"

And we went charging toward the pier at full steam ahead. The gangplank we had mangled as we pulled out the night before went flying into the air. The engines stopped just in time.

"You see, he brought us back," Lisyei said, turning up beside me. "And there you were, all worried."

Chapayev's machine gun carts were already lining up on the riverbank.* Rainbow stripes darkened and cooled on the bank from which the tidewaters had just ebbed. In a heap next to the pier were boxes of cartridges left by boats that had come and gone. Makeyev, the commander of one of Chapayev's squadrons, was sitting beltless on a box in a peasant shirt and a tall fur hat. Captain Korostelyov went up to him with outspread arms.

"I was a real idiot again, Kostya," he said with his childlike smile. "I used up all the fuel!"

---

*Vasili Ivanovich Chapayev, 1887–1919, was commander of the Pugachov Brigade that was fighting the counterrevolutionary troops in the area.

Makeyev was sitting sideways on the box, scraps of his fur hat hanging over the yellow, browless arches of his eyes. A Mauser with an unpainted butt was lying on his knees. Without turning around, he fired at Korostelyov, but missed.

"What can I say?" Korostelyov whispered, with wide, shining eyes. "So you're angry with me?" He spread out his thin arms farther. "What can I say?"

Makeyev jumped up, turned around, and fired all the bullets in his Mauser. The shots rang out rapidly. There was something more Korostelyov had wanted to say, but he didn't manage to. He sighed and fell to his knees. He tumbled forward onto the rim of the spoked wheel of a machine gun cart, his face shattering, milky strips of brain bespattering the wheel. Makeyev, bending forward, was trying to yank out the last bullet which was jammed in the cartridge clip.

"They thought it was a good joke!" he said, eyeing the crowd of Red Army men and the rest of us who had gathered by the gangplank.

Lisyei crouched and went sidling over to Korostelyov with a horse blanket in his hands, and covered him as he lay there like a felled tree. Random shots rang from the steamer. Chapayev's soldiers were running over the deck, arresting the crew. The pockmarked woman, her hand pressed to her cheek, stood at the railing, peering at the shore with narrow, unseeing eyes.

"I'll show you too!" Makeyev yelled up at her. "I'll teach you to waste fuel!"

The sailors were led down one by one. German settlers, trickling from their houses, came out from behind their barns. Karl Biedermayer was standing among his people. The war had come to his doorstep.

We had much work to do that day. The large village of Friedental had come to trade. A chain of camels was lying by the water. In the far distance, windmills were turning on the colorless, metallic horizon.

We loaded the Friedental grain onto our barge until suppertime, and toward evening Malishev sent for me. He was washing on the deck of the *Ivan Tupitsin*. An invalid with a pinned-up sleeve was pouring water over him from a pitcher. Malishev snorted and chuckled, holding his cheeks under the stream of water. He toweled himself off and said to his assistant, obviously continuing a conversation, "And rightly so! You can be the nicest fellow in the world, have locked yourself up in monasteries, sailed the White Sea, been a desperado—but, please, whatever you do, don't waste fuel!"

Malishev and I went into the cabin. I laid out the financial records in front of me, and Malishev started dictating to me a telegram to be sent to Ilyich.

"Moscow. The Kremlin. To Comrade Lenin."

In the telegram we reported the dispatching of the first shipments of wheat to the proletariat of Petersburg and Moscow: two trainloads, each twenty thousand *poods* of grain.

GUY DE MAUPASSANT

*I*n the winter of 1916 I found myself in Petersburg with forged
papers and without a kopeck to my name. Aleksei Kazantsev, a
teacher of Russian philology, gave me shelter.

He lived on a frozen, reeking, yellow street in Peski.* To increase
his meager income, he did Spanish translations—in those days the
fame of Blasco Ibáñez† was on the rise.

Kazantsev had never been to Spain, not even once, but his whole
being was flooded with love for the country—he knew every Spanish
castle, park, and river. Besides myself, a large number of men and
women who had fallen through the cracks of life flocked to him. We
lived in dire poverty. From time to time our pieces on current events
appeared in small print in the popular press.

In the mornings I lounged about in morgues and police stations.

But the happiest of us all was Kazantsev. He had a motherland—
Spain.

In November I was offered the position of clerk at the Obukhovsky
Factory,** not a bad job, bringing with it an exemption from conscription.

I refused to become a clerk.

---

* A poor suburb of Petersburg.
† Vicente Blasco Ibáñez, 1867–1928, was a Spanish novelist and anti-monarchist politician.
His novels, with their themes of war and social injustice, were particularly popular in Soviet
Russia.
** Steelworks founded in 1863. Its almost twelve thousand workers were to play an important
role in the Revolution.

Even in those days, at the age of twenty, I said to myself: Better to suffer hunger, prison, and homelessness than to sit at a clerk's desk ten hours a day. There is no particular daring in making such a pledge, but I haven't broken it to this day, nor will I. The wisdom of my forefathers was ingrained in me: we have been born to delight in labor, fighting, and love. That is what we have been born for, and nothing else.

Kazantsev patted the short yellow down on his head as he listened to my sermon. The horror in his eyes was mixed with rapture.

At Christmas, fortune smiled upon us. Bendersky, a lawyer who owned the Halcyon Publishing House, had decided to bring out a new edition of Maupassant's works. His wife, Raisa, was going to do the translation. But nothing had yet come of the grand enterprise.

Kazantsev, as a Spanish translator, was asked if he knew anyone who might be able to help Raisa Mikhailovna. Kazantsev suggested me.

The following day, donning another man's jacket, I set out to the Benderskys'. They lived at the corner of the Nevsky Prospekt by the Moika River, in a house built of Finnish granite trimmed with pink columns, embrasures, and stone coats of arms. Before the war, bankers without family or breeding—Jewish converts to Christianity who grew rich through trade—had built a large number of such spuriously majestic, vulgar castles in Petersburg.

A red carpet ran up the stairs. Stuffed bears on their hind legs stood on the landings. Crystal lamps shone in their wide-open jaws.

The Benderskys lived on the third floor. The door was opened by a maid in a white cap and pointed breasts. She led me into a living room, decorated in old Slavic style. Blue paintings by Roerich,* prehistoric rocks and monsters, hung on the walls. Ancient icons stood on little stands in the corners. The maid with the pointed breasts moved ceremoniously about the room. She was well built, nearsighted, haughty. Debauchery had congealed in her gray, wide-open eyes. Her movements were indolent. I thought how she must thrash about with savage agility when she made love. The brocade curtain that hung over the door swayed. A black-haired, pink-eyed woman, bearing her large

---

*Nikolai Konstantinovich Roerich, 1874–1947, was a Russian painter and popular mystic who gained international fame for the sets he designed for Diaghilev's Ballets Russes.

breasts before her, came into the living room. It took me no more than a moment to see that Benderskaya was one of those ravishing breed of Jewesses from Kiev or Poltava, from the sated towns of the steppes that abounded with acacias and chestnut trees. These women transmute the money of their resourceful husbands into the lush pink fat on their bellies, napes, and round shoulders. Their sleepy smiles, delicate and sly, drive garrison officers out of their minds.

"Maupassant is the one passion of my life," Raisa told me.

Struggling to restrain the swaying of her large hips, she left the room and came back with her translation of "Miss Harriet." The translation had no trace of Maupassant's free-flowing prose with its powerful breath of passion. Benderskaya wrote with laborious and inert correctness and lack of style—the way Jews in the past used to write Russian.

I took the manuscript home with me to Kazantsev's attic, where all night, among his sleeping friends, I cut swaths through Benderskaya's translation. This work isn't as bad as it might seem. When a phrase is born, it is both good and bad at the same time. The secret of its success rests in a crux that is barely discernible. One's fingertips must grasp the key, gently warming it. And then the key must be turned once, not twice.

• • •

The following morning I brought back the corrected manuscript. Raisa had not lied in speaking of her passion for Maupassant. She sat transfixed as I read to her, her hands clasped together. Her satin arms flowed down toward the ground, her forehead grew pale, and the lace between her struggling breasts swerved and trembled.

"How did you do this?"

I spoke to her of style, of an army of words, an army in which every type of weapon is deployed. No iron spike can pierce a human heart as icily as a period in the right place. She listened with her head inclined and her painted lips apart. A black gleam shone in her lacquered hair, parted and pulled smoothly back. Her stockinged legs, with their strong, delicate calves, were planted apart on the carpet.

The maid, turning away her eyes in which debauchery had congealed, brought in breakfast on a tray.

The glass sun of Petersburg reclined on the uneven, faded carpet. Twenty-nine books by Maupassant stood on a shelf above the table. The sun, with its melting fingers, touched the books' morocco leather bindings—the magnificent crypt of the human heart.

We were served coffee in little blue cups, and we began to translate "Idyll." Who can forget the tale of the hungry young carpenter sucking milk from the overflowing breasts of the fat wet-nurse. This took place on a train going from Nice to Marseilles, on a sultry midday in the land of roses, the motherland of roses where flower plantations stretch down to the shores of the sea.

I left the Benderskys' with a twenty-five-ruble advance. That evening our commune in Peski got as drunk as a flock of inebriated geese. We scooped up the finest caviar and chased it down with liverwurst. Heated by liquor, I began ranting against Tolstoy.

"He got frightened, our count did! He lacked courage! It was fear that made him turn to religion! Frightened of the cold, of old age, the count knitted himself a jersey out of faith!"

"Go on," Kazantsev said, wagging his birdlike head.

We fell asleep on the floor next to our beds. I dreamt of Katya, the forty-year-old washerwoman who lived on the floor beneath us. In the mornings we would go and get boiling water from her. I'd never had a good look at her face, but in my dream Katya and I did God only knows what. We consumed each other with kisses. The following morning I could not resist going down to her for boiling water.

I came face-to-face with a wilted woman, a shawl tied across her chest, with disheveled ash-gray curls and sodden hands.

* * *

From then on I breakfasted every day at the Benderskys'. In our attic we now had a new stove, herring, and chocolate. Twice Raisa drove me out to the islands.* I couldn't resist telling her about my childhood. To my own surprise, my tale sounded doleful. Her frightened sparkling eyes peered at me from under her fur hat. The reddish hairs of her eyelashes quivered mournfully.

I met Raisa's husband, a yellow-faced Jew with a bald head and a

---

* Islands of the Neva and the Bay of Finland, on which St. Petersburg was built.

lean, powerful body that always seemed poised to surge up into the air. There were rumors that he was close to Rasputin. The profits he had made from military supplies had given him the look of a madman. His eyes wandered the fabric of his reality had been rent. Raisa was embarrassed introducing her husband to new people. Because of my youth, it took me a week longer than it should have to realize this.

After the New Year, Raisa's two sisters came up from Kiev. One day I went to her house with the manuscript of "The Confession," and, not finding her there, dropped by again in the evening. They were in the dining room at the dinner table. I heard silvery neighing and the thunder of excessively jubilant men's voices. Dining is invariably boisterous in wealthy houses that lack pedigree. Their boisterousness was Jewish, with peals of thunder and melodious flourishes. Raisa came out to me in a ball gown, her back bare. Her feet tottered in wavering patent leather shoes.

"Oh, how drunk I am!" And she stretched out her arms draped in platinum chains and emerald stars.

Her body swayed like the body of a snake rising to music toward the ceiling. She shook her curly head, her rings tinkled, and suddenly she fell into an armchair with ancient Russian carving. Scars shimmered on her powdered back.

There was another explosion of women's laughter in the room next door. Out of the dining room came her sisters with their little mustaches, just as big-breasted and tall as Raisa. Their breasts were thrust forward, their black hair flowed free. Both were married to Benderskys of their own. The room filled with rambling female vivacity, the vivacity of mature women. The husbands wrapped the sisters in sealskin coats, in Orenburg shawls,* and shod them in black boots. Peering out from the snowy shields of their shawls were their burning, rouged cheeks, their marble noses, and eyes with a nearsighted Semitic sparkle. After some lively commotion, they left for the theater, where Chaliapin was appearing in *Judith*.†

· · ·

---

* Delicate lace shawls, fashionable in Russia at the time, knitted from goat wool by Orenburg Tatars.

† Chaliapin, the renowned opera singer. *Judith* is an opera by Alexander Nikolayevich Serov, 1820–1871.

"I want to work," Raisa jabbered, stretching out her bare arms. "We've lost a whole week."

She brought a bottle and two glasses from the dining room. Her breasts lay loose in the silken sack of her dress. Her nipples stiffened, the silk impeding them.

"A cherished vintage," Raisa said, pouring the wine. "A Muscatel '83. My husband will kill me when he finds out!"

I had never had any dealings with a Muscatel '83 before, and did not hesitate to empty three glasses one after the other. I was immediately wafted off to a little side street where orange flames flickered and music played.

"Oh, how drunk I am. . . . What are we going to do today?"

"Today we're doing 'L'aveu.' "

In other words, "The Confession." The hero of this tale is the sun, *le soleil de France*. Incandescent drops of sun, falling on red-haired Céleste, turned into freckles. Wine, apple cider, and the sun with its steep rays had burnished the face of Polyte, the coachman. Twice a week, Céleste drove into town to sell cream, eggs, and chickens. She paid Polyte ten sous for the ride and four to carry her basket. And on every ride Polyte winked at her and asked, "When are we going to have a bit of fun, *ma belle*?"

"What do you mean by that, Monsieur Polyte?"

"Having fun means having fun, damn it!" Polyte explained, bouncing on the seat. "A man and a woman, no need for music!"

"I don't like such jokes, Monsieur Polyte," Céleste answered, and swept her skirts, which hung over her powerful, red-stockinged calves, away from the young man.

But Polyte, the devil, kept guffawing and coughing. "We'll have fun someday, *ma belle*!" And tears of mirth trickled down his face, which was the color of rust-red blood and wine.

I drank another glass of the cherished Muscatel. Raisa clinked glasses with me.

The maid with the congealed eyes walked through the room and disappeared.

*Ce diable de Polyte** . . . Over a period of two years Céleste paid him

* "That devil Polyte."

forty-eight francs. Two francs short of fifty! One day at the end of the second year, when they were alone together in the buggy, Polyte, who had drunk some cider before they set out, asked her as usual, "How about having some fun today, Ma'mselle Céleste?"

"I'm at your service, M'sieur Polyte."

Raisa laughed out loud, slumping over the table. *Ce diable de Polyte!*

The buggy was harnessed to a white nag. The white nag, its lips pink with age, walked a slow walk. The joyful sun of France embraced the buggy, shut off from the world by a faded brown cover. The young man and the girl—they needed no music.

. . .

Raisa handed me a glass. It was the fifth.

"To Maupassant, *mon vieux!*"

"Aren't we going to have some fun today, *ma belle?*"

I reached over to Raisa and kissed her on the lips. They trembled and bulged.

"You're so funny," Raisa muttered through her teeth, tottering backward.

She pressed herself against the wall, spreading her bare arms. Blotches flared up on her arms and shoulders. Of all the gods ever crucified, she was the most captivating.

"Be so kind as to seat yourself, M'sieur Polyte."

She pointed to the reclining blue Slavic armchair. Its back was made of interlaced carved wood on which tails were painted. I stumbled toward it.

Night obstructed my youth with a bottle of Muscatel '83 and twenty-nine books, twenty-nine petards crammed with pity, genius, and passion. I jumped up, knocking over the armchair and bumping into the shelf. Twenty-nine volumes came tumbling onto the carpet, falling onto their spines, their pages flying wild . . . and the white nag of my fate walked a slow walk.

"You're so funny," Raisa growled.

I left the granite house on the Moika Canal after eleven, just before her husband and sisters came back from the theater. I was sober and could have walked a thin plank, but stumbling was far better, and I swayed from side to side, singing in a language I had just invented.

Mists of fog rolled in waves through the tunnels of streets girded with a chain of street lamps. Monsters roared behind seething walls. The carriageways cut the legs that walked over them.

Back at home Kazantsev was asleep. He slept sitting up, his haggard legs stretched out in felt boots. The canary down was fluffed up on his head. He had fallen asleep by the stove, hunched over a 1624 edition of *Don Quixote*. There was a dedication on the title page to the Duke de Broglio. I lay down quietly so as not to wake Kazantsev, pulled the lamp toward me, and began to read Édouard de Maynial's book *The Life and Works of Guy de Maupassant*.*

Kazantsev's lips moved, his head lolled forward.

• • •

That night I learned from Édouard de Maynial that Maupassant was born in 1850 to a Norman nobleman and Laure Le Poittevin, Flaubert's cousin. At twenty-five, he had his first attack of congenital syphilis. He fought the disease with all the potency and vitality he had. In the beginning, he suffered from headaches and bouts of hypochondria. Then the phantom of blindness loomed before him. His eyesight grew weaker. Paranoia, unsociability, and belligerence developed. He struggled with passion, rushed about the Mediterranean on his yacht, fled to Tunis, Morocco, and central Africa, and wrote unceasingly. Having achieved fame, he cut his throat at the age of forty, bled profusely, but lived. They locked him in a madhouse. He crawled about on all fours and ate his own excrement. The last entry in his sorrowful medical report announces: "*Monsieur de Maupassant va s'animaliser* (Monsieur de Maupassant is degenerating to an animal state)." He died at the age of forty-two. His mother outlived him.

I read the book through to the end and got up from my bed. The fog had come to the window, hiding the universe. My heart constricted. I was touched by a premonition of truth.

La vie et l'oeuvre de Guy de Maupassant was published by Société du Mercure de France in 1906.

PETROLEUM

I have a lot of news to tell you, as always. Sabsovich was given a prize at the oil refinery, walks about decked out in flashy "foreign" clothes, and has been given a promotion. When people heard about this promotion, they finally saw the light: the boy is moving up the ladder. This is the reason I stopped going out with him. "Now that he has moved up the ladder," the boy feels that he knows the truth hidden from us lesser mortals and has turned into "Comrade Perfect," so orthodox ("orthobox," as Kharchenko calls it) that you can't even talk to him anymore. When we ran into each other two days ago, he asked me why I hadn't congratulated him. I asked him whom I should congratulate, him or the Soviet government. He understood my point right away, hemmed and hawed, and said, "Well, call me sometime." But his wife was quick to pick up the scent. Yesterday I got a call. "Claudia, darling, if you need any underwear, we now have great connections at the Restricted Access Store." I told her that I was hoping to get by with my own underwear ration coupons till the outbreak of the World Revolution.

Now a few words about myself. You'll have heard by now that I am the section head at the Petroleum Syndicate. They dangled the position before me for the longest time, but I kept turning them down. My argument: no aptitude for office work, and then I also wanted to enroll at the Industrial Academy. Four times at Bureau Meetings they asked me to accept the position, so finally I had to accept. And I must say I don't regret it. From where I am I have a clear picture of the whole enterprise, and I've managed to get a thing or two done. I organized an expedition to our part of Sakhalin, stepped up the prospecting, and I deal a lot with the Petroleum Institute. Zinaida is with me. She's well. She'll be giving birth soon, and has been through quite a lot. She didn't tell her Max Alexandrovich (I call him Max-and-Moritz)* about the pregnancy until she was already in her third month. He put on a show of enthusiasm, planted an icy kiss on her forehead, and then gave her to understand that he was on the brink of a great scientific discovery, that his thoughts were far from everyday life, and that one could not imagine anyone less suited to family life than he, Max Alexandrovich Solomovich, but, needless to say, he wouldn't hesitate to sacrifice everything, etc., etc. Zinaida, being a woman of the twentieth century, burst into tears but kept her aplomb. She didn't sleep all night, gasping, her head thrashing about. The moment it was light, she put on a tattered old dress and rushed off to the Research Institute, looking dreadful, her hair in tangles. There she made a scene, begging him to forget what had happened the previous night, saying that she would destroy the child, but that she would never forgive the world—all this in the halls of the Research Institute, teeming with people! Max-and-Moritz goes bright red, then pale. "Let's discuss it on the phone, we'll get together for a chat," he mutters.

Zinaida didn't even let him finish, but rushed out and came running to me.

"I'm not coming to work tomorrow!" she told me.

I blew up, and, seeing no reason to control myself, bawled her out. Just think—she's over thirty, has no looks worth mentioning, no man worth his salt would even wipe his nose with her, and then this Max-and-Moritz fellow turns up (not that he's hot for her, he's hot for the fact that she's not Jewish and has aristocratic ancestors), she gets herself knocked up, so she might as well keep the baby and raise it. As we all know, Jewish half-castes come out quite well—just look at the specimen Ala produced. And when if not now does she intend to have a child, now when her gut muscles are still working and her breasts can still make milk? But she has only one answer to whatever I say: "I can-

* Two boys who terrorize the neighborhood with their funny practical jokes in the story in verse, *Max and Moritz,* by the German humorist Wilhelm Busch.

not bear the idea of my child growing up without a father." She tells me it's still like in the nineteenth century, "and my papa, the general, will come stalking out of his study carrying an icon and lay a curse on me (or maybe without an icon—I don't know how they used to curse back then), after which the women will take the baby to a foundling home or send it to a wet nurse in the countryside."

"Nonsense, Zinaida!" I tell her. "Times have changed, we'll make do without Max-and-Moritz!"

I was still in midsentence when I was called to a meeting. At that time the matter of Viktor Andreyevich had to be dealt with immediately. The Central Committee had decided to revoke the former Five-Year Plan and raise petroleum extraction in 1932 to forty million tons. The figures for analysis were handed to the planners, in other words to Viktor Andreyevich. He locks himself in his office, then calls me over and shows me his letter. Addressed to the Presidium of the Supreme National Economic Council. Contents: I hereby renounce all responsibility for the planning department. I consider the figure of forty million tons to be wholly unjustified. We're supposed to get more than a third of it from unprospected regions, which is like selling a bearskin not only before you've actually killed the bear, but even before you've tracked it down! Furthermore, from three oil refineries functioning today the new plan expects us to have a hundred and twenty up and running by the end of the Five-Year Plan. And all this with a shortage of metal and the fact that we have not yet mastered the extremely complex refinery system. And this is how he ended the letter: Like all mortals, I prefer to support accelerated production quotas, but my sense of duty, and so on and so forth. I read his letter to the end.

So then he asks me: "Should I send it, or not?"

And I tell him: "Viktor Andreyevich! I find your arguments and attitude completely unacceptable, but I do not see myself as having the right to advise you to hide your views."

So he sent the letter. The Supreme National Economic Council's hair stood on end. They called a meeting. Bagrinovsky himself came from the council. They hung a map of the Soviet Union on the wall, pinpointing new deposits and pipelines for crude and refined oil. "A country with fresh blood in its veins," Bagrinovsky called it.

At the meeting the young engineers of the "omnivore" type wanted to make a meal of Viktor Andréyevich. I stepped forward and gave a forty-five-minute speech: "Though I do not doubt the knowledge and good will of Professor Klossovsky, and even have the utmost respect for him, I spurn the fetishism of numbers that is holding him captive!" That was the gist of my argument.

"We must reject our multiplication tables as guidelines for governmental wisdom. Would it have been possible to foretell on the basis of mere figures that we were going to manage to fulfill our five-year crude-oil quarrying quota within just two and a half years? Would it have been possible to foretell on the basis of mere figures that by 1931 we would have increased the bulk of our oil export by nine times, putting us in second place after the United States?"

Muradyan got up and spoke after me, attacking the route of the oil pipeline from the Caspian Sea to Moscow. Viktor Andréyevich sat in silence, taking notes. His cheeks were covered with an old man's flush, a flush of venous blood. I felt sorry for him. I didn't stay to the end and went back to my office. Zinaida was still sitting there with clasped hands.

"Are you going to give birth or not?" I asked her.

She looked at me with unseeing eyes, her head shaking, and said something, but the words were soundless.

"I'm all alone with my sorrow, Claudia, as if they've just nailed my coffin shut," she tells me. "How quickly one forgets—I can't even remember how people live without sorrow."

That's what she said to me, her nose turning red and growing even longer, her peasant cheekbones (yes, some aristocrats do have them!) jutting out. I doubt Max-and-Moritz would get all fired up seeing you like that, I think to myself. I started yelling at her, and chased her off to the kitchen to peel potatoes. Don't laugh—when *you* come here, I'll have you peeling potatoes too! We were given such a stringent time frame for designing the Orsky factory that the construction crew and the draftsmen are working night and day, and Vasyona cooks them potatoes and herring and makes them omelets, and off they go to work again.

So off she went to the kitchen, and a minute later I heard a scream. I run—Zinaida is lying on the floor without a pulse, her eyes rolled up. I cannot even begin to tell you what she put us through—Viktor

Andreyevich, Vasyona, and me! We called in the doctor. She regained consciousness at night and touched my hand. You know Zinaida, how incredibly tender she can be. I could see that everything inside her had burned out and something new was about to well up. There was no time to lose.

"Zinusha," I tell her, "we'll call Rosa Mikhailovna (she's still our main specialist in these matters) and tell her that you've had second thoughts, that you won't go and see her. Can I call her?"

She made a sign—yes go ahead, you can. Viktor Andreyevich was sitting next to her on the sofa, taking her pulse incessantly. I walked away, but listened to what he said to her. "I'm sixty-five, Zinusha," he told her, "my shadow falls more and more weakly on the ground before me. I am an elderly, learned man, and God (God does have His hand in everything), God willed that the final five years of my life are to coincide with this—well, you know what I mean—this Five-Year Plan. So now I won't get a chance to have a breather or a quiet moment till the day I die. If my daughter didn't come to me in the evenings to pat me on the back, if my sons didn't write me letters, I would be unhappier than words could say. Have the baby, Zinusha, and Claudia Pavlovna and I will help raise it."

While the old man goes on mumbling, I call Rosa Mikhailovna—well, my dear Rosa Mikhailovna, I tell her, I know Zinaida promised to come see you tomorrow, but she's reconsidered. And I hear Rosa's sprightly voice on the phone: "Oh, I'm so happy she's reconsidered! That's absolutely marvelous!" Our specialist is always like this. Pink silk blouse, English skirt, hair neatly curled, showers, exercise, admirers.

We took Zinaida home. I tucked her in bed, made tea. We slept in each other's arms, we even cried, remembered things best forgotten, talked everything through, our tears mingling, until we fell asleep. All the while my "old devil" was sitting nice and quiet at his desk translating a German technical book. Dasha, you wouldn't recognize my "old devil"—he's all shriveled up, has run out of steam and become quiet. It really upsets me. He spends the whole day working himself to death on the Five-Year Plan, and then at night he does translations.

"Zinaida will have the baby," I tell him. "What shall we call the boy?" (It's definitely not going to be a girl.) We decided on Ivan. There are far too many Yuris and Leonids about the place. He'll most probably be a beast of a little boy, with sharp teeth, with teeth enough for sixty men. We've produced enough fuel for him, he'll be able to go on drives with young ladies to Yalta, to Batumi, while we've had to make do with the Vorobyovi Hills.* Good-bye, Dasha. My "old devil" will write you separately. How are things with you?

CLAUDIA.

P.S. I'm scribbling this at work, there's a great racket overhead, the plaster is falling from the ceiling. Our building still seems strong enough, and we're adding another four stories to the four that we have. Moscow is all dug up and full of trenches, pipes and bricks everywhere, a tangle of tram lines, machines imported from abroad are banging, rumbling, swinging their cranes, there's the stench of pitch, and there's smoke everywhere, like at a wildfire. Yesterday on Varvarskaya Square I saw a young man with sandals on his bare feet, his red, shaven head shining and his peasant shirt without a belt. He and I went hopping from one little mound to another, from one earth pile to another, climbing out of holes, falling back into them again.

"This is what it's like once a battle has begun," he tells me. "Moscow has now become the front, lady, Moscow is at the heart of the battle!"

He had a kind face, smiling like a child. I can still picture him before me.

* A Moscow neighborhood.

DANTE STREET

*T*he Hotel Danton, where I was staying, was rattled to its foundations by moans of love from five until seven in the evening. Experts were at work in the rooms. Having arrived in France with the conviction that its people had lost their spark, I was somewhat taken aback by their vigor. In our country, we do not bring women to such a boiling pitch. Nowhere near it.

"*Mon vieux,*" Monsieur Bienalle, my neighbor, once told me, "in our thousand years of history we have created woman, food, and literature. No one can deny this."

Jean Bienalle, a secondhand car dealer, did more for my knowledge of France than all the books I had read and all the French towns I had seen. The first time we met he asked me which restaurant I ate at, what café I went to, and which brothel I frequented. My answer appalled him.

"*On va refaire votre vie!*"*

And the changes were undertaken. We ate lunch at a tavern across the street from the Halles aux vins, frequented by cattle dealers and wine merchants.

Village girls in slippers served us lobster in red sauce, roast rabbit stuffed with garlic and truffles, and wine you could find nowhere else. Bienalle ordered, I paid, but I only paid as much as the French paid. It wasn't cheap, but it wasn't the foreigner's price. And I also paid the

* "We shall change your ways!"

Frenchman's price at the brothel funded by a group of senators next to the Gare St. Lazare. Bienalle had to put more effort into introducing me to the inmates of that house than if he had attempted to introduce me to a session of Parliament while a cabinet is being overthrown. We capped off the evening at the Porte Maillot at a café where boxing promoters and race car drivers gathered. My tutor belonged to the half of the nation that sells cars. The other half buys them. He was an agent for Renault and did most of his trade with the Balkans, those most ambiguous of countries, and with Rumanian speculators, the dirtiest of speculators. In his free time Bienalle taught me the art of buying a used car. According to him, one had to go down to the Riviera toward the end of the season, when the English were leaving for home, abandoning in local garages cars they had only used for two or three months. Bienalle himself drove a dilapidated Renault, which he drove the way a Siberian tribesman drives his sled dogs. On Sundays we drove 120 kilometers to Rouen in his bouncing vehicle to eat duck, which the locals there roast in its own blood. We were accompanied by Germaine, who sold gloves on Rue Royale. She spent every Wednesday and Sunday with Bienalle. She always came at five o'clock. Within seconds their room echoed with growls, the thud of tumbling bodies, frightened gasps, after which the woman's tender death throes began: "Oh, Jean . . ."

I added it all up: Germaine went into his room, closed the door behind her, they gave each other a kiss, she took off her hat and gloves, laid them on the table, and, according to my calculations, that was all there was time for. He wouldn't even have had time to undress. Not uttering a word, they bounced about like rabbits between the sheets. They moaned for a while, and then burst out laughing and chatted about everyday things. I knew as much as any neighbor living on the other side of a thin board partition. Germaine was having trouble with Monsieur Heinrich, the store manager. Her parents lived in Tours, where she visited them. On one Saturday she bought herself a fur wrap, on another she went to see *La Bohème* at the opera. Monsieur Heinrich had his saleswomen wear tailored dress suits. Monsieur Heinrich anglicized Germaine, turning her into one of those brisk, flat-chested, curly-haired businesswomen painted with flaming, brownish rouge. But her fine chunky ankles, her low, nimble laugh, the sharp gaze of her sparkling eyes, and that death-throe moan— "Oh, Jean!"—were all left untouched for Bienalle.

Germaine's powerful, lithe body moved before us in the smoke and gold of the Paris evening. She laughed, throwing back her head and pressing her delicate pink fingers to her breasts. My heart glowed during these hours. There is no solitude more desperate than solitude in Paris. This town is a form of exile for all who come to it from far away, and I realized that Germaine was more important to me than she was to Bienalle. I left for Marseilles with this thought in mind.

After a month in Marseilles, I returned to Paris. I waited for Wednesday to hear Germaine's voice.

Wednesday came and went, but nobody disturbed the silence of the room next door. Bienalle had changed his day. A woman's voice rang out on Thursday, at five o'clock as always. Bienalle gave his visitor time to take off her hat and gloves. Germaine had not only changed her day, she had also changed her voice. It was no longer the gasping, imploring "Oh, Jean!" followed by silence, the harsh silence of another person's happiness; it had turned into a hoarse domestic clamor with guttural exclamations. The new Germaine gnashed her teeth, flung herself heavily onto the sofa, and during the interludes pontificated in her thick, dragging voice. She said nothing about Monsieur Heinrich, growled until seven o'clock, and then got ready to go. I opened the door a crack to say hello to her, but saw a mulatto woman in the corridor with a cockscomb of horselike hair and large, dangling, hoisted-up breasts. She was coming down the corridor, her feet shuffling in worn-out shoes with no heels. I knocked on Bienalle's door. He was lolling about in bed in his shirt and washed-out socks, ashen and crumpled.

"So, *mon vieux,* you've pensioned off Germaine?"

"*Cette femme est folle,*"* he said with a shudder. "Mademoiselle Germaine does not care that on this earth there is winter and summer, a beginning and an end, and that after winter comes summer and then the opposite. She heaves a heavy burden on you and demands that you carry it—but where to, nobody but Mademoiselle Germaine knows!"

Bienalle sat up in bed. His trousers stretched over his thin legs. His pale scalp shimmered through his matted hair, and his triangular mustache twitched. A bottle of Macon, four francs a liter, lifted my friend's spirits again. As we waited for our dessert, he shrugged his shoulders

* "That woman is mad."

and said as if in answer to my thoughts, "There's more than everlasting love in this world—there are Rumanians, promissory notes, men who go bankrupt, cars with broken chassis. *Oh, j'en ai plein le dos!*"*

He grew more cheerful over a cognac at the Café de Paris. We sat on the terrace under a white awning with wide stripes running down it. The crowd streamed past over the sidewalk, blending with the electric stars. A car, long as a torpedo, stopped across the street from us. From it emerged an Englishman with a woman in a sable wrap. She sailed past in a cloud of perfume and fur, inhumanly long with a small, shining head of porcelain. Bienalle sat up when he saw her, stretched out his leg in his tattered trousers, and winked at her the way one winks at the girls on the rue de la Gaîté. The woman smiled with the corner of her carmine mouth, gave a barely visible nod with her tightly wrapped pink head, and, swinging and swaying her serpentine body, disappeared, with the stiff, crackling Englishman in tow.

"*Ah, canaille!*"† Bienalle said after them. "Two years ago anyone could have had her for an aperitif."

The two of us parted late. I had decided that I would go see Germaine that Saturday, take her to the theater, go to Chartres with her if she was in the mood. But as things turned out, I was to see Bienalle and his former girlfriend before then. The following evening, all the doors of the Hotel Danton were cordoned off by the police, their blue capes swirling through our vestibule. They let me go up after they verified that I was one of Madame Truffaut's lodgers. I found policemen standing outside my room. The door to Bienalle's room stood open. He was lying on the floor in a pool of blood, his lusterless eyes half closed. The stamp of street death was upon him. My friend Bienalle had been stabbed, stabbed to death. Germaine was sitting at the table in her tailored dress suit and her delicate, close-fitting hat. She greeted me and hung her head, and with it the feather on her hat hung too.

All this took place at six in the evening, the hour of love. There was a woman in every room. They hastily applied rouge and drew black lines along the edges of their lips before leaving half dressed, with stockings up to their thighs like pageboys. Doors opened and

* "Oh, I've had it up to here!"
† "Ah, the bitch!"

men with untied shoes lined up in the corridor. In the room of a wrinkled Italian racing cyclist a barefoot little girl was crying into the pillow. I went downstairs to tell Madame Truffaut. The girl's mother sold newspapers on the Rue St. Michel. All the old women of our street, the Rue Dante, misshapen piles of goiterous meat, whiskered, wheezing, with cataracts and purple blotches, had already gathered in the little office: market women, concierges, sellers of roasted chestnuts and potatoes.

"*Voilà qui n'est pas gai,*" I said as I went in. "*Quel malheur!*"*

"*C'est l'amour, monsieur. . . . Elle l'aimait.*"†

Madame Truffaut's lilac breasts tumbled in her lace blouse, her elephantine legs strode through the room, her eyes flashed.

"*L'amore!*" Signora Rocca, who ran a restaurant on Rue Dante, called out from behind her like an echo. "*Dio castiga quelli, chi non conoscono l'amore!*"**

The old women huddled together, all muttering at the same time. A variolar flame lit their cheeks, their eyes bulging out of their sockets.

"*L'amour,*" Madame Truffaut repeated, hobbling toward me. "*C'est une grosse affaire, l'amour!*"‡

A siren sounded in the street. Skillful hands dragged the murdered man downstairs and out to the ambulance. My friend Bienalle had turned into a mere number, losing his name in the rolling waves of Paris. Signora Rocca went over to the window and looked out at the corpse. She was pregnant, her belly jutting out threateningly. Silk lay on her protruding hips, and the sun washed over her yellow, puffy face and soft yellow hair.

"*Dio,*" Signora Rocca said. "*Tu non perdoni quelli, chi non amano!*"***

Dusk descended on the tattered net of the Latin quarter, the squat crowd scuttling into its crevices, a hot breath of garlic pouring from its yards. Darkness covered the house of Madame Truffaut, its gothic facade with its two windows, and the remnants of turrets and volutes, ivy turned to stone.

---

* "Well, this isn't very cheerful. How dreadful!"
† "It is love, monsieur. . . .She loved him."
** "Love! God punishes those who do not know love!"
‡ "Love is a nasty business!"
*** "God, you do not forgive those who do not love!"

Danton had lived here a century and a half ago. From his window he had seen the Conciergerie, the bridges strewn across the Seine, and the same cluster of little blind hovels huddling by the river. The same breath had wafted up to him. Rusty beams and signs of wayside inns had creaked, rattled by the wind.

DI GRASSO

I was fourteen years old. I belonged to the fearless battalion of theater ticket scalpers. My boss was a shark with an eye that always squinted and a large, silky mustache. His name was Kolya Shvarts. I fell in with him that dark year when the Italian Opera went bust. The impresario, swayed by the theater critics, had not signed up Anselmi and Tito Ruffo as guest stars, concentrating instead on a strong ensemble. He was punished for this, went broke, and so did we. To set things right, we were promised Chaliapin, but Chaliapin wanted three thousand a performance. So Di Grasso, the Sicilian tragic actor, came with his troupe instead. They were taken to their hotel in carts loaded with children, cats, and cages in which Italian birds fluttered.

"We can't push this merchandise!" Kolya Shvarts said when he saw the motley procession rolling in.

The moment the actor arrived, he went down to the bazaar with his bag. In the evening, carrying a different bag, he turned up at the theater. Barely fifty people came to the premiere. We hawked tickets at half price, but could find no buyers.

That evening Di Grasso's troupe performed a Sicilian folk drama, with a plot as humdrum as night and day. The daughter of a rich peasant became engaged to a shepherd. She was true to him, until one day the squire's son came visiting from town in a velvet vest. The girl chatted with the visitor, tongue-tied and giggling at all the wrong moments. Listening to them, the shepherd darted his head about like a startled bird. Throughout the whole first act he crept along walls, went off somewhere in his fluttering trousers, and then came back again, looking around shiftily.

"We have a turkey on our hands!" Kolya Shvarts said during the intermission. "This is merchandise for Kremenchug, not Odessa!"

The intermission gave the girl time to prime herself for the betrayal. In the second act she was unrecognizable. She became intolerant and dreamy, and eagerly gave back the engagement ring to the shepherd. The shepherd led her to a tawdry painted statue of the Holy Virgin.

"Signorina! It is the Holy Virgin's will that you hear me out!" he said in a bass voice in Sicilian dialect, turning away from her. "The Holy Virgin will give Giovanni, the visitor from town, as many women as he wills. But I, Signorina, need nobody but you! The Virgin Mary, our Immaculate Protectress, will tell you the same thing if you ask her."

The girl stood with her back to the painted wooden statue. As the shepherd talked, she tapped her foot impatiently. On this earth—oh, woe to us!—there isn't a woman who is not gripped by folly at the very moment when her fate is being decided. A woman is alone at such moments, with no Holy Virgin she can appeal to.

In the third act, Giovanni, the visitor from town, met his fate. The village barber was shaving Giovanni as he sat with his powerful masculine legs sprawled out over the proscenium. The pleats of his vest shone beneath the Sicilian sun. The stage set portrayed a village fair. The shepherd stood in the far corner. He stood there silently, among the carefree crowd. He hung his head, then raised it, and under the weight of his burning, fixed gaze, Giovanni began to fidget and squirm in his chair. He jumped up and pushed the barber away. In a cracking voice Giovanni demanded that the policeman remove all shady and suspicious-looking people from the village square. The shepherd—played by Di Grasso—hesitated for a moment, then smiled, soared into the air, flew over the stage of the Odessa City Theater, alighted on Giovanni's shoulders, and sunk his teeth into his neck. Muttering and squinting at the audience, he sucked the blood from the wound. Giovanni fell to the ground and the curtain came down in menacing silence, hiding the murderer and the murdered man. Not wasting a single moment, we rushed off to Theater Alley, Kolya Shvarts leading the pack. The box office was already selling tickets for the following day. Next morning the *Odessa News* informed the few people who had been at the performance that they had seen the most incredible actor of the century.

During his Odessa performances, Di Grasso was to play *King Lear, Othello, Civil Death,* and Turgenev's *Parasite,* convincing us with every word and movement that there was more justice and hope in the frenzy of noble passion than in the joyless rules of the world.

The tickets for these performances sold at five times their price. The public in its frantic quest for tickets ran to the taverns, where they found howling, red-faced scalpers spouting innocent blasphemies.

A stream of dusty pink heat poured into Theater Alley. Storekeepers in felt slippers brought green bottles of wine and casks of olives out onto the street. Macaroni was boiling in foaming water in cauldrons in front of stores, the steam melting into the distant skies. Old women in men's boots sold cockleshells and souvenirs, chasing wavering customers with their loud yells. Rich Jews, their beards combed and parted, rode in carriages to the Hotel Severnaya, and knocked discreetly at the doors of fat, black-haired women with mustaches—the actresses of Di Grasso's troupe. Everyone in Theater Alley was happy, except for one person, and that person was me. Disaster was hovering over me. It was only a matter of time before my father would realize that I had taken his watch and pawned it with Kolya Shvarts. Kolya had had enough time now to get used to the idea that the gold watch was his, and as he was a man who drank Bessarabian wine instead of tea at breakfast, he could not bring himself to return the watch, even though I had paid him back his money. That was the kind of person he was. His personality was exactly like my father's. Caught between these two men, I watched the hoops of other people's happiness roll past me. I had no choice but to escape to Constantinople. Everything had already been arranged with the second engineer of a steamer, *The Duke of Kent,* but before setting out to sea, I decided to bid Di Grasso farewell. He was to appear one last time in the role of the shepherd whisked into the air by an otherworldly force. Odessa's whole Italian colony had come to the theater, led by the trim, bald-headed consul, followed by fidgety Greeks and bearded externs staring fanatically at a point invisible to all. Long-armed Utochkin* was also there.

---

*Sergei Isayevich Utochkin, 1874–1916, an aviation pioneer, was a prominent and dashing Odessan figure.

Kolya Shvarts even brought his wife in her fringed, violet shawl, a woman as robust as a grenadier and as drawn-out as a steppe, with a crinkled, sleepy face peeking out at its borderland. Her face was drenched with tears as the curtain fell.

"You no-good wretch!" she shouted at Kolya as they left the theater. "Now you know what *real* love is!"

With mannish steps Madame Shvarts plodded heavily down Langeron Street, tears trickling from her fishlike eyes, her fringed shawl shuddering on her fat shoulders. Her head shaking, she yelled out for the whole street to hear a list of women who lived happily with their husbands. "Sugar puff—that's what those husbands call their wives! Sweetie pie! Baby cakes!"

Kolya walked meekly next to his wife, quietly blowing into his silky mustache. Out of habit, I walked behind them. I was sobbing. Catching her breath for a second, Madame Shvarts heard me crying and turned around.

"You no-good wretch!" she shouted at her husband, her fishlike eyes widening. "May I not live to see another happy hour if you don't give that boy back his watch!"

Kolya froze, his mouth falling open, but then he came to his senses, and, pinching me hard, shoved the watch into my hands.

"What does he give me?" Madame Shvarts's rough, tearful voice lamented, as it receded into the distance. "Low-down tricks today, low-down tricks tomorrow! I ask you, you no-good wretch, how long can a woman wait?"

They walked to the corner and turned onto Pushkin Street. I stayed back, clutching my watch, and suddenly, with a clarity I had never before experienced, I saw the soaring columns of the Town Council, the illuminated leaves on the boulevard, and Pushkin's bronze head with the moon's pale reflection on it. For the first time I saw everything around me as it really was—hushed and beautiful beyond description.

SULAK

*G*ulay's outfit had been crushed in the province of Vinnitsa in 1922.* His chief of staff was Adrian Sulak, a village schoolmaster. Sulak managed to cross the border into Galicia, and shortly thereafter the newspapers reported his death. Six years later, we found out that Sulak was alive, hiding in the Ukraine. Chernishov and I were commissioned to track him down. We set out for Khoshchevatoye, Sulak's village, with papers in our pockets saying that we were livestock specialists. The chairman of the village council turned out to be a demobilized Red Army man, a good, straightforward fellow.

"You'll be lucky if you can get your hands on a jug of milk in this place," he told us. "Here in Khoshchevatoye they chew people up, skin and bone!"

Chernishov asked him where we could spend the night, bringing the conversation around to Sulak's hut.

"Yes, that's an idea," the chairman said. "His widow's living there now."

He took us over to the edge of the village, to a house with a corrugated iron roof. Inside we found a dwarf in a loose white blouse sitting in front of a pile of sackcloth. Two boys in orphanage jackets sat with their heads bowed over books. A baby with a bloated white head lay asleep in a cradle. A cold monastic cleanliness lay over everything.

---

* General Diomid Gulay was the leader of the Ukrainian Liberation Movement. Vinnitsa is a province in west-central Ukraine.

"Kharitina Terentevna," the chairman said hesitantly. "I want to put these good people up with you."

The woman showed us the room and went back to her pile of sackcloth.

"This widow won't turn you away," the chairman told us when we were outside. "She's in a bind."

Looking around, he confided to us that Sulak had served with the Ukrainian nationalists, but had now gone over to the Pope of Rome.*

"What? The husband's with the Pope of Rome and the wife has a child a year?"

"That's life," the chairman said. He saw a horseshoe on the road and picked it up. "Don't be fooled just because the widow is a dwarf—she's got milk enough for five. Even other women come over for her milk."

At home the chairman fried some eggs with lard, and brought out some vodka. He got drunk, and climbed up onto the bench above the stove to go to sleep. We heard whispering and a child crying.

"Hannochka, I promise I will," our host whispered. "I promise I'll go see the schoolmistress tomorrow."

"Quiet up there!" shouted Chernishov, lying next to me. "We want to get some sleep!"

The bedraggled chairman peered over the edge of the stove bench. His shirt collar was unbuttoned and his bare feet hung down.

"The schoolmistress handed out some bunnies for breeding at school," he said apologetically. "She gave us a she-bunny, but no he-bunny. So there was the she-bunny, and then come spring, that's life, she hops off to the woods!"

"Hannochka!" the chairman suddenly shouted, turning to the girl. "I'll go to the schoolmistress tomorrow and I'll bring you a pair, and we'll make a cage for them!"

Father and daughter went on talking for a long time on the stove bench, and he kept shouting, "Hannochka!" Then he fell asleep. Next to me, Chernishov was tossing and turning in the hay.

"Let's go there now," he said.

---

* By the Pope of Rome he means the Polish partisans, who were Catholic, unlike the Ukrainian partisans, who were Russian Orthodox.

We got up. The moon shone in the clean, cloudless sky. The puddles were covered by spring ice. Bare cornstalks stood in Sulak's garden, which was overgrown with weeds and filled with scrap iron. A stable stood next to the garden. We heard a rustling noise coming from it, and a light shimmered through the cracks in the boards. Chernishov crept to the stable door, rammed it with his shoulder, and the lock gave way. We went inside and saw an open pit in the middle of the stable, with a man sitting at the bottom. At the edge of the pit stood the dwarf in her white blouse, a bowl of borscht in her hands.

"Hello, Adrian," Chernishov said. "Getting a bite to eat, are you?"

The dwarf dropped the bowl and hurled herself onto me, biting my hand. Her teeth were locked and she moaned and shook. A gunshot came from the pit.

"Adrian!" Chernishov shouted, jumping back. "We want to take you alive!"

Sulak struggled with the bolt of his gun at the bottom of the pit. The bolt clicked.

"I've been talking to you as a person," Chernishov said, and fired.

Sulak fell against the yellow, planed wall, scraping at it, blood flowing from his mouth and ears, and collapsed.

Chernishov stood guard. I ran to fetch the chairman. We took the dead man away that same night. Sulak's sons walked next to Chernishov along the wet, dimly shimmering road. The dead man's feet in Polish shoes with reinforced soles jutted out from the back of the cart. The dwarf sat stiffly by her husband's head. Her face, distorted by little bones, looked metallic in the dimming light of the moon. The baby slept on her tiny knees.

"Full of milk!" Chernishov suddenly said, as he marched down the road. "I'll show you milk!"

THE TRIAL

Madame Blanchard, a sixty-one-year-old woman, met Ivan Nedachin, a former lieutenant colonel, in a café on the Boulevard des Italiens. They fell in love. Their love was more a matter of sensuality than common sense. Within three months the lieutenant colonel had disappeared with Madame Blanchard's stocks and the jewelry she had given him to be appraised by a jeweler on the Rue de la Paix.

"*Accès de folie passagère*,"* the doctor diagnosed Madame Blanchard's ensuing fit.

Regaining consciousness, the old woman confessed everything to her daughter-in-law. Her daughter-in-law went to the police. Nedachin was arrested in a wine cellar in Montparnasse where Moscow gypsies sang. In prison Nedachin turned yellow and flabby. He was tried in chamber number fourteen of the criminal court. First there was a case involving an automobile matter, followed by the case of sixteen-year-old Raymond Lepique, who had shot his girlfriend out of jealousy. The lieutenant colonel came after the boy. The gendarme pushed him out into the light, as a bear is pushed into a circus arena. Frenchmen in badly sewn jackets were shouting loudly at each other, and submissively rouged women fanned their teary faces. In front of them, on the podium beneath the republic's marble coat of arms, sat a red-cheeked man with a Gallic mustache, wearing a toga and a little hat.

* "A fit of temporary insanity."

"*Eh bien, Nedachin*," he said, on seeing the accused man, "*eh bien, mon ami.*" And his fast burred speech washed over the shuddering lieutenant colonel.

"As a descendant of the noble line of the Nedachins," the presiding judge loudly proclaimed, "you, my friend, are listed in the heraldic books of the province of Tambov. An officer of the Czar's army, you immigrated with Wrangel* and became a policeman in Zagreb. Discrepancies in the question of what was government property and what was private property," the presiding judge continued sonorously, the tips of his patent leather shoes darting in and out under the hem of his gown. "These discrepancies, my friend, forced you to bid the hospitable kingdom of Yugoslavia farewell and set your sights on Paris."

"In Paris,"—here the judge ran his eyes over some papers lying before him—"in Paris, my friend, the taxi driver test proved a fortress you could not conquer, at which point you concentrated all the powers left to you on Madame Blanchard, who is absent from this hearing."

The foreign words poured over Nedachin like a summer shower. He towered over the crowd—helpless, large, with dangling arms—like an animal from another world.

"*Voyons,*"† the presiding judge said unexpectedly. "From where I am sitting, I can see the daughter-in-law of the esteemed Madame Blanchard.

A fat, neckless woman, looking like a fish jammed into a frock coat, hurried with lowered head over to the witness box. Panting, lifting her short little arms to heaven, she began listing the stocks stolen from Madame Blanchard.

"Thank you very much, madame," the presiding judge interrupted her, nodding to a gaunt man with a well-bred, sunken face, who was sitting next to him.

The public prosecutor, rising slightly, muttered a few words and sat down again, clasping his hands. He was followed by the defense attorney, a naturalized Kiev Jew, who ranted about the Golgotha of the Russian military officers in an offended tone, as if he were in the mid-

---

* Baron Peter Nikolayevich Wrangel, 1878–1928, commander of the White anti-Bolshevik army, was forced to evacuate 150,000 soldiers and civilians by sea from the Crimea to Constantinople in November 1920, which marked the end of the Russian Civil War.
† "Let's see."

dle of an argument. Incomprehensibly pronounced French words came sputtering out of his mouth, sounding increasingly Yiddish toward the end of his speech. The presiding judge peered blankly at the attorney for a few moments without saying a word, and then suddenly lunged to the side—toward the gaunt old man in the toga and the little hat—then lunged to the other side, to another old man just like the first.

"Ten years, my friend," the presiding judge said meekly, nodding his head at Nedachin, and hurriedly grabbed the papers for the next case, which his secretary slid over to him.

Nedachin stood rigidly to attention. His colorless eyes blinked, his small forehead was covered with sweat.

"*T'a encaissé dix ans,*" the gendarme behind him said. "*C'est fini, mon vieux.*"* And, quietly pushing the crowd out of the way, the gendarme led the convicted man toward the exit.

---

* "He's locked you up for ten years. It's over, old boy."

MY FIRST FEE

To be in Tiflis in spring, to be twenty years old, and not to be loved—that is a misfortune. Such a misfortune befell me. I was working as a proofreader for the printing press of the Caucasus Military District. The Kura River bubbled beneath the windows of my attic. The sun in the morning, rising from behind the mountains, lit up the river's murky knots. I was renting a room in the attic from a newlywed Georgian couple. My landlord was a butcher at the Eastern Bazaar. In the room next door, the butcher and his wife, in the grip of love, thrashed about like two large fish trapped in a jar. The tails of these crazed fish thumped against the partition, rocking the whole attic, which was blackened by the piercing sun, ripping it from its rafters and whisking it off to eternity. They could not part their teeth, clenched in the obstinate fury of passion. In the mornings, Milyet, the young bride, went out to get bread. She was so weak that she had to hold on to the banister. Her delicate little foot searched for each step, and there was a vague blind smile on her lips, like that of a woman recovering from a long illness. Laying her palm on her small breasts, she bowed to everyone she met in the street—the Assyrian grown green with age, the kerosene seller, and the market shrews with faces gashed by fiery wrinkles, who were selling hanks of sheep's wool. At night the thumping and babbling of my neighbors was followed by a silence as piercing as the whistle of a cannonball.

To be twenty years old, to live in Tiflis, and to listen at night to the tempests of other people's silence—that is a misfortune. To escape it, I ran out of the house and down to the Kura River, where I was over-powered by the bathhouse steam of Tiflis springtime. It swept over me, sapping my strength. I roamed through the hunchbacked streets, my throat parched. A fog of springtime sultriness chased me back to my attic, to that forest of blackened stumps lit by the moon. I had no choice but to look for love. Needless to say, I found it. For better or worse, the woman I chose turned out to be a prostitute. Her name was Vera. Every evening I went creeping after her along Golovinsky Boulevard, unable to work up the courage to talk to her. I had neither money for her nor words—those dull and ceaselessly burrowing words of love. Since child-hood, I had invested every drop of my strength in creating tales, plays, and thousands of stories. They lay on my heart like a toad on a stone. Possessed by demonic pride, I did not want to write them down too soon. I felt that it was pointless to write worse than Tolstoy. My stories were destined to survive oblivion. Dauntless thought and grueling pas-sion are only worth the effort spent on them when they are draped in beautiful raiment. But how does one sew such raiment?

A man who is caught in the noose of an idea and lulled by its ser-pentine gaze finds it difficult to bubble over with meaningless, burrow-ing words of love. Such a man is ashamed of shedding tears of sadness. He is not quick-witted enough to be able to laugh with happiness. I was a dreamer, and did not have the knack for the thoughtless art of happiness. Therefore I was going to have to give Vera ten rubles of my meager earnings.

I made up my mind and went to stand watch outside the doors of the Simpatia tavern. Georgian princes in blue Circassian jackets and soft leather boots sauntered past in casual parade. They picked their teeth with silver toothpicks and eyed the carmine-painted Georgian women with large feet and slim hips. There was a shimmer of turquoise in the twilight. The blossoming acacias howled along the streets in their petal-shedding bass voices. Waves of officials in white coats rolled along the boulevard. Balsamic streams of air came flowing toward them from the Karzbek Mountains.

Vera came later, as darkness was falling. Tall, her face a radiant white, she hovered before the apish crowd, as the Mother of God hov-ers before the prow of a fishing boat. She came up to the doors of the Simpatia. I hesitated, then followed her.

"Off to Palestine?"

Vera's wide, pink back was moving in front of me. She turned around.

"What?"

She frowned, but her eyes were laughing.

"Where does your path take you?"

The words crackled in my mouth like dry firewood. Vera came over and walked in step with me.

"A tenner—would that be fine with you?"

I agreed so quickly that she became suspicious.

"You sure you have ten rubles?"

We went through the gates and I handed her my wallet. She opened it and counted twenty-one rubles, narrowing her gray eyes and moving her lips. She rearranged the coins, sorting gold with gold and silver with silver.

"Give me ten," Vera said, handing me back my wallet. "We'll spend five, and the rest you can keep to get by. When's your next payday?"

I told her that I would get paid again in four days. We went back into the street. Vera took me by the arm and leaned her shoulder against mine. We walked up the cooling street. The sidewalk was covered with wilted vegetables.

"I'd love to be in Borzhom right now in this heat," she said.

Vera's hair was tied with a ribbon. The lightning of the street lamps flashed and bounced off it.

"So hightail it to Borzhom!"

That's what I said—"hightail it." For some reason, that's the expression I used.

"No dough," Vera answered with a yawn, forgetting all about me. She forgot all about me because her day was over and she had made easy money off me. She knew that I wouldn't call the police, and that I wasn't going to steal her money along with her earrings during the night.

We went to the foot of St. David's Mountain. There, in a tavern, I ordered some kebabs. Without waiting for our food to be brought, Vera went and sat with a group of old Persian men who were discussing business. They were leaning on propped-up sticks, wagging their olive-colored heads, telling the tavern keeper that it was time for him to expand his trade. Vera barged into their conversation, taking the side of the old men. She was for the idea of moving the tavern to Mikhailovsky Boulevard. The tavern keeper was sighing, paralyzed by uncertainty and caution. I ate my kebabs alone. Vera's bare arms poured out of the silk of her sleeves. She banged her fist on the table, her earrings dancing among long, lackluster backs, orange beards, and painted nails. By the time she came back to our table, her kebabs had become cold. Her face was flushed with excitement.

"There's no budging that man—he's such a mule! I swear, he could make a fortune with Eastern cooking on Mikhailovsky Boulevard!"

Friends of Vera's passed by our table one after another: princes in Circassian jackets, officers of a certain age, storekeepers in heavy silk coats, and potbellied old men with sunburned faces and little green pimples on their cheeks. It was pushing midnight when we got to the hotel, but there too Vera had countless things to do. An old woman was getting ready to go to her son in Armavir. Vera rushed over to help her, kneeling on her suitcase to force it shut, tying pillows together with cords, and wrapping pies in oilpaper. Clutching her rust-brown handbag, the squat little old woman hurried in her gauze hat from room to room to say good-bye. She shuffled down the hallway in her rubber boots, sobbing and smiling through all her wrinkles. The whole to-do took well over an hour. I waited for Vera in a musty room with three-legged armchairs and a clay oven. The corners of the room were covered with damp splotches.

I had been tormented and dragged around town for such a long time that even my feeling of love seemed to me an enemy, a dogged enemy.

Other people's life bustled in the hallway with peals of sudden laughter. Flies were dying in a jar filled with milky liquid. Each fly was dying in its own way—one in drawn-out agony, its death throes violent, another with a barely visible shudder. A book by Golovin about the life of the Boyars lay on the threadbare tablecloth next to the jar. I opened the book. Letters lined themselves up in a row and then fell into a jumble. In front of me, framed by the window, rose a stony hillside with a crooked Turkish road winding up it. Vera came into the room.

"We've just sent off Fedosya Mavrikevna," she said. "I swear, she was just like a mother to all of us. The poor old thing has to travel all alone with no one to help her!"

Vera sat down on the bed with her knees apart. Her eyes had wandered off to immaculate realms of tenderness and friendship. Then she saw me sitting there in my double-breasted jacket. She clasped her hands and stretched.

"I guess you're tired of waiting. Don't worry, we'll do it now."

But I simply couldn't figure out what exactly it was that Vera was intending to do. Her preparations resembled those of a surgeon preparing for an operation. She lit the kerosene burner and put a pot of water on it. She placed a clean towel over the bed frame and hung an enema bag over the headboard, a bag with a white tube dangling against the wall. When the water was hot, Vera poured it into the enema bag, threw in a red crystal, and pulled her dress off over her head. A large woman with sloping shoulders and rumpled stomach stood in front of me. Her flaccid nipples hung blindly to the sides.

"Come over here, you little rabbit, while the water's getting ready," my beloved said.

I didn't move. Despair froze within me. Why had I exchanged my loneliness for this den filled with poverty-stricken anguish, for these dying flies and furniture with legs missing?

O Gods of my youth! How different this dreary jumble was from my neighbors' love with its rolling, drawn-out moans.

Vera put her hands under her breasts and jiggled them.

"Why do you sit half dead, hanging your head?" she sang. "Come over here!"

I didn't move. Vera pressed her shirt to her stomach and sat down again on the bed.

"Or are you sorry you gave me the money?"

"I don't care about the money."

I said this in a cracking voice.

"What do you mean, you don't care? You a thief or something?"

"I'm not a thief."

"You work for thieves?"

"I'm a boy."

"Well, I can see you're not a cow," Vera mumbled. Her eyes were falling shut. She lay down and, pulling me over to her, started rubbing my body.

"A boy!" I shouted. "You understand what I'm saying? An Armenian's boy!"

O Gods of my youth! Five out of the twenty years I'd lived had gone into thinking up stories, thousands of stories, sucking my brain dry. These stories lay on my heart like a toad on a stone. One of these stories, pried loose by the power of loneliness, fell onto the ground. It was to be my fate, it seems, that a Tiflis prostitute was to be my first reader. I went cold at the suddenness of my invention, and told her the story about the boy and the Armenian. Had I been lazier and given less thought to my craft, I would have made up a drab story about a son thrown out by his rich official of a father—the father a despot, the mother a martyr. I didn't make such a mistake. A well-thought-out story doesn't need to resemble real life. Life itself tries with all its might to resemble a well-crafted story. And for this reason, and also because it was necessary for my listener, I had it that I was born in the town of Alyoshki in the district of Kherson. My father worked as a draftsman in the office of a river steamship company. He toiled night and day over his drawing board so that he could give us children an education, but we took after our mother, who was fond of fun and food. When I was ten I began stealing money from my father, and a few years later ran away to Baku to live with some relatives on my mother's side. They introduced me to Stepan Ivanovich, an Armenian. I became friends with him, and we lived together for four years.

"How old were you then?"

"Fifteen."

Vera was waiting to hear about the evil deeds of the Armenian who had corrupted me.

"We lived together for four years," I continued, "and Stepan Ivanovich turned out to be the most generous and trusting man I had ever met—the most conscientious and honorable man. He trusted every single friend of his to the fullest. I should have learned a trade in those four years, but I didn't lift a finger. The only thing on my mind was billiards. Stepan Ivanovich's friends ruined him. He gave them bronze promissory notes, and his friends went and cashed them right away."

Bronze promissory notes! I myself had no idea how I came up with that. But it was a very good idea. Vera believed everything once she heard "bronze promissory notes." She wrapped herself in her shawl and her shawl shuddered on her shoulders.

"They ruined Stepan Ivanovich. He was thrown out of his apartment and his furniture was auctioned off. He became a traveling salesman. When he lost all his money I left him and went to live with a rich old man, a church warden."

Church warden! I stole the idea from some novel, but it was the invention of a mind too lazy to create a real character.

I said church warden, and Vera's eyes blinked and slipped out from under my spell. To regain my ground, I squeezed asthma into the old man's yellow chest.

"Asthma attacks whistled hoarsely inside his yellow chest. The old man would jump up from his bed in the middle of the night and, moaning, breath in the kerosene-colored night of Baku. He died soon after. The asthma suffocated him." I told her that my relatives would have nothing to do with me and that here I was, in Tiflis, with twenty rubles to my name, the very rubles she had counted in that entrance on Golovinsky Boulevard. The waiter at the hotel where I was staying promised to send me rich clients, but up to now had only sent me taproom keepers with tumbling bellies, men who love their country, their songs, and their wine and who don't think twice about trampling on a foreign soul or a foreign woman, like a village thief will trample on his neighbor's garden.

And I started jabbering about low-down taproom keepers, bits of information I had picked up somewhere. Self-pity tore my heart to pieces; I had been completely ruined. I quaked with sorrow and inspiration. Streams of icy sweat trickled down my face like snakes winding through grass warmed by the sun. I fell silent, began to cry, and turned away. My story had come to an end. The kerosene burner had died out a long time ago. The water had boiled and cooled down again. The enema tube was dangling against the wall. Vera walked silently over to the window. Her back, dazzling and sad, moved in front of me. Outside the window the sun was beginning to light the mountain crevices.

"The things men do," Vera whispered, without turning around. "My God, the things men do!"

She stretched out her bare arms and opened the shutters all the way. The cooling flagstones on the street hissed. The smell of water and dust came rolling up the carriageway. Vera's head drooped.

"In other words, you're a whore. One of us—a bitch," she said.

I hung my head.

"Yes, I'm one of you—a bitch."

Vera turned around to face me. Her shirt hung in twisted tatters from her body.

"The things men do," she repeated more loudly. "My God, the things men do. So . . . have you ever been with a woman?"

I pressed my icy lips to her hand.

"No. . . . How could I have? Who would have wanted me?"

My head shook beneath her breasts, which rose freely above me. Her stretched nipples bounced against my cheeks, opening their moist eyelids and cavorting like calves. Vera looked at me from above.

"My little sister," she whispered, settling down on the floor next to me. "My little whorelet sister."

Now tell me, dear reader, I would like to ask you something: have you ever watched a village carpenter helping a fellow carpenter build a hut for himself and seen how vigorous, strong, and cheerful the shavings fly as they plane the wooden planks? That night a thirty-year-old woman taught me her trade. That night I learned secrets that you will never learn, experienced love that you will never experience, heard women's words that only other women hear. I have forgotten them. We are not supposed to remember them.

It was morning when we fell asleep. We were awakened by the heat of our bodies, a heat that weighed the bed down like a stone. When we awoke we laughed together. That day I didn't go to the printing press. We drank tea in the bazaar of the old quarters. A placid Turk carrying a samovar wrapped in a towel poured tea, crimson as a brick, steaming like blood freshly spilled on the earth. The smoking fire of the sun blazed on the walls of our glasses. The drawn-out braying of donkeys mingled with the hammering of blacksmiths. Copper pots were lined up under canopies, on faded carpets. Dogs were burrowing their muzzles into ox entrails. A caravan of dust flew toward Tiflis, the town of roses and mutton fat. The dust carried off the crimson fire of the sun. The Turk poured tea and kept count of the rolls we ate. The world was beautiful just for our sake. Covered in beads of sweat, I turned my glass upside down. I paid the Turk and pushed two golden five-ruble coins over to Vera. Her chunky leg was lying over mine. She pushed the money away and pulled in her leg

"Do you want us to quarrel, my little sister?"

No, I didn't want to quarrel. We agreed to meet again in the evening, and I slipped back into my wallet the two golden fivers—my first fee.

Since that day many years have passed, and I have often been given money by editors, men of letters, and Jews selling books. For victories that were defeats, for defeats that turned into victories, for life and death, they paid me a trivial fee, much lower than the fee I was paid in my youth by my first reader. But I am not bitter. I am not bitter because I know that I will not die until I snatch one more gold ruble (and definitely not the last one!) from love's hands.

THE JEWESS

"The Jewess" is an unfinished manuscript of a novel that was found among the papers of Babel's friend Lev Ilich Slonim, in whose apartment in Leningrad Babel often stayed between 1927 and 1934. It is particularly interesting to follow Babel's creative process in this work-in-progress. Some passages read like notes that will be developed: "He took Boris aside, and peering at him with his blinking eyes (blinded from within), told him (he did this in an attempt to bond with his nephew who had strayed from the family) . . ." Much of the writing, however, already possesses a mature stylistic finish. "The Jewess" was never published in Russia, except for a Yiddish translation that appeared in the 1980s. Phrases in parentheses are Babel's.

1.

In observance of custom, the old woman sat on the floor for seven days. On the eighth day, she rose and went out onto the shtetl street. The weather was beautiful. A chestnut tree, drenched in sunlight, stood in front of the house, the candles on it already lit. When you think about the recently deceased on a beautiful day, the calamities of life seem even more cruel and inescapable. The old woman was wearing an old-fashioned black silk dress with a black floral print, and a silk kerchief. She had dressed up as she would have for her husband, who was now dead, so that the neighbors would not think that he and she were wretched in the face of death.

Old Esther Erlich headed to the cemetery. The withering petals of the flowers strewn across the burial mound had begun to curl. She touched them with her fingertips, and they crumbled and fell apart. Reb Alter, an old cemetery fixture, came hurrying up to her.

"Madame Erlich! For my prayers for the dead!"

She opened her bag, slowly counted out some silver coins, and handed them to Reb Alter in solemn silence.

Reb Alter, disconcerted by her silence, walked off on his crooked legs, holding a hushed conversation with himself. The sun followed his faded, crooked back. She stayed alone by the grave. The wind blew through the treetops, and they bent forward.

"I'm having a very bad time without you, Marius," Esther said. "I can't tell you how bad." She sat by the grave until noon, clutching some wilted flowers in her wrinkled hands. She clenched her fingers until they hurt, trying to dispel the memories. It is terrible for a wife to stand before a burial mound thinking back over thirty-five years of marriage, of the days and nights of marriage. Vanquished by her battle against these memories that were so painful to face, she trudged back home (in her silk dress) through the squalid shtetl.

Yellow rays filled the marketplace. Misshapen old men and women stood by their hawker's stands selling sunflower oil, withered onions, fish, and toffee for the children. In front of the house, Esther ran into her fifteen-year-old daughter.

"Mama!" the girl shouted in that particularly Jewish desperate woman's voice. "You're not going to torment us, are you? Boris has come!"

Esther's son stood fidgeting in the doorway in his military uniform, his chest covered with medals. The broken old woman, her damp face flushed and feverish, stopped in front of him.

"How dare you come too late to your father's deathbed! How dare you do that to him!"

Her children led her into the house.

She sat down on a little stool, the same stool she had sat on for seven days, and, staring into her son's eyes, tortured him with the tale of his father's death throes. It was an extremely detailed account. She left out nothing: the swelling in his legs, his nose turning blue the morning of the day he died, how she ran to the pharmacy to get oxygen balloons, the indifference of the people who stood around his deathbed. She left out nothing—not even how his father had called out for him as he died. She had knelt by his bed, warming his hands in hers. His father had weakly pressed her hand, ceaselessly uttering his son's name. He had stared with shining eyes, had repeated the name clearly, over and over. That one word, "Boris," had droned through the still room like the droning of a spindle. Then the old man had choked, there was a hoarse rattle in his breath, and he whispered, "Borechka." His eyes had bulged, and he wailed and moaned, "Borechka." The old woman had warmed his hands and said, "Here I am, your son is here!" The dying man's hand had filled with strength and began clutching and scratching the palms that were warming it. He began to shout that one word—"Borechka"—in a changed voice, high-pitched in a way it had never been during his life, and died with that word on his lips.

"How dare you come too late!" the old woman said to her son, who was sitting turned away from her at the table. They hadn't lit the lamps.

Boris sat in the dark, which had flooded the stillness. The old woman sat on the stool breathing heavily (with anger). Boris got up, his revolver rapping against the edge of the table, and left the room.

Half the night he roamed through the shtetl, his native shtetl. Clear serpentine reflections (of stars) quivered on the river. A stench rose from the hovels that stood along the bank. The three-hundred-year-old walls of the synagogue that had once withstood Khmelnitsky's hordes* had been battered with holes.

His native shtetl was dying. The clock of the centuries chimed the end of its defenseless life. "Is this the end, or is it a rebirth?" Boris asked himself. His heart was filled with so much pain that he didn't have the strength to answer this question. The school to which he had gone had been destroyed by Hetman Struk in 1919. The house in which Zhenya had once lived was now the labor exchange. He walked past the ruins, past the squat, crooked, sleeping houses, a hazy stench of poverty seeping out of their gates, and bade them farewell. His mother and sister were waiting for him at home. A dirty samovar was boiling on the table. A bluish piece of chicken lay next to it. Esther moved toward him with weak steps, pressed him to her, and wept. Her heart was pounding beneath her blouse, beneath her flabby, clammy skin—as was his heart, for their hearts were one. And the smell of his mother's shuddering flesh was so bitter, so pitiful, so typical of the Erlichs, that he felt a deep and boundless pity. The old woman cried, the all-embracing [one word illegible in the manuscript], shaking on his chest on which two Red Flag Medals hung. The medals were wet with her tears. That was the beginning of her recovery, and her resignation to loneliness and death.

* Bogdan Khmelnitsky, 1595–1657, a rebel Cossack leader who had led a successful Ukrainian rebellion against Polish rule in 1648. His army's ruthless massacre of Jews was still remembered centuries later in the shtetls of the region.

2.

The relatives, remnants of a large and ancient clan, arrived the following morning. There had been merchants in the family, adventurers, and timid, poetic revolutionaries from the days of the People's Will Party.* Boris's aunt, a medical orderly who had studied in Paris while living on twenty rubles a month, had heard the speeches of Jaurès and Guesde.† His uncle was a pitiful, luckless shtetl philosopher. Other uncles had been grain merchants, traveling salesmen, and storekeepers, their livelihoods knocked out from under them, a herd of confused, pathetic men, a herd of men wearing long brown overcoats. Boris had to hear all over again how his father's legs had become bloated, where he had developed bedsores, and who had run to the pharmacy to get oxygen. The grain merchant, once a rich man, had been driven out of his house, and now wrapped his old, thin legs in military leggings. He took Boris aside and, peering at him with his blinking eyes (blinded from within), told him (he did this in an attempt to bond with his nephew who had strayed from the [one word illegible] family), that he had never expected that his father would manage to keep his body so smooth and clean. They had looked at him while he was being washed, and he was as well built and smooth as a young man. . . . And to think that some valve somewhere in his heart, some tiny one-millimeter vein . . . His uncle spoke these words probably thinking that as both he and the dead man were born of the same mother, he probably had exactly the same heart valve as his brother who had died a week ago.

The following day Boris's uncles asked him, first timidly, then with the shudder of long suppressed-despair, if he could give them a recommendation so that they could join the trade union. Because of their former prosperity, none of the Erlichs were now accorded membership in the trade union.

Their lives were indescribably sad. Their houses were collapsing with leaks everywhere, they had sold everything, even their cupboards,

---

* Narodnaya Volya, the revolutionary terrorist organization that had assassinated Czar Alexander II in 1881.

† Jules Guesde, 1845–1922, an early leader of the Marxist wing of the French Labor Movement, and Jean Jaurès, 1859–1914, French socialist leader, were the foremost leftist orators of the time.

and nobody would hire them. On top of that, they had to pay rent and water bills at much higher rates than members of the trade union. And they were old and suffering from terrible illnesses, harbingers of cancer and fatal disease, as were all members of ancient and dwindling Jewish families. Boris had long ago formed a theory about mankind—that people on their last legs should be put out of their misery as quickly as possible. But his mother was standing right next to him, her face resembling his face, her body like his was going to be in two or three decades, and through the closeness of his mother arose a feeling of fate, a feeling of their common fate, the fate of the bodies of all the Erlichs (in some respect all the same). He overcame his reservations and went to see the chairman of the Local Executive Committee. The chairman, a Petersburg worker, seemed to have been waiting all his life to tell someone how dismal it was to work on an Executive Committee in this damned former Jewish Pale of settlement, how difficult it was to resurrect these shtetls of the western provinces and lay the foundation for a new prosperity in these damned Jewish shtetls (of the damned southwest region) that were dying in misery (and like dogs).

For several days Boris kept seeing before him the cemetery of his native shtetl and the imploring eyes of his uncles, the former (devil-may-care?) traveling salesmen, who now dreamed of joining the trade union or the Labor Exchange. A few days passed. The Indian summer changed into autumn. A (slushy) shtetl rain was falling. Mud from the mountain, mud with rolling stones (like concrete) came flowing down from the mountain. The front room of the house was filled with water. Rusty bowls and Passover saucepans were put under the cracks in the roof. As they walked through the room they had to be careful where they stepped so they wouldn't trip over a bowl.

"Let's go," Boris said to his mother.

"Where to?"

"To Moscow, Mama."

"Aren't there enough Jews in Moscow?"

"Nonsense," Boris said. "Who cares what people say!"

She sat in the leaking room in her corner by the window from which she could see the pockmarked carriageway and her neighbor's collapsing house—and thirty years of her life. Sitting by the window and (sharing) her soul's tears and her old-woman's compassion for her sisters, brothers-in-law, and nephews, to whom fate had not granted a son like hers. Esther knew that sooner or later he would talk of going to Moscow and that she would give in. But before she did, she wanted to (torment herself and infuse her surrender with the sorrow of the shtetl . . .). She said that it pained her to death to leave without her husband, who had dreamed of Moscow as he had dreamed of leaving this godforsaken place to live (the rest of his life) more happily, from which you expect nothing more than peace and the happiness of others, to live with his son in this new (Promised) land. And now he lay in his grave, beneath the rain that had lashed down all night, while she was preparing to go to Moscow, where, word had it, people were happy, cheerful, spirited, full of plans (doing all kinds of special things). Esther said that it was hard for her to leave all her graves behind—of her fathers and her grandfathers, rabbis, *tsaddiks*, and Talmudists who lay under the gray (traditional) stones. She would never see them again. And how would he, her son, answer for her when her time came to die on foreign soil, among people who were so very foreign. . . . And then, how could she forgive herself if life in Moscow turned out to be pleasant? Her hands with their long (gout-ridden, twisted, soft, swollen) fingers trembled when Esther considered how unbearable it would be for her to be happy at such a time. Her damp, twisted fingers trembled, the veins on her yellow chest swelled and throbbed, the (shtetl) rain drummed on the iron roof. . . . For the second time since her son had come home, the little old Jewess in her galoshes wept. She agreed to go to Moscow because there was nowhere else for her to go, and because her son looked so (terribly) like her husband that she could not be parted from him, even though her husband, like everyone else, had had faults and pitiful little secrets, which a wife knows but never tells.

3.

Most of their arguments centered around what to take with them. Esther wanted to take everything, while Boris wanted to have done with it all and sell it off. But there was nobody in Kremenets to whom one could sell anything. The last thing the townsfolk needed was furniture. The dealers, angry men who had sprung up from God knows where, and who looked like undertakers, like visitors from the beyond, were only prepared to pay small change. They could only resell the mer-

chandise to peasants. But Esther's relatives were quick to lend a helping hand. No sooner had they gotten over (the first doleful stirrings of
soul) than they began to cart off whatever they could lay their hands on.
And as, deep down, they were honest people, and not petty (pettily
mercenary), the sight of this furtive (secretive) carting off was particularly sad (unbearable). Esther was taken aback. A sickly flush on her
face, she tried to grab a snatching hand, but the quaking hand was covered in such pitiful sweat, and was so wrinkled, so old (edged with broken nails), that she (staggered back and in a flash) understood everything. She was horrified that anyone would have to stop someone in
such a tormenting (offense), and that the people she had grown up with
had gone out of their minds, trying to carry off cupboards and sheets.

Everything was sent to Moscow by train. Her relatives cried as they
helped her tie her bundles. Sitting on the packed bales, they had come
to their senses (their hearts were touched), and they said that they
themselves would stay (in Kremenets)—they would never leave. The
old woman [one word illegible] packed a kitchen trestle and a tub for
boiling clothes. "You'll see, we'll need all this in Moscow!" she told her
son. "After sixty years of life, am I supposed to remain with nothing but
ashes in my soul and the kind of tears that flow even when you don't
want to cry?" As their belongings were taken to the station, the old
woman's hollow cheeks flushed, and a blind, urgent, passionate sparkle
glittered in her eyes. She hurried through the besmirched, ransacked
house, a force dragging her quaking shoulders along the wall from
which torn strips of wallpaper hung.

The next morning, the day of their departure, Esther took her son
and daughter to the cemetery, where, among oak trees that were centuries old, rabbis who had been killed by the Cossacks of Gonta and
Khmelnitsky* lay buried under Talmudic gravestones. Esther went to
her husband's grave, shuddered, and drew herself up. "Marius," she said
(in a gasping voice), "your son is taking me to Moscow. Your son does
not want me to be laid to rest at your side." Her eyes were fixed on the
reddish mound, its earth spongy and crumbling. Her eyes grew wider
and wider. Her son and daughter held her hands tightly. The old

---

*Ivan Gonta (d. 1768) and Bogdan Khmelnitsky, 1595–1657, were leaders of the Zaporozhian
Cossacks who rebelled against Polish rule in Ukraine and were known for their ruthless massacres
of Jews.

woman swayed, stumbled forward, and half closed her eyes. Her haggard hands, relinquished to her children, tensed, were covered in sweat, and grew limp. Her eyes grew wider and wider and blazed with light. She tore herself free, fell onto the grave in her silken dress, and began thrashing about. Her whole body was quaking, and her hand stroked the yellow earth and the withered flowers with greedy tenderness. "Your son, Marius, is taking me to Moscow!" she shouted, her shrill voice tearing through the Jewish cemetery. "Pray for him, that he will be happy!" She dragged her fingers, hooked and twisted as if she were knitting, over the earth that covered the dead man. Her son gave her his hand and she got up submissively. They walked along the path shaded by oak branches, and Boris's whole being blazed and surged as his tears pressed against his eyes and throat like rocks. He experienced the taste of tears that cannot break free and so must remain (inside a man). The old woman stopped by the gate. She freed her hand (pierced, drenched), on which sweat surged impetuously, like a subterranean spring, alternately boiling hot and deadly cold (frozen through), and waved to the cemetery and the grave as if she and her children were on a ship leaving port.

"Farewell, my sweet," she said (softly), without crying (or twitching). "Farewell."

And so the Erlich family left its native shtetl.

4.

Boris took his family to Moscow on the Sebastopol Express. He got tickets for a first-class compartment. They were taken to the station by Boychik, the shtetl comic, once known far and wide for his droll stories and massive black horses. He no longer had the horses, and his rickety cart was now drawn by a gigantic white jade with a drooping pink lip. Boychik himself had grown older, bent with rheumatism.

"Listen, Boychik, I'll be back next year," Esther said to his little bent back as the cart turned and pulled into the station. "You must keep well till then."

The hillock on Boychik's back became even more pointed. The white jade plodded through the mud on her stiff, gouty legs. Boychik turned around, his crimson eyelids raw and inflamed, his sash crooked, dusty tufts of hair growing out of the side of his face.—"(I don't think you will, Madame Erlich)," he said, and suddenly shouted to his horse: "The party's over! Off you go, now!"

The first-class railway car had been patched together out of several cars from Czarist times [one word illegible]. Through the wide, gleaming window Esther saw for the last time the huddled crowd of her relatives, rust-brown coats, soldiers' leggings, crooked smocks, her old sisters with their large, useless breasts, her brother-in-law Samuel, a former traveling salesman with his puffy, twisted face, her brother-in-law Efim, a former rich man whose withered, homeless feet were now wrapped in rags. They jostled each other on the platform (like . . .), and shouted words she could not hear as the train pulled out of the station. Her sister Genia went running after the train.

[One page of the original manuscript missing.]

[Boris showed] her Russia with so much pride and confidence, as if he, Boris Erlich, had himself created Russia, as if he owned it. And to some extent, he did. There was in everything a drop of his soul or of his blood, the blood of the corps commissar (of the Red Cossacks)— from the international train cars to the newly built sugar factories and refurbished train stations.

[Half a page in the manuscript crossed out.]

In the evening he ordered bed linen, and with childish pride showed his mother and sister how to turn on the blue night-light. With a big smile he revealed the secret of the little mahogany closet. Inside the closet there turned out to be a washstand—right there in the compartment! Esther lay beneath the cool sheets. Rocked by the oily bounce of the train's springs, she stared out into the blue darkness and (with her heart) listened to the breathing of her son. He tossed and called out in his sleep. Somebody, she thought, would definitely have to foot the bill for this palace hurtling through Russia with its lit chandeliers (and heated with sparkling copper tubes). This was a typically Jewish thought—such a thought would never have occurred to Boris. As they approached Moscow, he kept worrying whether Alexei Selivanov had received his telegram and would come to pick them up with the car. Alexei had received the telegram and did come with the car. The car was the Red Army headquarters' new thirty-thousand-ruble Packard, and in it the Erlichs drove to an apartment Boris had set up for them a while back in Moscow's Ostozhenka district. Alexei had even brought some furniture to the apartment. Esther was overwhelmed by the inexhaustible delight of the two-room apartment, as Boris showed her the kitchen with its gas stove, the bathroom with its own hot water boiler, and the pantry with its icebox. The rooms were beautiful. They were part of a house that had belonged to the deputy governor general of Moscow before the Revolution, and as Boris eagerly dragged his mother through kitchens, bathrooms, and mezzanines of the princely house, he was involuntarily fulfilling the call of his ancient Semitic blood. The cemetery and the grave of his luckless father, who had not lived to see happiness, had awakened in him the powerful passion for family which for so many centuries had sustained his people. At thirty-two, obeying this ancient command, he felt himself to be father, husband, and brother in one—the protector of the women, their breadwinner, their support—and he felt this with a passion, with the tormenting and stubborn tightening of the heart characteristic of his people. Boris was tortured by the thought that his father had not lived to see this, and wanted to make up for his having come too late to his father's deathbed by having his mother and sister pass from his father's hands into his own. And if his mother and sister were to fare better in his strong hands, that was simply due to the ruthlessness of life.

5.

Boris Erlich had been a student at the Institute of Psychology and Neurology (before the Revolution, all the other institutes had a restrictive enrollment quota for Jews). He had spent the summer of 1917 with his parents in the shtetl. He had trudged to all the restless villages nearby, explaining the basics of Bolshevism to the peasants. His propaganda rounds were hampered by his hooked nose, but not too much: back in 1917, people had more than noses on their minds. That same summer Alexei Selivanov, the son of a bookkeeper at the local council, came back from Siberian exile in Verkhoyansk. At home, while Alexei swallowed the cherry dumplings and liqueurs his mother made, he dug into the Selivanov family's history and found that they were descendants of

Selikha, a Zaporozhian Cossack commander.* Among the papers Alexei found there was even a lithograph of his ancestor wearing his Cossack jacket and sitting on a cardboard horse carrying his ceremonial mace. There was a faded inscription in Latin beneath the portrait, and Alexei claimed that he recognized the handwriting of Orlik, the Ukrainian chancellor in the days of Mazepa.† Alexei's romantic delving into the past coexisted with his membership in the Socialist Revolutionary Party.** His idols were Zhelyabov, Kibalchich, and Kalyayev.‡ At twenty-one, Alexei led a full life. His youthful passion fired up Erlich, the large-nosed student with the strange name. The two young men struck up a friendship, and Alexei became a Bolshevik when he realized that no other party in the world had as much battling, destroying, and rebuilding to do as the Bolshevik Party, filled as it was with mathematical and scientific passion. (Erlich supplied Alexei with books and the Communist Manifesto). After the Revolution, Alexei rounded up his shtetl friends: a nineteen-year-old Jew, who worked as a projectionist at the Chary Movie theater, a blacksmith, also a Jew, a few noncommissioned officers who were sitting around bored, and a few boys from a nearby village who had been discharged from the army. Alexei gave them horses, and their unit turned into the Insurgent Regiment of Red Ukrainian Cossacks. One of the former noncommissioned officers became the regiment's chief of staff, and Boris became its commissar. Alexei's regiment was fighting for a palpably good cause, its fighters lived together in camaraderie and died proudly in action, and each told taller tales than the next. Their ranks grew day by day, and the regiment experienced the fate of all the small rivulets that

---

* The Zaporozhian Cossacks, the Cossacks of the Dnieper River region, who during the sixteenth and seventeenth centuries had managed to stay politically autonomous both from Poland and Russia, briefly even forming a semi-independent state.

† Filipp Orlik, 1672–1742, served in the General Chancery of the Cossack government. Ivan Stepanovich Mazepa, 1644–1709, was a Cossack commander who became *hetman* (ruler) of Ukraine in 1687.

** The most important non-Bolshevik socialist party, suppressed by Lenin in 1921, after the Bolshevik victory in the Civil War.

‡ Andrei Ivanovich Zhelyabov, 1851–1881, Nikolai Ivanovich Kibalchich, 1853–1881, and Ivan Platonovich Kalyayev, 1877–1905, were leading members of the People's Will Party (Narodnaya Volya), a revolutionary terrorist organization. Kibalchich had been involved in the assassination of Czar Alexander II in 1881, and Kalyayev assassinated Grand Duke Sergei Alexandrovich, the governor general of Moscow in 1905.

flowed into the Red Army. The regiment turned into a brigade, the brigade into a division. Alexei's men battled renegade bands, Petlyura,* the White Army, and the Poles. By now all regiments already had their Political Divisions, Provision Units, Tribunals, and War Spoils Commissions.† In the campaign against General Wrangel's White Army, Alexei became a corps commander. He was twenty-four. Foreign newspapers wrote that Budyonny** and Alexei had invented new tactics and strategy of cavalry warfare. At the academy they began teaching the lightning raids of Alexei Selivanov. The students at the Military Academy went about solving exercises in strategy by studying the operations of the Ukrainian Cossack Corps. Alexei Selivanov and Boris Erlich, his irreplaceable commissar, were sent to study at the Military Academy, where they ended up studying their own operations along with the other students. In Moscow Alexei and Boris formed a commune with the former projectionist and one of the former noncommissioned officers. In the commune, as in the corps, honor and the spirit of camaraderie was high, and Boris clung to it with tormenting passion. Perhaps it was because his race had for so long been deprived of one of the most important human qualities—friendship, both behind the plow and on the field of battle. Boris experienced a need, a hunger for camaraderie and friendship—(to defend and be loyal to camaraderie)—with such vulnerability that his friendships were marked by fevered passion. But in his fervor, chivalry, and self-sacrifice, there was also something (attractive and) noble, which turned Boris's shabby room into a club for the "Red Marshals." This club truly blossomed when, instead of the standard-issue sausage and vodka, gefilte fish was served. The tin kettle was replaced by a samovar brought from Kremenets, and the tea was poured by the comforting hand of his old mother. It was many years

---

* Semyon Vasilevich Petlyura, 1879–1926, was one of the leading socialist leaders of Ukraine's unsuccessful fight for independence during the years of the Russian Civil War.

† In the new Soviet army, every regiment had representatives that reported back to Moscow and dealt with specialized day-to-day military issues. The Political Propaganda Division (Politotdel) dealt with the ideological education of the military, the Provision Units (Khoz-chast) with the acquiring and distribution of supplies, the Tribunals (Tribunaly) with military justice and the detection of counterrevolutionary activity in the ranks, and the War Spoils Commission (Trofeinaya Komissiya) was in charge of hindering looting and sending war spoils to the local military authorities.

** Semyon Mikhailovich Budyonny, 1883–1973, the commander of the First Cavalry and later a Marshal of the Soviet Union. One of the major figures in Babel's *Red Cavalry* stories.

since Alexei Selivanov and his brigade commanders had seen an old woman sitting behind a samovar. It was a pleasant change for them. The old woman was meek and timorous. And quiet as a mouse. But in her gefilte fish (and in her fingers that prepared the samovar) lay (the history of the Jewish people), a true history with a hefty dash of peppery passion.

6.

At first the gefilte fish caused trouble at their new apartment. One of the lodgers, a professor's wife, announced in the communal kitchen: God, did the apartment stink! And it was true. With the arrival of the Erlichs, even the hallway began to reek of garlic and fried onions.

I. BABEL.

ISAAC EMMANUELOVICH BABEL

A CHRONOLOGY

by Gregory Freidin

Isaac Babel, July 1930, sent by Babel to his sister in Brussels with the handwritten inscription, "My life is spent fighting this man."

1894   Isaac Babel is born (June 30) in Moldavanka, a poor district near the harbor of Odessa, to Feiga and Man Yitzkhovich Bobel, a dealer in agricultural machinery. Soon after, the family, now under the name Babel, relocates to Nikolayev (150 kilometers from Odessa). Babel studies English, French, and German; private Hebrew lessons.

1899   Babel's sister, Meriam, born on July 16.
1905   The October Manifesto of Czar Nicholas II establishes a constitutional monarchy. Pogroms in southern Russia, including Nikolayev, witnessed by Babel. But the family is untouched.
1906   Babel's family, now considerably more prosperous, moves back to Odessa and settles in the residential center of the city. Babel enrolls in the Nicholas I Commercial School in Odessa; begins writing stories in French.
1911   After an unsuccessful attempt to enroll at the University of Odessa (due to the restrictions on Jews), Babel enters the Institute of Finance and Business Studies in Kiev. Meets Evgenia Borisovna Gronfein, his future wife.
1913   First publication: the story "Old Shloyme."
1914   World War I begins.
1915   Babel follows his institute's evacuation from Kiev to Saratov.
1916   After graduating from the institute, moves to St. Petersburg, meets Maxim Gorky, and begins to contribute stories and sketches to Gorky's journal *Letopis* and other periodicals (stories: "Mama, Rimma, and Alla," "Elya Isaakovich and Margarita Prokofievna"). Babel's stories receive a favorable response from reviewers.
1917   Charged with writing pornography (story "The Bathroom Window"), but the charge is made moot by the political turmoil.
        The February Revolution.* Czar Nicholas II abdicates. Russia is ruled by the provisional government. Babel briefly volunteers for the Rumanian front. Bolshevik coup d'état in October.†
        Babel abandons the disintegrating front in November, returns to Odessa, and takes a dangerous journey to Petrograd** (his story "The Road," 1932). Reaches Petrograd in December 1917 and joins the newly organized Cheka for a brief stint as a translator for the counterintelligence department.
1918   In March, Babel becomes a regular contributor of sketches about life in the city to Maxim Gorky's anti-Leninist newspaper *Novaya zhizn* until the publication is shut down by the Bolsheviks on July 6 (Babel's last contribution is in the July 2 issue).
        Contributes stories to newspaper *Zhizn iskusstva* (Petrograd) in November.
1918–19 Serves in the food requisitioning detachments during the Civil War; returns to Odessa. Marries Evgenia Gronfein (August 9, 1919).
1920   Odessa Party Committee issues Babel the credentials of a war correspondent under the name of Kiril Vasilievich Lyutov, assigned to Budyonny's Cavalry Army on the Polish front. Babel spends June through September with the Budyonny Cavalry.‡
        Returns to Odessa severely ill (lifelong asthma). Travels with his wife in Georgia and the Caucasus, contributes to local periodicals.

* March, according to the Gregorian calandar, adopted subsequently.
† November 7, according to the Gregorian calandar.
** Formerly St. Petersburg.
‡In August 1920, the Red Army reaches the outskirts of Warsaw but is soon after repelled and by September defeated by Pilsudski's troops, aided by the Western powers; an armistice is signed in October 1921; the Treaty of Riga, finalizing the Russian-Polish border and ceding parts of the Ukraine and Belarus to Poland, is signed on March 18, 1921.

1921   End of the Civil War. The tolerant New Economic Policy replaces War
        Communism.
        Babel does editorial work for a publishing house, contributing stories and
        essays to Odessa periodicals.
1923   Most of the Benya Krik stories (the Odessa stories) written and published in
        Odessa.
        Father dies (July 13).
1923–24 After finishing the Odessa stories, Babel begins work on the *Red Cavalry* sto-
        ries (June 1923), the publication of his stories in the avant-garde *Lef* and the
        fellow traveler *Krasnaya Nov*; the beginning of Babel's fame.
1924   Lenin dies on January 21; Stalin, the Communist Party's General Secretary
        since 1922, begins his ascent to power.
        Budyonny's first attack on *Red Cavalry* stories (March).
        Babel publication in the first issue of Evgeny Zamiatin's independent jour-
        nal *Russkii sovremennik*.
        Meriam Chapochnikoff (Babel's sister) emigrates to Brussels.
1925   First two childhood stories (the cycle *The Story of My Dovecote*) are published
        with a dedication to Maxim Gorky.
        Evgenia Babel (Gronfein), Babel's wife, emigrates to Paris.
1926   *Red Cavalry* is published as a book. Babel's mother emigrates to Brussels.
        Babel is Russia's "most famous writer."
1925–27 Babel's liaison with Tamara Kashirina (later, Mrs. Vsevolod Ivanov).
1926   Mikhail (Ivanov) is born to Babel and Tamara Kashirina in July.
        Babel finishes his play *Sunset* in August.
        Works on the film script of *Benya Krik*; the beginning of Babel's career as
        a screenwriter (script based on Shalom Aleichem's *Roaming Stars* and others).
1927   The film *Benya Krik* is released and soon taken out of circulation. In subse-
        quent publications of the script, Babel disowns the film.
        Babel is in Kiev on family business; possibly works on *The Jewess* (a novel)
        of which only the beginning is extant. Plans a work on the French Revolution,
        hints that he is working on a novel about the Cheka; continues work on the
        "childhood" story cycle (referred to by Babel as "my true legacy").
        Babel leaves Russia for Paris in July; a brief affair with E. Khaiutina (future
        Mrs. Nikolai Yezhov) in Berlin; rejoins his wife in Paris.
        Sunset staged successfully in Baku (October 23), in two theaters in Odessa
        (October 25 and December 1).
1928   Moscow production of *Sunset* at the Moscow Art Theater II (February 28)
        fails.
        The Shakhty Trial. End of the liberal New Economic Policy era and begin-
        ning of the Stalin Revolution.
        Babel returns to Russia in October. General Budyonny resumes attacks on the
        Red Cavalry stories. Gorky comes to Babel's defense.
        The Chinese Mill, a film comedy based on a script by Babel, premieres in
        July.
        Continues work on the childhood story cycle (according to Babel, "part of
        a larger whole").
        Critic Alexander Voronsky, an early patron and admirer of Babel, chides

him in print for his low productivity, or "silence."

Completes the story "My First Fee" (1922–28); plans *Kolya Topuz*, a long narrative about an Odessa bandit who is reformed during the period of socialist construction (late 1920s–early 1930s).

1929   Trotsky is exiled from Soviet Russia in January.

Babel's daughter, Nathalie, born in Paris to Evgenia Borisovna Babel on July 17.

Red Cavalry is published in English translation in the United States (following German and French editions), preceded by the appearance of some stories in literary magazines.

1929–30 "In search of new material," Babel, like many other Soviet writers, travels in the industrial heartland to observe "socialist construction"; witnesses the brutal collectivization and famine in the Ukraine (February–summer 1930).

1930   Babel is publicly accused of granting an anti-Soviet interview to a Polish newspaper while on the French Riviera. He insists, apparently successfully, that the interview was a fabrication. Attempts to receive permission to return to Paris fail in part due to the author's continued "silence."

1931   Resumes contacts with Khaiutina.

Spends early spring in the Ukraine.

Publishes two more childhood stories (the *Dovecote* cycle) and a "collectivization" story, "Gapa Guzhva."

Impending publication of a series of stories is announced at the end of the year, only one of them subsequently published.

1932   Publication of the story "Guy de Maupassant." Babel lives in Molodenovo, a village outside Moscow, close to Gorky's summer estate.

Babel meets Antonina Nikolayevna Pirozhkova, a young engineer.

After many pleas, Babel finally is allowed to return to his family in France.

1932–33 In Paris, Babel sees his daughter for the first time. Collaborates on a script about a famous socialist-revolutionary double agent, Yevno Azef, for a French movie studio (continues this work later in Russia). Close friendship with Ilya Ehrenburg, who introduces Babel to André Malraux. Babel visits Gorky in Sorrento. Travels through France, Italy, Germany.

Returns to Moscow in August in response to Gorky's request for assistance in organizing the First Congress of Soviet Writers.

In the fall, Babel travels, with Antonina Pirozhkova, through the Caucasus on the way to Kabardino-Balkaria (a small Caucasus republic).

1934   Babel travels to the Donbass region (January).

During the 17th Communist Party Congress, "The Congress of Victors," opposition to Stalin becomes manifest, but is ultimately defeated.

Publication of Babel's story "Dante Street."

Osip Mandelstam recites his anti-Stalin verses to his friends and is arrested in May.

At the First Congress of Soviet Writers (August), Babel obliquely criticizes the cult of Stalin. Speaking about his modest output, Babel calls himself "a great master of the genre [of literary silence]." He is grateful to the

Soviet establishment for being able to enjoy the high status of a writer despite his "silence," which, in the West, would have forced him to abandon writing and "sell haberdashery." Babel spends time with André Malraux, who attended the congress.

Assassination of Sergei Kirov on December 1. Beginning of the great purges.

1935   Babel attends the Congress of Soviets in Moscow (February).

Babel completes *Maria*, his second play, which is published in March.

Babel and Pasternak are dispatched, on the insistence of André Malraux and André Gide, to the anti-Fascist International Congress of Writers for the Defense of Culture and Peace in Paris (June).

On July 14, Babel witnesses huge demonstrations in Paris (Popular Front and the pro-Fascist Croix de Feu*), seeing in them the signs of an impending revolution.

Along with his wife and daughter, Babel visits his mother and sister in Brussels (July). Babel makes plans to bring his entire family back to the Soviet Union. These plans do not materialize.

Babel returns to the Soviet Union (August) and travels, with Antonina Pirozhkova, to the Kiev region and on to Odessa. After returning to Moscow, Babel and Pirozhkova establish a household.

Ilya Ehrenburg, on a visit to Moscow from Paris, queries Babel about the mounting repression and the purges of the old Bolshevik intellectuals from the leadership. Babel attributes the changes to the preparations for war, which calls for a more decisive, military-style government and a kind of art that could best serve the goals of total mobilization of society.

Babel collaborates with Sergei Eisenstein on the film *Bezhin Meadow*, about a young peasant Communist who is murdered for denouncing his father as a kulak (winter 1935–36).

1936   Attack on Dmitri Shostakovich's opera *Lady Macbeth of the Mtsensk District* (January) inaugurates the "Campaign against Formalism," a purge in the cultural sphere.

Together with André and Roland Malraux, Babel visits Gorky in the Crimea and, along with Mikhail Koltsov, serves as Malraux's interpreter (March). Afterward Gorky complains to Stalin that the "Campaign against Formalism" represents a harmful cultural policy.

Babel spends time with André Gide in Moscow and occasionally interprets for him.

Maxim Gorky dies on June 18.

As one of the leading figures in the Writers' Union, Babel receives a country house (dacha) in Peredelkino.

Spanish Civil War begins in July.

The trial of Lev Kamenev, Grigory Zinoviev, and other famous party and military leaders, including several Civil War heroes (some friends of Babel's) takes place in August. The accused are sentenced to death.

*Ilya Ehrenburg, *Memoirs: 1914–1941*, translated by Tatyana Shebunina (NY: Grosset & Dunlap, 1966), p. 317.

Nikolay Yezhov (now the husband of E. Khaiutina) replaces Genrikh Yagoda in September as the head of the NKVD (Stalin's secret police).

According to an NKVD informer, Babel is critical of the trials, saying that the prosecution failed to make a convincing case against the accused.

1937   Daughter Lydia is born to Babel and Antonina Pirozhkova (January).

Babel publishes stories "Sulak," "Di Grasso" (thematically, part of the childhood story cycle), and "The Kiss" (a new concluding story of *Red Cavalry*).

Show trials of political and military leaders continue.

1938   In a meeting with Ilya Ehrenburg, Babel recounts how banned books are pulped in a Moscow factory. Ehrenburg, who has just been recalled to Moscow from Spain, suggests to Babel that if Fascism wins in Spain, the repressive USSR would be the only place left for people like Babel and himself, and "so much the worse for us."[*]

Last meeting with Ehrenburg (May).

Yezhov is replaced by Lavrenty Beria as the head of the NKVD and is soon afterward arrested. He gives evidence against Babel.

Babel publishes a story "The Trial" (August).

Collaborates on scripts for the film version of Gorky's autobiographical trilogy (he is chiefly responsible for the script of the volume *My Universities*, released in 1939–40).

Signs a contract for an edition of his collected works.

1939   Babel completes a film script for a military-industrial spy thriller, *Number 4 Staraya Square* (the title referring to the address of the Communist Party Central Committee Headquarters in Moscow).

Babel is arrested on May 15 and is soon charged with spying for France and Austria. The accusation is based, in part, on the evidence provided by Yezhov and Babel's fellow writers Boris Pilnyak and Mikhail Koltsov, who had been arrested earlier.

Molotov-Ribbentrop Pact is signed in Moscow in August. In September, the armies of Germany and the Soviet Union invade and partition Poland.

1940   Babel is executed in the Lubyanka prison on January 27.

1941   Germany invades the Soviet Union on June 22.

1948   Rumors circulate about Babel's imminent release from prison.

1953   Stalin dies (March 5).

1954   Babel is officially exonerated on December 23. The death certificate misleadingly states that he died under unknown circumstances on March 17, 1941.

1955   *Collected Stories by Isaac Babel*, with an introduction by Lionel Trilling, is published in New York.

1956   Nikita Khrushchev denounces Stalin at the 20th Party Congress (February).

1957   A volume of selected stories is published in Moscow with the introduction by Ilya Ehrenburg, at last opening the way for subsequent editions, albeit censored and incomplete.

---

[*] S. Povartsov, *Prichina smerti—rasstrel* (*Cause of Death: Execution by the Firing Squad*), M. 1966, p. 130.

1964 *Isaac Babel, The Lonely Years: 1925–1939: Unpublished Stories and Correspondence,* edited and introduced by Nathalie Babel. Revised edition published in 1995.

1966 *You Must Know Everything,* edited by Nathalie Babel, published in New York.

1989 *Vospominania o Babele (Babel Remembered),* edited by Antonina Pirozhkova, is published in Moscow, including Pirozhkova's essay "Years Spent Together (1932–1939)."

1990 The two-volume *Sochineniia (Works)* edition is published in Moscow, the most comprehensive uncensored edition of Babel to date, albeit incomplete.

   Details of Babel's interrogation and death begin to reach Soviet press (publications by Arkady Vaksberg and Vitaly Shentalinsky based on their research in the KGB archives).

1994 The centenary of Babel's birth is marked by international conferences in Russia and the United States.

1996 Pirozhkova publishes *At His Side: The Last Years of Isaac Babel,* translated by Anne Frydman and Robert L. Busch (Royalton, Vermont).

GREGORY FREIDIN

NOTES

EARLY STORIES

OLD SHLOYME
Original title: "*Starii Shloyme*". First published in *Ogni* 6, 1913.

AT GRANDMOTHER'S
Original title: "*Detstvo. U babushki.*" First published in *Literaturnoye Nasledstvo*, Nauka, 1965, dated: Saratov, November 12, 1915.

ELYA ISAAKOVICH AND MARGARITA PROKOFIEVNA
Original title: "*Elya Isaakovich i Margarita Prokofievna.*" First published in *Letopis* 11, 1916.

MAMA, RIMMA, AND ALLA
Original title: "*Mama, Rimma, i Alla.*" First published in *Letopis* 11, 1916.

THE PUBLIC LIBRARY
Original title: "*Publichnaya biblioteka.*" First published in *Zhurnal zhurnalov* 48, 1916, under the heading "My Notes." Signed Bab-El.

NINE
Original title: "*Devyat.*" First published in *Zhurnal zhurnalov* 48, 1916, under the heading "My Notes." Signed Bab-El.

ODESSA
Original title: "*Odessa.*" First published in *Zhurnal zhurnalov* 51, 1916, under the heading "My Notes." Signed Bab-El.

THE AROMA OF ODESSA
Original title: "*Listki ob Odesse.*" First published in *Vechernyaya zvezda*, March 8, 1918.

INSPIRATION
Original title: "*Vdokhnovenie.*" First published in *Zhurnal zhurnalov* 7, 1917, under the heading "My Notes." Signed Bab-El.

DOUDOU
Original title: "*Doudou.*" First published in *Svobodniye mysli* 2, March 13, 1917, under the heading "My Notes."

SHABOS-NAKHAMU
Original title: "*Shabos-Nakhamu.*" First published in *Vechernyaya zvezda,* March 16, 1918, under the subheading "From the Hershele Cycle." Babel was working on a series of stories on Hershele, a trickster figure in Jewish lore, who was also reputed to be the court jester Reb Borukhl Tulchiner, the grandson of the Baal Shem Tov, the founder of Hasidism. The manuscripts of these stories, however, have not survived.

In the *Red Cavalry* story "Rabbi," the narrator tells the rabbi, " 'I am putting the adventures of Hershele of Ostropol into verse.' 'A great task,' the rabbi whispered, and closed his eyelids."

See also *1920 Diary* entry for July 23.

ON THE FIELD OF HONOR
Original title: "*Na pole chesti.*" First published in *Lava* 1, 1920.

THE DESERTER
Original title: "*Dezertir.*" First published in *Lava* 1, 1920.

PAPA MARESCOT'S FAMILY
Original title: "*Semeistvo papashi Maresko.*" First published in *Lava* 1, 1920.

THE QUAKER
Original title: "*Kvaker.*" First published in *Lava* 1, 1920.

THE SIN OF JESUS
Original title: "*Iisusov grekhi.*" First published in *Na khleb,* August 29, 1921.

AN EVENING WITH THE EMPRESS
Original title: "*Vecher u imperatritsy.*" First published in *Siluety* 1, 1922, under the heading "From the Petersburg Diary."

CHINK
Original title: "*Khodya.*" First published in *Siluety* 6–7, 1923, under the heading "From the Petersburg Diary."

A TALE ABOUT A WOMAN
Original title: "*Skazka pro babu.*" First published in *Siluety* 8–9, 1923. The story is an earlier version of "The Sin of Jesus."

THE BATHROOM WINDOW
Original title: "*V shchelochku.*" First published in *Siluety* 12, 1923, with the subtitle "From the Book *Oforty.*" See also its earlier version, "A Story," in the section Variations and Manuscripts.

BAGRAT-OGLY AND THE EYES OF HIS BULL
Original title: "*Bagrat-Ogly i glaza ego byka.*" First published in *Siluety* 12, 1923, with the subtitle "From the Book *Oforty.*"

LINE AND COLOR
Original title: "*Liniya i tsvet.*" First published in *Krasnaya nov* 7, 1923, with the subtitle "A True Occurrence."

YOU MISSED THE BOAT, CAPTAIN!
Original title: "*Ty promorgal, kapitan!*" First published in *Izvestiya Odesskogo Gubispolkoma,* February 9, 1924. Signed Bab-El.

THE END OF ST. HYPATIUS
Original title: "*Konets sv. Ipatiya.*" First published in *Pravda,* August 3, 1924, under the heading "From My Diary."

A STORY
Original title: "*Moi listki. Raskaz I. Babelya.*" First published in *Zhurnal zhurnalov* 16, 1917. See also "The Bathroom Window," of which this is an earlier variant.

THE ODESSA STORIES

THE KING
Original title: "*Korol.*" First published in *Moryak,* June 23, 1921, with the subtitle "From the Odessa Stories."

JUSTICE IN PARENTHESES
Original title: "*Spravedlivost v skobkakh.*" First published in *Na pomoshch!,* August 15, 1921, with the subtitle "From the Odessa Stories."

HOW THINGS WERE DONE IN ODESSA
Original title: "*Kak eto delalos v Odesse.*" First published in *Izvestiya Odesskogo Gubispolkoma,* May 5, 1923.

LYUBKA THE COSSACK
Original title: "*Lyubka Kazak.*" First published in *Krasnaya nov* 5, 1924, with the subtitle "From the Odessa Stories."

THE FATHER
Original title: "*Otets.*" First published in *Krasnaya nov* 5, 1924, with the subtitle "From the Odessa Stories."

FROIM GRACH
Original title: "*Froim Grach.*" First published in *Vozdushnye puti,* Volume 3, New York, 1963.

THE END OF THE ALMSHOUSE
Original title: "*Konets bogadelni.*" First published in *30 Dnei* 1, 1932, with the subtitle "From the Odessa Stories," dated 1920–1930.

SUNSET
Original title: "*Zakat.*" First published in *Literaturnaya Rossiya,* November 20, 1964. The last page of the manuscript was missing.

THE RED CAVALRY STORIES

The stories are presented in the order in which they appeared in the first edition of the book *Konarmiya* (*Red Cavalry*), May 1926, by which time all the stories had been published in magazines and newspapers as indicated below.

CROSSING THE RIVER ZBRUCZ
Original title: *Perekhod cherez Zbruch.* First published in *Pravda,* August 3, 1924. Dated Novograd-Volynsk, July 1920.

Savitsky: The altered name Babel used in his later editions of the *Red Cavalry* stories for Semyon Konstantinovich Timoshenko, 1895–1970, the commander of the

Sixth Division of the Red Cavalry. He was later to become a Marshal of the Soviet Union and Commissar of Defense. He appears as Savitsky in the *Red Cavalry* stories "My First Goose," "The Commander of the Second Brigade," "The Story of a Horse," and "The Continuation of the Story of a Horse," and as Timoshenko throughout the *1920 Diary*. In the original publication of the stories, Babel used Timoshenko's name.

THE CHURCH IN NOVOGRAD
Original title: "*Kostel v Novograde.*" First published in *Izvestiya Odesskovo Gubispolkoma*, February 18, 1923.
 See also *1920 Diary* entry for July 15.

A LETTER
Original title: "*Pismo.*" First published in *Izvestiya Odesskovo Gubispolkoma*, February 11, 1923. Dated Novograd-Volynsk, June 1920.
 See also *1920 Diary* entry of August 9, 1920.
 Pavlichenko: The altered name of Iosif Rodionovich Apanasenko, 1890–1943, who took over the command of Division Six after Timoshenko. Mentioned throughout the *1920 Diary* and in the *Red Cavalry* stories "The Life of Matvey Rodionovich Pavlichenko" and "Czesniki." In the original publication of the stories, Babel used Apanasenko's name.

THE RESERVE CAVALRY COMMANDER
 First published in *Lef* 4, 1923. Babel changed the original title "*Dyakov*" to "*Nachalnik konzapasa*" ("The Reserve-Cavalry Commander") in later story editions. Dated Belyov, July 1920.
 See also *1920 Diary* entries for July 13, 14, and 16.

PAN APOLEK
Original title: "*Pan Apolek.*" First published in *Krasnaya nov* 7, 1923.

ITALIAN SUN
First published in *Krasnaya nov* 3, 1923. Babel changed the original title "*Sidorov*" to "*Solntse Itali*" ("Italian Sun") in later story editions. Dated Novograd-Volynsk, July 1920.

GEDALI
Original title: "*Gedali.*" First published in *Krasnaya nov* 4, 1924. Dated Zhitomir, June 1920.
 See also *1920 Diary* entries for June 6 and July 7.

MY FIRST GOOSE
Original title: "*Moi pervii gus.*" First published in *Izvestiya Odesskovo Gubispolkoma*, May 4, 1924. Dated July 1920.
 See also *1920 Diary* entry for August 9.

THE RABBI
Original title: "*Rabbi.*" First published in *Krasnaya nov* 1, 1924.
 See also *1920 Diary* entry for June 3.

THE ROAD TO BRODY
Original title: "*Put v Brody.*" First published in *Izvestiya Odesskovo Gubispolkoma*, June 17, 1923. Dated Brody, August 1920.
 See also *1920 Diary* entries for August 18 and 31.

THE *TACHANKA* THEORY
Original title: *"Ucheniye o tachanke."* First published in *Izvestiya Odesskovo Gubispolkoma*, February 23, 1923.

DOLGUSHOV'S DEATH
Original title: *"Smert Dolgusheva."* First published in *Izvestiya Odesskovo Gubispolkoma*, May 1, 1923. Dated Brody, August 1920.

Korotchayev: Was demoted by General Budyonny from provisional commander of the Fourth Cavalry Division to one of the brigade commanders of the Sixth Cavalry Division. See also *1920 Diary* entries for August 2, 8, and 13.

THE COMMANDER OF THE SECOND BRIGADE
First published in *Lef* 4, 1923. Babel changed the original title *"Kolesnikov"* to *"Kombrig 2"* ("The Commander of the Second Brigade"). Dated Brody, August 1920.

See also *1920 Diary* entry for August 3, in which Budyonny threatens to shoot Kolesnikov and Grishin. In the original edition of this story in *Lef,* Babel had used Grishin's name, which in later editions Babel changed to Almazov.

SASHKA CHRIST
Original title: *"Sashka Khristos."* First published in *Krasnaya nov* 1, 1924.
See also *1920 Diary* entry for July 28.

THE LIFE OF MATVEY RODIONOVICH PAVLICHENKO
Original title: *"Zhiznyeopisaniye Pavlichenki, Matveya Rodionicha."* First published in *Shkval* 8, 1924.

Matvey Rodionovich Pavlichenko: the altered name of Iosif Rodionovich Apanasenko, 1890–1943, who took over the command of the Sixth Cavalry Division in August 1920. Mentioned throughout the *1920 Diary,* particularly the entries for August 5, 8–13. See also Sketches for the *Red Cavalry* Stories, "Apanasenko's Life Story" (p. 482).

THE CEMETERY IN KOZIN
Original title: *"Kladbishche v Kozine."* First published in *Izvestiya Odesskovo Gubispolkoma*, February 23, 1923.
See also *1920 Diary* entries for July 18 and 21.

PRISHCHEPA
Original title: *"Prishchepa."* First published in *Izvestiya Odesskovo Gubispolkoma*, June 17, 1923. Dated Demidovka, July 1920.
See also *1920 Diary* entries for July 23, 24. See also the two sections on Demidovka in Sketches for the *Red Cavalry* Stories (pp. 482–84).

THE STORY OF A HORSE
First published in *Izvestiya Odesskovo Gubispolkoma*, April 13, 1923. Babel changed the original title *"Timoshenko i Melnikov"* ("Timoshenko and Melnikov") to *"Istoriya odnoi loshadi"* ("The Story of a Horse") in later editions. Dated Radzivillov, July 1920. The story was republished in *Krasnaya nov* 3, 1924.

In a letter to the editor, Parfenti Melnikov denied that he had ever written a letter renouncing his membership in the Communist Party. Babel wrote an apology, published in the literary magazine *Oktyabr.* See "A Letter to the Editor," (p. 362).

KONKIN
Original title: "*Konkin.*" First published in *Krasnaya nov* 3, 1924. Dated Dubno, August 1920.
See also *1920 Diary* entry for July 13.

BERESTECHKO
Original title: "*Berestechko.*" First published in *Krasnaya nov* 3, 1924. Dated Berestechko, August 1920.
See also *1920 Diary* entries for August 7 and 8.

SALT
Original title: "*Sol.*" First published in *Izvestiya Odesskovo Gubispolkoma*, November 25, 1923.

EVENING
First published in *Krasnaya nov* 3. Babel changed the original title "*Galin*" to "*Vecher*" ("*Evening*") in later editions. Dated Kovel, 1920.
See also *1920 Diary* entries for September 10 and 11.

AFONKA BIDA
Original title: "*Afonka Bida.*" First published in *Krasnaya nov* 1, 1924.
See also *1920 Diary* entry for August 1.

AT SAINT VALENTINE'S
Original title: "*U Svyatogo Valentina.*" First published in *Krasnaya nov* 3, 1924. Dated Berestechko, August 1920.
See also *1920 Diary* entry for August 7.

SQUADRON COMMANDER TRUNOV
Original title: "*Eskadronnii Trunov.*" First published in *Krasnaya nov* 2, 1925.
See also "And Then There Were Nine," "And Then There Were Ten," and the *1920 Diary* entry for August 30. See also "Sokal 1" and "Sokal 2" in Sketches for the *Red Cavalry* Stories (pp. 478–79).

IVAN AND IVAN
Original title: "*Ivany.*" First published in *Russkii Sovremenik* 1, 1924.
See also *1920 Diary* entry for August 3.

A CONTINUATION OF THE STORY OF A HORSE
First published in *Krasnaya nov* 3, 1924 as part of the story "*Timoshenko i Melnikov*" ("Timoshenko and Melnikov"), which Babel changed to "*Prodolzhenie istorii odnoi loshadi*" ("A Continuation of the Story of a Horse") in later editions.

THE WIDOW
First published in *Izvestiya Odesskovo Gubispolkoma* 15, 1923. Babel changed the original title "*Shevelyov*" to "*Vdova*" ("The Widow") in later editions.
See also *1920 Diary* entry for August 9.

ZAMOSC
Original title: "*Zamostye.*" First published in *Krasnaya nov* 3, 1924. Dated Sokal, September 1920.
See also *1920 Diary* entries for August 29 and 30.

TREASON
Original title: *"Izmena."* First published in *Izvestiya Odesskovo Gubispolkoma*, March 20, 1923.

CZEŞNIKI
Original title: *"Chesniki."* First published in *Krasnaya nov* 3, 1924.
See also *1920 Diary* entries for August 28–31.

AFTER THE BATTLE
Original title: *"Posle boya."* First published in *Prozhektor* 20, 1924. Dated Galicia, September 1920.
See also *1920 Diary* entry for August 31.

THE SONG
First published in *Krasnaya nov* 3, 1925. Babel changed the original title *"Vecher"* ("Evening") to *"Pesnya"* ("The Song"). Dated Sokal, August 1920.

THE RABBI'S SON
Original title: *Syn Rabbi*. First published in *Krasnaya nov* 1, 1924.
See also *1920 Diary* entry for September 12.

THE RED CAVALRY CYCLE: ADDITIONAL STORIES

MAKHNO'S BOYS
Original title: *"U batko nashego Makhno."* First published in *Krasnaya nov* 4, 1924, dated 1923.

A HARDWORKING WOMAN
Original title: *"Staratelnaya zhenshchina."* First published in *Pereval* 6, 1926.
See also *1920 Diary* entry for July 16.

GRISHCHUK
Original title: *"Grishchuk."* First published in *Izvestiya Odesskovo Gubispolkoma*, February 23, 1923, subtitled "From the *Red Cavalry*," dated July 16, 1920.
See also *1920 Diary* entries for July 14, 19, and 21–29.

ARGAMAK
Original title: *"Agarmak."* First published in *Novii mir* 3, 1932, subtitled "An Unpublished Chapter of the *Red Cavalry*," dated 1924–1930.

THE KISS
Original title: *"Potselui."* First published in *Krasnaya nov* 7, 1937

AND THEN THERE WERE NINE
Original title: *"Ikh bylo devyat."* First published in *Novii Zhurnal* 95, New York, June 1969.
See also "And Then There Were Ten," "Squadron Commander Trunov," and the *1920 Diary* entry for August 30.

AND THEN THERE WERE TEN
Original title: *"Ikh bylo desyat."* First published in *Petersburg 1918*, 1989, Michigan, Ardis Publishers.

A LETTER TO THE EDITOR
First published in *Oktyabr* 4, 1924.

STORIES, 1925–1938

THE STORY OF MY DOVECOTE
Original title: "*Istoriya moyei golubyatni*." First published in *Krasnaya gazeta*, May 18, 19, 20, 1925, evening edition. Dated 1925.

FIRST LOVE
Original title: "*Pervaya lyubov*." First published in *Krasnaya gazeta*, May 24, 25, 1925, evening edition. Dated 1925.

KARL-YANKEL
Original title: "*Karl-Yankel*." First published in *Zvezda* 7, 1931.

THE AWAKENING
Original title: "*Probuzhdeniye*." First published in *Molodaya gvardiya* 17–18, 1931, under the heading "From the Book *The Story of My Dovecote*." Dated 1931.

IN THE BASEMENT
Original title: "*V podvale*." First published in *Novii mir* 10, 1931, under the heading "From the Book *The Story of My Dovecote*." Dated 1929.

GAPA GUZHVA
Original title: "*Gapa Guzhva*." First published in *Novii mir* 10, 1931, under the heading "The First Chapter from the Book *Velikaya Krinitsa*." Dated spring 1930.

KOLYVUSHKA
Original title: "*Kolyvushka*." First published in *Vozdushniye puti*, Volume 3, New York, 1963.

THE ROAD
Original title: "*Doroga*." First published in *30 dnei* 3, 1932. Dated 1920–1930.

THE *IVAN AND MARIA*
Original title: "*Ivan-da-Mariya*." First published in *30 dnei* 4, 1932. Dated 1920-28.

GUY DE MAUPASSANT
Original title: "*Gyui de Mopassan*." First published in *30 dnei* 6, 1932. Dated 1920–22.

PETROLEUM
Original title: "*Nefts*." First published in *Vechernaya Moskva*, February 14, 1934.

DANTE STREET
Original title: "*Ulitsa Dante*." First published in *30 dnei* 3, 1934.

DI GRASSO
Original title: "*Di Grasso*." First published in *Ogonyok* 23, 1937.

SULAK
Original title: "*Sulak*." First published in *Molodoi kolkhoznik* 6, 1937.

THE TRIAL
Original title: "*Sud*." First published in *Ogonyok* 23, 1938, under the heading "From My Notebook."

MY FIRST FEE
Original title: "*Moi pervii gonorar*." First published in *Vozdushniye puti*, Volume 3, New York, 1963.